Sunday's SON

*To John,
with my compliments —
All the Best

Andy*

An Historical Novel

Andreas H. Vassiliou

DEDICATION

To my wife Marika,
my daughters, Alexia and Katia
and my grandchildren Nicolas, Trianna, Ava and Sofia

INTRODUCTION

Although this book is based, to a large extent, on real people and on actual events, historical or otherwise, it is still essentially a work of fiction. True characters, living or deceased, are not necessarily identified by their real names. Fictional characters and places as well as imaginary events and circumstances are also included. The story takes place primarily during the third quarter of the twentieth century.

Prologue

Practically every country in the world, no matter how small or large, is believed to have contributed foreign students or immigrants who came to the United States for higher education or a better life. Cyprus, the third largest island in the Mediterranean with a total population of about eight hundred thousand, has been the source of many students and over twenty-five thousand immigrants, most of whom live in the greater New York metropolitan area.

The event that eventually planted the seed that germinated into one such Cypriot foreign student, Nicolas Maos, took place in 1919, just six years before Cyprus was totally divorced from the Ottoman Empire. In the early summer of that year, 18 year old Kyriaki (Sunday) was promised to Mr. Maos, a well-to-do widower of 57.

The church wedding of Kyriaki Nicolaou and Thomas Maos took place two months later, without much fanfare, in the tiny mountainous village of Ora. The young bride moved into the groom's family home which was built exactly one hundred years earlier when the island's Greek population was toiling through its 249th year of a 307- year Turkish occupation and oppression.

In 1878 the British assumed the administration of Cyprus while the Ottoman Empire officially retained ownership of the island. When the Turkish sultan joined Germany against the allies during World War I, the British "punished" the Turks by usurping several of their long-occupied Middle East territories, including the island of Cyprus, which they eventually declared a British colony in 1925.

At the time of the marriage and for several years after that, Thomas Maos was a good provider for his family as one of the top three producers of olives, carobs and grapes in the village. However, by the mid-1930's, a couple of years before Nicolas was born, Mr. Maos was in his seventies and becoming more and more incapable of physically maintaining his agricultural property. He was forced to sell his land, his olive and carob groves, and his vineyards, one by one, in order to support his family. By the time the once-good provider died at the age of 84, the Maos family had zero land holdings and was one of the poorest in the village. Within the first year of her marriage, Mrs. Kyriaki Maos had her first child, her daughter Marina. Her next two children, both girls, came in rapid succession but both died in infancy. After that, she waited for five years before she had another child, another daughter whom she named Theodora. Another try, three years after Theodora, produced yet another daughter who died at the age of three. At this time, Kyriaki made a declaration to her family:

"I swear to the almighty Lord and to you, my family, my most important reasons for being, that I will never give up. I am determined to have a boy, no matter how long it takes. My boy, my son, will grow up to be an important man in this village... even in this whole country...he will be our savior, the savior of this family."

A couple of years after her declaration, Kyriaki Maos was in labor once again and, once again, her efforts produced another girl. She was named Nina, but few expected her to live very long. She was very tiny and frail and appeared to have other physical deformities, including a neck that was permanently bent to the left. However, Nina was still alive and well when her mother became pregnant with her seventh child three years later at the age of 36.

During her pregnancy, Kyriaki was praying several times daily for a healthy son. Mr. Maos simply wanted a healthy child, but often expressed his preference for a son since he was anxious to please his "long-suffering wife." The two older sisters were very eager to have a brother and even trained their little sister Nina to call out "brother" when appropriately prompted.

Finally, Kyriaki Maos went into labor, under the watchful eye of the old village midwife. Simultaneously, the suspense in the Maos household climbed to its highest peak. After what felt like eternity for the woman in labor, the midwife managed to pull out the latest offspring and, while gently slapping its derriere, proclaimed, "Bless the Lord, it's finally a boy."

"It must be a miracle…but I want to see it…with my own eyes," shouted the mother, apparently weak and exhausted, but unmistakably invigorated by the midwife's declaration. "Hold him up, please…hold him up for me to see."

The midwife raised the infant high up and with one finger pushed the tiny penis gently upwards.

"My God, it is true…it's a miracle…thank you Lord for my son…thank you Lord for Sunday's son."

Chapter One

Elementary school graduation was an event attended by practically every one of the nearly three hundred residents of Ora. Nicolas was the first of the graduates asked to stand on the ceremonial platform. Mr. Manolas, the village teacher, proclaimed loud and clear, "Nicolas Maos is the top student in a class of fourteen, the class of 1949, the largest graduating class in this school's history. Some of you call this boy Sunday's son and agree with his mother that his birth was a kind of a miracle. I can neither confirm nor deny his birth as such, but I can assure you of one fact: this boy's school performance has been close to miraculous. He is an exceptionally gifted candidate for higher education but, as you all know, his family is very poor. But this village can help…you must not allow his mind to remain uncultivated."

If any of the fourteen graduates planned to attend high school, they had to travel 32 miles to the district capital to do so. Tuition fees alone made the trip to higher education just about impossible for Nicolas. Deep in his heart, Nicolas always felt hopeful because his mother made sure of that.

"God has plenty and will always provide for us too," was one of Mrs. Maos' favorite phrases and her most frequent answer to any depressing comment concerning her son's limited chances for higher education or the family's complete lack of any finances. Every time she uttered the phrase, her voice sounded like a cantor's prayer and her arms and face turned towards the heavens. Invariably she would then turn toward her son to add, "You are the answer to my prayers, my Nicolaki…you bring joy and happiness to this family…soon you will also bring material wealth."

Nicolas loved to hear his mother utter words of great expectations for him in spite of the associated great responsibilities. She made him feel important and even indispensable because she reinforced a personal pact between them that brought him endless motivation to succeed, not only for his sake, but also for hers and that of his whole family.

"Thank you, Mr. Manolas, thank you sir, very much," said Nicolas in a low voice as he received his diploma from his seemingly proud teacher.

Mr. Manolas was a strict but effective teacher. He was known for dishing out unrelenting punishment to those that broke the rules. At the same time, he had a reputation that traveled beyond the bounds of the village concerning his exceptional ability to make history and literature sound and feel like everybody's favorite fairy tales.

Nicolas admired and respected this man, his first teacher, who truly sharpened his curiosity and desire for knowledge. His total estimation of him as a person had diminished considerably, though, after he suffered an incident of cruel punishment under him for kissing a schoolgirl and creating the village's biggest scandal in years. The student's mind traveled back, dwelling on the details of that scandalous incident.

Nicolas' mother referred to the punishment as an example of lack of sensitivity and compassion for young people. It took place two weeks after Nicolas' twelfth birthday and about ten days before Christmas.

The circumstances that led to the punishment began a few weeks earlier. Nicolas was in sixth grade and so was Stella. Just about everybody in school over the age of eleven was in love with Stella.

"She has dark brown eyes like large almonds, wavy, light brown hair with silky luster, and a figure that proclaims her a true daughter of Aphrodite. What's her name?"

"Stella…Stella," all boys shouted in unison, during a class break in the school yard, in response to Costa's question.

"I just learned she has been promised to Sodiris. Goodbye beautiful Stella," added Costas.

At twenty-one, Sodiris was the hunk of the village. Tall, muscular, with good facial features, curly black hair and a brush mustache, the village perception of the ideal stud. Since grade school graduation, he was working with his father, ironsmith Komodromos, who specialized in shoeing donkeys and mules. Sodiris earned his muscles through his trade.

When the news finally sank in, Nicolas felt saddened and depressed, but most of all betrayed. He could see the practicality of the match. Besides his physical endowments, Sodiris had a good trade and came from a very well-to-do family. In addition to the lucrative shoeing business, the Komodromos family usually had the biggest carob crop production in the district.

Like so many other boys in school, Nicolas was in love with Stella but, in his case, there was a big difference—he was certain she only loved him.

Stella was one of nine students assigned to Nicolas that semester by Mr. Manolas for math tutoring. The tutor made sure that Stella always sat next to him for the entire hour of group tutoring. The trouble was that he couldn't talk to her about his feelings for her during tutoring, or during any other time for that matter.

In Cyprus during the forties, and for a couple of decades

later, dating or openly expressing love for somebody that was not promised to you or engaged to you was strictly unacceptable social behavior. Despite the prohibition, many young people did express their love for each other secretly, mostly through trusted intermediaries. Occasionally they even managed to have physical contact, perhaps a kiss or two. But if their secret should become known to the community, the girl's reputation and, therefore, her chances for a proper marriage, would be practically ruined. Romantic love was typically conducted through eye flirting and only from a safe distance.

After half a dozen tutoring sessions, Nicolas gathered enough courage to write little notes on Stella's slate, expressing first his admiration for her rare beauty and pure character, and then his personal intentions in winning her love. She totally ignored those notes, wiping them fast and clean with the little sponge attached to the slate. She told nobody about the love notes and that was a very good omen for him.

One late afternoon, towards the end of the last tutoring session, Nicolas must have grown very desperate and bold at the same time. Uncharacteristically, he violently pulled her slate away from her hands. She looked very surprised but said nothing. He brought it close to his chest for privacy, drew two hearts that covered the whole writing area, wrote first his name inside one heart and then hers in the other, and placed it in front of her face.

She looked at the hearts for a moment, then turned those big brown eyes towards him. It felt like his eyes were burning in the brightness of hers. She pulled the slate away from him, rather gently, drew a long, bold arrow across both hearts and placed it in front of his face. He had only a moment to marvel at the revelation before she quickly erased the whole art work.

The slate incident became the start of the great "Nicolas and Stella" love affair, filled with love notes and romantic glances. For his part, he didn't even dare hope for a touch, a holding of hands, let alone a kiss.

Within a few weeks, after the brief love notes became long accounts of true love and total devotion forever, the young lovers recklessly did dare for a quick kiss, behind the wall of the school vegetable garden, not far from the corner rock where they commonly hid their love letters.

"Yesterday I became a young woman," she whispered as she planted that first kiss on his right cheek. "You are my choice…the one I love…I promise I will always be yours," she added as she turned quickly and ran towards the front school yard.

Her promise, the first romantic oral communication they ever had, put him in seventh heaven, but he was totally puzzled by her other statement. *How can a girl become a woman literally overnight? Was it because of love or declaration of love?*

It took several days before she was able to answer his question in her letter, tactfully explaining the start of her menstruation cycle. It was the last one she wrote before the matchmaking was announced, declaring that the Varellas family made an agreement with the Komodromos family that Stella and Sodiris would be formally engaged, in a church ceremony, after her elementary school graduation in mid-June.

The formal announcement increased Nicolas' frustration considerably. He had about seven months before graduation, seven months to do something, but what? He was too young to formally declare his love and intentions to marry her. In any case, he thought he would never be able to compete with Sodiris in terms of the promise of giving her a good and comfortable life.

He started praying for guidance from God, perhaps a miracle. Instead, he finally subscribed to the work of the devil, the temptation to create a scandal that would break the engagement. His mind was searching for the right scandal and the right moment.

"*Yia sou* Stella, *yia sou* Maria, good morning to you both."

It was mid-morning break and the two inseparable friends were sitting at the top of the marble stairs, leading to the main school entrance, as Nicolas greeted them. Their legs were uncrossed, wide apart, and their feet rested on the step below. Their blue-and-white striped skirts, imitating the Greek colors, were stretched to the limit over their bent knees, concealing everything but a small part of their black knee socks and shoes. Local hand-woven wool sweaters lay folded across their legs. "You look like you are enjoying this warm December sun," he added, sitting himself at the bottom of the stairs. Both girls smiled and nodded in agreement.

He turned around to face them. The bright sun was shining straight at them. Blinding glare, reflected from their white blouses, practically concealed their facial features. Maria turned her legs to the side while Stella kept her original posture. From his vantage position at the bottom, the strong sunlight kept escorting his eyes along a bright path up Stella's skirt, revealing smooth, complexion-perfect legs whose ends were framed by the outline of white panties.

As he remained fixated at the highly intoxicating vision, he remembered Stella's revelation about the onset of her period and her passage into womanhood. The combination of the two produced an exhilarating feeling of desire that kept flashing through his body like fast moving waves. It was his first personal encounter with his own raging hormones.

The trip up the path of desire lasted for a minute or two. Maria stood up and Stella seemed ready to follow when, like a flash of lightning, Nicolas sprung up the five stairs and grabbed Stella by the shoulders, simultaneously causing her to lie on her back and pressing his lips against hers. The first quick kiss was followed by several more, with the total lasting less than half a minute.

"She is mine forever," Nicolas shouted on top of his lungs, turning around to face the large student crowd that kept approaching the scene.

Stella, perhaps in a state of disbelief, remained completely motionless and speechless. So did Maria. Within hours, the whole village was talking about the incident, primarily described as "the act of a degenerate, dirty person." The village priest added "unholy" to the list. Nicolas' mother referred to it as "a simple expression of impulsive love by our youth."

At first, just about everybody blamed Nicolas alone as "the shameless attacker." Later, after Stella's best friend Maria, under pressure, revealed all she knew about her friend's secret romance with Nicolas to the teacher and then to others, most people included Stella as an active participant in the dirty incident.

The teacher never discussed the incident publicly, but he was under great pressure from Stella's family and from many others in the village to punish Nicolas through a combination of severe beating and permanent expulsion from school. Nicolas was absolutely certain that Mr. Manolas would abide by the rules. *He is very regimental, perhaps stubborn, and quite predictable. I expect him to eventually subject me to considerable punishment of some sort.*

The young student broke two of the most important conduct rules of the school as well as those of society in general: He publicly kissed a girl that wasn't promised to him and, even worse, he publicly kissed a girl that was promised to someone else. Yet, in spite of the prospect of severe punishment, he felt relieved and exhilarated. *The whole thing seems to be worth it if, in the end, I manage to keep Stella from getting engaged to someone else, some brute almost twice her age.*

Some villagers thought that both Stella and Nicolas should be punished or expelled. *Typical old hypocrites...they probably did something similar or even worse in their youth.* For some reason, neither Sodiris nor any member of his family made any public statements about the incident. Whenever Nicolas thought of Sodiris, he literally shivered with fear, knowing that the muscleman was expected to avenge the honor of his future fiancé.

Two days after the kissing incident, on a Friday afternoon, Mr. Manolas dismissed the lower two grades early and addressed the remaining student body in the main school room.

"Today, I want you all to witness punishment...punishment of one of your fellow students, Nicolas Maos...punishment befitting conduct strictly unacceptable for him or any member of our student body."

Nicolas was asked to stand on the wooden platform, next to the teacher's desk, facing the students. He was glad that apparently only students were allowed to be present during the punishment. It seemed that, in spite of considerable pressure from community members, Mr. Manolas refused to allow any of them to witness the event.

He picked up the "punishment stick" from under his desk. The famous stick was part of a flexible olive tree shoot, close to four feet long and a little over one inch in diameter at its thickest. It was dreaded by any student who was unlucky enough to experience its devastating effect across the bottom cheeks or on the open palm.

"The punishment will consist of twenty across the bottom and ten on each palm," he announced as he motioned Nicolas to bend over the desk.

I must be brave. I must receive my punishment without expressing fear and without complaining. I wish Stella was allowed by her parents to attend school...I wish she was present to witness the silent testimony of my love for her.

After the end of the first round, the end of the first twenty strikes across the bottom, Nicolas was told to straighten up and open his palms. The pain on his buttocks was unbearable, but he was still surprised that he felt dizzy and could hardly stand up straight. *I guess I'm not as tough as I thought.*

He opened his eyes for another look at the audience. He expected to see signs and motions of approval, perhaps admiration, for the way he silently endured severe pain. Instead all he could see was stillness and countless pairs of eyes floating in the room.

My God, can that be?... all these sad, pitiful eyes...they express only pity...nothing but pity. They fail to see the personal sacrifice for the sake of love.

As the punishment continued, Nicolas was very much surprised by the intensity of the pain across the open palms. He never experienced anything as utterly unbearable as that at any time before. He kept his arms more or less stretched out straight and his mind reasonably clear until about halfway through the punishment. Then he passed into a daze, somewhat of a soothing daze, apparently a semi-conscious state.

As if in a nightmarish dream, he could hear numbers but he could not follow the order of the count. Even worse, he could not shut out that ominous command, alternating in perfect coordination with the sound of each slash on the palms, "Arms up...up and straight...arms up...up and straight..."

After the students had been dismissed, Nicolas tried to sit at his desk and wait for his mother who was notified to come and pick him up. But he quickly discovered that sitting was highly uncomfortable. While standing, the teacher had him soak his puffed-up, achy palms in a bowl of cool water placed on the teacher's desk. Then, in a surprisingly tender, apologetic voice, Mr. Manolas analyzed the situation with," Nicola...Nicola...the whole thing could have been avoided...if only the people of this village were more understanding...more sensitive to young people's social needs...more sensible..."

In a way, Nicolas understood the teacher's position—the fact that he had a job to do, the idea that he had to keep traditions and maintain discipline. The student was never really angry with his teacher personally, and he was about to forgive him when his mother pulled him away and angrily proclaimed, "Damn you... Mr. Manola...damn you for being insensitive and cruel."

Nicolas was expelled for the ten days remaining before Christmas break. He needed the time to recover both physically and mentally. He returned to school in early January, having matured practically overnight. *I feel like a veteran ancient warrior who triumphantly survived some horrible encounter with a deadly beast.*

Ironically, in spite of the brutal punishment, Mr. Manolas' teachings still dominated his thoughts and influenced his imagination. He was now determined to concentrate totally on the remaining school work, always obeying rules and keeping traditions.

Stella did not return to school after that December day, the day of the infamous kisses. She never graduated. About four months later, during Easter feast, the third week of April, Stella was officially engaged to Sodiris. The wedding was to follow a little over a year later.

It was obvious to Nicolas that he lost Stella forever. His last few months in elementary school were both lonely and miserable. He missed lively Stella, her beautiful face, and especially her eyes that so warmly and charmingly flirted with his at every opportunity in the classroom or in the school yard.

Eventually, he somehow did manage to convince himself that life should go on even without Stella being physically present in his immediate environment. However, he did not manage to convince himself to keep Stella out of his thoughts and his dreams.

"Nicolas Maos," called the teacher out loud, "please lead the graduates back to the auditorium."

Instantly, his mind joined his body back at the graduation ceremonies. As he walked towards the crammed school room, first he saw his sister's youthful face, full of joy. Nina, who was three years older than him, was quite petite at four-feet eight and eighty pounds. She was born with one eye smaller than the other and of different color. For some reason, the combination translated into poor eyesight.

I wish Marina and Theodora were here today for my graduation...

my older sisters hardly come to the village any more...but we should be thankful for the baskets of food they send us for Christmas and Easter...I don't even remember the first time they moved to Larnaca to work at Shapiro's button factory.

He then focused on his mother. Tears were running down the shallow valleys of her cheeks. The bright Cyprus sun made sure that widow Kyriaki's face looked much older than her forty-nine years.

"Mother, why the tears?"

"They're tears of great pride and joy, my son." *Unfortunately they also express plenty of sadness too because I cannot provide for my son's higher education...but then God never fails to provide for us.*

Nicolas sat between his mother and sister. Nina planted quick kisses on each of his cheeks and forehead, grabbed the rolled-up diploma from his hand, opened it, placed it very close to her face, and then looked at him to proclaim with obvious pride,

"Congratulations brother Nicola, congratulations graduate Nicola."

"Thank you Nina. Oh how I wish you could have had your diploma too...I guess it wasn't easy for you...everybody knows that..."

"I don't want you to believe what some people say about your sister Nina, my son. She is not slow. She is really quite smart, you know. I took her out of school early because I need her around the house. Look at me. Everybody knows I never went to school but does anybody doubt I can take good care of my family?"

In her turn, his mother, after a long hug and many kisses for the graduate, asked to see the diploma. She placed it open in front of her face and stared at the words for a while as if she could read.

"Show me your name...show me 'Nicolas Maos' on this diploma."

She stared at the name for a long time and then, turning towards her son, made a loud proclamation, one which Nicolas found quite embarrassing:

"The very best graduating student...my Nicolaki...nobody in the whole village is really surprised...Mr. Manolas boasted about his top student many a time at the village coffee shop...and to imagine that all the time until you entered school, everybody in the village expected you to be a very poor student, to have been stupefied because you had too much of your mother's milk."

"Mother...please..."

"I knew otherwise...I nursed you, I gave you milk from my breasts until you were close to four...how can that give you anything else but strength and love...You do remember nursing from your mother, don't you Nicolaki?"

He responded with, "No, mother, I do not remember," but in fact he wasn't sure.

He could clearly envision an embarrassing incident which his sisters related whenever they planned to make fun of him. Did he actually remember experiencing the incident himself or did he vividly recall just the story embedded in his mind by his sisters? In any case, the incident was back in his thoughts once again:

It was a lazy afternoon in early summer. His mother was sitting in front of their house, embroidering, under the shade of the grape vine porch. She was facing one of the main streets and she had to stop her work at times in order to greet and chat with various people. When her toddler stood in front of her silent for several minutes, she couldn't ignore him because she knew what he wanted. She had him lie in her lap and then covered him with her apron, hiding him completely from anybody's view. He started nursing away as she continued embroidering.

Little Nicolas was hardly at it for a minute or two when he heard the distinct voice of aunt Marina. She was not a relative but she was very wealthy and often gave his family all kinds of necessities such as sugar, carob syrup, pork lard, and most important for his mother, hard-to-get ground coffee.

Probably because of that, aunt Marina seemed to have some control over his mother's thoughts and actions. She was a giant of a woman, dressed in the widow's long, black garments. It was her husky voice that intimidated Nicolas the most.

Aunt Marina must have sensed something or saw movement under the apron. The minute she pulled the apron and threw it over the mother's face, the young boy was up and running away like a rabbit chased by a dog. He heard part of what she said: "Shame on you to nurse a big boy like that…in a couple of years he could be helping out in the fields…"

A few days later, the whole village knew about the family secret of Nicolas' prolonged nursing. It became a current topic of gossip. His mother had an explanation for all the curious, "I tried to persuade my Nicolaki to stop at two, at three and then again at three and a half. I used all kinds of incentives, including rubbing hot pepper on my breasts. He became very ill. The doctor said that maternal milk was critical to his health and ordered me to continue nursing until my Nicolaki decides to stop on his own."

Nicolas did stop for good on his own, alright. He did it very soon after aunt Marina exposed his secret and he became the village topic of ridicule. *Nine years passed since then and yet I have the feeling that some people never forgot my early weakness, my total dependence on mother's milk. Perhaps they even interpret my present devotion to her as a continuation of that early weakness…I wish they could understand as well as I do that a mother's milk provides more than just simple nutrition, it provides love.*

"Let's go Nicolaki, let's go Nina…stand up son, graduation ceremonies are over and it's our turn to move out of here," she said, pulling her son by the arm.

Out in the school yard, comments and sighs of relief could be heard all around. The sun had just disappeared behind the mountain-lined horizon and it felt much cooler, much more comfortable than in the stuffy classroom. Mother was still holding the open diploma, this time pressed against her chest. The off-white color of the paper provided some visual relief from her totally black attire which so monotonously covered her slight body from head to toe, symbolizing the permanent plight of every woman who became a widow. She turned her face towards her son. This time she appeared calm and content and her eyes were beaming with happiness.

"The Lord guided you through the first step in your education, my son…I know He will be there to guide you through many more accomplishments…I'm sure God will prepare you to one day take good care of your helpless sister Nina…in her future she has nobody else but you to care for her…"

"Mother, I protest! I will always take care of you too! You are the one first and foremost in my future plans."

His protests were in vain. Mother would never include herself under his future care, always explaining, in a rather somber tone, that she would probably be gone before he was ready to take care of her. Strangely enough, she would always make one exception. She would proudly tell just about everybody that she expected the fulfillment of a promise her son made to her when he was only six. The young graduate's promise to his mother came about one late autumn afternoon when he was allowed to accompany her to their old olive grove at Laxia to fetch firewood for cooking and home heating. At the time, just about every family in the village owned a donkey. The beasts of burden were used mainly for cultivating fields but also for transporting harvest crops and firewood, often for long distances, along winding paths over numerous hills and valleys in the surrounding mountainous terrain.

Nicolas' family could not afford such a luxury. On occasion, his mother borrowed a neighbor's donkey through an exchange of labor deal whereby she had to help harvest carobs or olives at the appropriate time. At his first outing with her, they had no beast of burden to help carry the firewood back home. He watched his mother, a short, skinny woman of very limited strength, he thought, exhibit constant bursts of unlimited energy in order to gather a large bundle of dried branches and small logs, twice her size, sometimes climbing up rough tree trunks or steep rocky hills. After tying up the heavy bundle, she had it rest against a tree trunk as she knelt and placed it across her shoulder.

She carried it home, a distance of almost three miles, completely on her own and with just three or four short rest stops. She was in a hurry to go home and cook on the open-air hearth before darkness set in. At one point when she appeared completely exhausted, her son offered to help carry the bundle.

"It would kill me if this bunch of dead wood breaks your delicate back, my Nicolaki," was her response.

At a quiet moment later on at home, Mrs. Kyriaki stretched her legs seated at the edge of one of the small wicker chairs, strategically placed close by the rejuvenated hearth fire. With her eyes almost totally shut, she was sipping her necessary demitasse of Greek espresso. Nicolas occupied another wicker chair next to his mother while his sister remained standing as she closely watched potatoes boil in a large metal pot whose outside surface was totally blackened by the fire and smoke.

The wood gathering excursion made Nicolas hungry. He could hardly wait for the salad of sliced potatoes and black olives, mixed with chopped, garden-fresh parsley and scallions and dressed with plenty of virgin olive oil and lemon. Add to that a crusty end-slice of that round, aromatic wheat bread, and you have a perfect meal at any time.

Mrs. Kyriaki baked four loaves of bread, the family's weekly supply, earlier that day. Her son watched her burn all of their remaining pile of firewood that morning, pushing piece by piece into the labyrinthine mouth of their semi-circular sandstone furnace. Its dome, the size of a wagon wheel, stood like a monument in the middle of the cobble-covered yard.

Eventually, Nicolas stood up and moved around to face his mother. The fire between them continued to produce a symphony of bright red and yellow flames, radiating warmth and color well into the late autumn dusk. His mother's bony face exhibited many years of toil but, at the same time, it also radiated back a saintly glow. When he started to speak, his heart was filled with gratitude and lots of love of course but, curiously, his dominant feeling for her was one of boundless admiration.

"Do not worry, mother...I promise...I promise I will buy you a donkey of your own some day...some day soon."

"Wait until you see what the evening will bring for you, my Nicolaki...wait until you see what I prepared for you to celebrate your graduation."

The first unusual thing Nicolas noticed was that his home, a typical mountain- village dwelling built over a hundred and twenty years earlier when Cyprus was part of the Ottoman empire, was decorated for the occasion with wreaths of fresh rosemary and wild Mediterranean lavender. Even the aging outhouse shack and the wooden poles and rope spool of the water well were similarly decorated.

Nicolas' older sisters often referred to the two-room house as "the cave" because its back walls were carved out of the side of a dense clay hill. His mother liked to refer to the larger of the two dirt-floor rooms as "our palace." It served as the living room, the dining room, and the bedroom, all in one. The smaller room housed the chickens and the rabbits as well as the occasional goat.

As soon as the young graduate entered the palace, he noticed the huge red-clay vase in the middle of the dining table. It contained a large bunch of multi-colored wild flowers, the beauty of rural Cyprus in late Spring. *Mother must have visited the nearby hills during the morning.*

The family dinner was unusually rich. Not one but two of Nicolas' favorite dishes were lined on the small, rectangular table.

Its unpolished pinewood surface was covered by the seldom used family tablecloth.

Closer to him, at one end of the table, was a large wooden bowl of homemade noodles sprinkled with chopped mint and grated halloumi, a cheese exclusive to Cyprus. A deep plate of stew, made with rabbit meat and shredded onions sautéed in olive oil, tomato sauce and vinegar, was at the other end of the table.

"Congratulations Nicolaki, and may the Lord guide you through many more paths of success, my son. Let's drink to that, pick up your glasses. The sherry is richly flavored and sweet. It's from aunt Marina's best stock."

The dessert, a rare item for them, consisted of raised dough patties, deep fried and smothered with aunt Marina's carob syrup.

Good food shared with those I love most, Nicolas thought, feeling reasonably content but not totally happy. *Happiness will never be complete...unlike some of my friends, I see no high school in my future.*

The mother seemed to be able to read her son's thoughts. She tried to console him with a pleasant announcement.

"Your uncle Thomas agreed to hire you as a mason apprentice in his construction company in Larnaca, with pay of course, provided you have a place to live in town. I will go with you to Larnaca in mid-August, the time your uncle starts a new project... I'm sure your sister Marina and her husband Makis will take you in, give you a place to live until you can afford your own place." She paused for a sip of wine before she continued,

"They now rent the first floor of one of the municipal buildings built for the town's working people...imagine two large rooms plus kitchen and an indoor bathroom...your brother-in-law Makis often works for your uncle...you can even have a ride to work on his bicycle."

The announcement raised Nicolas' hopes. He could now envision a different future than the one expected from life in the village where it meant most probably a career as a farm laborer or crop harvester. New and exciting thoughts began turning in his mind.

They say that Larnaca has three high schools…living there means being closer to the possibility of going to school…eventually…somehow… this is good…this is even more than good…this is great…there is now real hope.

The next day, one day after graduation, Nicolas was already searching for ways to make some money, raise a few shillings for his trip to Larnaca. For the first time in his life he thought of having some new clothes and perhaps even a new pair of shoes instead of the altered hand-me-downs from his great Aunt Eleni with family connections in America.

He couldn't ask his mother for money. His family had no monetary income. He actually saw his mother use money only once or twice a year, specifically when his older sisters sent her some for the holidays. The family survived by exchanging food, mostly local produce, for his mother's labor in harvesting crops or doing laundry.

Purchases of absolute necessities at the village grocery store were paid through barter trade. Eggs or chickens or rabbits were often exchanged for flour or salt or sugar. Occasionally Mrs. Kyriaki treated her son and daughter to a smoked, salt herring imported in wooden crates from Norway for the poor folks of the British colony. Grilled over open flames and seasoned with plenty of olive oil and lemon, a side dish of herring meat with crunchy blackened skin would greatly enhance the taste of plain beans or lentils.

He asked his mother's advice.

"Do not worry, Nicolaki, things will fall in place once you get there…I pray that God is always with you…of course some secondary harvesting of a cash crop will put a few shillings in your pocket, give you some buying power for the things you want. I will help gather some almonds for you, this year's crop appears to be plentiful."

He also spoke to his best friend Chris who was essentially thinking along the same lines, some pocket money for his trip to another town to attend high school. But Chris was very lucky. His parents could afford to send him to the Commercial Lyceum in the town of Larnaca.

Chris agreed with Nicolas and Mrs. Kyriaki. Their best bet for cash was the gleaning of almonds, an excellent cash crop that would be in season in a few weeks. Carobs and olives were also popular crops for gleaning but their season would be well after the two boys left the village. The summer before both boys made over sixteen shillings each after selling the almonds they had gathered in partnership throughout most of July and August.

The almond gathering venture was not as successful as the two boys had thought it would be. By the first week of August they had only earned one pound, twelve shillings less than the year before. They both reasoned out that their earnings were negatively effected by the lower price of the nuts due to the bigger than usual harvest as well as by the fact that a larger number of kids than usual was out there partaking in the secondary harvest.

Fortunately, another opportunity arose that would allow the two partners to increase their earnings.

On most evenings, Nicolas and Chris, along with many of the village residents, would listen to the news program, a short wave broadcast from the National Radio Service of Athens. At the time, there was only one radio in the village. Since there was no electricity, it was powered by a car battery and housed in the Farmers Association building which also served as a public coffee house.

There was a lot of interest in the news broadcasts from Athens because of the civil war in Greece, between the communists and the royalists, that began soon after the German occupiers left the country at the end of World War II. Some of the younger residents showed an even greater amount of interest in the Sunday afternoon broadcast of the latest Greek popular songs.

Nicolas and Chris did not remember who mentioned it first, but they were both in agreement that one could make lots of money if one owned a radio and were to charge a small fee to those interested in listening to radio programs. They agreed to build a radio and charge a fee of fifty almonds to kids interested in listening to a half hour of news and music.

The two entrepreneurs were aware of the fact that the Farmers Association people replaced their radio a few months back and that the old, broken-down device was still gathering dust behind the association's kitchen counter. They were also well aware of the fact that the original boxy radio was essentially a piece of junk but it had sentimental value as the village's first radio. The boys paid five shillings for it, or one fourth of their summer's earnings.

The execution of their plan was smooth and quick. Using loose ceramic bricks piled in Chris' back yard, they built a drywall, four-feet wide and six-feet high, to cover the entrance to his family's empty chicken coop which consisted of sun-dried brick walls and a roof of loose aluminum panels.

The radio was built into the brick wall, approximately three feet above the coop floor, with its front panel protruding a couple of inches out of the wall surface. To enter the "radio room," the boys would climb the back wall, push aside one of the aluminum panels and drop down onto the coop floor. Chris' mother was definitely unhappy with the wall. It took a while for her only child to convince her to let the wall stand. Then came the bigger problem of convincing her to allow the boys to bring the family's gramophone into the "radio room."

The hand-winding gramophone, the only one in good order in the village, plus a couple of 78 rpm records, were sent to Chris's mother by her sister Maro from Virginia where Maro's husband owned a restaurant.

Many a time Chris would invite Nicolas to his house to listen to music. The boys would place the gramophone on the upstairs patio and make sure that half the village heard the songs they played over and over. Their favorite American songs, in spite of the language barrier, were two by Bing Crosby, *Sweet Laylanie* and *White Christmas*.

Chris' mother, Mrs. Phanari, acquired a few Greek records as well. Everybody in the village, within hearing distance of the music, loved the Greek songs whose lyrics they could understand. The song representing an ode to the sea and seamen and the one about a girl who looked lovely as her long hair was blown by the breeze were favorites.

For their inaugural program, after posting a couple of announcements on the posts of the dirt soccer field, they had nine customers, each paying fifty almonds to listen to news and music.

The area in front of the radio room was prepared so that at least twenty kids could sit comfortably on burlap sacks filled with straw. The first audience appeared to be thrilled with the program and, through word of mouth, the later audiences grew larger and larger and so did the entrance fee.

During the program, Chris would be outside the radio room, seated by the radio panel, announcing the program while controlling the radio dials. At the right word signal, Nicolas, hidden behind the brick wall inside the coop, would summarize or paraphrase some of the actual news he heard a day or two earlier at the Farmers Association building or he would play a couple of records.

Nicolas would camouflage his voice to a much deeper tone by speaking through a large funnel. At the right signal, he would also use a flashlight to direct light from the back of the radio to the front panel, giving the impression that the radio was turned on for the program.

At times, Nicolas would also make up stories that he thought would interest his audience. One of his favorite topics was about the human abuse of animals, wild or tame, and how these animals often escaped to find their freedom in the wild or in a happier home among humans. The capacity audiences loved the stories and demanded more.

Nicolas's conscience would bother him at times, thinking that perhaps he was taking advantage of poor, naïve kids. But his mind would fire back. *These kids are quite smart. They do know, of course, that the "radio" is fake and that I'm pretending to be the "radio announcer" but somehow they don't care...most probably because the "radio show" is the only novel entertainment option they have...it's the remedy to their boredom.*

So the kids continued to flock to the show, some of them many times repeaters, in spite of the fact that the entrance fee was raised to one hundred almonds per kid. By the time Mrs. Phanari put a stop to it, the two boys had raised two pounds and five shillings through the sale of the almonds.

Nicolas was quite content with the money he earned from the radio enterprise. However, upon his mother's strong insistence, he agreed to go for another nut-gathering trip, this time accompanied by her only. She specifically wanted to check out an old almond tree growing in their olive grove of Kouris.

When they arrived, it was obvious that, like many of the olive trees there, the almond tree was practically dead and must have been in that condition for some time. Nicolas thought that his mother must have known that, even before she explained, "Observe closely, my Nicolaki...nothing was cultivated at Kouris for over fifteen years...The wild brash and weeds had taken over. Neither I nor your elderly father, during his last few years with us, had the energy or the means to care for the property."

On their way back, mother led her son through an adjacent olive grove owned by the church, the biggest landowner in the village. The olive tree branches, heavy with fruit, bent close to the well-cultivated soil.

"This is out of our way, Nicolaki, but I wanted you to see this magnificent property originally owned by your father when he was a rich landowner," she said with obvious pleasure in her eyes as she outlined the perimeter of the property with an extended arm. She always seemed to enjoy referring to those prosperous times, especially when it was harvest time in the village. Then she added, after switching to a much more somber disposition, "Unfortunately, your father fell into hard times in his later years and was forced to sell his land, piece by piece, to support us."

"Did he actually sell this land to the Church?"

"No, Mr. Domazos bought it from your father and kept it for a few years before he donated it to the church for the soul of his son who was killed during the big war."

His mother's comments reminded Nicolas of the village priest, Papa Christodoulos who, at the end of many a Sunday's liturgy, would ask for volunteers to help cultivate the church groves or collect the Lord's crops. The elderly priest himself was always the first to volunteer, doing hard field work alongside all the other volunteers. It was the only time people could see their priest without his black vestments and miter.

Towards the end of the church property, mother and son came across an area of almond trees, laden with fruit, not yet harvested. Mother, without any hesitation, proceeded to harvest parts of each tree that she could reach without climbing, trying to fill up a large weed basket. Nicolas was astonished and speechless and did nothing to help his mother.

I cannot believe what I see with my own eyes...my mother is actually stealing from the Church...my own mother, my role model for honesty and good behavior...my role model for religious piety.

"Papa Christodoulos and his family partake of this fruit, God's fruit, all the time," she said, feeling the need to explain her behavior. "The priest is a decent man and the servant of God and he deserves what he gets. But God loves all his children. We are God's children and the Lord would want us to partake of his plentiful fruit in our hour of need. I'm sure that it was God who guided your father to plant these trees many years ago, perhaps for a special purpose such as this."

Apparently, the widow did not expect any opposing argument from her son. She proceeded to fill both baskets to the brim. However, she must have sensed his concerns and probable disapproval, for she never asked him to participate in the improper harvest.

Nicolas was not fully satisfied with his mother's explanation and decided to continue looking for additional reasons that would further justify her unexpected and improper behavior. He did not express his thoughts on the matter to her or anyone else. However, from that time on, a slightly revised picture of his loving mother's character and religiosity entered his mind.

I can still see my mother as the decent and kind woman whose thoughts and actions usually reflect both her love and fear of God. At times, however, her thoughts and actions may also reflect a certain out-of-character practicality. In other words, she will not hesitate to bend rules and regulations, whether human or divine, when it comes down to a question concerning the welfare of her family.

Chapter Two

Nicolas arrived in the big town alone. His mother promised to join him in a couple of weeks. It was only a little after nine in the morning, but the mid-August temperature and humidity of coastal Larnaca were already high. Of course the sun was shining, it usually never fails to do so every day in Cyprus from early May to late September. Rain would help a lot but it seldom comes to the lowlands during this five-month period.

For shade relief, the youth moved his solitary bundle to the corner across the street from the bus depot. He was told that his brother-in-law, Makis, would pick him up in front of the depot but he had to take a chance and move away from the hot sun. In spite of the light clothing, khaki shorts, linen short-sleeve shirt and sandals, the boy was sweating profusely even in the shade. His hair, now much longer than the usual crew-cut of his school days, was moist all around but was dripping wet around the ears and the neck.

His misery started evaporating the moment he saw Makis approaching on his bike. He had spent some time with his twenty-eight year old brother-in-law twice before and thought of him as the most likeable male adult he ever met. To avoid sweat's wet contact, their hug was loose and quick.

"Welcome to our town, Nico."

"Thank you, Maki, I am quite excited to be here…is it always so hot in August?"

"Actually not. We have been having a heat wave for about a week now, since last Friday. It should be over soon."

They tied the bundle on the back metal seat and, with Nicolas sitting on the front cross bar, started for home. Makis and Marina did not live in one of the relatively new municipal buildings that Mrs. Kyriaki thought they did. They were still on a waiting list for that kind of dwelling. In the meantime, they were renting two rooms in a modest five-room townhouse. The larger of the two was used as the couple's bedroom and the other, originally intended to be the family room, was now designated to be Nicolas' own. A cot was promised but the young apprentice did not mind at all sleeping on the couch. For the first time in his life, he did not have to share his bed or his sleeping quarters with anyone.

Nicolas was excited about his new home with marble floors, painted walls and many modern facilities. He was impressed with the outhouse that boasted a fancy tank-and-chain system for indoor water release. He was equally fascinated with the bathhouse that had a fancy bathtub as well as an overhead shower, something completely new for him. The ever present sun simply heated water in a metal tank placed on top of the roof.

He was told that solar energy was not effective for a few cold winter weeks but, if a bath was deemed necessary, water could be heated on top of the kerosene stove.

Nicolas' first few days with his sister and brother-in-law in the vast metropolis of close to twenty thousand people were more pleasant than any of his most optimistic expectations. It appeared to him that both Marina and Makis were truly happy to have him stay with them. They appeared to treat him as their son, especially his thirty-one year old sister whose personality and behavior reminded him so much of his mother.

"Nicolaki…my dearest Nicolaki…you are God-sent. I've been

trying to have a child of my own ever since we got married, over six years ago. Doctors tell me I may still have one. In the meantime, you are here to fill the void...you are truly God-sent."

The young apprentice began work two days after he arrived in town. Construction work hours were long but bearable: weekdays from 6:00 a.m. to 7:00 p.m., with three hours break for lunch and an optional siesta. He used the scheduled two-hour siesta time for a swim and relaxation at the nearby beach. For a boy who grew up in a mountain village, this was a great treat.

Saturdays were always anticipated with pleasure. The work ended half an hour before high noon and the pay was distributed soon after. That was the most satisfying part of a working week. By pay time, all kinds of vendors of baked goods and sweet snacks were gathered at construction sites or outside factory gates all over town to take advantage of the workers' appetite as well as their filled pockets. Nicolas felt plenty of self-satisfaction because, for a change, he had earned money for a treat.

One aspect of his work was a bit disappointing. He was part of a team of three boys, none older than thirteen, whose main job was to mix mortar and then transport it by hand, two buckets at a time, to one of several masons, sometimes climbing up two or three floors on primitive wooden ladders.

The fact that this work was very hard was not the main disappointing aspect of the job. Nicolas was promised work as an apprentice, watching a master mason at work. Instead, he was one of several construction laborers, of all ages, who performed routine chores. However, he did not dare complain to his uncle. He was grateful he had the job.

On his third payday, in early September, an unexpected pleasure awaited him at home. His mother had arrived that morning for a few days' visit. Marina, who did not work at the button factory that day, appeared unusually jovial. Nicolas suspected that something more than just her mother's visit was motivating her. Eventually, after Makis also came home from construction work at a nearby British base, Marina announced,

"I have something wonderful to share with you...I just found out this morning...I am pregnant. The Lord listened to my prayers...I am finally going to have a child of my own!"

When the congratulations and the overall excitement subsided, Nicolas went out into the back yard and sat on the bench built around the trunk of the tall eucalyptus.

The sun was exhibiting its usual mid-afternoon bright face. The boy's body must have appreciated the cool tree shade even though his mind was restless and apparently oblivious to any physical comforts or discomforts.

Thank you God for making my sister so happy...Lord, I do know that You will answer my prayers too...but when? School starts soon and I still have no prospects...I see no chance of attending school this year..."

Mrs. Kyriaki startled her son as she approached from behind and placed her hand on his shoulder. As he turned around to face her, her hand moved to the top of his head which was richly endowed with thick, wavy hair.

"Do not lose your faith, my Nicolaki. God never fails to open doors for those who believe in Him. On Monday you and I will visit the town's high schools. Let's test them. Let's see if they dare refuse financial assistance to worthy students like you..."

Nicolas was not surprised that his mother was always able to read his mind, nor was he surprised that she was always there when he needed her.

God, please do not let me disappoint my mother...she thinks so highly of me and my abilities as a student.

"Thank you for your faith in me, mother. I look forward to visiting the Lyceum, the six-grade Greek "high school" for boys. The Catholic "Nun's High School" is for girls only. Perhaps we should even consider the only other remaining option and visit "the Americans" as well.

"Let's try our own people first, my son. Maybe we will not have to solicit help from the Americans."

On Monday morning, mother and son were the first to enter the Lyceum offices, a few minutes before nine. Their first impression of the school was positive. The administrative assistant, a courteous middle-aged woman, assured both mother and son that the school offered several scholarships to elementary school graduates who qualified for and excelled in the Lyceum's "special entrance examinations."

"Please take a seat, madam. Mr. Loukaides, the assistant principal, will review your son's transcript and then invite you into his office to discuss his qualifications and, hopefully, schedule him for the scholarship exam."

The assistant principal, a balding, gray-bearded squab with midnight eyes, appeared to Nicolas to be the personification of proper, serious behavior and stern discipline. Immediately, the boy equated the man's appearance with a bad omen.

"I am Mr. Loukaides, please take a seat." He approached and offered his hand to Mrs. Kyriaki for a handshake. She shook hands with obvious reverence and a nervous smile but said nothing.

The assistant principal then moved to face Nicolas who tried to stand up but was pushed back in his seat with a gentle push on the shoulder. Nicolas felt intimidated by the man and became even more so the moment he turned his head up to directly face the school official's dark face and small, piercing eyes which were much too close for comfort.

Mr. Loukaides was indeed the bearer of bad news. His deep voice, the angling of his thick, black eyebrows and his formal speech, all correlated well with the morbid disposition already assigned to him by the boy. He spoke slowly and clearly but with no apparent compassion in his voice, first congratulating the boy on his good academic record and recommendation from his teacher and then explaining the school's position:

"I am afraid I'm going to disappoint you young man. Unfortunately, you do not qualify to compete for the Lyceum academic scholarships. Your transcript shows that you never had English."

"Sir, English is not taught in our village school," interjected Nicolas.

"I suspected that but there is nothing we can do. By council decree, the Lyceum scholarship entrance examinations incorporate questions based on a requirement of at least two years of basic English language in elementary school. Therefore, upon failing the questions on the English language portion of the exam, your score will not be good enough for a scholarship."

"Don't you think it's unfair for a Greek school to require English in its scholarship examinations? This unfair policy will definitely exclude worthy students who come from small villages where the English language is not taught at all," pointed out Mrs. Kyriaki, narrowing her eyes and raising her upper lip, signs of anger and disgust.

The administrator made no additional comment. He opened his arms and shook his head, clearly conveying the feeling of helplessness.

"Good day to you," he said as he opened the office door, essentially signaling that they should exit.

Mrs. Kyriaki was visibly upset and barely managed not to let her anger take total control of herself. She did murmur something in a very unfriendly tone, however, which caused Loukaides to stare at her for just a moment before he closed the door behind her.

Both mother and son appeared to be in a cloud of total disappointment. He spoke first as they were about to exit the Lyceum grounds.

"I suppose it's useless going to the American Academy...if

the Greek Lyceum requires English, I can't imagine why not the Americans..."

"Somehow I have a good feeling now about the Americans. It's only a short walk from here, let's give it a try, son...what do we have to lose at this point? Remember never to underestimate the workings of the Lord. Sometimes He closes a door, creates an obstacle in the present, so that He may open more doors and create more opportunities in the future."

They entered the grounds of the American high school, a non-profit secondary school of seven grades, founded by the Reformed Presbyterian Church. They passed through an ornamental iron gate which was framed under a semi-circular arch of the same material. Flat, cast-iron letters in red were attached to the front surface of the arch, spelling "American Academy." The founding date of 1908 was displayed in black numbers below the name.

They decided to walk around the campus first before contacting any administration officials. The campus appeared quite extensive in area, with all structures widely scattered. The larger of these were two two-story buildings of carved limestone blocks, typical of colonial times. A more modern concrete block building and at least four barracks-like structures made up the rest of the main campus buildings.

From across the main street that formed much of the campus perimeter, they could see a long, narrow path, lined on both sides by tall Cypress trees, leading to the principal's residence. The home was not visible from the street. A little building down the street from the tree-lined pathway served as the school's evangelical chapel.

Mrs. Kyriaki approached and asked one of the students, "Why are so many students on campus today, ten days before the school is scheduled to begin classes?"

"Those who live in the school's dormitories and some of those who play varsity sports arrive a few days earlier than the others."

"I see only boys around. Are girls admitted to this school?"

"Yes they are. The school is coeducational, but only male students can live in the dormitories."

Mother and son came to rest at a bench by a concrete pathway, midway between the two limestone buildings. There was no shade anywhere in the vicinity, but because of a cool breeze, the sun was bearable for a short while. They both knew that eventually they had to walk over to Carithers Hall, the building facing the main street, because it housed the administration offices. To avoid hanging around for hours, they had to do it before lunch break. But Mrs. Kyriaki didn't seem to be quite ready to see an official yet.

At one point, she closed her eyes and lowered her head. Nicolas could hear her praying but he couldn't make out all the words. However, the direction of her prayer was obvious to him upon hearing phrases such as "my son's destiny…open a door …"

Finally mother and son stood up, ready to walk towards Carithers, but they both sat down again, simultaneously, when they saw a tall and lean gray-haired man walking along the pathway towards their position. As he came within a couple of yards, they could tell he was American. His formal blue suit and tie, his height, his blue eyes, his light complexion, with cheeks and forehead reflecting a reddish hue in the hot son, all betrayed his heritage.

Because both mother and son were certain they could not communicate with the tall American, they felt it was alright to keep staring at him as he approached. When he stopped and spoke to them, they both practically went into shock.

"Good day madam, good day young man. Welcome to the Academy. Can I help you with anything? My name is Weir, I am the director of the school." He spoke in a friendly and courteous manner in perfect Greek. They both stood up in reverence. Very uncharacteristically, mother remained silent.

"Good day sir. My mother, Mrs. Kyriaki Maos, and I, Nicolas Maos, are here to see if your school offers any scholarships for needy students."

With a broad smile, he shook hands with both of them before answering.

"The Lord sent you to the right place at the right time. For the first time in our school history, we offer a full-tuition scholarship for all seven years, or until graduation, to the needy student who performs best in a specially prepared scholarship exam."

"This sounds good but I am very much afraid to ask if knowledge of basic English is part of the exam."

"I can understand your concern, young man, I assume you come from a small village where English is not taught. You do not have to be concerned with basic English. The school's admissions policy is to consider every qualified student in Cyprus irrespective of English language background. This policy applies to the scholarship as well."

Mother Kyriaki's eyes became swollen with tears of joy and raised her arms to give thanks to the Lord. When she lowered them, she grabbed the principal's left hand and kept it sandwiched between hers while she sobbingly proclaimed,

"This is the Lord's miracle…He never forgets those who trust in Him…my good sir, you are a good man…you are a messenger of the Lord…"

Mr. Weir was visibly moved with the mother's faith and devotion and, above all, her characterization of him as "a messenger of the Lord." Representing the founding church, this was his 25th year at the Academy with the mission to educate the youth of Cyprus as well as to bring to them the Lord's message of redemption through Christ.

"Thank you mother Kyriaki…your name brings to mind the

Lord's day...the English translation of your name is "Sunday"... thank you Mrs. Sunday, if I may call you by your English name, for your kind words." He turned to face Nicolas whose eyes were also watery.

"Young man, I believe you have a rich heritage, you are Sunday's son. I am sure you think that poverty is currently a disadvantage for you but here is your chance to change your disadvantage into an advantage...poverty, your apparent disadvantage, qualifies you to get in there and try to win that scholarship."

Mother and son were escorted to the office where the boy was registered for the exam by the school's administrative assistant, Mrs. Moissides, a very kind and patient lady. She informed them that, in spite of the limited publicity about the "Scholarship of the 500th," a large number of elementary school graduates were expected to participate in the competition which was to be held in about three days, on Thursday morning at eight.

Answering Nicolas' question, she also informed them that math problems, Greek spelling and grammar, and a written essay on a given topic would be the main part of the exam. The boy was quite curious about the name of the scholarship, "the 500th," but did not ask for an explanation.

Thank you God...thank you for opening a door of opportunity for me.

The word that Nicolas was to compete for a scholarship spread very fast among relatives, friends and neighbors. His sister Theodora and her fiancé Gogos joined the rest of the family at sister Marina's in order to celebrate. The celebration went on and on and Nicolas began to worry.

"You all seem to celebrate as if I won the scholarship...please remember that all that's happened thus far is that I was given the opportunity to compete. I'm scared to death...I hope I do not disappoint you."

"You better get to work and start studying hard until Thursday's exam," advised sister Marina. Most of the others seconded the idea. Nicolas tried to explain.

"The exam is based on fundamental knowledge...you can't really study for it. You either have it by now or you don't."

"I agree with my Nicolaki," added his mother. "All he has to do now is join me in prayer...day and night...the Lord is bound to listen. He can't abandon us now after giving us today's miraculous opportunity."

⁂

Math was the first part of the exam which consisted of three parts and four pages. The time allocated for all three parts was sixty minutes.

The first part required the completion of fifteen multiplication functions, with multiplicands and multipliers progressively increasing from four to eleven digits. The second part was similar to the first except that, in this case, the emphasis was on division, with six-to-eleven-digit dividends to be divided by divisors which progressively increased from three to seven digits. The third part required the solution of fifteen word problems. The detailed solutions were to be entered on blank page four.

When the exam proctor called out, "Time is up, stop writing, all pens down." Nicolas was halfway through a check-up of his solutions to the word problems. While exiting the large auditorium/classroom he felt butterflies stirring in his stomach. He completed all the functions and word problems but he did not have enough time to review all his work.

Was I fast enough?...is my work accurate?...look at some of these sophisticated students all around me...they probably had plenty of time to spare.

Most students were hanging around the auditorium hallway waiting for the call to sit for the second part of the exam. Nicolas was moving slowly among the candidates without talking to anyone.

At one point, he stood next to a group of five well-dressed, tall boys that seemed to know each other very well. By comparison to the group, Nicolas appeared small and unsophisticated. They were in the middle of a very lively discussion about their performance in the exam they had just finished.

Besides their dress, the boys' language betrayed their big-town origin. With the exception of one of them who claimed he finished "almost everything" on the exam, the rest admitted they only did a good portion of it.

The biggest and probably the oldest in the group kept emphasizing that it was not the amount completed that counted the most but the amount that was correct. At one point, he noticed Nicolas standing next to him and addressed him with a fake smile and in a rather sarcastic tone,

"Hey, little village boy, how many of those functions and problems you were not able to finish?"

The rest of the boys turned around, with a grin on their face, apparently interested in Nicolas' answer. At first Nicolas thought that, for the sake of humility, he should purposely play down his exam performance. However, the apparent sarcasm and the overall condescending attitude of the boys convinced him to tell the truth.

"I completed everything and rechecked most of the answers. I don't expect any major errors."

The immediate effect of Nicolas' answer was expressions of serious disbelief frozen on five faces. The later effect was a burst of comments expressing ridicule, followed by lots of belly laughter.

Six days later, classes began at the Academy but Nicolas had not as yet received any notification concerning the results of the scholarship exam. The echoes of the five boys' comments of ridicule began to resonate in his ears. Even worse, most family members started predicting disaster. His mother, however, refused to go along with the others and continued to express hope and optimism and trust in God.

On the second day of classes, Nicolas borrowed Maki's bicycle for another personal visit to the school. He had to find out about the scholarship one way or another.

When he entered the school's grounds, the bell was ringing for students to assemble in the Main building for the morning assembly and prayer. He made his way to Carithers Hall. Mrs. Moissides, who saw him in the lobby, literally ran over to him and hugged him a couple of times before she joyfully exclaimed,

"Congratulations Nicola! Good work...great work young man! We expected you to come for registration a couple of days ago... what happened?"

Nicolas could hardly speak. Deep emotions of happiness and pride as well as consequential tears of joy temporarily blocked his power of speech.

God, I feel blessed...I feel Your presence...thank You...

Finally, the young student managed to explain to the administrative assistant that he never received any notification concerning the scholarship. Eventually she discovered that the notification letter was mailed to his permanent address, the village of Ora, instead of his present address in Larnaca.

Right in the middle of registration, the director, Mr. Weir, entered the office and asked his administrative assistant for the "final number." Nicolas, who was seated with his back towards the office entrance, recognized the director's voice and immediately stood up and turned around to greet him.

Mr. Weir did not wait for any introductions since he recognized the boy and extended his arm for a handshake.

"Congratulations, Nicolas, the son of Kyriaki Maos. You are the 500th...you and your mother and her faith won...God is triumphant...but come, come with me to the assembly. You can finish registration later."

The assembly hall was packed with students and staff and the program was already underway. Mr. Weir took his usual position on the front elevated platform, to the right of the podium, after he placed Nicolas in one of the first row seats. When time came for "the director's report," Mr. Weir approached the podium. After his usual greetings to the students and staff, his voice tone changed abruptly to convey lots of personal pride and satisfaction.

"And now, I am very pleased indeed to share some great news with all of you here in this assembly. Today, the second day of the new semester, the beginning of the 41st academic year of our school, the final enrollment figure stands at 511, a new record for our beloved Academy. Until..." He paused for several seconds, waiting for the loud applause to die down.

"About fifteen days ago, the enrollment figure stood at 499. Even though it was still a record for our school, the school administration decided to round the figure to 500 by offering a full-tuition competitive scholarship to be named 'the 500th.' For some reason, after the scholarship was announced, the enrollment did increase to 5ll. Nevertheless, the competition for the "500th" did take place as planned."

Mr. Weir paused to motion to Nicolas to come up to the platform. The boy did not understand the details of the announcement since it was in English but he had a pretty good idea what it was all about. He stood by the side of the towering director who then continued his speech.

"Here he is, Nicolas Maos, the winner from among several dozen applicants who sat for the scholarship exam." Another thunderous applause. "A few days ago, I met Nicolas and his mother, Mrs. Kyriaki Maos, seated at the bench outside Carithers. They were visiting the Academy to inquire about scholarships. I personally informed them about the exam for the 500th to be held in three days...I had a good feeling...there was something special about this boy and his loving mother."

The director turned to face Nicolas and added, in Greek, "Congratulations Nicolas, the son of Kyriaki." He then faced the audience once again and added, in English, "Let's hear it once again for the winner of the 500th, let's hear it for Sunday's son." The acclamation for the boy resonated throughout the Main Hall.

They shook hands and the boy whispered, "Thank you, sir." It was his first communication in English. Mrs. Moissides taught him the words earlier that morning.

At the end of his first school day, in mid-afternoon, Nicolas came back home carrying several books and other needed school supplies in his hands or under his arms. They were all part of his scholarship winnings. His whole family and many close relatives and friends as well as neighbors were already there waiting for him. Earlier that day, Mrs. Moissides had sent a personal messenger to inform the family about "Nicolas' triumph."

While waiting, most were celebrating by drinking local red wine and eating slices of fried halloumi cheese and smoked sausage on pieces of sesame *koullouri*, the Cyprus version of a sesame bagel.

As usual on such occasions, one could hear several very loud conversations going on at the same time. To a foreigner, such loud discussions would appear to be unfriendly arguments but, in reality, they represented mostly serious exclamations of praise for the scholarship winner and the family's good fortune.

For some reason, mother Kyriaki did not appear to be celebrating. Nicolas found her seated on a tree-trunk stool at one of the far corners of the back yard, all by herself. They hugged for quite a while. When she let go, Nicolas could see tears rolling down her cheeks.

"No one, no one on this earth could be happier than I am. I celebrate my own way…far from the noise of the crowd…I celebrate with thoughts of my good fortune for having a son like you…thoughts of finding favor in the eyes of the Lord…"

Another special morning assembly on Nicolas' second day of school. The assistant director had an important announcement for the student body.

"The Academy council has awarded another full-tuition scholarship to the Turkish Cypriot who achieved the highest score from among several Turkish Cypriots who participated in the scholarship exam." He asked a young girl, in a front seat, to join him on the platform. "Here is Yiasmin Ibrahim, from our town of Larnaca. She is the winner of the scholarship. She is the..."

The Turkish students, about ten percent of the student body, interrupted the introduction to give the winner an extensive and very loud standing ovation. There was a polite, almost silent applause from the rest of the assembly.

As soon as the assembly was dismissed, there was an immediate exchange of comments among the students. Some of the most outspoken of the students thought that her scholarship merely represented an obvious "gift of pacification" to the Turkish community. Some others referred to her, jokingly, as a "hanoum" or "harem girl." A few well known cynics thought she deserved it because she looked spectacular in her national Turkish costume.

Nicolas felt isolated and quite frustrated because he could not understand what most of the older students were discussing or arguing about. The Academy had a very strict rule that students, above the third grade, must always converse in English when on school grounds. If caught by a teacher breaking the rule, a student would receive demerit points on conduct. So, without much choice at this time, Nicolas kept to his own thoughts.

The two scholarship winners, Nicolas and Yiasmin, together with several other students who lacked English language fundamentals, were placed in the "Beginners Class" instead of the First Grade. English vocabulary and grammar were practically the only subjects taught, several hours a day, during the first semester. During the second semester, all subjects, with the exception of Greek or Turkish, were taught primarily in English.

Topics like geography, history and social studies were taught a couple of times a week. However, since the Academy could be described as a "missionary school," the study of the Bible was scheduled at least for one class period per day. A rather detailed march through sections of the Old and New Testaments, together with an analysis of the contents, was essentially expected to be completed by graduation time.

Many students referred to Nicolas as a "book face" because he typically received the highest grades in class. Yiasmin surprised just about everybody, except Nicolas, with her class performance. He somehow did expect her to be the outstanding student that she actually was. She hardly socialized with anybody, including other Turkish students, in or outside the classroom.

Yiasmin's cultural behavior, her aura of mystery and her beauty fascinated Nicolas to no end. He often sat next to her in class but only managed to exchange a few greetings or glances with her a handful of times. She even totally ignored the class gossip linking her and Nicolas romantically. The gossip started, slowly at first, because they were placed next to each other as late comers to class but skyrocketed to higher levels after the social studies teacher kept referring to the two scholarship winners as the "freebie couple."

The first five years at the Academy were routine and generally uneventful. Nicolas concentrated on his studies in order to maintain a good grade point average and class rank, both necessary in order to continue as a scholarship recipient. He also literally subscribed to the school motto, "To Grow and to Serve," by volunteering lots of time and effort in the work of school associations. He especially cherished the work of the "Boys' Brotherhood" where he proudly helped to raise funds and disseminate food during the holidays to the town's needy families.

He also made sure he found time to visit his village, especially during school holiday breaks. He always looked forward to these visits, essentially hooked on his mother's special attention and pampering. She seldom failed to declare her pride or express her feelings about her son.

"You are the pride of my life, my Nicolaki, and my life in this village is complete only during your visits."

During most of the long summer school breaks, he managed to get employment at the nearby British base of Dhekelia, first as a construction laborer and later as a clerk assistant. There was a minimum age requirement to begin work at the base so his brother-in-law Makis arranged for him to get the job after he convinced or bribed the village mouhtar to produce a "new" birth certificate that increased Nicolas' age by two years. With time, this fake earlier date became Nicolas' official birthday.

Summer work was especially time-consuming because not only did it involve all weekdays and most of Saturday, but it also had excessive overtime requirements that often used up most of the weekend. Nicolas also discovered the pleasures of weekend visits to the beach with his new friends and especially the joy of Saturday evening open-air cinema. Nevertheless, he still preferred weekend visits to his mother and youngest sister, especially in late July and August when the figs and grapes were in season.

The spring of 1955 was Nicolas' last semester in the "prep-grades" of the Academy. He had to make a decision about the remaining two grades. He explained to Marina and Makis:

"I decided against entering the Commercial Section of the Academy, generally believed to be the most practical of the two choices. Instead, I signed up for the U.P. or University Preparatory Section...I expect..."

"I heard that the Commercial Section usually provides immediate employment with banks and other businesses upon graduation. Isn't that important to you?" asked Makis.

"Of course it's important to me...and to my mother and Nina and everybody in our family...but I also have a dream... a dream about university studies. Someday I have to prepare myself for that no matter how improbable it may appear to be...I know that the U.P. classes will be quite competitive and even difficult but I also expect them to be quite exciting and perhaps..."

"That's right, little brother, do follow your dream. I wish that your dream does come true for your sake and that of our mother. I hope and pray that my son has similar dreams," interrupted Marina.

"Thank you sister. You know of course that throughout my life I will make sure that my nephew, our little Andros, is given similar chances for higher education as you and other people have given me."

That spring of 1955 was also one of the most eventful in Nicolas' middle school life. In fact, that whole year produced some of the most influential, character-building events and circumstances in the young man's life.

The early part of the semester brought him sadness when it became apparent that, for some unknown reason Yiasmin, the Turkish scholarship winner abandoned her Academy education. It was strange that he felt like that because, in reality, he never had a close relationship with her, except perhaps in his imagination. During the almost five years the two "freebies" shared classes, real and perceived cultural differences did not allow them to exchange more than a couple of words of greetings at a time.

Nobody among the Greek students seemed to know why "the hanoum" left school. Rumors and cynics with ideas did abound, however.

"A rich, old Turkish pasha bought her for his harem," said a known wiseguy.

"The Turkish gal was removed because she favored and flirted with Greek boys," added another.

No one thought of asking the Turkish students whether they knew the real reason of her departure because, at this time, the relationship between the Greek and Turkish communities was deteriorating fast.

The Greeks, who made over eighty percent of the island's population, were reaching a very high pitch in their demands, through frequent public demonstrations, that the British colonial forces leave Cyprus and allow the island to unite with Greece. The Turkish minority felt abandoned and insecure and demanded separation of the two communities through partition under the protection of Turkey.

Nicolas had several friends among his Turkish classmates but still did not dare ask them about Yiasmin lest they misinterpret his curiosity as a culturally and politically unacceptable romantic interest in a Turkish maiden. But one day, several weeks into the semester, unexpectedly and out of the blue, his friend Ali, the tall, muscular Turk who gave him plenty of competition in the classroom, volunteered some information:

"Yiasmin had no choice but to immigrate to America...with her mother and little brother. Her mother has a sister whose family owns a Turkish restaurant in New York."

Nicolas was curious why Yiasmin had no choice and why her father was left out of the story. He was about to ask but Ali was faster with additional information.

"You read in the paper, of course, about the suspicious construction accident in the Greek section of town that killed her father last December."

Nicolas never heard of the accident but immediately realized that, whether justified or not, the Turks had already classified it as a product of the violent aspect of their community conflict with the Greeks. He decided not to prolong this type of conversation where the two communities blamed each other for any and all serious mishaps that each experienced. "Oh, yes...an unfortunate, horrible accident...but tell me Ali, what do you know about life in New York, about its colleges...you think that you or I could ever study there?"

"Everything is possible. I hope you can do it, if that's what you want...I plan to go to England, I want to enter London University...that's why I plan to take several G.C. exams during my U.P. years."

The other most extraordinary event of the semester was the declaration on April 1st, through the dissemination of tens of thousands of leaflets all over Cyprus, that the struggle of E.O.K.A. (National Organization of Cypriot Fighters) had began. The Greeks, especially the high school students, poured into the streets to demonstrate their total support for the organization and its noble struggle for freedom. The Turks rejected the organization and its aims as anti-Turkish and the British colonial government soon declared E.O.K.A. as a terrorist organization.

With time, the leaflets and the peaceful protests were being replaced by shootings and bombs and ambushes. Middle-school education, essentially the island's top educational level at the time, was being disrupted by leaps and bounds.

The Greek students, primarily those attending the gymnasiums, would often abandon their classes, pick up a Greek flag and parade into the town main streets in order to proclaim their loud support for E.O.K.A., Archbishop MAKARIOS and *ENOSIS* or "Union with Greece."

In the beginning, the student demonstrators appeared to enjoy their newly-found role in the struggle for freedom. However, with time, the demonstrations became more violent, primarily through rock throwing, and the British security forces were at times disbursing the students with tear gas bombs and bullets. The casualties were mounting and the "fun part" of the demonstrations was disappearing.

Under the declared state of emergency, Greek students from all over the island were being arrested or wounded or killed. Some young people were even sentenced to be hanged for attacking British emergency security forces or merely because they were caught carrying a firearm.

Between April 1st and the end of the semester in mid-June, the American Academy, primarily because of its American character and international student population, appeared to be immune to all the disruptions effecting all other schools. Only a handful of its students joined in the demonstrations of the other schools in town and the school itself was not shut down, even once, because of a school-wide protest or a call to strike. However, things changed drastically in the next semester.

Because of a violent summer, with frequent EOKA ambushes of security patrols in towns and especially in remote rural areas, all resulting in a large number of deaths on both sides, the Greek gymnasiums and lyceums of the island began the new Fall semester with continuous protests and classroom strikes.

At the same time, because the British colonial rulers needed the Turkish population to staff the police, they convinced the Turkish minority that its security and, indeed, its survival depended on a successful elimination of the Greek terrorist organization E.O.K.A. that demanded *ENOSIS* or Union with Greece, something that would bring disaster to the Turks.

As a result, large numbers of young Turks joined the uniformed or secret "Special Police Forces" whose aim was the apprehension and destruction of the "terrorists" under the leadership of British officers. This of course exacerbated the feeling of distrust between the Greek and Turkish communities.

The great majority of the student body of the Academy was

Greek and, eventually, many of these students would join their counterparts, primarily the boys and girls of the Larnaca Lyceum, in their almost daily demonstrations against the British.

However, the Academy itself still managed to avoid disruption of its classes for well over a month into the semester. All classes were available for those of its students who wanted to attend. But a relatively minor incident changed all that.

Upon arrival on campus, on a chilly morning in mid-October, the Academy students were surprised to see a huge Greek flag, instead of the official Academy banner, flying high from the central campus pole. When the bell rang for classes as per schedule, everybody assumed that the administration decided to hold classes and ignore the illegally placed flag.

However, after lunch break, the students found all classroom buildings closed when they tried to return to their classes. Hand written signs taped on the front door of each building explained the administration's "new" policy: *NO CLASSES WILL BE HELD UNLESS THE GREEK FLAG, ILLEGALLY RAISED ON THE CENTRAL SCHOOL POLE, IS REMOVED*

It was rather obvious to everyone that the Turkish students and their community leaders must have protested very strongly and very effectively in order to convince the administration to close the school unless the Greek flag is removed. Two Turkish community leaders, accompanied by several Turkish students, were seen entering the administration building a few minutes after the lunch break bell.

No student, Greek or otherwise, was expected to dare remove the Greek flag.

Everybody assumed that the flag was there because of a directive from E.O.K.A. which was known to always punish, often very severely, those who opposed its directives.

Most Greek students at the Academy believed that Ali, Nicolas' outspoken classmate, a Turkish tough with an impressive bodybuilder's physique and a quick temper, was a member of a secret Turkish police unit whose aim was to report Greek student agitators to the British authorities. Everybody expected "fearless" Ali to be the first to try and remove the illegal flag.

But Ali surprised just about everybody with his unexpected and quick disappearance from campus that early afternoon. Nicolas, who respected his Turkish classmate not for his physical prowess but for his intelligence and excellent academic performance, was pleased with Ali's show of restraint.

By one thirty, the rest of the commuting students left the campus. The dormitory residents kept the vigil going till late at night, watching the flag from their dormitory windows. Nothing or no one was seen to disturb the flag except for the night breeze.

When the students arrived back to school the next day, the Greek flag was gone. Once again, the AA banner was in its proper place.

"Your Turkish friend Ali, a coward, must have done it under the cover of night," whispered Maro into Nicolas' ear, with some concern in her voice and eyes. "I'm sure he will receive the punishment he deserves...you better stay away from him this time..."

"Ali can be a lot of things but I doubt he is a coward nor would he seek the cover of darkness to remove the flag. He happens to be a shameless exhibitionist who would love to remove the flag in front of an audience. I have a feeling he was restrained by some promise he made to the administration," he responded rather loudly, attracting some bystanders who entered the conversation and eventually supported the young woman's theory.

Later on, during the morning assembly, it was announced that a staff member of the school had been asked to remove the flag. No name was mentioned. Speculation as to who removed the flag continued until the morning of the third day when another Greek flag was raised. School classes were disrupted once again until the flag was removed overnight. This went on back and forth for several weeks.

Nicolas began to worry and confided his feelings to his good friend Savvakis, a graduating senior and president of the Boys' Brotherhood committee:

"I'm afraid for the loss of the whole semester, perhaps the whole year or even more than a year unless something happens to end this nonsense. Don't you agree that the whole thing is ridiculous?"

His friend appeared puzzled but said nothing. Nicolas was encouraged to continue: "We both need to graduate soon...you have less than a year to go. We both have families to support, especially you with two younger sisters and no parents. How long can relatives and friends help support your family? Is there anything we can do to end this ridiculous game with the flag?"

Savvakis, a soft spoken and rather shy young man with exceptional good looks, was suspected by many as a behind the scenes leader and organizer of student demonstrations against the British. Uncharacteristically, he was visibly quite disturbed, his face exhibiting anger at Nicolas for what he had just said. At first, without uttering a word, he began to walk away but changed his mind and returned to confront Nicolas.

"I am surprised, in fact I am shocked that you selfishly look at this noble struggle for freedom as a ridiculous game...as nonsense...I have always assumed that you and I, two good friends who shared family values, also shared common ideals about our ethnic heritage and the future of our homeland. I see now that my assumptions were wrong...terribly wrong. Apparently you are not the patriot you pretend to be."

Nicolas was not given a chance to respond to his friend's comments. The words kept echoing back to him for days and sounded more and more like serious accusations. He felt deeply hurt. But Savvakis would not talk to him or even respond to a simple greeting from Nicolas as the two crossed paths on the school grounds or in the library. Even worse, some students started accusing Nicolas as being totally indifferent to the noble Greek cause and even labeling him as a Turkophile.

～

On a Monday morning, in early December, Nicolas arrived on campus expecting another school closing, so typical of most week beginnings. From a distance he could see a large crowd of students around the school flag pole but he could not hear the usual loud cries of support for E.O.K.A. and *ENOSIS*.

He stopped seeking an explanation as soon as the flag on the pole became visible. Instead of the Greek flag, blue and white stripes with a blue cross in the upper left corner, the bright-red Turkish flag, with a white half moon and a star in the same corner, was waving high in the cool breeze of the clear day.

Nicolas pushed through until he reached the inner perimeter of the circle of students. He wasn't totally surprised to see his Turkish classmate, tough Ali, standing by the pole in a bodybuilder's sleeveless T-shirt. A dusty, roughly folded bundle of fabric was lying on the bare ground in front of him. The colors of the bundle revealed the identity of a Greek flag which he undoubtedly lowered from the pole earlier that morning. Ali's right foot was resting on the flag as he kept proclaiming over and over, while flexing his bulging biceps and triceps,

"I dare you...I dare anybody to come and lower the magnificent Turkish flag. I dare anybody to come and face a Turk...is there anybody who is strong enough to face the power of a Turk? Bold enough to try and remove the Turkish flag? The blood-red flag that instilled fear in its enemies for centuries, the flag that was never conquered...I challenge you..."

Nicolas stood there practically motionless for five or ten minutes, along with the rest of the large crowd of students. Suddenly, the silent spectators produced a wave of louder and louder whispers expressing surprise and awe, followed by one of deafening cheers. Nicolas was walking, slowly but steadily towards the flag pole and the tough Turk guarding it.

Ali responded by moving to intercept his puny classmate before he reached the pole. They both stopped abruptly at about three feet from each other.

"I can clearly see surprise, perhaps even disappointment in your eyes and face classmate Ali…my counterchallenge to you is mostly symbolic but necessary…I know very well that you can easily beat me, perhaps beat me badly, but I still have to face you for personal and other reasons…"

"Classmate Nick, I have always respected you for your intelligence but mostly for your apparent fair attitude towards all others, including us Turks. You can turn around and walk away totally unharmed…you can even take that Greek flag with you… you can look like a winner…"

Ali turned and walked to the pole, picked up the Greek flag, dusted it, refolded it neatly and then returned to hand it to Nicolas. Instead of picking up the flag, Nicolas landed a rather quick and surprisingly powerful right on Ali's chin. The Turk fell flat on his back. The Greek spectators went berserk with cheers, calling out the name of their unlikely hero.

But the powerful Turk quickly got up and immediately jettisoned himself, head first, right into his Greek classmate's stomach. Nicolas' back reached the ground with a loud thump. Within a couple of seconds, Ali locked his opponent's torso motionless by sitting on his stomach and by pressing his muscular shins against the frail Greek's sides. At the same time, the Turk relentlessly delivered fierce blows at his victim's head and ribs.

In less than a minute, the language of the crowd cheers went from Greek to Turkish. Nicolas was in big trouble, he looked like his life was in jeopardy.

But Nicolas must have had a blessing because his life was

spared just in the nick of time. His "former" friend Savvakis appeared suddenly at the fight scene and, like a lightning bolt, struck from behind and violently unsettled and jettisoned the Turk who fell flat on his face and stomach.

Once again, the language of the cheers was Greek. However, none of those cheering the new hero expected him to last very long. Like Nicolas, they thought that the taller but similarly frail Savvakis would soon succumb to the blows of the formidable Turk.

However, the Greek cheers continued to grow louder and louder. Everybody was amazed at Savvakis' great ability to avoid the Turk's powerful fists while he himself managed to land formidable blows all over his opponent's body with both his hands and feet.

"He must have had considerable training in the martial arts," someone in the audience suggested and many others agreed.

Within a couple of minutes, the Turk appeared to be hurting and was literally boiling with anger and frustration. He eventually pulled a British army knife from his pants' side pocket. Savvakis seemed to be well trained not only to avoid hand blows but knife blows as well.

The fight came to an abrupt end when, after a close-knit arm struggle for control of the knife that culminated into a tight body entanglement on the ground, Savvakis managed to stand up alone.

At first, Ali remained flat on his back, silent and motionless, with the knife handle and part of the blade protruding out of his right side. But within seconds, he started to groan out loud as he slowly raised his right arm and, in a quick burst of energy, pulled the knife out. For a moment, he kept his arm high with knife in hand, as if in protest or perhaps a challenge, but the arm dropped suddenly with a thumb and stayed motionless. The knife remained loosely in his grip. The rush of blood from his open wound covered much of his body and his vicinity in bright red.

No policemen were found in the vicinity. They must have

all been called to the downtown area where a typical violent demonstration was taking place.

No person from the large crowd of student bystanders approached the three combatants, even after the end of the fight. They all stood at considerable distance around the flag pole in eerie silence. This wouldn't surprise a keen observer who would notice a rather large number of well organized student "security officers" maintaining tight control of the crowd. They apparently protected Savvakis who must have placed them there before he decided to save Nicolas by openly attacking tough Ali.

In the meantime, the winner Savvakis proceeded slowly and calmly to lower the Turkish flag. After folding it lengthwise a couple of times, he used it to bandage Ali's wound by tying it tightly around his waist. He then called out for four Turkish student volunteers to come forward quickly and take their wounded hero, who was still groaning faintly, to the town hospital, less than a block down the street.

Savvakis finally approached Nicolas who was still lying on the ground, fully conscious but apparently unable to move much. Smiling, he padded Nicolas on the shoulder before he placed the folded Greek flag over his chest. He whispered something to his onetime close friend and patiently waited for an answer before he called out to Greek student volunteers to take "hero Nicolas Maos" to the hospital.

As Nicolas was being carted away by three students, Savvakis approached and faced the crowd which responded with a thunderous applause. He bowed his head and then calmly walked away. He was never seen on the Academy campus again.

The next day, all three of the island's leading Greek newspapers had extensive coverage of the flag protest and knifing, as told by several of the Greek students and a school staff member, all present during the event.

One newspaper openly proclaimed Savvakis as an E.O.K.A. operative, a veritable hero of the liberation cause against the British. Another, praised Savvakis for fighting and perhaps eliminating a well known Turkish agent who was constantly bullying and threatening the Greek students of the Academy. The papers also included a footnote explaining that even though tough Ali was badly wounded, he was still expected to live by most expert accounts.

The Greek newspapers also suggested that because of the knifing incident, hero Savvakis will probably join other hard core E.O.K.A. guerilla fighters in one of their secret hideouts across the island. The three papers had a less extensive reportage on Nicolas' participation but they all proclaimed him either a "patriot" or a "courageous young man."

At the same time, the main Turkish newspaper had a front page account of the flag incident. It included school I.D. photos of both Savvakis and Nicolas, labeling them as well-known bullies who tried to kill, without any provocation, a quiet and studious Turkish student who constantly performed at the top of his class as an honor pupil.

Nicolas lost five weeks of classes recovering from his wounds. He had several broken ribs and a severe concussion. Ali took much longer to recover and never returned to the Academy to graduate. He wasn't seen in Larnaca for a long time and rumor had it that he left Cyprus, probably for Turkey and most probably in order to join the Turkish army.

The struggle for liberation was getting more widespread and bloodier during Nicolas' last two years of tenure at the Academy. He managed to stay out of trouble through complete non-participation in school demonstrations or politics in general. He was able to do this for one main reason.

He was closely shielded by his three new friends. These were the three strong student volunteers, all three well-known as devoted boy scouts, who carried him to the hospital after that severe beating he received from Ali. They were chosen for the task by his savior Savvakis, his last act before he vanished.

"I know that there is a purpose in your friendship, I know that you constantly shield me and protect me and you don't let me get into trouble...you are my three musketeers, and I appreciate it very, very much, but why?"

The answer was always the same, and the spokesman was always "the friendly giant" Andros. "We are here to see that you graduate. You can never predict these Americans...they may decide to take your scholarship away if you get into trouble again."

Nicolas eventually completed all the requirements for the University Preparatory diploma in 1957, after almost eight years at the Academy. He was definitely ready for college but no opportunities seemed to present themselves right after graduation. At the same time, no one was predicting an imminent end to the already two-year-old struggle for liberation from the British and the associated violence. In the meantime, a good job and the opportunity to save some money for a hopeful trip abroad to attend college seemed very appealing to him.

His Academy diploma and his clean record of no arrests for violent demonstrations against the British landed him a relatively good-paying job at the nearby British base, specifically the RASC Petrol Depot, as civilian clerk, grade C.

He also took advantage of his new position and applied for and received a passport. On its hard cover, it exhibited the royal crown of Great Britain and was identified with "BRITISH PASSPORT" above the crown and with "CYPRUS" under the crown. On the first page, Nicolas Maos was designated as "British Subject: Colonies," obviously intended to further differentiate the bearer from a "British Citizen."

Nevertheless, Nicolas was happy because the passport was

valid for travel to all countries in Europe and the United States of America for a period of five years.

Anything can happen in five years...including a trip to higher education.

Chapter Three

For almost a year after graduation, life could not have been any better. For the first time in his life, Nicolas tasted the fruit of great personal satisfaction and accomplishment for being able to contribute to the happiness of those he loved most. He was making good money in his new job and, even though he knew he had to save practically all of it in hopes of a future trip to a college education, he actually spent much of it on his mother and younger sister in the village.

He also contributed modestly to his sister Marina's household expenses since she continued to house and feed him while he worked at the Dhekelia army base.

When he visited his mother and Nina in the village every other Sunday, he would bring a couple of deep baskets filled with food necessities and an occasional luxury item such as fancy ground coffee or sugar or pastries. He would also occasionally bring fashionable clothing for his younger sister, carefully chosen by his older sisters. Nina would often display her new items around the village and celebrate her good luck for days.

For many years his mother wore only her widow attire, an ankle-length cotton skirt and light jacket and a pair of worn-out ankle boots, all in black. It was very difficult to bring her something fashionable. Nevertheless, he once brought her a pair of stylish shoes, in black of course. She was thankful to her son and praised the Lord for her good fortune but thought of the shoes as too fancy for herself. She had them altered to fit young Nina.

But Nicolas' greatest joy was to watch his mother's eyes and facial expression, a combination of total disbelief combined with amazing satisfaction, when he occasionally handed her a pound note (approximately three dollars) and once even a five-pound note. His mother practically never handled paper money before, she was used to handling coins, a few shillings at a time. She appeared reluctant to take such big sums of money.

"Thank you son, I always knew that prosperous times would eventually come to this family…of course, this money will be more useful to you and your personal needs now and in the future, my Nikolaki. But I'm willing to serve as your money's keeper."

At the time, Nicolas didn't know what she really meant by the latter statement and she casually avoided all his requests for any further explanation. Nevertheless, that was the golden year of his relationship with his beloved mother and sister in the village.

During the same period, after graduation, the friendship bond between Nicolas and his "three musketeers," who were still attending the Academy, became stronger and stronger. Typical of the youth of Cyprus at the time, the four friends pledged "unending friendship and devotion and even personal sacrifice, if needed, for each other."

The three students spent a couple of their off-school hours riding their bicycles around town. Working Nicolas joined them only on some late afternoons or evenings, or on weekends. The reason for riding around town appeared the same for all of them, but in reality there were differences.

Yiannis was tall and slim, like a young cypress tree and, according to most, the best looking of the four. School regulations did not allow for long hair, but he made sure that a lock of his black, wavy hair fringed across his forehead, much like Tony Curtis. No one disagreed that he was outgoing and likable and had a great sense of humor.

Yiannis rode his bike around town more than all the others, by far, because he loved to flirt or make eye-contact with girls who were usually seated on their balconies or porches facing the street, often pretending to read or knit.

To be fair, Yiannis did have a favorite girl. By all accounts she was not a beauty but she was a lovely and lively petite maiden that also practiced the art of charming everybody with her beautiful eyes. It also meant a lot to Yiannis that her family was one of the oldest and richest in town, so he readily ignored a number of cynics who referred to her as "the perfect snob, the richest flirt in town."

Yiannis hardly ever rode around town all by himself. Even though all the other three rode with him at times, he preferred Nicolas. Andros, "the friendly giant," was not a good choice for a riding companion because he, too, was ruggedly handsome and popular. Some girls thought he owned the most fascinating pair of "bee-brown" eyes in town.

Lakis appeared to be too mature and serious for his age and was very reluctant to ride "aimlessly" around town unless he was going to school or to the conservatory where he was studying the violin. The beauty of his deep blue eyes, a great rarity for Cyprus, was masked by the ever present thick lenses of his spectacles.

Nicolas, who was a couple of inches shorter than the others and of average good looks, was himself a natural for eye flirting, aided by his bright hazel eyes. He was not interested in any of the town girls at the time and only pretended to flirt in order to please his friend Yiannis who did not perceive Nicolas as a serious threat to his multiple conquests through distant flirting.

Only a couple of girls, who got to know Nicolas quite well as a private tutor of English, recognized his intelligence and good sense of humor and acknowledged having a crush on him. In any case, Nicolas was going along for the ride in order to provide a unique service to his friend.

"Nick, Nick...is she looking at me? Is she smiling?...Tell me, tell me, what is she doing now?" This was Yiannis' typical request whenever the two friends approached a candidate for flirting during their bike tours or whenever they attended Sunday services.

The church was a perfect place for flirting since young men stood in the front, close to the altar, facing mostly sideways, and young girls lined up on the upper level known as "the balcony," facing the altar. Yiannis was near-sighted and could hardly recognize the girls on the balcony. However, he refused to wear glasses.

"It's totally unromantic to flirt or exchange glances with a girl through glasses," Yiannis often rationalized. He would actually sit through a motion picture and listen to it, without glasses, rather than watch it with glasses on, just because his favorite girl might be sitting a few rows in front of him and may turn to flirt with him at any time, especially during a love scene in the film.

During an evening at an open-air theater showing *Love in the Afternoon* with Audrey Hepburn and Gary Cooper, a film expected to provide many opportunities for romantic glances, an innocent joke by Andros revealed Yiannis' secret of having acute myopia.

Andros and Nicolas were watching the movie while Yiannis was essentially listening to the soundtrack. Lakis came a little late and was sitting a couple of rows behind his friends.

"Is she looking over here? Is she looking?" asked Yiannis softly, during a romantic interlude in the film, turning towards his friends. Andros rushed to respond first. He had an intentional surprise in his voice.

"It appears to me that she has been staring at a handsome guy behind us for quite a while now...I wonder who the devil this good-looking guy is..."

Yiannis was quite upset because he uttered a loud, "What?" as he stood up, put on his black-rimmed glasses and looked in the direction pointed to him by Andros. As soon as he recognized his friend Lakis and the joke played on him, he turned around, his face showing no signs of being upset but exhibiting a faint smile, ready to scold Andros.

Right at that moment, however, the theater lights went on because of an intermission. His favorite girl and many of her companion friends were already staring at Yiannis, some smiling and some laughing. For a moment he blushed and turned his head down but within seconds straightened up again and resumed flirting, apparently pleasantly surprised that he could enjoy it so much better with his glasses on. He would seldom remove his glasses again until contact lenses became popular many years later.

In February of 1958, Nicolas' hosts, his sister Marina's family, were approved to move into a new home in the municipality housing development. By incredible coincidence, Yianni's family moved into the same housing development and Nicolas and Yiannis became next-door neighbors. The two friends were now in contact several times more a day than before by walking next door to visit at each other's homes or by talking across the dividing fence.

Their usual Sunday routine started very early in the morning. They rode together a few blocks to the local bread bakery to deliver their family's Sunday meal for "oven roasting." In the absence of home electric ovens at the time, the bakery provided the service of its ovens for a small fee. Typically, this popular Sunday pork roast was complemented with a salad of seasonal greens and freshly baked bread.

After the bakery delivery, the two friends attended the last two hours of the morning church service which ended around noon. However, they seldom attended services at the local church. They rode their bikes for close to two miles to the town main Cathedral of Saint Lazarus because that's where Yiannis' favorite girl usually attended. On their way home from church, they picked up the roast from the bakery.

Sunday's lunch around one o'clock, the main meal of the day, was a veritable family affair. Together with a Greek espresso and dessert, a combination of seasonal fruit or custard, the meal sometimes lasted for over two hours. Yiannis was restless and itching to go bike-flirting well before lunch was over, but he had to wait for Nicolas who couldn't get enough of this Sunday family affair.

On a windy and unusually cool Sunday afternoon in early March, after a long bike tour around town, Nicolas did not expect Yiannis to suggest that the four friends meet, as usual, at Phinicoudes that evening. During good weather Sundays, just about every citizen of Larnaca participated in the traditional walk up and down the palm-lined Phinicoudes boulevard by the seashore. The general idea behind the walk was to exchange glances and greetings with many a fellow citizen who may be walking up and down or sitting at one of the many sidewalk cafes.

When the four friends met at the boulevard, they started the walk, arm in arm as they always did, almost totally alone because not too many people ventured out during a cold and windy evening. Nicolas suspected that something very unusual was in the air because his three buddies refused his offer to buy them souvlaki, something he practically always did every Sunday since he started working. Yiannis spoke first after he got all four to face each other in a tight circle:

"Nico, all four of us swore to be close and true friends for life. But there is something that keeps all four of us from being closest in all respects. Three of us are members of E.O.K.A., we swore to fight for freedom until the end...you have been the odd man out and now we want you to join us. In a few days we will let you know concerning the time and place of your swearing-in. Congratulations, Nikolaki!" He ended his speech with a long hug. The others followed suit without saying much.

Nicolas did an excellent job of hiding the fact that he was terribly upset, in fact a little angry. He was, of course, concerned about the many serious risks of joining a guerilla organization, but he mostly was angry at Yiannis who gave him no choice, no option as to whether he would like to join or not. Even worse, his friend assumed that he had no choice and proceeded to talk about scheduling his swearing-in. He decided to say something that was bound to disappoint his friend, but Andros jumped in before him.

"With all due respect to you, Yianni, our section leader, I think you should have given Nico an option. Perhaps he is not ready… perhaps he is not even interested…"

"You are right, Andro…I am sorry Nico, did I assume too much? Did I take advantage of our friendship? It's your choice, of course, whether you want to join us or not. In any case, we do trust you."

Given Yianni's apology and his choice of words, Nicolas now looked at the invitation under a different light.

"I'm honored, of course, for your trust in me and for giving me the opportunity and the privilege to serve with you all…my brothers."

Three days later, late in the evening, the four friends met at the local church. The elderly priest, the only other person present, administered the oath of E.O.K.A. to Nicolas, behind the holy altar. Numerous secret sessions of indoctrination and training, including survival tactics and the use of firearms, followed. After several weeks, Nicolas was given his graduation "certificate", a secret code name and the rank of assistant to the assistant section leader.

Even after finishing his training as an E.O.K.A. operative, Nicolas was still not asked to participate in any action, not even in the relatively simple and innocuous task of propaganda leaflet distribution. He almost always could tell whenever one or all of his three friends participated in some kind of operation because they would be unavailable for several hours and sometimes even completely disappear for one or more days.

Perhaps I'm thought of as incapable of carrying out a mission...even worse, perhaps I'm not considered trustworthy.

On a Sunday afternoon in mid May, Nicolas felt lonely and depressed primarily because none of his friends was available. Not even the exceptionally beautiful light-blue sky or the soothing warm sun could help elevate his spirits. He found himself digging up a watering ditch around the long line of banana trees in his backyard in preparation for the long, hot summer. He abandoned the task halfway through when the sound waves of a strong explosion vibrated through his ear drums, painfully stimulating his auditory nerves. He knew right away that the explosion was practically in the neighborhood.

From his second floor balcony, Nicolas could see a funnel of black smoke almost a mile away. It was rising from the edge of a dirt road that crossed the "reed and cane swamp." He knew the area quite well since he and Yiannis often hunted birds, with sling and stone, in the tall cane groves.

Within minutes of the explosion, special auxiliary police were slowly traversing neighborhood streets announcing an immediate curfew for everybody in a two-mile radius area from the location of the incident. People went inside and closed doors and windows. About an hour later came the dreaded loud knock on Nicolas' front door.

"All males between the ages of 17 and 30 must come out for questioning," announced a Turkish police officer, in broken Greek. He acted as interpreter for two British soldiers standing in front of the house gate, with clip-loaded Sten Guns at the ready.

As he came out, Nicolas was ordered to climb into a canvas-covered army lorry parked at the corner of the block. Homes that produced one or more males of the suspect age were visited again by the authorities, a few hours later, for a thorough search.

All detainees were taken to the Larnaca central police station. Of the dozens of young men standing in the large interior courtyard, only a handful raised their hands in response to the question of whether they spoke English fluently. This small group, which included Nicolas and his friend Yiannis, were taken to a nearby army camp.

The camp consisted of a couple of dozen tents in a round clearing in the center of a eucalyptus grove close to the coast line. The English-speaking detainees were placed in a large tent with no place to sit except the canvas-covered floor. Armed guards standing around the perimeter of the tent made sure that none of the detainees spoke to each other at any time. After several hours of detention, Nicolas was escorted to a smaller tent for questioning.

"You may stand right there," began the Second Lieutenant whose light blond hair reflected a blinding silver glow under the solitary naked bulb hanging from a central wire. "Some of the information you gave us on the questionnaire is interesting. You have security clearance to work for the R.A.S.C. petrol depot at Dhekelia and you graduated from an American high school...Tell me, Mr. Maos, do you want the British to leave Cyprus?"

"Yes, sir."

"Did you ever participate in a violent demonstration or any other violent act against the colonial government of the island?"

"No, sir."

"Do you know anybody in your neighborhood or elsewhere who believes in the violent overthrow of the government?"

"No, sir."

"Did you see or hear anything suspicious before, during or after the explosion near your neighborhood yesterday afternoon?" He didn't wait for an answer and added, "That was a cowardly act...a powerful device detonated by remote control from a distant cane grove...two young soldiers, about your age, on routine patrol duty, badly wounded...a cowardly, criminal act. Don't you want to help catch these terrorists?"

"Sir, I do indeed feel sorry for the two soldiers but I don't think I can be of any help to you. I did hear the explosion, I was in my back yard cultivating my banana plants at the time, but I did not see the explosion go off...I'm sorry, sir, I do wish I could help."

After a few more questions, some of which sounded like pleas for help, Nicolas was returned to the large holding tent. He quickly checked the dozen or so faces in the tent looking for his friend. Yiannis was not back yet. He sensed that dawn was near and decided to try and catch a few minutes of sleep. He sat and stretched his legs on the canvas floor.

When Nicolas woke up a couple of hours later, all the detainees were seated like him, their eyes fixated on a couple of soldiers, one placing a small table by the tent entrance and the other holding a large tray with mugs and a couple of plates. A sergeant appeared at the entrance.

"Come and get it, it's tea and biscuits. You have ten minutes before boarding," he yelled, as if addressing his troopers.

There was plenty of milk but no sugar in the tea. The sweet wafers made up substantially for its absence. The snack boosted Nicolas' energy. He hadn't eaten anything since yesterday's breakfast. At the same time, he was seriously concerned about his friend.

Why is Yiannis being interrogated so much longer than all the others? he asked himself again and again.

The sergeant returned soon, as promised, and guided everybody to a waiting army lorry. As he entered, Nicolas couldn't be more pleasantly surprised. His friend was already seated towards the front of the truck facing backwards. The best part was that Yiannis was exhibiting his trademark broad smile.

For a few moments, the two friends were back in the best of times. Yiannis was enjoying the wafers that Nicolas "stole" for him as if he knew he would find his missing friend desperately hungry. They began to talk about their night's experiences at the army camp but were rudely interrupted by another of the sergeant's piercing yells.

"Nicolas Maos, step down from the lorry immediately. You are under arrest."

Nicolas remained motionless and speechless for quite a while. He was in shock and so, apparently, his friend. Everybody else in the lorry was totally surprised about Nicolas' arrest. Two military police officers grabbed Nicolas by the arms, pulled him out of the truck and, standing behind him, literally pushed him with the barrels of their guns towards one of the larger tents.

The new interrogation tent had a rough plywood floor and contained a solitary steel desk whose top was clean except for an empty paper pad and a couple of pencils. Several chairs were lined along the tent's perimeter. Nicolas was asked to stand about four feet from the desk. A large, middle-aged bald man in loose civilian shirt and pants entered and sat at the desk. He avoided looking at Nicolas as he thoroughly studied a folder that the earlier interrogator, the young lieutenant, brought to him.

The man finally turned his head up and began to slowly examine Nicolas from top to bottom before letting his eyes enter into a continuous stare with those of the youth. His deep-seated black eyes appeared small but still quite penetrating and totally intimidating. His thick, black eyebrows and huge, untrimmed mustache, his large nose, his bony face and dark complexion, all betrayed his probable non-British heritage.

"Nick Maos, it says here that you were cultivating bananas in your back yard, digging a watering ditch, at the time of the bomb explosion close to your…"

The man was interrupted by the lieutenant who handed him a piece of paper. In the meantime, Nicolas was wondering about the man's heritage. He spoke to Nicolas in Greek, pretty good Greek but with an accent. *Most probably a well-educated Turk.*

"Tell me young man," the interrogator continued in English, this time with a noticeable Turkish accent, " how did you acquire the loaded handgun that was found in that very ditch that you were digging yesterday? How long did you have the gun?…and what did you plan to do with it?"

At first, Nicolas was simply puzzled when he heard the accusation but, within seconds, the puzzlement changed into shivers of horror. The mere idea that they thought he owned a gun was absolutely terrifying. Under the declared state of emergency, proven possession of a loaded gun carried a mandatory death penalty.

"Sir, I never owned a handgun in my life and I do not know anybody in my family who ever owned one. In fact, I never saw a gun close enough to touch it."

"We shall see about that soon enough. Our experts are already correlating finger prints found on the handgun…but tell me, how do you think the gun got into your banana ditch?"

"Sir, all I can think of right now is that perhaps somebody put it there, a place where it can easily be seen…or perhaps somebody, some passerby, most probably threw it there out of necessity or for whatever reason…the grove is only about ten feet from the side street."

"I want you to tell me all about your probable enemies as well as your friends in your neighborhood…full names and addresses." Nicolas had no choice but provide the information requested of him. He mentioned Yiannis as a next-door neighbor and friend but was prompted by the interrogator to further describe him as "my closest friend." He then went on to answer many more questions until well after mid-day.

At dawn the next day, he was transferred to the Larnaca central police station where he occupied a small prison cell, all by himself. During his stay there, several uniformed and non-uniformed police interrogated him for short or extended periods at all hours of the day or night. At first, his solitary daily meal consisted of two slices of bread smeared with a margarine spread and plenty of water. As time progressed, the bread and water rations were halved and the spread was eliminated.

Late one Friday afternoon, after three weeks and two days of jail confinement with absolutely no contact whatsoever with anybody except his interrogators and without being formally charged with any crime, Nicolas was informed that he was being released. He was told that he would be under constant police watch and that he could not leave town, at any time, without written police permission.

Nicolas' family, his two sisters and their husbands, tried very hard to appear happy, rejoicing for his release from prison. However, their facial expressions, the tone of their voices, and their body movements suggested otherwise. Makis volunteered to explain:

"Your friend Yiannis was arrested about a week ago. Two days after his arrest, the newspapers reported that he had been charged with "gun possession" plus the attempt to conceal evidence in a terrorist act by throwing the gun in our back yard…"

"I never knew that," interrupted Nicolas.

"Not according to one of the papers which claims to have information from a confidential source that you, his best friend, essentially told the police during your interrogation about Yiannis' involvement…"

"Absolutely false and cruel accusations," Nicolas managed to say before he ran out of the house, totally devastated by what he had just heard. At first he didn't know where he was going, he did not plan any destination, but eventually he wound up at Andros' house. His friend truly earned the nickname of "gentle giant." He managed to console Nicolas with hugs and soothing words and gestures before he even uttered the revealing explanation:

"The right people, all your friends and partners in the struggle for liberation, do know that you did not betray Yiannis, that you are not a traitor. Our E.O.K.A. leadership does not want the general public to know that Yiannis himself, a section leader, surrendered on his own and confessed to the police."

"Is the handgun truly his?"

"I guess you may say that. He and others used that handgun one time or another."

Nicolas felt better for a while until a cold sadness enveloped his spirit. In a way, he could understand and proudly appreciate his friend's act of self sacrifice in order to save an innocent friend. He felt he would probably do the same for his friend under similar circumstances.

As he walked back home, Nicolas thought of Andros and the fact that he never really denied that the gun may have been in his possession at the critical time. Perhaps he threw it in the banana grove himself, instead of Yiannis, on his way to his uncle's home which was less than a block away from Nicolas' back yard.

"This is absolutely an extraordinary idea," Nicolas whispered to himself, "Yiannis may be totally innocent and yet he sacrificed himself for a friend...for me."

Tears of sadness and proud satisfaction rolled down his cheeks.

A couple of days later, Nicolas got permission from the town police to visit his childhood home in Ora. Because of his recent arrest and detention as a suspect terrorist, he lost his job at the British base. At this point he needed to visit his mother but he also wanted to find some peace and quiet in the normally peaceful village.

Friends and acquaintances did not project their usual warmth and welcome to Nicolas when he returned to the village. It was obvious they read the newspapers. Even Nina, his sister, appeared to him to behave a bit differently than usual. Perhaps he was paranoid but then again why didn't he notice any negative change in his mother's behavior?

"Of course I trust you fully my son. I brought you up to be truthful and loyal not only to your family but also to your friends. No one can live a satisfying life without good friends…and always remember that friendship is not casually given or taken, it's earned. Your father, God bless his soul, used to say it differently: 'If you want to make a friend, you have to first become worthy of that friendship.'"

For several days, Nicolas did find peace and quiet. He seldom left home and had no interaction with anyone except his family. For much of the time, he was busy drafting letters to colleges in the New York City area, telling them about his status and his desire for higher education. He was also asking them for application forms and financial aid information for the Fall '58 semester. However, he knew very well he couldn't make it that soon so he never mailed any of the letters.

He was often asked why he favored the New York City area. His answer always emphasized the fact that he would have more opportunities for part-time employment in a big city. He also pointed out that he had a close family relative living in that area, a great aunt who immigrated to America and lived with her family in Brooklyn for the last four years. Perhaps she would provide room and board for him for the critical first couple of semesters when he was not allowed to work as a foreign student.

On the second Sunday of his village stay, Nicolas attended the morning church service. He was pleasantly surprised to see that his old friend Chris, from his almond gathering days, was also attending church.

At the end of the service, they exchanged information about

the latest changes in their lives. Nicolas was very pleased not only because Chris had a good job with a bank in Nicosia, but also because he expressed total disbelief concerning the accusations leveled at his friend. They agreed to meet at one of the village coffee shops, after lunch, for a game of *tavli* or backgammon.

The two friends had a history of fierce competition in that game since they were six years old. This time, Chris triumphed by winning the set by three points. As a consolation prize, Nicolas was invited for a visit and a cookout. Chris was particularly anxious to show his friend his new hybrid tangerine trees in his back yard, loaded with fruit.

Making their way through the narrow cobbled streets that were made to serve strictly pedestrians and their occasional beast of burden or goat, they encountered and greeted several villagers. However, the atmosphere changed drastically when a young, obviously late-stage pregnant woman was approaching.

My God…can it be?…Yes, it's Stella! Same gorgeous eyes, same beautiful, fascinating face…now that of a woman in her prime…I haven't seen her since the elementary school days, since the kissing incident…

Stella stopped very close to the two young men. As she stood motionless directly opposite Nicolas, both men thought they were watching a beautiful apparition. Her face was radiant and calm, exhibiting a faint smile and a slight blush when she extended her hand for a handshake.

"Welcome back to our humble village Nicola…I'm so happy to see you after so many years…congratulations on your many educational accomplishments. Chris, as a neighbor I see you more often, but I'm happy to see you once again."

Chris greeted her back with courtesy. Nicolas put on a nervous smile as he shook hands but remained speechless until she started to walk away. He turned and shouted, more or less repeating the same phrase a few times over,

"I'm happy too…me too…" She did turn back twice to wave with a smile.

"Chris, a few years back I promised my mother that I wouldn't talk to Stella or even think about her but now I broke my promise...I couldn't help it...isn't she an incredibly attractive young woman? Please tell me, how many children does she have with tough guy Sodiris, or is this her first child?"

"She has no other children...everybody knows she is expecting and everybody knows Sodiris is not the father...nobody really knows who the father is...there are rumors but nobody knows for sure..."

"Chris, are you serious? Please do not make fun of such things...you shake your head...my God, this is incredible, you are serious. Please explain quickly...please."

"It goes back now several years, the night of the wedding of Sodiris and Stella. A spectacular wedding...a joyous celebration... but perhaps, more accurately, it was the morning after their wedding night...Sodiris did not even wait for dawn, he abandoned his bride forever, in the middle of the night, because he discovered she was not a virgin."

"This is even more incredible and absolutely unbelievable... Stella not a virgin? There is no way I can believe that..."

"In her own words, thirteen year old Stella painfully described to her parents how her uncle Tomazos sexually abused her before she was nine...she was afraid, but mostly ashamed to say anything at the time. You do remember, I'm sure, when widower Tomazos immigrated to England a couple of years before we graduated elementary school and took with him his son Dimitri, our friend? It now appears he also took with him Stella's chastity."

"Where is Sodiris now? How do you know he is not the father?"

"Sodiris left alone for Greece a few days after the wedding was annulled. He came back more than a year later and tried to reconcile and take Stella back with him as his wife. She refused and he left the village again, this time for the town of Limassol. As far as I know, he visits his parents in the village only occasionally. I saw him at the Panos coffee shop only yesterday."

Nicolas couldn't stay in the village much longer, living so close to his first innocent love, his gorgeous Stella, who now became a fallen, tarnished angel. He returned to Larnaca and got another job in construction with his uncle Thomas.

In his first day back in Larnaca, Nicolas was quite disturbed to find out that his friend Andros was also arrested. It wasn't clear why until Lakis came to visit him.

"All I could find out is that Andros was suspected to be somehow involved in the attempt to shoot a British government official a few months back. You probably remember that incident when, according to the government news release, two men on bicycles passed by the official's home, late in the evening, and fired one bullet at his residence before they sped away. It appeared to be an act of intimidation…no one was intended to be killed or injured."

"I do remember hearing about that incident but I also remember reading that two high school students, Lyceum I believe, were arrested for that incident a few days later. In any case, it looks bad. Our two closest friends are in serious trouble…they are now in confinement somewhere in town and there is nothing we can do."

"There is one ray of hope," responded Lakis. " Newspapers quote official British sources that the British government plans to meet with top level government officials from Greece and Turkey to seek a solution to the Cyprus problem, perhaps as early as December."

"Yes, I did read about that. In fact, one newspaper added that Archbishop Makarios, who has been in Athens for over a year now and is closely working with the Greek government, may be also invited to participate in the talks. This sounds good but still…my conscience bothers me to no end. I feel guilty for Yiannis' arrest…he sacrificed himself for me even though he is probably innocent."

"I am really surprised you feel guilty about Yiannis. Didn't Andros explain the situation to you when you met with him right after you were released? I guess not. Here is the whole story. Yiannis did indeed throw the handgun in your backyard…"

"Wait a minute. Did Yiannis tell you that? How come you are so sure and…"

"Among our circle of friends, you seem to be the only one who doesn't know that it was Yiannis. After your confinement lasted for weeks, we all thought you may lose your life for something you didn't do. So Andros, who also took part in the ambush, announced that he was willing to give himself up and confess to be the owner of the gun. Of course Yiannis would not hear of it. A quick throw of a coin resolved the problem. Yiannis won the toss and surrendered to the police as the guilty party."

"My God, this is more incredible than I thought. I have to be the luckiest guy in the world…not one but two of my friends were willing to sacrifice everything to save me…I don't know how I will ever get a chance to reciprocate."

"I don't think you should worry about reciprocity. We both know they did it in the name of friendship."

For a long time, Nicolas' mind refused to abandon the story of his friends' sacrifice.

December finally arrived. Just about everybody was looking forward to Christmas but more so to the end of the year, the end of 1958, the bloodiest since hostilities had begun almost four years earlier. Dozens of Greeks and British died fighting each other but also dozens of Turks and Greeks lost their lives because of inter-communal riots. These statistics of death and destruction eventually came close to home and touched Nicolas' life.

It was mid-afternoon, Christmas day in the village. The whole Maos family was enjoying the traditional festive dinner of *avgolemono* soup, pork roast and chicken *tava* (chicken pieces with rice and green peas and lots of spices baked in a sealed brick oven).

The "cave palace" seldom saw such a big crowd seated at its modest pine table. Nicolas and his two sisters and their families came to the village to celebrate with mother and sister Nina. They brought with them most of the ingredients for cooking.

After dessert, Nicolas was on his way to visit his friend Chris who also came to the village to celebrate Christmas with his mother. On his way, he chose to pass by Stella's street. His heart began pounding like jungle drums when he saw her standing by the street entrance to her home. He slowed down somewhat as they greeted each other silently, with head bows and faint smiles.

Early evening before darkness set in, on his way back home, Nicolas found himself outside Stella's home once again. He nervously anticipated seeing his old flame once more, but this time the front door was closed. He passed by without knocking but hardly moved a few feet when he heard her call out,

"Nico...Nico...please wait for a moment. Do come in the house...I have a surprise for you."

The young man was shocked speechless by the totally unexpected request. He appeared to hesitate as he slowly followed her into the house. Once in the stone-walled family room which was dimly lit by an active fireplace and a small kerosene lamp on the mantle, he saw the silhouette of a tall, lean man approach him. Nicolas remained totally clueless and somewhat intimidated even after the bearded young man embraced him.

"My dear Nico, you don't seem to recognize your old friend Savvaki...how are you my friend? It's been years since I saw you last."

"Savvaki...My God, I can't believe it's you...here in my village..." He felt a bit relieved and immediately reciprocated with a hug. "It's been over three years since the Academy flag incident...I didn't even get a chance to thank you properly for saving my life."

The two friends talked incessantly for several minutes, mostly about the good old times at the Academy. Savvakis never commented about his actions as an E.O.K.A. guerilla fighter, but Nicolas surmised that his friend had a hideout or hideouts somewhere in and around the rugged terrain of his mountain village. But his mind went back and forth, unable to satisfactorily explain his handsome friend's connection or relationship with Stella until, "I guess I forgot to introduce Stella, not of course in terms of who she is, I know that you are good old friends, she told me all about your elementary school romance. I want you to now meet Stella as my wife of two years…of course our marriage is still secret and will remain so even though, as you can plainly see, we are expecting our first child. I hope this struggle ends soon but not before we gain our freedom."

Savvakis eventually told the story of how he met Stella. In a way, Nicolas was very much surprised and at the same time very much impressed to learn that quiet, timid Stella has been working as an effective E.O.K.A. courier for the Savvakis fighter group which hid and operated somewhere in the vicinity of Ora.

I'm happy for Stella. She married a good man, a friend. Her child is after all legitimate…I'm also sad, I feel a great sense of loss…Stella is not available once again…I always hoped that she and I would renew our romance some day…"

At one point in their conversation, Savvakis pointed out that, if apprehended, he expected to die fighting rather than surrender or allow himself to be captured. Upon hearing that, Nicolas proclaimed his support and admiration for his fighter friend by promising that, if his friend were to make the ultimate sacrifice, Nicolas would see to it that Stella and her child were properly taken care of.

Savvakis must have had a chilling premonition. A few days later when Nicolas was back in Larnaca, he heard on the government radio that "terrorist Savvakis Couros was killed by security forces after he was apprehended in the narrow streets of Ora and refused to surrender."

The Greek newspapers reported a fierce hour-long battle between Savvakis and a vastly superior force of British regulars who trapped him in a dead-end street. The papers also hinted that national hero Savvakis was probably betrayed by someone who knew that the fighter often visited a woman in the village, a woman to whom he was secretly married. No mention was made of the woman's name at the time.

Nicolas was very much concerned about his promise to his dead friend Savvakis that he would somehow look after his widow and child but he wasn't sure how he would realistically approach the matter. Her parents weren't exactly friendly to him ever since the kissing incident in the sixth grade. A couple of weeks later, it appeared that his problem pretty much resolved itself when newspapers reported on the birth of "the daughter of hero Savvakis and his wife Stella," noting that, like so many other widows and children of fallen heroes, the mother and child would be looked after by a national fund established for such a purpose. Still, Nicolas made up his mind to visit Stella in the village and check things out for himself.

I owe that much to my friend Savvakis and his widow...he sacrificed himself for our freedom...also, it will be great to see his baby daughter... and mother Stella too.

Nicolas never made it to the village. Instead, his mother and sister Nina preempted his plans by coming to Larnaca for a rare visit.

"Nicolaki, my son, I had to come here as fast as I could. You're in grave danger, especially if you set foot in our village...leaflets and posted proclamations in Ora claim that you are the one who betrayed the hero Savvakis...you are the one who informed the British about his frequent visits to Stella's home..."

"You don't believe that, do you mother?"

"Of course not. But lots of others do seem to believe it. Many claim they saw you at the coffee shop sharing refreshments with British soldiers and participating in long discussions with them in their language...I'm very much concerned...I'm afraid for your life."

"I was just being hospitable! I wanted to show these soldiers that some of us villagers are educated and, in a way, as civilized as they think they are...I actually discussed English literature with them, but only one of them, a lieutenant, was well informed on the subject. I wonder what Stella thinks about the idea that I betrayed her husband..."

"Stella left the village just before the leaflets came out," interjected Nina. "I believe she is here in Larnaca with her baby... they say she is visiting her husband Savvakis' family."

"I know where Savvakis' home is...perhaps I should visit Stella and the family."

I don't think it's a good idea, son. I came here to see that you go into hiding immediately...go to a place where those terrible people are not likely to find you...leave our beloved island if necessary."

"Do you suspect anybody in the village, anybody in particular who is after me?"

"Your friend Chris told me that some people in the village believe that Sodiris is behind the leaflets...these same people think that Stella's first husband is a bitter, vindictive liar but they're afraid to say so publicly because he is quite powerful...he heads the largest guerilla group in our region."

"I can see the situation clearly now. I happen to know certain things about the loyalties of Sodiris' guerillas...they would not hesitate to kill me if their leader tells them so...I guess I better be on my way. Mother, I won't be able to get in touch with you directly but I shall find a way."

Within an hour Nicolas said good-bye to his mother and the rest of his family and left word for his friend Lakis. His mother handed him a handkerchief tied into a bundle and asked him to open it when he was well on his way. He placed it into the small duffle bag, along with all of his other absolute necessities and boarded a bus for the town of Limassol. He had no plans concerning a final destination.

When the town of Larnaca was well behind him, Nicolas untied his mother's handkerchief. It contained a tiny gold cross and chain and paper notes totaling thirty-five pounds. There was a short message:

My dearest Nicolaki,

Please wear the cross wherever you may go. It will bring you closest to our Lord and hopefully remind you of your loving mother too.

Nicolas estimated that the money represented much of what he gave her during his employment after high school graduation. He recalled her words, the very first time he gave her any money: "I'm willing to serve as your money's keeper."

⁂

During the first two months of 1959, the prime ministers of Greece and Turkey held negotiations on the future of Cyprus—first in Paris and then in Zurich, where they formulated an agreement in principle. They took their agreement to London where they reached a suitable accommodation with the British government.

The "Cyprus Agreement" as conceived by the three sponsor countries of England, Greece and Turkey required the approval of the two main Cypriot communities, the Greek majority and the Turkish minority. The latter, along with the Armenian and Maronite minorities, made up close to twenty percent of the population. The two main communities were required to sign the agreement but were not invited to participate in the agreement negotiations.

The leader of the Greek community, Archbishop Makarios, was forced to sign on the dotted line when faced with an ultimatum from the British Colonial Secretary and tremendous political pressure from the Greek government. The Turkish leader, Dr. Kutchuk, also signed the agreement after facing similar pressures from England and Turkey.

Makarios, who was deported and lived in exile first in the Seychelles islands, in the Indian Ocean, and then in Athens since March of 1956, returned to Cyprus on March 1, 1959. It appeared that the whole Greek population of the island showed up in Nicosia, the capital, to give him a tumultuous hero's welcome. For all practical purposes, the British colonial regime of Cyprus came to an end, the violence against the British was over and all political prisoners were slowly being released.

For the first time in twenty-seven centuries, Cyprus had become an independent country. The Constitution of the Republic of Cyprus was drafted a year later in accordance with the twenty-seven points of the Zurich and London Agreements between the three sponsor countries.

Unfortunately, the independence of Cyprus and its drafted constitution could not resolve, and actually helped magnify, the centuries-old inherent problems of cultural and religious animosity and distrust between the Greek and Turkish communities of the new republic. More future communal bloodbaths were inevitably looming on the horizon.

After being released from detention camps, popularly referred to by the Greek youth as "British concentration camps," both Yiannis and Andros returned to their studies at the Academy. They had matured considerably in a relatively short period of time and never quite went back to their old casual attitudes and interests. Education and career concerns were high on their lists.

Yiannis also made sure that the newspapers printed the true story about his arrest and about his friend Nicolas who actually never betrayed him. But he couldn't do much about Nicolas' reputation in the region of Ora, where he was still posted as a traitor. Yiannis as well as Andros and Lakis, did, however, vow to work on their friend's case until his name was cleared. At the same time, nobody seemed to know where Nicolas was or whether he was even alive. But it would not be so for long.

Yiannis received a personal oral message from Nicolas through a Greek sailor whose ship anchored in Larnaca. He, in turn, passed the highlights of the message to Nicolas' mother:

"When in Limassol, Nicolas joined the crew of a Greek freighter. His home port is Piraeus but he is mostly at sea traveling to and from various Mediterranean ports. He plans to join another ship which is scheduled to visit England next month. He is in good health and he sent you this money."

Chapter Four

Three Years Later

Like countless thousands before him, Nicolas felt goosebumps invade his body temporarily as the ship that brought him from Cyprus sailed past the Statue of Liberty and into New York Harbor. It was late morning in mid-September, but it felt hot and humid, more like mid-August. The New York City skyline was bathing in a cloud of mist, its outlines barely visible from a distance. But, as the ship came closer and closer to the harbor, the unique spectacle of the skyline unfolded and became permanently etched by the sun's rays in the young man's mind:

What an extraordinary vision of endless vertical lines…like long rows of tall Cypress trees bathing in the sun at a river's edge.

The spectacle faded quickly once he was out of the ship and onto the pier. With passport in hand, Nicolas stood in the line designated for non-citizens seeking entry into the United States. He reached the checkpoint thirty-five long minutes later.

The port official checked the passport and visa carefully, glancing back and forth a couple of times between the travel document and the young visitor's face.

"Mr. Maos, please confirm the following information you

provided on the entry form: you are a resident of London and you seek entry as a foreign student planning to attend school in the City of New York. You gave a relative's residence in Brooklyn as your New York address."

"Yes, sir, that's exactly so."

"Here is your passport. Welcome to the United States, Mr. Maos."

Next, the passenger was directed towards the customs platform. It was chaotic, to say the least, with all kinds of anxious people expressing their frustrations in languages other than English while nervously searching for their luggage.

Nicolas was lucky to find his solitary suitcase rather quickly at a remote section of the platform. But he still had to convince a customs agent to come over and inspect his belongings. This turned out to be the toughest task.

Twice he stood behind an inspector and assumed to be the next in line, only to find out that the inspector shook hands with somebody else who arrived later than Nicolas and followed him to his luggage. At first it was a mystery but soon Nicolas realized that a tip must have been exchanged during the handshake.

*Money talks…even in America, the land of plenty…*He had hardly finished his thought when his third choice inspector obliged politely. The official made a chalk mark on the luggage, signifying customs clearance. He did not inspect the contents.

Most of the Mavros family members appeared happy to have Nicolas live among them. The great aunt was strict but accommodating and quite generous. The two older daughters, one a freshman and the other a junior in high school, were genuinely excited to have a "cousin" of college age come "from the other country" to live with them. The other two girls, both in grade school, were happy to have the benefits of a "big brother." Mr.

Mavros appeared pleasant but was, in fact, quite uneasy with Nicolas' living in his household. His elderly mother, referred to by the children as *yiayia,* the Greek word for grandmother, could not hide her disapproval of Nicolas' "intrusion into her family."

The Mavros children were extremely sheltered and their lives totally regulated by their mother, especially that of the oldest daughter Dora. Unlike her chubby siblings, Dora was slim and fit and a veritable beauty in all respects. Eleni Mavros was proud of her children, especially her "beautiful Dora."

For some reason, Aunt Eleni wanted Nicolas to know all about her plans for her Dora:

"Nico, don't you agree with me? Of course you do. It's my duty as a decent mother, a God-fearing mother, that I must find a suitable husband for her, a man from a good family...a man with a good position in our community and preferably a man of some wealth."

"Now that I have seen Dora and got to know her a little bit, I think you will have absolutely no problem at all with your plans, Aunt Eleni."

"Confidentially, I was already offered a match for her...a good, a very good man...runs his family's two restaurants. He was married before, but the main problem is his age, a bit too old at forty-two. I turned him down..."

"You made a good decision, Eleni," interjected *yiayia.*

"You took part in the decision too, *yiayia*...anyway, right now I'm excited about the fact that my Dora will have the option to become an *Americanida* when she turns eighteen."

"An American citizen in a little over a year, good for her and for you Aunt Eleni!"

To Nicolas' surprise, the grandmother practically never interfered or disagreed with her daughter-in-law. In fact, she always tried to enforce Aunt Eleni's rules. The father appeared somewhat indifferent to the details of everyday home life. He seemed totally happy and content to leave all decisions to his wife. After dinner, he would sit in front of the television and take a nap until it was time to go to bed. Besides complaining about his customers, his limited contribution to family conversation always ended with,

"I can't believe it's nine thirty already…goodnight everybody…I better go to bed. I have to get up at five to open up the store."

It's incredible, Nicolas thought every time he heard Mr. Mavros' goodnight.. *This man never seems to give credit to his wife who usually gets up at the same time and accompanies him to the store. The whole family knows that she is the one that makes the morning coffee and helps prepare the shop for the day's business. As soon as the waitress arrives for the breakfast rush, she returns home to take care of her kids.*

Towards the end of his first semester in college, Nicolas began to seriously consider leaving his aunt's home in Brooklyn, perhaps renting a room in the vicinity of the Morningside Campus, in spite of the fact that his aunt promised him free room and board for at least two semesters.

Actually, the room and board were not strictly "free." Mr. Mavros asked him to "pay for part of his keep" by providing his free services as the coffee shop dishwasher one day a week, when he had no classes, and during most of the weekend. Maureen, the "permanent" waitress, would not consent to the idea of having Nicolas as her assistant waiter. She was not willing to share tips .

Nevertheless, he knew very well that the arrangement with his aunt was much more affordable than having to pay for food and rent. The money he brought with him, after working for two and a half years in a fish-and-chips restaurant in London, was totally allocated for his first year's tuition and fees. He couldn't earn his room and board since foreign students were not permitted to work during their first academic year.

However, certain circumstances and a couple of incidences provided incentives that prompted him to consider just such a financially difficult move to Manhattan.

The subway ride to school and back provided a good incentive for the move. At a total cost of fifteen cents each way, the train ride was a great bargain, but not for someone counting every penny in his budget. The two-hour plus trip was also time consuming, requiring transfers to three different train lines before reaching the campus station at 116th Street and Broadway.

The commute meant that Nicolas would catch the usual breakfast of toast and coffee offered to him at home, but he would always miss the family lunch. Most of the time, because of library or laboratory study projects and the occasional evening lecture, he would also miss the six o'clock family dinner. This meant that he would essentially have very little to eat for the day.

Nicholas knew very well that when it came to a choice between staying late on campus for library work or for completing assignments versus arriving home on time for dinner, he really had no choice but to choose the former even if it meant hunger. The reality was that he could not afford to take the risk of losing his competitive edge for an academic scholarship. He had to win that scholarship in order to stay in school.

He couldn't afford lunch or dinner on campus but he occasionally indulged in the uniquely delicious taste of a piece of apple pie at the college cafeteria or a whole wheat donut and coffee at Choc Full O' Nuts. He also discovered that his favorite fruit, the fig, was the main ingredient in a fig Newton. That satisfying cookie served as his lunch or dinner many a time.

Of course there was nothing more satisfying than eating a delicious and nourishing dinner at home, even if it meant doing it under the watchful and critical eyes of Mr. Mavros' mother. At times, Nicolas would very much enjoy leftovers if he was lucky enough that his aunt was home, instead of helping at the store, when he arrived home late. Yiayia, on the other hand, seemed to take pleasure in pointing out that there were no leftovers to be served.

An incident that pushed freshman Nicolas even further to contemplate an early departure from Brooklyn took place on a Sunday in mid December, two weeks after his 20th birthday. After waking up late that morning, he went downstairs for a glass of water. As he walked through the narrow corridor, towards the kitchen, he thought,

It's very quiet. Everybody must be at St. Demetrius for the morning service.

He was about to fill a glass from the faucet when he heard grandma's voice in the adjacent dining room. He couldn't make out what she was saying. He approached the door leading to the dining room. It was partially closed. He stood there for a moment contemplating his next move. She began to talk again. He could now hear her clearly.

"You've got to convince Eleni to get rid of that Maos…you've got to try again and again…promise me…swear on your father's name, God bless his soul."

"We're going back and forth here to no end. You know I asked my wife several times. She will not ask him to leave, at least not before another semester. She promised him and his mother, her dear cousin Kyriaki. I think we can afford to have him here for a few more months."

"You could actually rent that upstairs room he occupies for free. Or you can ask him to pay rent or pay for the food he eats. Did you notice how much food he devours? More than all your kids put together…but there's something else that bothers me even more. Did you notice how close he gets to your girls? Aren't you concerned about your daughters?"

Nicolas could not listen any longer. He went back to his room.

The idea, the terrible notion this old woman has…that I could take advantage of innocent girls, my cousins no less…it's absolutely devastating. It's actually my character and my honor that are being molested here…I better find a way to move out of here.

A chance meeting with Luke, a childhood friend, at a Christmas time social at St. Demetrius church hall in Jamaica provided Nicolas with the first true hope that his move to Manhattan could become a reality.

Both boys had attended the Ora elementary school. After the fourth grade, Luke, his mother, his younger brother and baby sister moved to Brooklyn to join his father who immigrated to the States a few years earlier. Because of his father's illness, Luke became the manager of his family's restaurant, the Canal Diner in Lower Manhattan, shortly after high school graduation.

"Hey Nick, come and visit me at the diner. It's very easy to get there. Just take the "A" train and get off on Canal Street. Come and have something to eat, plenty of good food. It's best to come on Saturday. We are closed on Sundays. It's a short and relatively slow day on Saturday—we close at two in the afternoon. I work the grill…I do most of the short-order cooking."

Between Christmas break and the end of exam time in mid-January, Nicolas visited the diner several times. He could count on being served a satisfying breakfast and, a couple of hours later, on his way out, he could also count on a rich take-out lunch. And, on top of all this, when Nicolas was ready to leave, Luke would never fail to say,

"Hey, Nick, you need any money?" Without waiting for an answer, he would approach and push a $5 bill into Nick's pocket saying, "Of course you need money."

During his Saturday visits, Nicolas would offer to help out with restaurant chores but his offer was only accepted once when an employee failed to show up. He was asked to deliver take-out orders to customers in neighboring buildings and to help wait on tables during the lunch-hour rush. For his help, he was paid $15 and earned an additional $4.65 in tips.

It didn't take more than a few minutes after payday for Nicolas to realize that a move to Manhattan could become a reality only if Luke was willing to hire him to work Saturdays on a regular basis. He was optimistic about Luke's support but he thought it would be best to wait until after the final grades were posted in late January.

Perhaps my semester's grades will not be quite good enough to deserve the type of support I'm asking from my friend...or the type of legal trouble Luke and I may face by breaking the rules of the Immigration and Naturalization Service.

At the time, INS would not allow foreign students to work during their first year in the States. Applications for full-time employment during the summer break or part-time employment (up to twenty hours per week) during the school year were accepted by INS only after the freshman year was completed.

On Wednesday mid-morning, five days before the Spring semester was scheduled to begin, Nicolas found himself on the "A" train going towards Manhattan. It was a nerve-racking trip. First he had to make a quick stop uptown, on campus, to check a couple of final grades. Would he earn a close to A average for the semester? He was very concerned about one of his courses. Then he would go back downtown to visit Luke on Canal street. He had to find out from him that day whether he could count on a regular Saturday job for the upcoming semester.

The long ride made him doze off a little. He definitely needed to catch up on his sleep since he had to forgo quite a lot of it during the past two weeks of exams. But his mind had other plans. It was busy reliving the semester's highlights of his course experiences and academic performance.

Out of the five courses he registered for that semester, a total of 16 credits, English Composition, Math and Sociology were by far the easiest to digest because of his American Academy background. Columbia admitted him with "advanced standing" for having passed several General Certificate of Education exams administered by London University.

The Math course, analytical geometry, was at a higher level of detail than the geometry course he had at the Academy but, nevertheless, it was easy to follow. The instructor, a portly lady that began and ended most of her sentences with a broad smile, included two optional problems in the midterm and in the final, thus allowing Nicolas the opportunity to earn an average of 104 percent. His grade was a gratifying A+.

Most of the credit goes to Mr. Moissides, my geometry teacher at the Academy. He introduced theorems and proofs not only with a sense of organized thought but also with a sense of humor. He made a typically boring subject interesting and fun to follow.

English composition was Nicolas' favorite course. His knowledge of the language has always been good, especially in sentence structure and grammar in general. His vocabulary and his standing in terms of the number of books he read in American literature was not as rich or as high as some of the other students in the section, but he had lots of practice in terms of writing competitive essays.

The instructor of the section, an adjunct lecturer who was working towards his Ph.D. in American Literature, evaluated Nicolas' work after reading two of his essays to the class: "Nicolas Maos has good imagination and the ability to synthesize his ideas grammatically in an easy to read style." He awarded Nicolas with one of the four A's in his section.

Sociology was relatively easy in spite of the amount of outside reading required and the term papers assigned. The lecturer, a full professor with a distinguished publication record including a multitude of refereed journal papers and edited volumes, was not an effective instructor for undergraduate students. A classmate summarized the general student sentiment with,

"The professor's lectures seem to be intended primarily for advanced students. The details he presents and discusses, based primarily on his own publications, are definitely beyond the scope of an introductory course."

Nicolas' midterm grade of 88 percent was above the class average and he felt he did much better in the final. However, he was unhappy with his performance on the first term paper. The teaching assistant who read the paper assigned a grade of B- with an explanation: *Your discussion is based strictly on the assigned textbook. The number of references used is not adequate.*

With that in mind, Nicolas took steps to enhance his chances for a better grade in the final term paper. He included a relatively large number of references to the professor's publications and those of a few other workers. He was pleasantly surprised to see an A posted next to his name on the bulletin board. He checked it out twice.

The journey uptown was primarily in order to check the posted grades for the other two courses. They were much more of a concern. The natural science course, General Chemistry, was quantitative and straightforward and the derivative principles relatively easy to understand even though Nicolas had no high school background on the subject.

The professor, a bearded giant of a man, apparently near retirement and a close double for Santa Claus, was generally known as a distinguished researcher in atomic and molecular structures but, surprisingly, his lectures were easy to follow and very informative.

The difficulty with the chemistry course was its accompanying laboratory, a required part of a four-credit course. The lab exercises were demanding and time-consuming and the assigned lab manual was too complex to follow without professional guidance. Unfortunately, the graduate teaching assistant provided very little of that.

He did, at least, provide safety information on the handling of reagents.

Nicolas scored 92 percent on the lecture midterm but his average of the lab exercise reports he submitted produced an average of only 79 percent.

"If you score in the nineties in the final exam, you do have a good chance of earning an A- or even an A in the course," the T.A. informed him.

But, in reality, he was most concerned and fearful of the results for an upper level classics course, a study of Homer's Iliad in the original Greek. Nicolas chose it, thinking that it would be relatively very easy for a Greek, a cinch for an A. He had a pretty good background in reading and analyzing ancient Greek text.

The class was responsible for translating large sections of the classic Homer poem at a time. The use of a Homeric dictionary was recommended. The students would be asked to "read" from the ancient Greek text but, in actuality, they only read from an English translation which they memorized.

Nicolas, according to his high school training, had to read the Greek text first, sentence by sentence, analyze the complex sentence structure, and translate one sentence at a time. He was way "too slow" for the class.

At a conference with the young instructor, a part-time lecturer who was still working on his Ph.D. dissertation, Nicolas expressed his concerns about the nature of the course. Unfortunately, he also told the instructor, with an apparent absence of humility,

"I believe that I am the only one in class who could properly read, analyze and translate the ancient Greek text."

An argument also ensued between the student and the instructor concerning the right pronunciation of words in the ancient language. Nicolas had the last word:

"What do you think is more probable, the relatively modern Greek pronunciation that we know was apparently used for over a thousand years, way before the Byzantines, or the Anglo-Saxon version essentially "created" during the Enlightenment period in Europe, a couple of hundred years ago?"

Nicolas earned a C+ in the midterm exam and did not expect much better in the final since he only translated about half of the Greek text given. He dreaded the idea of checking out the posted final grade. *It's so ironic that a Greek course that was expected to boost my chances for a scholarship may have, instead, drastically diminished them.*

~

"Hey, Nick, good to see you...ham n' eggs with home fries and a large orange juice, coming up." This was Luke's usual greeting whenever Nicolas entered the diner any time before noon.

Luke knew exactly what each of his usual customers preferred, whipping and frying everything from pancakes to eggs to all kinds of meat and home fries on the hot grill at great speeds, right behind the serving counter where everyone could watch. He even remembered the occasional variations in his customers' orders: "Hey, Nick, what is it going to be today, rye toast or English muffin?"

Nicolas was seated at the counter seat furthest from the grill. He was just about halfway through his late breakfast, when Luke approached him.

"Hey, Nick, the lunch crowd should be here in about twenty minutes. Can you stay after breakfast today? Can you help out, work a couple of tables? My brother Jimmy couldn't come in today."

"Yes, yes...of course I will stay and help," Nick responded with evident enthusiasm in his voice. Right away he thought of posing the critical question, asking his friend about regular Saturday employment, but he hesitated too long and Luke was already back at his grill.

Near closing time, late in the afternoon, Nicolas got another opportunity.

"Luke, I want to share something with you, something that makes me feel proud and humble at the same time. Proud because it is a personal accomplishment and humble because it could not have been done without the will of God and the support of my family and that of many friends like you."

"Hey, Nick, don't go sentimental on me…go ahead, tell me all about this accomplishment. But I bet I know what it is…it's about your final grades, right?"

"Right. You already know about my grades in math, English and sociology. Today, to my surprise, I found out I received an A- in chemistry. But can you guess what I got for the Greek course, after going into the final with a C+ ?"

"Hey, the professor knows that you are the only student who can read and write and really understand the Greek language. He probably felt sorry for you and gave you a good grade because you are, after all, a Greek. He probably gave you an A, right?"

"Well, not quite but I'm very happy to have received a B. This gives me a G.P.A. well above the minimum for the Dean's list."

"Good job Nick, congratulations…you are well on your way to a scholarship for next September…but you must keep up the good work for another semester, right?"

"Right…but I need some help…I need a favor from you… actually, I need a job to pay for a room on campus…of course you do know how the INS feels about my getting employment at this time…would you risk it? Can you use me on Saturdays on a regular basis?"

"I'm sure we can use you. Jimmy was always looking for an excuse not to work on Saturdays…he wants to pick up wrestling. Can you start as early as five thirty?"

"Of course I can. I will be here at five, the time you get here to set up for breakfast."

The next day, Nicolas checked the University bulletin for furnished rooms. He finalized the renting of one on 120th street and Amsterdam Avenue. It was very tiny, but clean and tidy, and, above all, the price was right. Mrs. Saltzman was asking for only twelve dollars per week.

In Nicolas' mind, the start of the second semester looked promising in terms of relative financial prosperity. After all, he did secure a good-paying Saturday job at Luke's diner. However, it didn't take more than a couple of weeks into the semester before the young student began to realize that even minimal financial security was to remain an elusive commodity.

After he paid for his rent and laundry and of course his constant companion, his Marlboros, he had enough money left over for three good meals per week, usually a hamburger with French fries or franks and beans at an off-campus restaurant on Broadway. For the rest of the week, he relied on Fig Newtons or donuts and also took advantage of the free tea and cookies served to students once or twice a week by various campus organizations.

Nicolas tried to make up for the loss of good nutrition during the week by having a good breakfast and very rich lunch at Luke's diner on Saturday. But, no matter how rich, a meal could not satisfy hunger for more than a day or so.

But even a bigger problem than food was looming on the horizon. In early March he realized that he would not be able to make his last tuition installment at the end of the month. He needed an additional 180 dollars, but where would he get such a big sum of money?

In a letter to his mother, he mentioned his financial problems not because he expected her assistance but because his conscience demanded that he should explain to her why he was not able to send her a few dollars now that he worked at the diner. The mother's response to his problems was typical:... *as for your financial difficulties my Nicolaki, please continue to trust in the Lord. He will provide for you at the right moment of critical need...watch for and acknowledge the Lord's miracles with thanks...*

Nicolas was on the look-out for a miracle but did not recognize the beginnings of one, at first, when he met Stanley during the weekly Friday afternoon tea served by the Eastern Orthodox Christian Association. Within a very short period, Nicolas considered Stanley, also known by his Greek name of Stelios, a good and generous friend in spite of the fact that just about everybody else in the Hellenic Student Association thought of him as an insensitive and spoiled rich boy, the only child of a tanker captain from the Aegean island of Chios.

Nicolas concluded that the other Greek students were simply jealous of this tall and fit young man, with a dark Mediterranean complexion and a handsome face. His good looks appeared totally unaffected by his deeply receding hairline.

There were also questions about Stanley's morals. Most Greeks and some other foreign students concluded that Stanley had an ongoing romantic relationship with his aunt, the very young wife of his elderly paternal uncle who, like his father, was also involved in shipping and traveled extensively. She would visit her nephew on campus quite often, usually on Friday evenings.

Even though Nicolas agreed with the others concerning Mrs. Koulados' flaming sexuality and had his own suspicions about her relationship with her nephew, he neither commented on his suspicions nor did he openly share the views of those who participated in the gossip.

Instead, he went into great lengths to defend the moral standing of his new-found friend. In reality he thought of Stanley as a kind of a guardian angel sent down from above, probably because his mother demanded it of God several times a day, to help him survive on campus.

Stanley was indeed a guardian angel. On many occasions, typically when he made other dinner arrangements and would not use his prepaid dormitory meal plan, he would invite Nicolas to have a meal, in his place, at the campus cafeteria.

Stanley was even more generous with frequent invitations to

Nicolas to have coffee and donuts with him at the Choc-Full-O-Nuts coffee shop, sometimes in late afternoon and other times in late evening following the closing of the university library.

Nicolas felt, on the one hand, somewhat uncomfortable because of the almost total absence of reciprocity on his part in terms of inviting his friend for dinner or a for a snack. But, on the other hand, he felt quite comfortable in accepting all those invitations because he knew that his friend Stanley was well aware of his financial predicament.

⁂

The workings of a second miracle began to surface after Nicolas was directed to appear before the University Foreign Student Advisor in early May, just two days before the beginning of the final exam period.

"Good afternoon, Mr. Maos. Last time we met in this office, a little over a month ago, you requested the meeting in order to discuss your financial situation, specifically your inability to make the tuition payment due that month."

"Yes, Mrs. Morrison. And, if I may, I would like to take this opportunity to again express my deep appreciation for your courtesy and kind consideration for making arrangements so that I can postpone the payment until after my summer employment."

"Well then, please explain to me why Mr. David Robertson, your host for the 'Thanksgiving with an American Family' program, called this office two days ago to inquire about possible tuition payment problems you may have. Did you mention your problem to him or perhaps even asked for assistance specifically from him since our last meeting?"

An intercom communication blocked Nicolas' chance to provide an answer.

"Please excuse the interruption. I should be back in a couple of minutes."

As he sat there waiting the return of the advisor, he began to recall highlights of his fellowship with the Robertson's:

Thanksgiving with the Robertson's turned out to be a pleasant surprise even though I expected a formal and boring afternoon when I first arrived in their home in North Plainfield. The winning combination of my hosts' simple courtesy and warmth made the difference. By the time spring rolled around, I visited the Robertson's three more times. The visit schedule was always the same: church from eleven to twelve for the family of devout Baptists, a casual conversation or two, a few games or puzzles with their two boys and then Sunday dinner around three. The dinner was identical every time. Roast leg of lamb, served with potatoes and string beans, plus home-baked apple pie for dessert. "This is always a great feast for me even though I'm not particularly partial to lamb but I'm a bit surprised that the Robertson family loves lamb so much. I heard that Americans eat beef almost exclusively." Evelyn and David laughed as if they heard a funny joke and the two boys could not hide a grimace on their face. The lady of the house spoke first. "I'm sorry we laughed out loud but, in a way, it's funny since both David and I much prefer beef to lamb and Michael and Peter do not even like lamb at all. I guess we never even considered the idea that you may not be partial to lamb since our minister advised us that lamb is sort of the national food of the Greeks." "I thank you for your courtesy and consideration very, very much. I do appreciate the family's silent sacrifice, especially that of the boys, in order to please a Greek." "No, it is not a sacrifice at all...it has been our pleasure to try and provide you with something that we thought will make you more comfortable in a foreign environment." "What about the apple pie? I hope it was not forced upon you because of my expressed fondness for it." "No, not at all. This family loves apple pie."

The Foreign Student Advisor returned in about six minutes.

"Back to my last question. Did you mention your financial difficulties to the Robertson's and perhaps even asked for their help?"

"During my last of several visits with the family, in late-March, Mrs. Robertson initiated a conversation during which she asked me a few questions about my family back home in Cyprus and how we make our living there and..."

"What about your answer to her question concerning your ability to pay your tuition fees?" she interrupted abruptly.

"I simply pointed out that I managed to raise the money I needed for the freshman year primarily through several years of employment after high school graduation. I also told her of my aspirations for a scholarship that would cover my remaining years in college. I did not mention my specific problem of being unable to make the last tuition payment this semester."

"I think I know now how Mr. Robertson found out about your difficulty to make the tuition payment in March. I am the one that told him, unintentionally of course."

"If this is so, why this meeting and why your effort to find out if I told the Robertson's about my financial difficulty?"

"You see, I simply wanted to find out if I was the first to tell him that. After all, he called here first and I assumed that he already knew the story concerning your tuition payment difficulties when, in fact, he was merely seeking to obtain general information about your financial standing."

"So, how did you wind up telling him about my specific problem and our arrangement for a deferred payment?"

"At one point in our telephone conversation, he indicated that he was also planning to call the bursar's office for more information on your ability to regularly pay tuition and fees. I then suggested that it was not necessary since I was the one who made arrangements with the bursar concerning the postponement of the last tuition payment until after you earn money during the summer break. After that, our conversation was practically over."

"I'm sorry Mrs. Morrison, perhaps it's not right for me to pry further into your private conversation, but since the incident involves me too, I would very much like to know Mr. Robertson's comment or comments right after you told him about my difficulty with the March installment payment."

"He said something to the effect that this well-endowed, great university should provide financial assistance to its worthy and needy students, whether American or foreign."

The two-week exam period went by very fast. While waiting for grades to be posted, Nicolas began to evaluate his experiences and the quality of life throughout the whole spring semester.

Besides my physical endurance, my patience and even my faith were tested many a time but, at the critical moment, my mother's soothing voice echoed in my ears and made me think and believe and hope. Life outside the classroom was dull and lonely. But Stella's beautiful image was a constant companion, promising excitement and endless love for the future.

Minutes after the grades were posted, Nicolas submitted an application for a scholarship. His devotion and exceptional motivation to succeed did not let him down. His class performance earned him A's in each of the three second-semester-sequence courses in math, English and sociology. In chemistry he earned a B+. Instead of the Greek classics, this time he registered for an introductory level course in Greek archaeology. He easily earned another A.

He did not expect an answer from the Dean of Students concerning his scholarship application until weeks later, perhaps in mid-to-late June. In the meantime, he made arrangements for a job at a Catskills summer camp for teenagers.

Life at the camp was not only profitable and educational but also very pleasing and, in a way, quite exciting. Three good meals a day plus the pleasure of supervising science workshops and other activities such as camp fires, hay rides and trail walks for a wonderful group of American teenagers who happened to be mostly of the female sex made it most enjoyable.

For the first two weeks at camp, happiness was not total, however, because the outcome of the scholarship application was still pending. Then the letter from the dean arrived. In fact two letters from Columbia arrived. The second one was from the Foreign Student Advisor.

The Dean's letter informed Nicolas that, due to his excellent academic performance in his freshman year, he was awarded a full-tuition scholarship for the sophomore year. It was also noted that the scholarship would be essentially in effect for the remaining undergraduate years, provided his academic performance remained at the appropriate level of excellence.

The student's immediate reaction to the letter came as a whispered prayer.

God, I thank You for this, the greatest triumph in my life's modest achievements! My mother knew it all the time, she told me again and again that You will never forget me, never abandon me, no matter how discouraging or impossible things may appear to be...thank you.

The excitement consumed his total being for quite a while. He did not open the Foreign Student Advisor's letter until bedtime. When he read it, his first reaction was to jump up with joy but, almost simultaneously, a cold wave of realization ran through him, troubling his conscience. He thought he had imposed his personal problems on his kind friends. The letter informed him that Mr. and Mrs. David Robertson had paid his outstanding tuition balance for the past Spring semester.

A double miracle! I dare say it's even beyond my dear mother's wildest expectations. One day I shall have to pay the Robertson's back...double.

Chapter Five

1964 — Three Years later

"I love your outfit, Nicolas," said Mrs. Saltzman, Nicholas' landlady, as he left the apartment. "You look great in that navy blazer. Dark blue is a good color for your complexion…it looks like a great day for graduation! Then she added, "I envy that girlfriend of yours," with a certain passion in her voice as the door was closing behind him.

"Why the envy?" he whispered to himself, somewhat puzzled. "She is a very handsome, middle-aged lady with a voluptuous figure that many a younger woman would envy," he added somewhat louder.

Mrs. Saltzman's older friend across the hallway, the one with the heavy makeup and towering hairdo, was standing by her door in her usual light pink terry robe, with matching slippers. She approached him as he waited for the elevator.

"Young man, you do plan to move after graduation, don't you?" She did not wait for a reply and added, "Monika Saltzman inherited plenty after old Saltzman died last January. No one knew the old man put away a small fortune. She won't need your fifteen dollars rent any more."

"It's actually twenty now, madam."

"No matter...the point now is, what will the neighbors think? A lone widow like her, sharing her apartment with a stud like you. Mind you, I am not talking about myself having such thoughts...I am not that kind of a neighbor..." Nicolas reluctantly nodded in agreement as he entered the elevator.

It was sunny but uncharacteristically chilly that early morning in late May when Nicolas entered the campus College Walk. He walked towards the granite sundial and reluctantly sat on its cool, polished surface.

Graduation day at last. Commencement exercises on historic Morningside Heights campus...finally I'm to attend as an active participant, a bachelor's degree recipient...impossible dreams do become reality sometimes.

As the morning progressed, many more people started to gather and watch the workers place the endless rows of chairs on the plaza. Some students recognized him and a few greeted him but he felt a bit uneasy in his ivy league outfit which also included the required khaki pants and the penny loafers.

At the age of twenty-seven, Nicolas sported long, wavy hair instead of a fashionable crew cut, and his sculptured face and straight Greek nose were uncharacteristic of the preppy, ivy league image. His off-and-on girlfriend bought him the outfit, piece by piece, as past birthday and Christmas gifts. Today he had no more excuses. He had to wear it to please Vivian.

In a way, Nicolas attended these graduation ceremonies before, as a campus observer at the end of his freshman year. From a distant elevated position, a sixth floor window on campus, the seated guests on the spacious plaza appeared like a multitude of heads of all shapes and sizes oscillating like small craft on a choppy sea. Most faced their larger than life, green-tarnished, Alma Mater and the great steps leading to the domed temple of Low Memorial Library with its circular rows of classic columns.

Several more buildings that imitated classic architecture,

including the impressive Parthenon-like Butler Library with its majestic Greek columns, could be seen outlining the plaza. This panoramic view reminded him of his first guided tour of the campus when he had just arrived:

"I understand you are of Greek heritage," said the Foreign Student Advisor, turning towards him and placing her hand on his shoulder. He turned up to face her and signified his agreement with a quick smile.

"Mr. Nicolas Maos. I don't think I have encountered the name "Maos" before. I imagine it's a Greek name, but what does it stand for? Does it have any special meaning?"

"Yes, it's actually a local version of *"magos,"* the Greek word for "magician.""

The towering lady, her graying long hair rolled into a knot at the back, pointed specifically towards Butler Library where large carved letters on the marble frieze spelled the names of Greek and other classic philosophers, and then added,

"You must feel very much at home in these surroundings."

Mid-day, and the chairs and banners seemed to be all in place for the late afternoon graduation exercises. The chill in the air was gone and the warmth of the sun energized Nicola's body and helped liberate his spirit. He could now clearly visualize himself sitting among the graduates, tossing his cap up in the air, breathing the atmosphere of excitement and great accomplishment, surrounded by his loved ones as proud observers.

But reality set in once more. No mother, no family, no loved ones to celebrate with him. Even worse, his beloved Stella had been lost once again. *It's a shame not to be able to share this milestone with lovely Stella...is it possible that in spite of all these setbacks in our relationship, I'm still destined to share an even greater event with her sometime in the future?... Right now it doesn't look likely.*

Even his American girlfriend, even Vivian, could not attend the graduation ceremonies. Something about family commitment kept her home on Long Island.

The College Walk was bustling with walkers and stationary onlookers. Families were already dispersed all around the plaza taking pictures of graduates in front of landmarks of the academic acropolis.

Nicolas' stomach started pushing for some nourishment. He was trying to cut down on the Marlboros and his appetite was growing out of bounds. He immediately thought of the Choc-Full-O'-Nuts coffee shop at the Broadway end of the College Walk. *A robust cup of coffee sounds good, especially if it's combined with a cream-cheese-and-walnuts sandwich on raisin bread.*

The restaurant was favored by himself and many of his friends, especially for an afternoon or evening snack of whole wheat doughnuts and that delicious cup of coffee that so enhanced the taste of cigarettes.

The restaurant was very busy so he picked up some potato chips and a coke from a nearby vendor and crossed over to Riverside Park. Seated on his usual bench, with a magnificent view of the Hudson River unfolding in front of his eyes, a pleasant shiver of anticipation came over him when he thought of Vivian and their date later on that evening.

⁓

Nicolas left the park bench to return to his off-campus room on Amsterdam Avenue. He still had close to three hours before commencement exercises but he told himself that he needed to freshen up a bit and perhaps relax some more in the privacy of his room. But the real reason was that he felt very anxious to put on his graduation gown and return to proudly parade among the crowds on campus, like so many other graduates did.

Half way through the crowded College Walk he ran into

Stanley. Neither of the two was surprised since they either kept running into each other or met purposely during most days of the school year. After the essential hug, they found space to sit on a step well below the crowded College Walk Sundial.

Stanley should have been graduating at the same time as Nicolas with a degree in electrical engineering but, at the last minute, he was not certified because of poor or failing grades in a couple of required humanities courses.

"I'm sure you do know, Stanley, that I still have a ticket for you in case you changed your mind and now want to join me for the commencement exercises...I already told you I even have one for your aunt. Since it's Friday, is she by any chance visiting you today?"

"No, no change of mind about attending the graduation ceremonies. I assure you I'm happy and excited about your graduation without having to attend the formal commencement exercises. I don't even plan to attend my own. I want to finish up this fall and get out of these damn dorms and this cold campus immediately, as early in January as possible." He paused for a minute, stood up and then added,

"Excuse me, Nick, I have to run over to Hamilton. Just wait for me here for a couple of minutes."

It was obvious that Stanley was still upset with the Dean of Students' decision not to certify him for graduation because of a couple of poor grades he received in courses that Stanley described as "totally unrelated and unimportant to my area of concentration." Whether purposely or not, Stanley had avoided the question about his aunt.

Stanley's aunt was believed to be no more than six or seven years older than him. Mrs. Koulados, the third wife of his paternal uncle, came mostly by train from Mattituck, eastern Long Island, to visit Stanley on many a Friday evening and sometimes stayed overnight, presumably in a midtown hotel.

Adjectives such as "suspicious," and "sexual" were used by

Greek and other students to describe Stanley's close relationship with his attractive aunt.

"She is a good looking woman with a charming disposition, highly expressive black eyes and an all-around good figure," explained George.

"I believe that you are missing one important item," volunteered Hagop. "The fact is that her figure is crowned, so to speak, by an attractively plump derriere which she often showcases by wearing tight skirts."

"I'm sure that a cute ass like that must attract Stanley's constant attention," added George.

" I think we all agree that she exhibits, perhaps even projects a certain sexuality that would arouse any vulnerable young man, let alone a young Greek," philosophized Alexander.

One Friday evening, Nicolas came upon Stanley and his visiting aunt walking along Amsterdam. While Stanley remained uncharacteristically quiet, she insisted that Nicolas should join them for some pizza at the small but cozy, below street level, Amsterdam Avenue Pizzeria.

The place was frequented almost exclusively by coeds and their dates. Nicolas felt out of place. It was a strange ten or fifteen minutes during which the couple faced each other, seemingly totally absorbed by their thoughts, as if in a different world. With the exception of a few polite comments from her about the weather and the tasty pizza, Nicolas' presence was practically ignored. He managed to eat a slice and promptly excuse himself on the way out.

At the exit door, he regretted turning around momentarily to observe the couple once again. They were still staring into each other's eyes but the distance between their faces had diminished considerably and their hands, intimately entangled in the form of a rough sphere, were now pressed against their lips.

Stanley returned with a small rectangular box in his hands. He handed it to his friend with a simultaneous hug and lots of congratulatory remarks on his graduation. It was a fine pen and pencil set with a silver luster, accompanied by a string of silvery-white worry beads. Nicolas reciprocated with another hug and lots of remarks expressing deep appreciation.

"Nick, did you get any more graduation presents?"

"No, but I'm expecting one from my boss, Rusty Weisman. He asked to see me tomorrow at the office, even though Saturday is not one of my scheduled three days of work this week. My landlady, Mrs. Saltzman, told me a few times already that she has a graduation present for me. Of course, I can't wait to see what Vivian gets me."

"Well, how is your relationship with Vivian, these days? You seem to be on and off and on again…is it because you can't seem to forget your first love Stella? I guess not, especially since she ignored you again and went all the way to England to marry somebody else…I'll have to assume that you are on again with Vivian if you expect a present from her, right? Is she still insisting on remaining a virgin until matrimony?"

"The best answer I can give you is that things haven't changed much since she and I became an item. It feels like yesterday but, in reality, I was completing my sophomore year and she was finishing her freshman year at Barnard…I have a date with her tonight. I assume she is taking me to dinner at an undisclosed location. Imagine, she is actually coming up to my room…"

"You told me that your landlady would not allow women come up to your room."

"Mrs. Saltzman is visiting relatives on Long Island and she is not expected back until tomorrow evening. I'm going to chance it. I told Vivian she can visit."

"I was under the impression that you are just about ready to move out of that room and into an apartment. Didn't you come to an agreement yet with that graduate student from India to share his apartment on 115th Street and Broadway?"

"Yes, I did come to an agreement with Sanjay. I will sublease one of the two bedrooms with its own little bathroom and share the kitchen for $165 a month. He told me that his share of the rent will be slightly higher since he has a bigger piece of the pie, another small room he plans to use as a study."

"I know it's a good building but it still sounds like too much rent. Did he show you the lease? Do you really trust this guy? You know how selfish these Indians often are…real operators too…"

"I have no cause to mistrust him, he seems like a nice person, very polite and considerate. Besides, he knows about my financial difficulties and told me he has similar problems himself trying to work his way through graduate school."

"How can you afford the rent?"

"I was under the impression that I told you about graduate school. I was accepted here by the Graduate Faculties with an offer of a Graduate Teaching Assistantship in Geological Sciences. With free tuition and benefits plus a good salary, I should be able to easily afford the rent starting in September."

"I was also under the impression that you are only planning to get a masters degree and then go get a job to support your mother before it's too late."

"Yes, that's exactly what I plan to do."

"Then explain the teaching assistantship. I thought that good graduate schools typically give assistantships only to Ph.D. candidates…you yourself told me that."

"That's exactly right. I applied for the Ph.D. program in order to qualify for the teaching assistantship, but as soon as I get the masters I will leave the program and try to get a job…at this point I can't afford to be totally honest. My mother taught me that I can sometimes bend the rules if a situation demands it for the sake of protecting the welfare of my family."

"You have another big problem. Since you only hold a Foreign Student Visa, how would you manage to get a full-time job, let alone keep it long enough to support your family?"

"That's going to be one of my biggest problems...of course there's always what appears to be an easy solution..."

"We all know what that is. Marry an American citizen or even a permanent resident and then apply for a green card through your wife. It looks like you have it made if you care to marry your girlfriend Vivian...at least for a while...unless you want to pay some woman a thousand bucks or more for a fake marriage."

"I prefer to pay out for a fake marriage rather than deceive a girl like Vivian. If I marry Vivian it will be because I want to stay married to her for all time."

"To change the subject, do you plan to move in Sanjay's apartment in September, the start of the new semester?"

"No, I plan to move in earlier. I made arrangements for June 1st...in about six days. Of course I do hope I find a full-time summer job by then."

"Things are finally looking up for you...your own bedroom plus bathroom and kitchen privileges in a private apartment. It sounds like paradise...it should be much easier for you now to seduce Vivian!"

"I do not plan to seduce Vivian there..."

"You do not seem excited about the prospects of spending time with her in a private setting. Don't you dream about sleeping with a woman like the rest of us? Is it true then that you do not want to sleep with Vivian?"

"No, that's not true. You know very well I always wanted to make love to her. God knows I did try to seduce her. But now I know better. I grew to respect her as a considerate, loving person, and especially to respect her wishes to abstain from intercourse until marriage."

"Sometimes I do not understand you, Nick...are you sure you are Greek?'

"You and I should understand this very well, it's strictly part of our culture to expect a woman to totally abstain from sexual intercourse until marriage. Hell, we even use the graphic term 'destroyed maiden' to describe a young woman who inappropriately loses her virginity before marriage!"

"So, I have to assume that you do plan to be a true gentleman, as they say, when she visits you in your room tonight."

"Yes, actually I do. But most of all, I do want to explain to her, up front, that I am unable at this time, or in the near future, to commit myself to any formal engagement or marriage. First I have to support my family back home before I think of creating another family. I cannot afford to be selfish at this time…I will not abandon my mother and handicapped sister…"

"I think that you also believe deep in your heart that Stella will come back in your life one of these days. In any case, I also think it's a shame you decided to give up on the pleasures of seducing such an attractive maiden as Vivian. What a figure! What a fuck! I think that if you insist a little more, you can have her. Why do I think that? She may play hard to get, but I happen to know she is totally crazy about you."

Nicolas was quite upset with his friend for what he said and for the way he said it.

I can't very well show my anger to a friend that has been so supportive of me in so many practical ways. I can't educate or change my friend either. I still remember my mother's wise saying: "You can't make a king out of a gypsy."

Instead, he chose to display an understanding smile and then asked Stanley,

"How do you know that Vivian is crazy about me? Did she share her feelings about me with you?"

"I found that out a few months ago when you asked me to escort Vivian to the fraternity party, remember? All this time, I didn't say anything about it to you. I guess I am still pissed off with the way she acted, the way she behaved towards me."

"I remember…I do remember asking you that. I was looking for a way to dump her when I asked you to escort her that evening… it was all because…"

"I never saw you so excited before or since that evening. You somehow managed to get a date with that sexy Barnard girl…was it Sylvia? What curves! What a pair of tits!"

"Yes, that was Miss Sylvia Rosenberger. Very, very popular with the boys. I'm sure I was infatuated with her. I met her during the afternoon tea at the International Student Center the day before. My condition worsened considerably when she accepted my invitation and came out to sit with me, later that day, at a Riverside Park bench. I made out with her."

"Did you get to enjoy those incredible tits?"

"No, it was mostly light stuff, a few embraces and a couple of quick kisses. Believe me, it was much more than mammary glands that attracted me to her. She was fascinating all around. Did I tell you she is the entertainment editor of her school paper? She invited me to join her at the Radio City Music Hall where she was assigned to review a Cary Grant movie."

"Knowing about you and your love for films, you probably didn't even take a break from watching the movie, perhaps to touch and feel and enjoy all those goodies right next to you."

"You are right, Stanley, you do know a lot about my personality, my likes and dislikes. I did enjoy *Walk, Don't Run* without initiating any interruption. As a reviewer, Sylvia had to concentrate on the movie and I respected her position."

"What a waste!"

"But I did make up for it tenfold later on, after the movie, when we went back to the park bench. We were there until dorm curfew time, a little over an hour, literally interwoven into each other both on and under the bench. I leave the rest to your imagination which you certainly have plenty of concerning such matters."

"I can't believe it. Did you actually go all the way?" He waited for an answer but it wasn't forthcoming, so he added, "I do remember your mentioning that you never saw Sylvia again…but I do not remember the reason. How come?"

"A couple of days after the movie, she wouldn't take my calls or even see me when I went over to the Barnard dorms, more than once. I found out that Juliana, Vivian's friend, told her about my going steady for a long time and that I was about to be engaged to Vivian. Of course the latter wasn't true but the damage was already done. But what about Vivian? Tell me about her behavior with you at the fraternity party."

"When Vivian arrived at the fraternity house, I was there to greet her as you suggested. She seemed very pleased to see me but all hell broke loose the minute I told her that you were tied up for the evening."

"Did you tell her that I had a date with someone else?"

"I didn't mention anything about your having another date... well, maybe I hinted that you did, I don't exactly remember. She sat on a couch and I joined her. Right away I could see her eyes swollen with tears and it got worse and worse. A few times I was ready to walk out on her and leave her there, all alone on the couch, but then I thought of you and our friendship and my promise to be a good escort. I finally forced myself to escort her back to her dorm."

"Oh, my God, you never told me this! What specifically got worse and worse?"

"Her crying, her sobbing…nonstop for a long time…maybe hours. Well, close to an hour anyway. I tried to tell her that I was there just for her…that I, Stelios, the magnificent Greek god of the Aegean, was there totally for her protection, but mainly for her entertainment…to make sure she had a good time. But all she would say over and over was, 'But you are not Nick'…"

"What a jerk I was then…what a selfish, inconsiderate brute… after dating a girl for over two years, I took her for granted, I tried to brush her off so that I could romance another woman. No wonder she avoided me for two months after the incident. She even came a few times to our favorite hangout, the Butler Library smoking lounge."

"Did she come alone? Did she talk to you at all?"

"No, she was not alone. As usual, she was accompanied by her friend Juliana, each escorted by a Sikh. She did not talk to me, but I caught her a few times staring at me with a pair of very sad eyes. She even took up smoking...anyway, things are back to normal now. I have to go...I'll see you around, my friend, and thanks again for the graduation present."

Back in his room, Nicolas took advantage of Mrs. Saltzman's absence to have an extra shower, at least fifteen minutes longer than the usual ten minutes allotted to him every other day. He returned to the campus plaza with cap and gown.

Most graduation guests were already seated, occupying the rear half of the plaza. He joined his classmates who assembled in front of Butler Library. They marched with music, as a group, to their designated space in the front area of the plaza, essentially parading by and through the rows of seats occupied by family members and friends.

After all graduates from the various colleges and schools of the University took their designated positions, the faculty procession began. Students and guests were in awe of the long line of distinguished faculty faces, the pride of the University, parading in their varied and fanciful doctoral caps and gowns.

The graduates and everyone else seated on the plaza faced the university administrators and their guest dignitaries, all in their multicolored regalia, all seated on the temporary platform built over the upper steps and decorated with flower bouquets and flowering plants. The rear perimeter of the platform was outlined by the colorful banners representing the various colleges and schools of the university.

He knew most of the graduates around him quite well, but not the one seated to his right. He had seen him before of course, several times, at the International Student Center. Though he had never talked to him, he had been told that he was a foreign student from Turkey.

The Turk made the polite first move by introducing himself as Hassan Faik from Izmir. The Turkish town was familiar to Nicolas with the older name of Smyrna. When Nicolas introduced himself as a Greek Cypriot, he expected the conversation to end right then and there. Indeed, nothing was exchanged between them for quite a while.

In the mid-1960s Cyprus was often in the news. It was a young republic, having achieved its independence from British colonial rule about four years earlier, after the Greek Cypriot majority conducted a bloody four-year struggle against the colonialists. Practically all the Greek Cypriots, however, were unhappy with the constitution of their small republic, imposed and protected by the three sponsor nations of England, Greece and Turkey, because it gave veto rights and excessive privileges to the small Turkish minority of eighteen percent. The majority of the Greek Cypriots favored the dissolution of the republic and demanded *ENOSIS*, or union with Greece. Many other Greek Cypriots, including the President of the republic, Archbishop Makarios, supported the new independent Republic of Cyprus, but demanded modifications or additions to the constitution so that it may become more in line, as it should be, with a ruling majority—in this case the Greek Cypriots.

The government of Greece openly supported the former group, the "Enosis" group, and their constant demands for the union of Greece and Cyprus, two lands that have been inhabited predominantly by Greeks since before the ancient times of Homer.

At the same time, the Turkish Cypriot minority, fearing union with Greece and the eventual loss of their privileges under the republic's constitution that that might bring, was often conducting violent demonstrations against the Greek Cypriot majority, demanding partition of the island into Greek and Turkish independent states. Their demands were strongly and openly supported by Turkey, the biggest power in the region.

Nicolas wanted to show his Turkish classmate that he considered him like any other individual on campus and, as such, he was not responsible for his ethnic origin nor was he responsible for the perceived age-old hatred between the Greeks and the Turks.

Incredibly, Hassan was thinking along the same lines. He wanted to express his feelings, to show courtesy to someone that was a neighbor on campus, but also, more importantly, a permanent homeland neighbor.

Even more incredibly, both men felt more comfortable in each other's presence than in that of any of their non-Greek or non-Turkish associates in America. Apparently people like them inevitably share and adopt a large number of regional, cultural traits in their formative years that create strong regional bonds between them when they become expatriates. Nicolas was the first to interrupt the silence.

"So, you come from Smyrna, Mr. Faik. For me, your home is one of the most interesting regions in the world. You see, I like fresh figs with a passion and, as you know, Smyrna is reputed to be the world's best and biggest producer of that heavenly fruit."

"I agree with you about figs, they are heavenly. I also agree that my home, the Izmir region, produces the best in the world. I can't wait to taste the early June crop in a few days when I return home. Please, call me Hassan. I may see you again next fall when I will probably be back for some additional courses in preparation for graduate school. A mutual acquaintance, Hagop, told me you have already been accepted for graduate work here."

Nicolas was about to confirm his admission to the Graduate Faculties, but Hassan was faster with some additional comments: "By the way, I know you will be interested to know that my mother was born in Larnaca, Cyprus. She lived there until she was married at fifteen and moved to our present home just outside Izmir."

"Thank you Hassan. Of course, you too can call me by my first name, Nicolas or Nick. I'm glad you are planning to return to the States in the fall and I, too, hope to see you again. By the way, I'm sincerely happy for you, happy that you have some Cypriot blood in your heritage." He paused to smile. Hassan did the same.

"Perhaps, now that we know we are compatriots in a way, you can do me a big favor," said Nick. "Do you think you can bring me a couple of those incredible figs when you come back in September? After all, I assume you do know that those great fig trees in Smyrna were planted by the Greeks, just before they had to leave Smyrna in a hurry back in 1922."

Nicolas took a big chance, of course, with the last statement because he assumed that Hassan had a sense of humor. Hassan proved that he did. His initial response was a loud burst of laughter. Then he capped his laughter with,

"No wonder my father told me that a couple of our oldest fig trees are well over forty years old. They hardly produce any fruit any more, but we keep them alive for historical purposes. I will make sure that I bring back some figs for you, provided I do find some Greek ones." This time they both burst out into loud laughter.

With the exception of a few glances of approval and some coordinated clapping during some of the speeches, the two young men then concentrated on the proceedings and hardly said anything else to each other.

The president of the University, Dr. Grayson Kirk, first bestowed the bachelors degree to each of the undergraduate colleges of the university, as a group, then the higher degrees to each of the graduate or professional schools. When their college and degree were announced, Nicolas and Hassan tossed their caps high up in the sky above them. It took a while before they managed to retrieve them.

The college reception and the handing out of diplomas, through alphabetical roll call, began at 6:45, a little later than originally scheduled because the university-wide festivities went overtime. Nicolas had already decided he wasn't staying for the reception after he received his diploma because of his date with Vivian at 7:30.

He was just about ready to walk out of Low Memorial when Hassan approached him, accompanied by a middle-aged man. The man looked like an older, exact replica of his younger escort. Dark complexion, medium height and broad shoulders, and small, black piercing eyes, deep-set in a face that was chiseled with high cheek bones and a slightly elongated, hook nose. The older man's gray curly hair and broad mustache provided a sharp contrast to Hassan's jet-black hair coloration.

"Your father, I assume?"

"No, actually my father's brother. I would like you to meet my uncle, Mr. Mehmet Faik...he immigrated to America with his wife and their ten year old daughter thirteen years ago."

Nicolas shook hands with the uncle and greeted him, using a couple of Turkish phrases in the process. The uncle appeared pleased, evidently quite impressed with Nicolas' use of Turkish words. In return for the compliment, the older gentleman uttered the well known Greek greeting of *"yia sou."* Hassan continued to dominate the conversation.

"My uncle is part owner of a Turkish restaurant downtown. He provided me with the affidavit of support that I needed to come to school here. He and my aunt make me feel as if I am home with my parents back in Izmir. Of course I earn my keep, in a way, by helping at the restaurant."

A tall, curvy woman with short, jet-black hair, tightly packaged in a white pleated skirt and pink blouse, approached the three men. She greeted the two Turks affectionately with hugs and kisses. The older Faik made the introduction.

"This is my daughter Nora."

"She graduated Barnard two years ago," added Hassan.

Nicolas greeted Nora with a warm "hello" and an extended arm for a handshake. She reciprocated with similar warmth and asked a couple of questions about his plans to do graduate work and about his home and family back in Cyprus. She spoke English with a slight Turkish accent.

All the essential characteristics of an eastern Mediterranean heritage...a nice young woman and a veritable Turkish beauty, he thought. He was also impressed with the fact that she had a graduate teaching assistantship with the archaeology program at NYU. In a way, archaeology was part of his graduate work too.

At one point when Nicolas turned around, he was surprised to see another young woman standing next to Hassan who had his right arm around her waist. This one was relatively short and quite skinny, with light brown hair that reached down to her shoulders. She wore a very becoming, light-blue, crinkle cotton dress.

"Nick Maos, this is my other cousin, Yasmin."

Nicolas moved closer to Yasmin. When he looked straight into her sparkling, brown eyes, he felt as if a blood flash invaded his face. *"Can this be true?...Is she my Academy classmate, Yiasmin Ibrahim, the co-winner of the scholarship?"* He offered a similarly warm "how do you do?" to her and extended his arm for a handshake. She refused to shake hands, offered a sour face instead of a greeting and walked away.

Both Nora and Hassan showed some concern about Yasmin's behavior. Nora also offered a simple but understandable explanation.

"Yasmin's younger brother, cousin Halil, was killed a little over a year ago in a Greek-Turkish communal riot in Larnaca. He was only eighteen."

The older gentleman offered no regrets for his niece's behavior. However, he volunteered to elucidate her relationship to the Faik family. He had a heavy accent but his grasp of English and his communication skills were quite acceptable for a man with only elementary school education.

"The Faik family live many, many years in Izmir, Turkey. Before the English steal Cyprus from Ottoman Turks, our family travel to Cyprus to pray at the Tekke Mosque in Larnaca many, many times. My parents continue the family tradition and took my brother, the father of Hassan, and me to Larnaca in 1936. Also our parents had one more thing in their mind. They arrange marriage for my brother with a girl from a Turkish family there in Larnaca." He paused for a moment. His nephew grabbed the opportunity to take over the story..

"When they visited the Larnaca family, my grandparents were pleasantly surprised to see three beautiful sisters, all of marriage age, in their mid-to-late teens. The oldest of the three sisters, Yasmin's mother, was already engaged. Eventually the two brothers married the remaining two sisters."

"Is Yasmin here with her whole family?" Nicolas asked of Hassan. Nora was faster to respond.

"Yasmin and her mother and brother came to the States, from Cyprus, to live with us after uncle Ali died in a construction accident about ten years ago. Yasmin's brother returned to Larnaca to visit friends and relatives. Whether it was fate or perhaps bad timing, he was killed during a riot."

"I am truly sorry for the loss of her brother…such a waste…but tell me please, do you know whether she attended the American Academy in Larnaca?"

"If I recall correctly, she did—for four years. Her English was excellent when she arrived in New York…I believe she won a full scholarship at the Academy," responded Nora. "Did you get to know her at the Academy?" she added quickly.

"Yes, I knew her as a student in some of my classes, but I never really got to know her well enough…too many cultural and religious conflicts of the times. I never got the chance to say much more than a 'hello' to her."

"You do have a chance to see Yasmin again…perhaps even say more than just a "hello" to her. She is entering the School of Architecture this fall, here at Columbia.

"I hope she changes her mind and talks to me then…but please excuse me, I have to run. I'm supposed to meet a friend in about… well, according to my watch I am over fifteen minutes late already. I guess I literally have to run now. It was indeed a pleasure to meet you all and I do hope to see you all again." After another round of handshakes, he exited the rotunda in a big hurry.

Nicolas made it to 120th street and Amsterdam in less than fifteen minutes. The old elevator wasn't responding fast enough, so he ran up six flights. He was breathing hard when he stood alone in front of the apartment door at almost ten after eight.

He was surprised and disappointed that Vivian was not there. He was quite sure she would be there waiting for him even if he was more than half an hour late. When he opened the door, he saw a piece of paper on the floor. As usual, her note expressed courtesy and plenty of understanding.

Dear Nick,

Please don't worry about being a little late. I'm sure you couldn't help it. Graduation ceremonies and receptions usually run overtime. It's a little after eight and I am going back on campus to make a call home. I am coming right back. I decided to stay in the city tonight (probably with Juliana if I find her). See you soon.

Vivian

Nicolas felt like a louse for screwing up his date with Vivian, but then again he kept rationalizing that he had to pick up his diploma and it wasn't his fault that the reception ran late. Also, he convinced himself that the delay was well worth it since he was given the extraordinary opportunity to meet and get to know some interesting Turks, of all people, for the first time since he arrived in New York. Even more extraordinary was the fact that one of the two beautiful Turkish women, with Cypriot heritage no less, was the sweet Yiasmin of his early high school years.

His noisy stomach kept reminding him that he was starving. He avoided most of the refreshments at the reception because he was expecting Vivian to take him out for a big dinner. He refreshed himself with a quick wash, then lay stretched on his bed. At first, a pleasant shiver of anticipation came over him when he thought of Vivian coming up to his room. Moments later, body and mind entered a state of relaxation. He wandered back close to the end of his sophomore year, exam time in mid-May when he first spoke to Vivian.

"Please be my guest," said Nicolas, standing up and pointing to the empty spot next to him on the sofa.

By the time she thanked him, sat down, crossed her legs and pulled her skirt over her knees, her face and her figure silhouette were already etched in his mind. His mind was very pleased indeed.

She picked up the *CUE* magazine from the side table. Nicolas could tell she was checking the movie listings and the mini-reviews. Since he was a big movie buff and did the same thing every time he came to the tea lounge, he decided he was going to interrupt and say something, perhaps about *Lawrence of Arabia,* since everybody seemed to be raving about that film. However, she beat him to it and said, turning towards him and offering her hand,

"I am Vivian and you are Nick, right?"

He was very surprised she knew his name. He managed to nod and smile but said nothing before she continued,

"The lounge is very crowded today. I guess you never miss the Friday afternoon tea at Earl Hall, right? Every time I come here I see you with one or another of the same group of friends. I don't see them today…I met your Iranian friend the other day…Darius right? He told me your name…"

"Would you like a cookie?" was his delayed first response to all her "right?" statements. Then he managed to explain in a rather formal tone,

"This is the semester's last tea and most people try not to miss it. I hope that the Eastern Orthodox Student Association continues sponsoring the tea next fall."

All of Nicolas' friends, mostly foreign students, attended these tea parties to meet girls, primarily Barnard coeds like Vivian who seemed to have a preference for international relationships. He liked to socialize too, but, during those lean times, he was there primarily for the tea and those deliciously satisfying cookies, so graciously served by faculty wives.

He had seen Vivian in the lounge a few times before, of course, but always in the company of the same three people. — a tall, full-bodied, blonde woman, spectacularly attractive in spite of a red birth mark that covered a good part of her forehead, who was practically always by the side of a black-bearded Sikh who came very close to personifying the term "tall, dark and handsome," and another Sikh, assumed to be Vivian's boyfriend, was a rather bigger, fuller man who appeared to be much older than his handsome friend. Every time Nicolas saw their turbans stand above most other heads in the lounge, he visualized countless scenes where Errol Flynn or Victor Mature wore them in movies that depicted British colonial times in India.

After several minutes of small talk, mostly about movies and her life in the dormitories, Nicolas asked her about her presumed boyfriend.

"Harbinder is not my boyfriend. He is just a friend of a friend of my best friend Juliana. She is terribly in love with Jaspal. Julie also encourages me to fall for Harbinder by painting endless, fabulous pictures of us two best friends living happily ever after with those two best friends."

"I'm so glad you are not involved with that...big guy." His tone was one of relief, and "big guy" was a last second substitution for "gorilla." "Perhaps I shouldn't be, but I guess it's my nature to be concerned about you, Vivian…you seem to have plenty of spirit, you are so lively and yet so petite and innocent-looking and perhaps even vulnerable in the company of such big…wolves…"

"I suppose I am safe with you," she interrupted with a wide and wily smile.

He quickly changed the subject. "I'm quite fascinated with your eyes," he said with a smile as he moved closer and locked into a direct stare with her. He thought that her eyes were rather small but beautifully radiant and penetrating, and appeared to perfectly complement her small head and petite torso. "I like the color but I'm not sure how to describe such a color. Is it green? Perhaps a mixture of green and brown?"

"I'm fascinated too," she responded with another direct stare and a smile, "You and I share the same uniquely identical color… it's called hazel."

Almost two hours of pleasant tea time finally came to an end. They left the lounge together and walked slowly towards the Barnard dormitories. At first, he hesitated, but eventually he dared hold her hand as they walked. She responded with a tight hand squeak of her own.

A knock on the apartment door brought Nicolas back from his sophomore year.

"It must be Vivian," he thought, with passionate anticipation. Alas, it was only a neighbor asking for Monica Saltzman. Within a couple of minutes, Nicolas was back on the bed reminiscing about his early days with his girlfriend.

After his first encounter with Vivian at the tea lounge, Nicolas could not see or talk to her for four days or until his last final exam was over. He knew he would have plenty of relative leisure time to see her after that, close to four weeks, before traveling to the Catskills for the second year in a row to begin summer work as a counselor at a summer teen-age camp.

During those four weeks, he never once asked Vivian out on a date. He did not have to. Just about every night of the week, between seven and ten, she would join him at his regular hangout, the smoking lounge on the third floor of Butler Library. They often shared a table, occasionally a sofa. He spent most of the time there getting acquainted with a text in a forthcoming course in crystallography and she was doing assigned reading for a summer session course in history, her subject of concentration.

At times, they both felt they could not only smell but also physically taste the heavy lounge atmosphere, laden with smoke from cigarettes and pipes. Nicolas was a significant contributor to the room's atmospheric composition, but Vivian was not a smoker at that time. The social atmosphere of the lounge was quite informal and casual. They couldn't carry out their usual highly animated discussions, but they could converse in a low voice and they both seemed to enjoy each other's company immensely.

A few other couples frequented the lounge, as well as some women on their own. Men, reading or studying by themselves, made up the largest group. Some of the men were smokers and others never smoked. It was obvious to Nicolas that they were all there to watch and even pick-up coeds.

Once when Vivian could not make it to the library, he shared one of the small round tables, lining up the center of the room, with a man in a suit and bow-tie. Nicolas had seen this rather formally dressed, good-looking older man—probably in his late thirties or early forties—many times before, practically always seated at one of the low-lying couch chairs facing the room's interior.

"The classics, Greek literature and philosophy, are favorite topics and essential basics to my dissertation studies, here at Columbia, on the early Roman Empire," the older man pointed out after Nicolas commented on the Homeric Dictionary in front of him. "I also teach a couple of sections of a western civilization course, Greek and Roman History and Culture, at City College," he added.

"Why the smoking lounge? You do not appear to be a smoker. I never saw you smoke here."

"I like the casual atmosphere. Even more, I like to watch all those attractive women who frequent this lounge. You ought to know. A gorgeous young woman accompanies you here all the time. Some of these women are very generous in sharing their usually hidden, physical beauty endowments with people like me."

"Another way of saying that you are a voyeur, I suppose," responded Nicolas with considerable authority, recalling many a time when he enjoyed doing the same thing. Of course it was different in his case, Nicolas rationalized, because he never actually planned it. It had to be an accidental occurrence of the moment.

The man did not deny the characterization. Instead, he excused himself and moved rather quickly to a vacated couch chair. Suddenly, Nicolas could see the man and many others like him, spying like predators, patiently waiting for their next prey to cross or preferably, to uncross her legs.

Later on that night, as he lay in bed recalling events of the day, two seemingly contradictory items stood up in his mind. On the one hand, he was pleased and rather proud that somebody referred to his girlfriend as "gorgeous" and, on the other hand, he was very much concerned that Vivian kept her private physical endowments hidden from everyone but him.

I suppose this is one way jealousy is acknowledged by one's mind, he thought.

The next day, when he saw Vivian again, he tried very hard, using abstract symbols and analogies, to warn her about the lounge predators.

"I love the way you dress, Vivian. You know that in the Greek Orthodox Church, icons are exhibited to remind us of important religious figures. In my mind's temple, I happen to have your icon, that of a very attractive and in many ways innocent girl in pleated skirts and blouses. Just remember that there are many predators out there, especially in our smoking lounge at Butler, who are ready and just waiting to take advantage of you, to salivate over you."

At first she appeared puzzled and he wasn't sure she understood his concern about the lounge voyeurs. He was ready to be more specific when she responded, in a rather serious tone, "Nick, I am actually tickled to death that you want me all for yourself. I want you all for myself too...I promise you...I promise you my body is for your eyes only."

At that moment, Nicolas was sure he saw sparks of passion in Vivian's eyes. He never felt so utterly romantic since his innocent romance with Stella back in elementary school. But he knew something was quite different this time. He looked at the relationship more as a sexual conquest. He realized he must have finally acquired that all-conquering Casanova mentality of the young male species, so often seen portrayed in the movies.

Even though he had kissed Vivian several times before, whenever he dropped her off at the dormitories, those kisses were polite and casual and practically passionless. This time, her impassioned words alone were much more powerful and much more physically arousing than her kisses, and caused new types of visions to parade in front of his mind's eye...visions of bodies intimately entangled, making passionate love.

Romantically speaking, the remaining two weeks before summer camp represented a milestone. Nicolas became thoroughly acquainted with the pleasures and frustrations of his sexuality which, until the end of his sophomore year, he almost totally ignored. He was much too busy studying, practically day and night, mostly in isolation in his tiny rented room, to be thinking about sex. He had to stay focused on school in order to earn and maintain a GPA that was good enough for a full-tuition academic scholarship.

Passionate necking, usually after the library closed, provided sexual pleasures for both but also sexual frustrations for Nicolas and perhaps even for Vivian. They often made-out at a Riverside

Park bench, but their favorite place was one of the semi-private lounges of the Barnard dormitory.

Men were not allowed to visit co-eds in their dormitory rooms at any time, but were allowed to visit in one of a series of tiny lounges, lined along the ground floor corridor, on a first-come-first-served basis. The couch was comfortable and inviting, but the lounge had no doors to close for complete privacy. Security personnel patrolled the corridor, especially during the last couple of hours before curfew.

Many a time, Nicolas thought of bringing Vivian to his room for more privacy. Even though she made it abundantly clear that she wanted to remain a virgin until her marriage, his main concern was his hosts, the Saltzmans, who also made it abundantly clear that he could not bring women to his room at any time.

But now, during the evening of his college graduation day, he was expecting Vivian to visit him in his room at any moment. After all, he was permanently moving out of the room in six days and, better yet, the widow Saltzman was not expected to return until the following evening.

As usual, Nicolas' imagination, already traveling ahead of him, was projecting visions of a passionate encounter in his head as well as literally bringing sweat and shivers over his whole body.

Chapter Six

A gentle knock. Nicolas looked at his watch, it was 8:50. As soon as he released the latch, the door was pushed open from the outside and, within seconds, Vivian was in his arms, which were already fully opened and extended to receive her. She began kissing him all over the face while whispering all sorts of congratulations. He reciprocated with plenty of kisses of his own as well as loud expressions of "thank you" and "I am so happy you are here."

When they finally calmed down, still in the apartment corridor, she was the first to speak.

"Nick, I do have a graduation present for you, a surprise, but you have to wait until later. We have plenty of time, I am staying in the city tonight. In the meantime, I think we should better get something to eat, I'm famished. What about you?"

"I am too…totally starved…where shall we go?"

They walked down to the Caravan Restaurant, on 110th Street and Broadway, where they shared and thoroughly enjoyed a dish of sautéed chicken wings with wheat pilaf, reserved only for Greek customers, and a dish of baked pork chops and French fries. They also shared a piece of apple pie with their coffee. Vivian insisted that dinner was part of her graduation present. She wouldn't even let Nicolas contribute to the tip.

They returned to the L-shaped building on 120th Street. His room, about eight feet from the entrance and to the right of the narrow corridor, was tiny, but had a window facing a similar 12-story building. The window overlooked a narrow concrete yard between the two buildings that was apparently used by the tenants primarily as a depository of unwanted household items. Stanley described Nicolas' room as "a walk-in closet with a window."

A total of seven items made up the room's furnishings, including the silver-painted steam radiator under the window. The radiator was quite noisy, mostly hissing sounds, when going into full steam early in the morning. Two piles of books and several folders, paper pads, note books and pens and pencils, together with a lamp fixture mounted on a green Chianti bottle, covered most of the top of the cherry veneer desk.

The desk was situated close to the window, partly concealing the radiator. It had no drawers and no shelves. Another much taller pile of books lay on the faded hard-wood floor by a folding metal chair, the only one in the room.

A cot with a rather fancy knit cover, placed against the right wall as you entered, protruded slightly into the room entrance and served both as the bed and as a sitting couch. An old mahogany armoire apparently had lost not only its polish luster but also its doors, with hinges still in place. It covered the narrow wall towards the interior of the apartment and provided drawer and shelf space. A rod installed just under the top shelf provided space for clothes hangers.

The final and most colorful item in the room was a shoe-box size, plastic AM radio in a light pink and white color combination. It was on the desk when Nicolas moved in, but he relocated it to the top shelf of the armoire. Mrs. Saltzman pointed out that she picked up the radio as well as the armoire and the lamp at a flea market. She expressed the hope that the radio would inform and entertain her young tenant.

Vivian whispered something that included the word "cozy"

while she was turning the tuning knob. She stopped at 1050. At that moment, the announcer, with a heavy put-on French accent, announced that WNEW 1050 was continuing with *la music avec la difference*. Almost instantly, the program became the symbol of their romance.

They both sat on the bed almost simultaneously. She made the first move by caressing his left leg with her left hand and the back of his head with her right. Nicolas needed no additional encouragement.

With gentle prodding, he had Vivian lie on her back and, within seconds, they were both experimenting with all kinds of intricate body entanglements. His hands were practically everywhere, exploring every hidden curve, every sensuous inch of her body.

The sounds of the encounter, especially those emanating from Vivian, were quite loud and apparently difficult to suppress since they continued in spite of her apologies. She finally motioned that she needed to stand up.

"Now for the big surprise," she said in a trembling voice as she shook her skirt off and started unbuttoning her blouse. "These buttons in the back…Nick, I need your help."

"Sure…of course," he responded with an even more obvious trembling in his speech. She presented a spectacular, inviting panorama as she stood there only with her bra and panties on.

"I'm all yours…please make love to me…I want you to be the first to make love to me…I am…your graduation present!"

Nicolas was motionless for a few moments, totally surprised, in fact totally shocked by what he saw and heard. But the shock was quickly changing to a feeling of total delight, a feeling of anticipated exhilaration.

He undressed down to his Jockey briefs and then pulled her towards him. While they were both dispensing a fury of kisses on the face and neck, he labored to unhinge her bra from the back. As the bra finally fell on the floor, he could feel her hardened nibbles creating sinkholes in his chest.

Nicolas had touched and felt Vivian's boobs on several occasions before, but always while confined in her bra. This was the first time her breasts were hanging totally exposed before him. He gently pushed her a few inches apart for an unobstructed look.

For a petite woman, she is generously endowed with plump breasts… the aroused breasts of a young woman in her very prime create a vision of passion that never quite leaves a man's mind. He was totally surprised he even had such thoughts, knowing very well that he was hardly a great devotee of mammary glands.

In his early childhood, in the village, women would not hesitate to take out a breast, right in front of him, in order to nurse an infant. Then, of course, he also nursed on his mother's breasts until he was almost four. Perhaps because of this experience, big boobs never quite aroused his passions as they seem to do for men in America, a breast-obsessed culture. Long, lean legs topped by a well-shaped derriere, round and tight, were his favorite passionate distractions on a woman.

Finally, after Nicolas discovered and, surprisingly, fully enjoyed the pleasures of Vivian's breasts, he moved his concentration elsewhere. He directed her to lie on her back and he stood there above her. His eyes feasted on the panorama only for a few seconds since his hands could no longer resist the temptation to participate. Her black, satin-soft bikini panties, with a red heart covering the whole front, greatly enhanced the pleasures of watching and feeling. Soon, the rest of his senses joined the party.

They practically lost track of time as they continued to indulge in the pleasures of the flesh, as if in a dream, with Nicolas unable to control or conceal an episode of wet orgasm. They had gone through this kind of intense foreplay, fully clothed, a couple of times before on a couch in Juliana's apartment. However, this time one thing was different. Nicolas was much more comfortable with his surroundings and definitely had the intention of going all the way.

The endless passion made him completely and totally forget his earlier promise to himself and to his friend Stanley that he would not take advantage of her and that, instead, he would explain first his inability to commit to any formal relationship with her before he would even consider intercourse.

So, with promises and commitments thrown aside, he began to pull down her panties ever so slowly. But things did not go his way. At the critical moment, she impulsively stopped him cold by pushing him away from her and abruptly crossing her legs tight. He stood up immediately. His face did not seem to express disappointment, or even anger. It was the face of a man who had just rediscovered something totally forgotten, something valuable.

"Oh, my God...I'm terribly sorry, Nick, please forgive me, I did not mean to do that...force of habit, I guess," she said in a rather loud, agitated voice. She quickly straightened and opened up her legs, at the same time extending an invitation with her arms.

"Here, here I am all ready for you...come back to me..." she added as she assumed her original position on the cot.

Nicolas kept his standing position in front of her with an expression of uneasiness, remaining both motionless and speechless for several more seconds. Two fiercely opposing forces were fighting for control of his body and mind. It was the age-old battle between the passionate desire of the flesh and the morality of the mind. When he spoke, it was obvious that the latter had won.

"I'm the one who should be sorry, who should apologize...I forgot myself, my promise to myself to respect your moral wishes... in spite of your decision to sacrifice your virtue, to give yourself to me. I do appreciate your notion of sacrifice, offering yourself as the ultimate graduation present...but your reaction to my advances made it quite clear that your vows of purity until marriage were still quite strong...much stronger than the desires of the flesh. As for me, the passions of the flesh took over my willpower.

I was ready and willing to take advantage of you...please forgive me..."

Her immediate response was in the form of a few tears running down her cheeks as she slowly began to cover herself with the top sheet. Nicolas placed her panties and bras on top of her covered chest and continued his lament, still standing naked by her side. At the same time, she began to put on her underwear under the cover of the sheet.

"I'm sorry, dear Vivian, I am sorry I cannot accept your graduation present at this time…of course I do appreciate the offer…I most certainly do…it's the best, the most personal and the most exciting I have ever received…and I do believe that you meant it. And I also want you to know that it was the most difficult decision I ever had to make…please remember that it's the thought that counts." He stopped for a moment to pick up his clothes and, as he dressed, he continued his explanation.

"I think it's also fair for you to know something else…I decided a few weeks back, when I was accepted to graduate school, that I cannot make any commitment to you for a permanent relationship…I cannot do it now or in the near future. Perhaps you see my decision as selfish…it probably is…but it also represents a commitment to my family back in Cyprus…"

"Nick, it's o.k., I do understand. You do not have to make any commitments to me. I did not expect you to do so…I offered myself to you because I love you and I don't want to lose you. I'll always love you…and my offer still stands…anytime…"

He knelt by the bed and kissed her lightly on the lips. Before he withdrew, she put her arms around his neck and kept him there for a closer, longer kiss.

"How about coming to bed, darling Nick? Don't you think we can share this bed for the night without worrying too much about the consequences of our passions? Don't you think we are mature enough to face the consequences if we decide to make love? I think we can make beautiful love by being in each other's arms…even without resorting to actual intercourse…it's up to you…"

He sealed her mouth with another kiss and then began

undressing down to his briefs. He practically leaped onto the narrow cot, essentially joining his body with hers in a very tight embrace. It was the first time they were sharing a bed together. The night was long and, even though they strictly planned to avoid it, they still partook of the forbidden fruit of the flesh. It was a truly unique and exhilarating experience for both.

At a little before six, relatively very early for a Saturday morning, Vivian left the apartment very quietly and without using the bathroom facilities. She expected to do that at her friend Juliana's apartment on 112th Street. During the night, a few minutes after midnight, the young lovers heard somebody come into the apartment and assumed, of course, that it was Mrs. Saltzman, returning earlier than expected. Vivian concluded that it would be prudent for her not to chance an encounter with the landlady.

Nicolas shaved and showered and left the apartment around eight, without seeing his landlady. He was on his way first to the Canal Diner for breakfast and a short visit with his friend Luke. But the most important tusk of the day was his early afternoon meeting with his boss, Rusty Weisman.

Nicolas finished his breakfast rather quickly and explained to his friend that, because of his uptown appointment with Mr. Weisman, he had to leave right away. This was not strictly true since his appointment with Mr. Weisman was well after lunch, at one-thirty, but he planned to take in a relaxing movie or two on 42nd Street's theater-row before he met his boss. It was his way of rewarding himself for his accomplishment.

He was almost certain that Luke, being very busy at working the counter, had somehow forgotten about his graduation. As usual, pride wouldn't allow him to remind his good friend and benefactor, lest he interpret the move as a call for a graduation present. However, as he got off the counter stool and started towards the exit door, Luke came from behind to pull him back for a quick congratulatory hug. He also quickly and secretly placed a small envelope into the graduate's blazer pocket. On his way back to the counter, Luke turned to exclaim in a loud but joyful voice,

"Hey, Nick, you did great! Congratulations...and good luck in graduate school."

Nicolas did not notice or feel the envelope in his pocket until he entered the 8th Avenue subway train for the 42nd Street, Times Square, station. For a Saturday morning, the uptown "A" train was quite crowded. He rushed to sit down on the solitary corner seat as soon as it became available. The concave, hard plastic seat was rather warm but comfortably smooth.

A quick look into the envelope revealed a typical graduation greeting card and two $20 bills. It was signed "Luke and family," with no additional personal message.

Nicolas arrived on 42nd Street, his favorite place to be whenever he felt a bit sad and somewhat depressed or lonely, or even whenever he felt upbeat and happy. He could catch any one of twenty-five or more movies, old and recent, shown in a dozen theaters, all lined-up on both sides of the street between Broadway and 8th Avenue and all open twenty-four hours.

The marquis of the Selwyn, the westerns theater, was showcasing two of the finest westerns of all time, 1948's *Red River* and 1959's *Rio Bravo*, both with John Wayne and both directed by the great Howard Hawks. Two weeks earlier, he saw two of John Ford's best, 1949's *She Wore a Yellow Ribbon* and 1956's *The Searchers*, also starring John Wayne in two of his best performances.

As usual, the price for the double feature was 55 cents. According to the posted time schedule, 1959's *Rio Bravo* was to begin in six minutes.

Nicolas had seen *Rio Bravo* three times before but it was still as diverting and entertaining as the first time. The theme music during the showing of the titles and credits was especially moving, almost haunting, and it beautifully set the sentimental story of loyalty and devotion among friends.

As the story unfolded, Nicolas, who made friends easily because he valued friendship as one of the greatest acquired privileges in life, couldn't help reminisce about the close friends he left behind in Cyprus. Images of the film, interwoven with those of his friends, kept bouncing in his head for quite a while after the end of the movie.

There was not enough time to get his full money's worth, to see the entire second feature. He exited the theater and walked over to the north end of 42nd and Broadway and ordered the famous snack at Nedick's: a grilled, greasy hot dog in a toasted, rectangular bun, smeared with lots of mustard and covered with relish. A cool orange drink, from an agitated glass-tank dispenser served as the perfect liquid complement to the meaty snack.

Nicolas reached the Columbus Circle station with plenty of time to spare before the appointment. He crossed over to the northeastern exit of the huge, interconnecting station in order to enter Central Park. It was a pleasant late-May day and he looked forward to sunning himself seated on a rock outcrop that provided a good view of the small lake in the park.

As soon as he placed himself on top of the hill, he recognized the almost eerie-like duplication of the moment. He was in the exact same spot, taking in the sun, almost three years earlier, killing time before his employment interview with the same man he was about to see this day.

He couldn't avoid comparing the two days. This day he was as happy and content as ever, with a strong feeling of accomplishment and pride. On that earlier day everything was different except for the vitreous luster of the schistose rock on which he was sitting. That day's prevalent mood was one of hopelessness combined with deep disappointment and frustration derived from the self realization that he had just been a victim of unfair play and prejudice. He couldn't keep his thoughts from dwelling on the events of that earlier day:

It was mid-September, the beginning of his sophomore year, when he began his search for part-time employment. The University Placement Office gave him two contacts: Radio City Music Hall and Weisman Ski Gloves, Inc.. Both employers were offering the minimum hourly wage.

His first choice was easy. Selling popcorn and candy at the city's top showcase theater, dressed in a colorful uniform, was personally very attractive. So many possibilities to enjoy great films as well as live shows free of charge. He set up an interview for a Friday morning.

The interview was conducted in the spectacular main lobby with a gold leaf ceiling, standing not too far from a candy counter. At first, the interviewer, a middle-age man with gray hair, dressed in black suit and bow tie, appeared to be impressed with Nicolas' educational background. Then, astonishingly, he asked the Ivy Leaguer,

"Can you handle American money? That is, could you add numbers in your head and give back the right change?"

"Sir, I know you are making a joke, even though your face expression suggests otherwise…sir, I assume that you do have a sense of humor by asking me that…"

"I am not making a joke. I like to point out that the theater's audience is typically made up of English-speaking, middle-class Americans and I would prefer not to subject the patrons of this theater to employees with language barriers or heavy accents."

Nicolas could easily confirm the man's apparent prejudicial hiring practices with one quick look around the concession counters in the lobby. But he could not agree with the man's characterization of the theater's audience.

"Sir, my aunt ,who lives in Brooklyn, brought me here to my first Radio City show. She proudly told me how she and the other neighborhood Cypriot immigrant ladies, who could hardly be classified as English-speaking middle-class Americans, loved to come to the Music Hall, the showcase of the nation, a couple of times a year. They did this because they enjoyed the luxury of the theater itself as well as the spectacular live musical show…and in spite of the fact that they did not fully understand the language of the movie."

The interviewer did not respond to the young man's comments. He excused himself and said he would be right back. Instead, a young man of college age, looking very much like a king-size Alan Ladd, introduced himself simply as an assistant to the supervisor and explained how Radio City Music Hall could not hire Nicolas at this time. When pressed for a reason, he added, "We have plenty of other applicants without language or cultural barriers."

There's still plenty of time, it's only 10:30. Perhaps I should call and schedule an interview with that glove company. It probably won't work, though. My mother said it all along—that 'you can tell early at dawn if a day will turn out to be a good one.' This first terrible interview, this awful disappointment, probably set the pace for the day.

The interview with the ski-glove company was set for 11:30. He had plenty of time to walk a few blocks from 50th and 6th Avenue to 60th and Broadway. He chose to do part of the walk through Central Park, using the pathways adjacent Central Park South. He took a few minutes to rest on a Manhattan schist rock outcrop overlooking the man-made lake. Very unusual for a typically optimistic young man, he felt quite pessimistic about his chances of getting a job that day.

The building housing the Weisman Ski Glove company was midway between Broadway and 8th Avenue. Rusty Weisman was seated at the desk of the sparsely furnished front room of the second floor office. As soon as Nicolas entered, Mr. Weisman got up and moved towards him, with a slight limp.

He was tall, very tall indeed, a late-middle-age athletic man, a former top skier, with a light pinkish complexion, numerous freckles or age spots and plenty of rusty-red hair that chose to grow only on the back and sides of his head. He introduced himself simply as "Rusty" and welcomed his prospective employee with the courtesy of a wide smile and the personal warmth of a strong, lively handshake. He also introduced Mrs. Bauman, seated at a typewriter to his left, as his part-time secretary. She greeted the young man politely and continued typing what looked like sales invoices.

The interview consisted of only one question, with the interviewer seeking to verify whether the candidate was in fact sent by Columbia, his Alma Mater. After the verification, Rusty offered Nicolas the part-time job. "My dad started this company. We manufacture and sell ski gloves, but we also represent and sell other ski equipment. Your job involves the shipping of our gloves to retail shops around the country, but mainly to the Northeast." He then added that Nicolas could work any day of the week or as his school schedule allowed, averaging about twenty-five hours per week.

Rusty also explained that his own job was to initiate sales either by phone or by actually visiting customers, using the company station wagon. Nicolas was to be given a key for access to the office when no one else was there.

Nicolas tried to hide his disappointment when Rusty showed him the layout of the back room which he described as "the inventory and shipping room." *What a mess!* was his first thought.

It consisted primarily of large, open cardboard cartons, some in a bad state of deterioration, scattered in a haphazard fashion all around the room. They contained what Rusty described as "our bread and butter, half a dozen different ski glove and ski mitten models, designed and manufactured by our own company." The gloves were organized in the cartons by model and according to five different sizes. If a carton was filled to the brim, any additional gloves were piled or scattered on the floor around the carton.

Samples of other types of merchandise included ski parkas and ski pants displayed on free-standing, stainless steel display fixtures near the far end wall of the room. Ski boots and bindings and other hardware were exhibited in the form of little mounds in one of the corners. The only seemingly well organized and colorful display was the wooden ski rack, placed against the east wall, exhibiting "various types and sizes of popular and experimental skis."

It did not take long for Nicolas to realize what a great part-time job he landed. It not only paid well, but also allowed for plenty of personal independence and great flexibility in his otherwise busy academic schedule. But the most important realization was the fact that Rusty Weisman, whom he thought of as "the cool giant" the first day he met him, was fast becoming his all-American best friend and guardian.

With time, he even came to consider his rejection by the Radio City Music Hall a blessing, confirming his belief in his mother's saying: "Every obstacle in your present path creates a better opportunity for you in the future."

After a couple of months on the Weisman job, Nicolas reorganized the shipping room or stock room not only for aesthetic reasons, but also for greater efficiency in shipping as well as in inventory taking. But most importantly, within a year or so, his position had evolved from a "simple shipping clerk" to a "do-it-all employee." He received substantial salary increments as well as many unexpected benefits and merit awards.

When Mrs. Bauman retired nine months after he joined the company, Nicolas took over the typing of the sales invoices, the balancing of the checking account monthly statement, the management of the petty cash account, and the shipping arrangements with the trucking companies.

When Rusty was on the road, Nicolas also handled telephone communications dealing with factory production problems, with accounts receivable or simply with customers' questions. He often gave "expertise" advice to callers concerning the proper use of equipment on the slopes even though he never did any skiing himself.

Rusty usually described his employee as "indispensable." He also gave full credit to Nicolas' idea of using space-age insulation material developed by NASA in one of the ski glove lines, even though Rusty himself spent fourteen months in the development of the final product and the securing of the NASA licenses. Eventually, the "space-age ski glove" became the company's best seller by far.

The sophomore job interview day events and three years of employment experiences with the Weisman Ski Glove company paraded in front of Nicolas' mind quite fast. The pleasant park surroundings and the warm sunshine made the trip to the near past very comfortable.

"It's now time to go see why Rusty called today's meeting on a Saturday," he whispered as he began walking towards 60th Street.

As soon as Nicolas entered the 2nd floor office, Rusty rushed over to greet him with his usual jovial laughter and powerful handshake.

"Congratulations, Nick, and welcome to the club." He pointed to his Columbia ring, class of '38, and added, "One day you may purchase one of these, a symbol of pride for some, an ego trip for others. In the meantime, this is much better for you." He handed Nicolas an envelope.

The young graduate could not have imagined a more exciting graduation present, even in his wildest dreams. He stood there, speechless, staring at the airline ticket packet he took out of the envelope. Rusty broke the silence.

"In case you are wondering why EL AL airlines, they had a special excursion to Tel Aviv for half the usual price. My mother received the promotion brochure for the excursion in the mail. I guess it's because I had her use the airline twice before for trips to Israel. Personally, I never visited Israel and my mother, like a good Jewish mother, wanted me to take advantage of the low fares."

"I think mothers know best...you should always listen to your mother's advice."

"She is always after me to do something. She is most persistent in trying to get me to marry... probably anybody...just as long as she gets a grandchild from her only child, before it's too late for her. Anyway, I immediately thought of you, especially since you made me aware of the fact that Israel and Cyprus have good trade relations and several scheduled flights between them."

Nicolas kept looking at the airline ticket. Rusty came closer and added, pointing to the latter part of the packet.

"Take a look at that Nick...the connecting flight to Nicosia is with Cyprus Airways...I thought you might like that..."

"Rusty, my friend...I do like that and I do like the whole thing very, very much indeed. It's the most incredible thing that ever happened to me...it's phenomenal...the timing is unbelievable... imagine, I can see my mother...my whole family after seven years of total separation and before I begin a new chapter in my life, before I begin graduate school."

Nicolas approached for a close embrace. Rusty was a little uncomfortable with hugging, he always preferred handshakes. "Thanks a million Mr. Weisman...from me and my mother and my whole family."

"It's Rusty, remember? And it's my pleasure to do this for you Nick, you deserve it. I'm sure you noticed that you only have three days to prepare for the trip. And you do need a visa to land in Israel."

The two men walking together towards the exit, close but not touching, projected quite a picture of contrasts. A bald, part rusty, part graying, six-foot-plus giant walking with a slight limp next to a young man of average height but good posture, flaunting a full head of dark-brown hair.

At the exit door, another of Rusty's strong handshakes was accompanied by his trademark laughter. "This is our slow season but, still, don't forget to come back in about four weeks. Oh, I almost forgot. Here is your paycheck...enjoy the trip and your homecoming!"

Nicolas returned to the 59th Street station and entered the Uptown Broadway local, bound for home. All of a sudden, he had too many things on his mind, too many things to take care of. First and foremost, he had to find out if in fact it was safe for him to actually return to his homeland.

As soon as he got a seat on the train, he began examining his airline ticket once again. *An incredible graduation present! This is a very significant contribution to Nick's happiness. What a good, kind gentleman...of course he has always been more than just a boss, a close friend indeed...I'll be indebted to Mr. Weisman for ever...I hope I can make use of this ticket.*

"*Apistephto!* Unbelievable!" he cried out in both Greek and English as soon as he took a look at his paycheck. He didn't even notice that he attracted the attention and stares of some of the passengers. The check was obviously for five weeks' pay instead of just one. Mr. Weisman was essentially giving him a four-week paid vacation to which he was not normally entitled as a part-time employee.

Back on campus, Nicolas' first order of business was to call Cyprus. He had to find out whether he was still "a targeted traitor" in his village. Last time he found out anything about his latest standing on the matter was over a year earlier when his friend Yiannis wrote, "My people are still working towards clearing your name." He knew he had to talk to Yiannis again before embarking on a "happy homecoming."

A campus public phone was not very convenient for an international call. Stanley's phone was his first choice, but his friend was nowhere to be found. Time was of the essence, so Nicolas reluctantly decided to ask his landlady. He never expected her accommodating answer: "Consider this phone call part of my graduation present to you."

He placed a person-to-person call. As he waited for the operator to ring him back, he told Mrs. Saltzman that his conversation would be in Greek. She offered no objection.

Instead, she directed him to sit next to the little telephone table, and then brought him a cold refreshment. In less than five minutes, the operator rung to say that Yiannis could not be reached. A new call was placed, this time for Andros.

"You caught me on the way out for an after-dinner visit with my aunt's family. You probably won't believe it, but I'm actually leaving on Tuesday for the States. You know about my girlfriend in California. I'm…"

"Let me guess. You are going there to marry Christine."

"That's right. By the way, I plan to visit you during my extended New York stopover on Wednesday. The coincidence of this call is amazing. I was planning to call tomorrow and leave a message with your friend Stanley."

"Well, that would be great but I may be leaving for Cyprus around the same time. I got a ticket, a graduation present, for Tuesday. That's the reason I'm calling…I need information about the situation in Ora. Is it safe to visit at this time?"

"Before I answer, let me congratulate you first, on behalf of all of your friends here…as for Ora, and similar rural regions on the island, a lot of things are happening but nothing final or decisive yet. Sodiris, your nemesis, is still the powerful leader of the local insurgent group that supports union with Greece. They do not hesitate to intimidate and even kill those that oppose them, those who support Makarios and the Republic."

"What about the Makarios' government? Can't they do anything about the intimidation and the violence?"

"They can't do much when people are afraid to testify against the group…my advice to you is to postpone your trip."

"I'll have to take my chances. I can't pass this great opportunity to visit my family and my friends. I'm very sorry I won't get to see you. Thanks and best regards to all."

"O.K. but don't count on going to the village. Just stay here in Larnaca."

⤴

Nicolas thanked his landlady and left the apartment without entering his room. He had to go on campus to make a few local calls concerning his trip.

His future roommate, Sanjay, was not very pleased about the five-week delay in moving in, even though Nicolas reminded him that his original posted offer to sublet was for September. Nevertheless, Sanjay emphasized the fact that he might not be able to hold the room for Nicolas if someone else became interested.

"I'll take my chances," was Nicola's quick response.

Vivian was, on the one hand, very excited and happy for Nick's good fortune but, on the other hand, she felt a certain sadness creep in as she realized she would miss him something terrible for several weeks. She insisted on spending time with him on Monday and Tuesday, even escorting him to Idlewild International Airport via subway and bus for his early evening flight on Tuesday. She even threw in the idea of spending Monday night with him if she managed to arrange for the use of Juliana's apartment.

"I'll miss you something terrible too," was Nicola's quick response, even though, for some strange reason, he didn't quite have the feeling that he was actually going to miss her that much. *The desire to spend some time with my family back home must be overwhelming, canceling out all other feelings or desires*, he rationalized. But he readily told his girlfriend, with an obvious excitement in his voice, that he would be very happy indeed, to spend time with her on both days, including Monday night.

His aunt offered to store his belongings until his return and suggested that he should visit her in Brooklyn the next day for

Sunday service, with her family, at St. Demetrius. He agreed it was a very good idea and needed no convincing to also accept to stay for Sunday dinner.

He finally finished his calls and left campus around 4:30 to return to his room to freshen up. He made arrangements to meet Stanley for dinner at 6:30 at the campus cafeteria. They also planned to attend Hagop's party later on.

In his room, he found a message from his landlady. Unbelievably, she was actually inviting him to "a special dinner to celebrate your graduation." It was to be served at 6:00 in her dining room.

It's not a bad idea to accept the dinner invitation, especially since it gives me the opportunity to properly say goodbye to her and to thank her for allowing me to share her apartment for over three years. She has been a...

He wanted to add to his thoughts that she had been a generous and considerate landlady but he couldn't do that without greatly exaggerating. She was friendly enough though and definitely liked to talk. She was often interesting to listen to, especially whenever she discussed, or rather argued, her views on world politics, using good English that was flavored with a noticeable Slavic accent.

For all those months as a tenant there, whenever Nicolas crossed the living room on his way to the bathroom before going to bed, he would most often see Mrs. Saltzman watching television, seated on one end of the couch, always wearing the same dark blue, velvet-like robe that concealed her body all the way down to the ankles.

The room was rather dark but the television glow revealed the strikingly handsome face of a mature woman. Whenever she stood up, her silhouette shadow outlined the well proportioned figure of a much younger woman.

During all that time, he only saw the elderly Mr. Saltzman twice or maybe three times. In all cases, he was dressed in his gray flannel pajamas lying on the couch next to her, with his legs and feet covered with a blanket. He must have been asleep because he never said a word or looked up or even responded to his tenant's greetings. When he first met them, Nicolas assumed that Mr. Saltzman was her father instead of her husband.

As soon as the young graduate's thoughts came back to the present, he decided to forgo his earlier plans for the evening and walked down the hallway to accept her dinner invitation. He called out, "Hello, Mrs. Saltzman," before entering the living room which was exceptionally well lit. She was standing by the couch. He couldn't believe his eyes.

She looked like a movie goddess, a Doris Day of the fifties. Her below-the-knee skirt of light beige and her similarly tight, low-cut, silk blouse of pure white, outlined every curve of her full but statuesque figure. As soon as she took a few steps on her stiletto-high heels, her confined body curves seemed ready to break loose at the seams. Her usual long, dark brown hair was now much lighter and quite short and her full, round cheeks and gray-blue eyes appeared highlighted with lots of bright make-up.

Nicolas definitely planned to keep his surprise and personal thoughts about her new look to himself but, for some reason, some of his thoughts came out as an audible whisper when she came close with her arm extended for a handshake. "Great look! Can it be true? All this just for me?" After a congratulatory handshake and an unexpected but warm hug, she thanked him for the compliment and explained,

"I guess you can say that this is all for you. It's part of the celebration…it's part of your graduation present."

The dining area next to the narrow kitchen was tiny but cozy. They sat at the small round table. She lifted her glass of Beaujolais and made the first toast to Nicola's success and happiness. He reciprocated with best wishes for happiness in her life.

They sat there for several minutes sipping wine and talking. As usual, she dominated the conversation but Nicolas did not mind it at all. He was totally fascinated with her life story and pushed for more and more. The wine was having its effect on both of them but she was obviously becoming more and more accommodating. She finally got up to serve dinner. In the meantime he immersed in his thoughts.

What an amazing story...what an incredible life...a refugee from Poland...how could she, a young woman of twenty-four, marry her father's business partner, an old jeweler, a man in his late fifties? I guess she had no choice after losing her soldier husband, after losing her whole family...imagine the coincidence of meeting the old man in Zurich...he must have been lonely and miserable himself after losing his own family... but I have a feeling she was in love with somebody else she met in Zurich. I have to find out about that..."

The dinner reminded Nicolas of the beef stew he sometimes ate at the Caravan Restaurant, except that in this one the beef was replaced by plenty of tasty kielbasa. He had seconds but she hardly touched the food. Instead, she kept staring at her guest while sipping wine, practically going through a second bottle all by herself.

Nicolas had to interrupt her. He was definitely embarrassed and could no longer take the direct, unblinking stare of her icy cool grays. He stood up and asked to be excused.

"Good...after you wash your hands, take a seat in the living room. We'll have dessert there."

She brought out a plate with a generous piece of apple strudel and vanilla ice cream for Nicolas. No mention of coffee or tea. For herself, the dessert was in the form of more wine. She offered some to him, but he chose a glass of water instead. He managed to bring the conversation back to her life story. He knew he had to move fast before she got too tipsy or forgetful to relate details of the story.

"Gary Saltzman was always good to me...a decent man. He managed to take out most of his jewels to Amsterdam just before the Nazis invaded Poland. His plan was to eventually move to

London but he somehow wound up in Zurich. My father, who served in the Polish cavalry as a young man, did not believe in fleeing the country. Both he and my husband of a few months died during the initial German invasion."

Nicolas was becoming extremely fascinated with her story and wanted to hear more. But he could also see the wine's influence on her language articulation. She was losing more and more of her ability to speak clearly.

"I believe you said earlier that both of your parents and your younger brother died during the war and that a Catholic family hid you for a while in their home until, eventually, you got out of Poland. How..."

"My father was Catholic but my mother was Jewish..." She stopped for another sip of wine and once again covered her eyes and most of her face with her hands. Her head and body movements together with an occasional sigh suggested that she fully relived those earlier tragic moments in her life. When she continued her story it was as if she left a whole chapter behind.

"Gary Saltzman brought a lot of comfort into my life in Zurich, something I didn't have for a long time. He did it by trading diamonds and other jewels. He kept telling me that half of what he had was mine. I couldn't accept that, but I did agree that we should both try and make it to Palestine or, preferably, to America, the land of opportunity..." She paused for a few seconds, as if she lost her train of thought.

"When we arrived in New York, several months after the end of the war, we pretended we were married. We did get married three years later when he opened his jewelry store on Amsterdam Avenue. We had a pretty good life together ...unfortunately he suffered during the last few months...he was dying of lung cancer. When he heard "lung cancer" Nicolas was puffing on a Marlboro. He felt very foolish as well as guilty because he had earlier allowed her, a non-smoker, to light up one of his cigarettes. She did not seem to grasp the significance of the moment and continued sipping wine and puffing smoke. She made it clear she did not want to talk about her life anymore.

Slowly but surely, as she gulped more and more wine, much of her conversation deteriorated into the form of disconnected phrases. She labored to keep her body straight up while seated on the couch and was pushing herself closer and closer to her guest. Eventually she leaned in and placed her head face up on his lap. She then quickly pulled his head down, by stretching her arms and locking her hands around his neck, while lifting up her head as high as she could. Their lips met for a few seconds before she let go. Nicola's blood rushed to his head and stayed there for several seconds. He also felt another fast-moving, high-frequency wave rush through the rest of his body. He was absolutely flattered to death that a good looking woman with a fascinating life history that encompassed half of Europe was actually trying to make love to him.

"I'm yours...take me...for your graduation. I want to be your best graduation present..."

"Please Monika, you know I have a girlfriend...you know I'm..."

"I know your girlfriend, I saw her...I saw you making out on the bench many an afternoon...I was careful that you not see me in the park. She cannot satisfy you. I saw the stress in your face, even hours later when you came home..." She got off his lap and the couch and started towards the bedroom door. "I wait for you in the bedroom. I become comfortable...I wait for you Nicola..."

Another major battle between passion and morality. This one lasted for almost ten minutes. Passion was triumphant. He moved towards the bedroom determined to make passionate love. Somehow the sadness he associated with this woman and her obvious surrender to him increased his libido by leaps and bounds. He entered without knocking.

She lay flat on her stomach, fully clothed, her face concealed. Her tight skirt was slightly pulled on one side, exposing a small part of a well-proportioned, milky-white leg. He sat at the edge of the bed, causing her body to slide slightly towards him. He reached and gently caressed her exposed leg. She did not move at all but he was convinced he felt a reaction, a fast-moving pulse in his palm. He was encouraged to make his next move.

He unzipped and gradually pulled her skirt down her legs and feet. Hid did the same to her black, silky slip, exposing a pair of lacey, high-cut briefs of apparently the same fabric and color. He hesitated for a while but eventually gathered enough courage to pull down her panties. Her round bottom was very inviting and his hands began performing a sensuous massage on her soft, pulsating cheeks. He couldn't help comparing this with the smaller, tighter derriere he massaged the night before.

He also unhinged her strap, but did not pull her bra from under her chest. He then had to stop and breathe hard, trying to absorb the total panorama, before he began, once again to touch and caress her whole body. All kinds of uncontrolled body and mind waves propagated through him. She remained motionless.

Should I wait for her to turn over, to make the next move, or should I take control and turn her over myself? Why is she so quiet and motionless?

He made up his mind to turn her over but he thought it would be more appropriate for him to also undress first. He took a glimpse of his naked body in the tall, rectangular mirror leaning against the end wall. Maybe the mirror was slightly distorting. He thought he looked too skinny and bony and somewhat taller than usual but he was happy to accept the apparently enhanced size of his highly agitated sexual organ.

He kneeled on the bed and gently rolled her body towards him, allowing her to assume a face-up position. Her eyes were shut tight. She was in deep sleep. All physical and mental symbols of his passionate state collapsed within seconds. He pulled the bed cover from under her, covered her all the way to the neck, and left the room with his clothes in his arms.

For a while, he lay naked on his cot, highly disappointed at his bad luck. However, as he kept reliving the events of the last twenty-four hours, he came to realize and became absolutely convinced that he was indeed one of the luckiest men in the world. During this time, two women, each a veritable beauty in her own right, offered themselves to him as graduation presents. How many men could even boast of just one such offer?

In reality, by making those offers, the two incredibly attractive women helped saturate his mind with beautiful and passionate scenes that would provide enough ammunition for his personal, physical gratification for a long time to come. He closed his eyes and allowed his imagination to guide his body through one such personal and highly passionate trip.

Nicolas moved out of the apartment early on Sunday morning without seeing Mrs. Saltzman. He planned to be back for a proper goodbye on Monday. He carried all his books and his traveling suitcase to Stanley's room and the rest of his belongings to Brooklyn where he spent Sunday with his aunt's family.

Sunday in Brooklyn was interesting and, in some ways, somewhat strange, even for Nicolas. After church, he and his college-age cousin Dora went downstairs to the church community center for the usual refreshments, consisting of several types of Greek sweets and freshly brewed coffee. Dora took Nicolas to a table occupied by the Pentaris family. After the introductions, he was asked to sit next to the family's only daughter, Maro, who had just completed her freshman year at Hunter College.

Nicolas was definitely very pleased to meet such an attractive and articulate Greek-Cypriot American. His aunt eventually joined them and sat next to Mrs. Pentaris. Almost immediately, the two women began whispering to each other incessantly, while closely eyeing what they loudly referred to, at one point, as the "young, good-looking couple."

He was visibly embarrassed when he became aware of the fact that his meeting with Maro and her family, which included her father and her younger sister, was by design. Specifically, the meeting was arranged by his aunt, already a well known matchmaker in the Cypriot community. However, his aunt said nothing specific to him about the "match" until much later, after dinner.

Sunday dinner with his aunt's family was often a pleasant affair. This time, it seemed a bit overwhelming or too crowded. The seven members of the Mavros family were joined by six members of another family of Greek-Cypriots, the Savvides, who also immigrated from the village of Ora.

Before dinner, they all raised their glasses of wine or soda to congratulate Nicolas on his graduation from a "first-rate American college," referring to the event as "quite an accomplishment," especially since several of those present did not even attend high school. Both families contributed for the graduation present, a small leather suitcase.

Nicolas was seated at the extra table set up for the Savvides. He was placed next to their daughter Tina, a petite high school student that appeared much younger than her proclaimed age of seventeen. Little Tina had a slight problem with acne but she was very cute and quite lively, seemingly absorbed in a world of her own, very much like a typical teenager.

Like so many young immigrants who arrived in America in their early teens, before having had the chance to finish a gymnasium or high school in their country of birth, Tina spoke English with a Cypriot accent and Greek with an American accent. Also characteristic of the immigrant community, her American vocabulary included many Anglicized Greek words that often became a topic of ridicule by the more sophisticated Greek Americans.

Again, judging from the behavior of his aunt with Mrs. Savvides, Nicolas could tell that he and little Tina were the subjects of a matchmaking in progress. Not too long after dessert, the Savvides were preparing to leave. While exiting, Mrs. Savvides turned to address Nicolas, making sure that everybody heard what she had to say to him.

"Nicolas, my dear young man, make sure you visit my parents when you arrive at our village. They will be ready to welcome you with open arms...ready to offer you all the riches of our home... our family...and don't forget our best regards to your mother and all your family."

Nicolas Maos had to wait until the end of the *Ed Sullivan Show* before his aunt took him aside to reveal her plans for him.

"You know, of course, that I am looking out for you, I want the best for you, the best for your future in this great country..."

"Thank you Aunt Eleni, I do appreciate everything you have done for me..."

"You also know that lovely Tina is one of our own, she was born in our village and finished school there before coming to this country. Her mother told me that little Tina will become an American citizen in a few months. The Savvides are a well-to-do family, they already own a restaurant and a barber shop in this country...they will take good care of you and even care for your mother and sister in the village. God knows your mother and sister need help."

"Aunt Eleni, first I want you to tell the Savvides that I very much appreciate their invitation to join their family. Tina is of good stock and, of course, quite lovely...I am really flattered, I am truly honored...but I am not ready yet...I want to wait for..."

"I understand, you probably want to discuss this with your mother...but if you prefer a more mature, a more sophisticated maiden who was born and raised here in America under her family's strict supervision, think of Maro Pentaris. She is not from our village but she is a beautiful girl and her family is very rich and wonderful. They want you as their son-in-law, the son they never had. You met Maro at church this morning...don't you agree she is beautiful and well educated?"

"Of course I agree. She is probably too good for me. But I have to insist that I'm not ready for marriage yet…I do not know how I will feel about all this in a couple of years."

"Fine, I will explain to both families that you need some more time to think about it…to discuss it with your mother."

Nicolas chose not to continue the conversation so he nodded and let his aunt have the last word. He said his goodbyes and started back for the city. He arranged to sleep at Hagop's apartment for the next couple of nights before his trip back home.

On Monday around lunch time, Nicolas rang the bell at his former residence. Mrs. Saltzman opened the door halfway and stood in the opening, wearing her usual dark blue robe. Her short hair was neatly combed, very much like Saturday night, but her face was free of make-up. He originally planned to greet her with an intimate "dear Monika."

However, her stern look and seemingly unfriendly facial expression changed his mind very quickly.

"Good morning, Mrs. Saltzman. I'm sorry to bother you at this time. I had to move out in a hurry yesterday because of my plans to attend church services and visit my aunt in Brooklyn. You seemed asleep at the time so I did not disturb you. I hope you found the key to the apartment. I left it on the desk…anyway, good bye and many thanks for everything."

She managed a half smile and a loose handshake. She also managed to whisper, "Goodbye and good luck," before she closed the door.

A few minutes later he called Vivian at her home in Hicksville. She rather abruptly informed him about "a very difficult situation at home" and about her apparent inability to meet with him, as promised, before his flight the next day. To his great surprise and disappointment, she could not or would not explain further, but promised to do so upon his return from his trip to Cyprus.

Chapter Seven

Nicolas' original itinerary for the Cyprus homecoming trip showed July 21st as the return date back to New York. He missed the date by a month and five days when he arrived at Idlewild International Airport in late August.

He had enjoyed the extra time back home with his family and friends but he was seriously concerned about the effect this delay could have on some of his New York friends, especially his girlfriend Vivian and his boss Rusty. Unfortunately, because of one excuse or another, he had not communicated with them about his itinerary changes.

He called Vivian at her Hicksville residence the very first evening he arrived at his temporary residence at the midtown YMCA.

"It's so great to hear your voice again, Nick. I'm so happy you are back."

Nick was also happy to hear her say that she missed him but, at the same time, he suspected that something was not quite the same as usual, something was missing. The ever present warmth of her voice was not quite there. She sounded too serious and uncharacteristically reserved.

His suspicions of a change in the air were confirmed as soon as she turned down his invitation to meet with him in the city at any time during the next three or four days or even during the upcoming weekend.

"I'm terribly sorry Nick…the truth is that I do want to see you…I want to talk to you…unfortunately I can't right now. I hope we do get together some other time soon…I can explain everything then."

"I'm moving into Sanjay's apartment tomorrow. I will call you from my own telephone as soon as I can…perhaps we can get together the following weekend…how about dinner and perhaps even a French film at the Thalia? You have a few days to think about it…"

"Nick, I can't wait to see you…I will talk to you soon."

By ten-thirty the next day Nicolas had completed the move to the new apartment. Sanjay showed Nicolas the facilities and explained the rules regarding the sub-letting.

"Nick, I want to stress the point once again that, for all practical purposes, I am your landlord. The two remaining days in August are free but, starting September 1st and on the first day of each month, you must pay the sum of $165 to me personally. I will add my portion, the same amount, and then take the total to the landlord. As I explained to you last May, the lease is in my name and I prefer that the landlord knows nothing about this sub-lease."

"Thanks a lot for everything Sanjay, especially your willingness to take a chance with me, to have me as a roommate. I also appreciate the fact that you kept the room for me until I returned from Cyprus even though you had several other offers in-between."

"Nick, also please remember that I did not ask for any security deposit, typically a month's rent, which I had to pay to the landlord when I moved in, but you are still responsible for any damage to the furniture or the fixtures."

"No problem at all, my friend. If I break it, I'll pay for it. By the way, I have to run. I plan to see my part-time employer before noon, before he goes out to lunch. Then I have to visit the Geology Department...I plan to see my program advisor and perhaps even pick up my first teaching assistantship check."

"I imagine you also need to register for the semester."

"True, I still have to make up my course schedule...but I guess there's plenty of time till classes start in about two weeks. See you later."

⁐

Nick arrived at the building that housed the Weisman Ski Glove Company a little later than he expected. It was almost ten minutes past noon.

It's unlikely I'll find Rusty in the office...he always leaves for lunch at twelve unless something out of the ordinary happened.

Something unusual did indeed happen, because not only was Rusty still in his office, but he also appeared to be emptying his desk and packing its contents. Some personal office furnishings, especially his collection of original sketches and paintings of the New York City skyline, were piled up on the floor.

Rusty dropped everything and literally jumped over to greet his part-time employee, exhibiting his trademark wide smile while offering his hand for his usual handshake.

"Nick, this is indeed a pleasant surprise. I'm happy to see you...for a while I wasn't sure you were coming back."

"I'm very happy to see you too, Rusty. Also, I must apologize for not communicating with you earlier...it was inconsiderate of me, to say the least...I really can't offer a good excuse. All I can say is that I was so overwhelmed with the joy of visiting with my mother and my family, thanks to your generosity, that I totally neglected some of my responsibilities...I'm truly sorry..."

"Nick, don't be sorry…things happened unexpectedly and I really didn't need you as much as I thought I would in prep for the fall shipment rush. I'm sure you never expected to hear this, but I sold my business…I got an offer I couldn't resist."

"You're right, I never expected to hear this and I still can't believe it. You yourself told me a few times how you got good offers in the past and how you would never sell something you enjoy doing…there must be more than just what you're telling me…"

"O.K., well, I'm also doing this for my health. I already found a nice place in southern California, a co-op in the San Diego area. The climate there is what I need…I'll miss New York, especially the Broadway theaters and the restaurants, but life must go on. I can't go into details now, but I do promise that I shall keep in touch…even if you change the address and phone you just gave me. I know how to reach you through our Alma Mater."

"When do you actually leave and what about your friend Janet, if I may ask?"

"Janet is coming with me to San Diego, for a while anyway. We are leaving in about ten days. We are actually driving together all the way to San Diego. We both decided we want to take our time and see some of this great country. Personally, I spent all my life in the Northeast and traveled extensively to California and other western states, but I think it's time to see middle America as well, the great Midwest, and the Rockies."

They said their goodbyes, they shook hands a few times and Nicolas forced a couple of hugs on his former boss and close friend. As soon as he exited the office, Nicolas released a few tears. His heart was heavy with sadness, not only because Rusty was going away, but also because he suspected that, in all probability, his fifty-eight year old boss had serious health problems he didn't care to reveal.

There goes the best American friend I have…my security blanket… it's a funny feeling…it's as if part of me, part of my body is leaving me.

Nicolas was so devastated with the idea of losing Rusty that he changed his plans about seeing his program advisor that afternoon.

I can always do it tomorrow or the day after...there's plenty of time... right now I can use a break...I can't think of a better one than a double feature on 42nd Street theater row.

⇀

Nicolas entered his advisor's office feeling very upbeat and confident that he would do a good job as a Graduate Teaching Assistant, no matter what the assignment. He had not met Professor Bower before. This initial advisor, the chairman of the Department, was assigned on a temporary basis, or until he selected a Ph.D. thesis topic under the direction of one of the faculty and, therefore, his own permanent advisor.

"Mr. Maos, in your application for a teaching assistantship you state that you prefer teaching intermediate or upper level undergraduate laboratories. Are you sure you can do the job of a laboratory instructor?"

"Yes, sir, I am quite confident I can do a good job."

"I'm afraid I'm unable to grant your stated preference for teaching intermediate or upper level laboratories...I'm afraid I can't even assign you to teach introductory level laboratories for that matter. It's a matter of general policy here not to assign teaching positions to foreign students who may have a language barrier. I'm afraid I have already assigned curatorial work for you."

"Professor Bower, perhaps if you stopped being 'afraid' and checked out or tested my ability to make clear presentations in English, you wouldn't have been quite as concerned about 'language barriers.' Once before, a few years back, somebody used the same phrase to turn me down for a job application."

"I assure you, it's a legitimate concern for some jobs."

"Perhaps it is in some cases. But it seems to me that some

people in this country confuse accent, which we all have to one extent or another, with knowledge of the language or the ability to communicate clearly...unless, of course, it's not really a case of confusion but one of xenophobia."

"I'm afraid this has always been my general policy with regards to foreign students, even though I must agree that some, like yourself, appear to do much better than others. Please see the departmental secretary who will provide details concerning the type of curatorial work assigned and the weekly time schedule recommended...you still have eleven days before classes begin. Remember, there are one hundred and forty graduate students in this department...I'm afraid there is plenty of competition for these assignments."

Nicolas was visibly upset—his face felt like it was on fire—but he knew he had to control himself. He couldn't afford to jeopardize the assistantship. He had already received the first monthly check for September and had spent a good portion on the apartment rent. "Thank you sir, I accept my assignment and I intend to do my best...I intend to do a good job." He shook hands and left the office with a plan in his mind.

I'm afraid, if I may use my advisor's favorite expression, I'm afraid I will have to speed up the process of presenting a thesis proposal... whether I plan to finish it or not. I need a new program advisor as soon as possible.

"Stanley...Stanley...I can't believe I met you here by accident after trying to locate your whereabouts ever since I returned from Cyprus...it's been almost two weeks!"

"Oh, well, you know that Choc-Full-O'-Nuts is on top of the list of favorite places for both of us...we were bound to meet here eventually."

"So, what's new? What happened to you anyway? Were you

out of town? Alexander thought that you went back home to Chios for a while. For a moment I thought you might have decided to skip the fall semester.

Stanley kept staring mostly in his coffee mug. " No, I did not visit Chios. All I did was to accompany my aunt to Toronto…to visit a cousin of hers. Then we decided to also spend a few days in Montreal." He lifted up his head. There were sparkles in his eyes when he added, "What a town! It's like being in Paris."

"They say that Paris is great when you are there with a special someone…when you're in love…of course there was nothing like that for me in Cyprus…"

"You practically spent all the summer in Cyprus, right? How is your family, your mother? Did you see all your friends?"

"When I got off the plane and walked by the fenced waiting area, I could recognize the faces of quite a few of the people there… it took me a few seconds to realize that most of those visitors were there to welcome me back home. My mother and my sisters and their families were all there, plus some of my aunts and uncles and at least half a dozen of my cousins."

"Of course you never got to see your first love Stella, I imagine…you knew already that she left for England a few years back…unless she returned."

"I was told that she did return to Cyprus, but I did not get to see her because she no longer lives in the village. I spent lots of time with my family and, of course, with my mother. She and I had several unforgettable 'mother-and-son moments.' Close to three months went by incredibly fast."

"What about Yiannis and the other friends you so looked forward to see once again?"

"Several of my friends had already left the island for further studies and other reasons. Lakis has been in London for a while, studying nutrition and physical therapy. Andros, who worked as a flight steward for Cyprus Airways, had already left for California just one day before I arrived."

"Is he planning to attend college in the States?

"He actually went there to marry his girl, an airline stewardess, whose family home is in Sausalito, a suburb of San Francisco"

"What about Yiannis?"

"I did get to see Yiannis, but I was very sad to see what he let himself get into." Nicholas paused to light a cigarette and take a sip of coffee. At that same moment, Stanley stood up.

"I'm sorry Nick, I have to go, I didn't realize I'm already late for a four o'clock meeting. But I do want to hear more about your friend Yiannis." He was practically out of the restaurant when he turned back to add, "I also want to here more about Stella too."

Nicolas left the coffee shop with lots of troubling thoughts in his mind. *I wonder what Stanley is up to. Four o'clock on a Friday afternoon, the time he usually picks up his aunt at the train station. Can it be she is back already for a visit after an apparently very cozy trip alone with him that ended only yesterday? It looks like things are really getting hot and complicated for my friend.*

When Nicolas returned to his apartment, he went straight to the mini refrigerator to retrieve his dinner, a large container of Greek salad purchased earlier that Friday afternoon from a Broadway delicatessen. His roommate entered almost simultaneously.

"I'm about ready to start cooking for my date. I'm making that curry chicken that I had you taste the other day. By the way, I brought some nice hard rolls for the dinner. Here, try one."

"Thanks a lot, Sanjay, this roll should go well with my salad. It's so great to have kitchen privileges, a kitchen of your own in a way. But I guess you've had such privileges for quite a while and probably take them for granted. Who is the lucky girl tonight, is it that tall, lean black girl I saw you with last Friday? She is almost as tall as you are. What a beauty! I bet she is from eastern Africa, Somalia perhaps?"

"Your guess is pretty good. She is actually from eastern Africa, specifically from the Eritrea region of Ethiopia. This is her second year at NYU's graduate program in psychology. She is here on a Fulbright Scholarship."

"Very impressive."

"But what about you? You don't have a date this weekend?"

"I'm glad you ask. My girlfriend Vivian may be visiting me here in the apartment tomorrow. I just want you to know that we may need to use the kitchen. She often promised that she would cook something special for me as soon as one of us had kitchen privileges."

"That's quite alright. Kerenia and I will be attending a party at a friend's house in Queens this Saturday. I'm sure we shall stay out till very late."

Nicolas went through the salad very quickly. After a quick clean-up, he sat on the bed which also served as the couch, placed the two pillows on top of each other against the wall and leaned on them for a moment of relaxation. His TV set, a 19-inch black and white portable that belonged to his former boss Rusty, was staring at him with a myriad of reflected light rays. The set, a parting gift from Rusty, was delivered to his apartment two days earlier.

I guess this television set will always remind me of Rusty...it will always raise my spirits thinking about my good friend and mentor... perhaps an interesting program or two would entertain me this evening... keep my mind occupied on things other than the question of whether Vivian will call me or not.

One TV show after another, but no telephone interruption, no call from Vivian.

He was so much looking forward to seeing Vivian after a long period, a whole summer. However, he could clearly see a shadow cast over his sunny anticipation. *This is definitely not the Vivian I have known for over two years...she always exhibited considerable excitement at the idea of meeting with me...never turned down a date with me...*

Vivian kept his mind well activated long after midnight. As a result, his body refused to enter into a relaxing sleep. He tried to move his thoughts elsewhere. Soon he was back in Cyprus, reliving moments from his recent homecoming trip.

After a separation of seven years, Nicolas was thrilled to be surrounded by family and friends in his sister's home in Larnaca. His mother was beaming with joy, apparently totally happy. But his own happiness was not complete. None of his three closest friends was there. Andros had already left for California the day before, and Lakis for England a few months earlier. Yiannis was definitely expected to be there. His absence was a mystery since none of those present knew why.

The "welcome home" party for Nicolas lasted close to two days. As soon as he got a chance, he walked over to Yiannis' home to personally inquire about his friend.

"My son has been visiting with his grandparents in the village of Pervolia for the last few weeks. I can send word to him right away."

"Please don't do that Mrs. Gregoriou. I'll wait for a few more days…I don't plan to leave town anyway…if he does not return to Larnaca soon, I shall pay him a surprise visit at Pervolia."

A few days later, Nicolas surprised Yiannis at his grandparent's village.

"My God, Yianni, it's so great to see you." Hugs and kisses followed. "My friend, I have to say that I am deeply concerned about the apparent condition I find you in…you look like an unkempt hermit suffering from malnutrition…when was the last time you shaved?"

"It's nice to see you too, college educated big shot! At this stage in my life I do not keep up appearances, but I do expect things to change…not because of my new vocation of placing bets on the British football pools, but simply because our friend Andros now lives in California with his American wife. I hope to get a visa for the States, any kind of visa, through his support."

"Well, we both know that if anybody can do it for you, it's Andros…but tell me, I'm still waiting to find out what brought you to this laissez-faire attitude about life. Last time you corresponded with me, I believe it was last April just before Easter, you were enjoying life as a happy go-lucky A.U.B. junior in Beirut. Why did the American University of Beirut throw you out before the end of the semester?"

"A.U.B. never threw me out. I left Beirut of my own accord...well, o.k., there was pressure involved...but not from the university...it was from a bunch of hoodlooms." Yiannis stopped right there and tried to change the subject. But Nicolas was relentless...he had to find out what had caused such big changes in his friend's life...in his friend's attitude about life. He did suspect that a woman had to be involved at some point in the story. He revealed his suspicions and pressed on for more explanation.

"You college geniuses think that you know it all...well, this time it was a good guess...there was a girl. Nico, you should have seen that woman...no description can do justice to her beauty... truly beyond description. I saw her in a nightclub, a fancy night spot on Busch Square. She was there with a bunch of other good-looking women. I approached her with a couple of my usual jokes and she actually went for me."

"Did you communicate with her in English? Is her heritage Arabic or European? How many more times did you see her?"

"It was instantaneous mutual attraction, a pure animal attraction, you know...she is the type you do not fall in love with, you just fall into bed with. We saw each other two and sometimes three times a week, but she refused to go out, even to a local restaurant. We only met in my room. I practically shut out my roommate...poor Costakis..."

"What about her heritage, her language skills, did she speak English? What about her age...and was she single or married?"

"My God, you should hear yourself! You sound like a stupid policeman. Yes, she spoke perfect English and her heritage is not Arabic. In fact, I was fascinated with the idea when she first told me that she descended from the sea-faring ancient Phoenicians. She is, in fact, a Maronite. As you know, there is a Maronite community in Cyprus."

"Yes, I do know about the Maronite minority in Cyprus…when it comes to inter-communal problems or divisions, they always side with us Greeks against the Turks, much like the Armenian community does. But what about your Maronite woman's age? As far as her marital status is concerned, I have my suspicions."

"Her age was never a problem. Just a few years older than me. Unfortunately, she did not reveal her marital status until weeks after we met. She was and is indeed married—married to a much older, but very well-to-do man."

"Now I know why Lakis wrote, just before he left Beirut for England, that you came to own, sort of suddenly, beautiful clothes and shoes and other luxuries such as a gold watch and a gold cigarette case."

"It's true. She was as generous with expensive gifts as she was with her love for me. But, with the exception of some clothing, they made me leave all the gifts behind."

"I think I know the rest of the story. Her old man hired a couple of hoodlums to threaten you, probably with your life, unless you left Beirut immediately. That much is obvious to me. What surprises me is that you actually left immediately without putting on a fight. Why?"

"Because I believed they would have carried out their threats."

"If I may change the subject, do you have any new information about the situation in my village with the Sodiris insurgent group, particularly whether the group is still blacklisting me as a traitor?"

"The timing is very interesting. Only yesterday I heard from my EOKA contacts that Sodiris was about to be arrested by the state police…something about one of his men being willing to testify against him for ordering or personally carrying out several murders…"

"You can't imagine the relief…this means I can go back to the village with my mother and sister…"

"You better wait until the arrest takes place...Sodiris will not hesitate to harm you. I believe that this whole thing, his hate for you, has to do with Stella, the fact that you and Stella were childhood lovers..."

"You can hardly call us 'lovers'...just because of one innocent kiss. He probably hated Savvakis much more because she fell in love with him, married him and had a child with him. I never said this before to anyone, but I always thought that Sodiris was most probably the one who betrayed Savvakis to the British. He is accusing me because I was conveniently present in the village at the time and also happened to have visited Stella and her husband at her house, their occasional secret hideout."

"Others have also thought of that particular scenario...let's wait and see..."

The ringing of the phone brought Nicolas's thoughts back to his room. He checked the time. It was one twenty. *Vivian, finally...better late than never.* It wasn't meant to be. It was the wrong number. Once again, he was fully awake and once again his thoughts traveled back to Cyprus.

He could see himself entering the village of Ora, with his senses acknowledging mostly pride and self-fulfillment. His mother was on his side as he walked through the village center, a relatively wide street lined with coffee shops and grocery stores and other part-time service shops. The village school capped one end of the two-block street while the magnificent limestone church edifice, with its lean and tall bell tower, enclosed the other end.

Just about everybody on the street or in coffee shops and stores literally ran over to shake hands with Nicolas, and some even with his mother. Their greeting carried one consistent message: Their pride in a village son, Sunday's son, who managed to go to America and study in one of the best universities that the country had to offer.

The villagers also declared the young college graduate as a kind of a long- suffering regional hero who was wrongly accused and persecuted for years by an evil man. Sodiris had been arrested. According to the press, more than one of his men were expected to testify against him.

Nicolas spent most of his days in the village with his mother and his sister Nina. His other sisters and their families came to the village a couple of times, including St. Marina's day on the 17th of July.

The Savvides family, especially the grandparents of little Tina who was offered in marriage to Nicolas back at his aunt's in Brooklyn, went way out of their way to please "their prospective grandson-in-law." Nicolas politely protested and tried to explain his position of non-commitment but, alas, they wouldn't listen to him.

There was one note of sadness throughout his stay in the village. He could not see Stella. He was told that she did return to her parents' home in Ora soon after she changed her mind about marrying the elderly man who invited her and her daughter to England.

"Nina, I'm quite mad at you because you promised. You promised to write and keep me abreast of everything major that concerned Stella's life. How can you not inform me that Stella and her daughter left the village? Are they now living with her husband's parents?"

"I'm sorry brother. My friend Stella also made me promise that I would never write to you about her leaving of our village. She said she didn't want to worry you with small details about her life...she was planning..."

At this point, Nicolas's mind left Cyprus without completing the thought. His body was finally winning the battle for some sleep.

The next day around mid-morning, Vivian called. It was a very fast call and her voice lacked the usual animated excitement.

"I will be over at your place at four. I can't stay too long...I'll bring some Danish...perhaps we can have a pleasant tea hour together, like old times."

After that, time moved like a turtle, far too slow for Nicolas. Sure he was looking forward to the reunion, but not with the customary passionate anticipation. In a sad way, he was also impatient to find out the reason for her apparent coolness towards him.

The only pleasant, fast-moving part of the day was his late morning visit to the Canal Diner. It was always a pleasure to talk to his friend Luke and, after a long absence, the bacon and eggs with home fries tasted exceptionally good.

At three-thirty in the afternoon, already back in his apartment for a couple of hours, he approached his sash window which faced the U-shaped front of the building and stood in front of it. He pulled up the shade high enough to allow himself full view of the wide corridor leading to the building entrance. From his vantage point on the seventh floor, he would be able to see Vivian the moment she arrived.

At 4:20 he became restless. She was never that late before for any of their dates. He began pacing the space parallel to the window. By 4:45 he was convinced that his girlfriend would not show up.

He was about to give up his window watch when he saw people approaching from across the street. As soon as they stepped on the concrete corridor, he let out a sigh of relief and a loud whisper, "It's Vivian, finally...with her friend Juliana...and the two Sikhs. I wonder why she brought them along."

When he opened the door, Vivian stood there alone. He expected to see her in her trademark skirt and blouse. Instead, she was in blue jeans and white sneakers plus a tight V-neck sweater. Her hair had a new look. Much longer and definitely much lighter. She did not carry anything that resembled a bakery box with Danish. She did carry a rather serious expression on her face.

"Welcome to my apartment, Vivian, it's so great to see you again..."

She interrupted by literally leaping onto him, like a tiger, planting kisses all over his face and neck while mumbling the same phrases over and over, "I can't help it, Nick. I can't control myself when I see you...I missed you so..." Nicolas remained practically motionless until her greeting was over. Then he reciprocated with a steady shower of hugs and kisses.

After a quick tour of the apartment, the young couple sat on the bed close to each other, their bodies gently touching. Seconds later, Vivian explained, "I'm very sorry, Nick...I do apologize for being late...I was running back and forth all day...I'm sure you noticed..."

"Never mind Vivian, no further explanations necessary. Let's go to the Caravan and grab an early dinner. We can talk about our lives, our relationship, later on, after dinner. It's Saturday, we have plenty of time...and you can always stay over if you like...it should be lots of fun if you do."

"I fully agree with you, it should be tons of fun, it should be very exciting to spend the night here with you...the idea makes my hair stand up...look, look at my arm."

"Alright, then, let's get the show on the road. I'm starved."

"I'm afraid we only have time for one thing. We can go out to eat and talk during dinner or we can stay here and talk. I promised Julie and the others to meet them at 6:30." She paused to check her watch. "We only have an hour and fifteen minutes..."

"I guess I can forgo food for a couple of hours. I prefer that we talk in a private setting. I have a feeling I will be the recipient of bad news. Perhaps you can simply tell me, if you like, why you are apparently ending our relationship."

"I've been under great pressure both from my family and my friends. I made the decision after undergoing a lot of personal pain and agony throughout the whole summer...perhaps my decision would have been different if only you were here, if only we had been able to communicate at times..."

"Your decision and your choice...they are now obvious to me and, once again, I apologize for not getting in touch with you all summer...but tell me, please, why the pressure from you family and friends to do this, and what kind of pressure are they exerting?"

"My parents separated last May, just a couple of days before your graduation. My stepfather simply left my mother. Now, a few months later, they have decided to divorce. My mother has been in a state of depression since May. She now has to go back to work and I have to help take care of my little brother—he is only eight."

"I am terribly sorry to hear that about your parents. I guess you are not coming back to college this semester."

"I received a leave of absence for the semester but I'm pretty sure it will be extended for another one or two semesters."

"I know that college will be a financial burden to your mother... tuition, dormitory living and so much more...in spite of your partial tuition scholarship."

"It's not just the financial problem, which is considerable. It's just that my mother needs me and I want to be there for her...she has been there for me all my life." At this point, her self-control collapsed, with running tears exposing her emotions.

Nicolas took advantage of the moment to put his arms around her and pull her closer towards him. She placed her head on his left shoulder. They kept that position for several silent minutes. With the exception of his left hand moving slowly through her hair, they also remained motionless. He was the first to interrupt the interlude.

"I am so sorry Vivian, I hate to push you further on this, but it seems to me that your parents' divorce and your impending absence from campus are not the main reasons for ending our relationship...please explain the role of Julie and your Sikh friends in your decision..."

"Julie and Jaspal got married in a civil ceremony in the city last July. Harbinder and I were the official witnesses. All four of us did a lot of socializing together throughout the summer. In mid-August, during a foursome dinner party given by Julie and Jaspal, Harbinder asked me to marry him. My immediate response was that I needed some time to think about it..."

"Let me guess. You finally decided to marry the Sikh...under lots of pressure, of course, from your dear friend Juliana who always pushed you towards such a relationship...and I dare say, probably in order to gain favor in the eyes of her husband and his best friend."

"You are probably right about Julie, but it's my turn to dare say that you've been wrong about Harbinder. You referred to him a couple of times as "a big gorilla," but he is actually as gentle as a koala bear...and very considerate and loving too."

"Well, congratulations are in order. But I'm still curious as to how these two graduate students plan to support their spouses."

"They started a business partnership, imports-exports between the States and India, about two years ago. They are now doing very well and they both plan to continue their graduate studies. I must say that they have been very, very generous to Julie and myself."

"There isn't much else to say, except perhaps our goodbyes." He moved further away from her.

"My friends agreed that I should have this time with you to personally explain things and say goodbye to you. Actually, Julie expressed her doubts to me privately. She wasn't sure she could trust me stay alone with you for more than an hour under any circumstances...I see we still have close to thirty minutes, but I guess it's best if I leave right now..."

"I wish you stay a little longer...I must find the words to thank you for your love and friendship these last couple of years... you have been a true and devoted friend...and lover...a real sweetheart...and I've always loved you."

That's all she needed to hear. She moved closer to him, sobbing. He reciprocated with a continuous hug and plenty of tears. Within seconds, their lips were locked together and their hands were busy removing clothing, allowing their half-naked bodies to become intimately connected.

She hesitated to leave when her time was up and he encouraged her to stay a little longer, perhaps another hour. She agreed and they both took advantage of each other's inexhaustible passion. They made love again and again.

Nicolas began his first semester in Graduate Faculties determined to concentrate and do well in all his courses and, in fact, to excel. He knew, first hand, that graduate work would be much more demanding on his time since, as an undergraduate, he did take a couple of graduate courses. However, this time he had a slight advantage: Vivian was gone, taking with her many of the tempting demands on his concentration.

It took quite a while for him to get used to campus life without Vivian. Even after he found out that she got married, he couldn't convince himself that she would never again be part of his life. No matter how hard he tried to concentrate totally on his studies, he could not completely escape memories of her love, her companionship. He decided not to let himself enter into any new, serious, romantic relationship, until at least most of his graduate studies were completed.

As predicted, the semester's work demanded maximum effort on his part. His schedule included two lecture/laboratory courses and one seminar-type course that required individual classroom presentations of library researched topics. At the end of the semester he earned top grades, much higher than the minimum grade of B required for matriculation in graduate school.

The three-week break between semesters was highly anticipated. He already made plans to celebrate his academic achievement by visiting the Times Square area a few times, each time treating himself to a "flame steak" at Tad's and a double feature at the movies. However, certain sobering and unwelcome events, all occurring within that short period of three weeks, would limit the planned celebrations considerably. An ancient Greek saying came to mind: *Many extraordinary things can happen within an hour even though nothing of the sort may happen within a whole year.*

One of the events that introduced sad notes to the otherwise gay music of the semester break, was the bidding of farewell to his friend Stanley who was going home after his January graduation.

"I just can't believe it…you and I will probably never see each other again. I can't imagine how dull and boring campus life will be without you…I hope that you do plan to visit the States once in a while. After all, you do have family here, you do have your dear aunt."

"Nick, it's guaranteed, we shall see each other again…you are right, I did promise my aunt that I would visit a couple of times a year, even though she prefers that we meet in Europe, preferably in Paris. By the way, my father thinks that I have a good chance of getting a job with his shipping company, probably to be stationed in Marseilles."

"Good for you, Stanley, and for your dear aunt. That romantic Paris rendezvous looks more like a reality now."

"I do detect a bit of sarcasm in your words, Nick, but I'm going to ignore it because I can also detect a note of sadness in your face and your expression. I imagine it can't be because of Vivian, you guys separated way back in September…it must be something else. What is it then? Is everything o.k. back home?"

"I didn't realize it was that obvious…it's a couple of things. First of all, back home, everything is o.k. with my family, thank God."

"I'm glad to hear it…what is it then that bothers you?"

"It's actually political problems back home in Cyprus…"

"What else is new?"

"Well, this time it's a lot worse than usual. About a month ago, on December 21st, an incident in Nicosia, involving an exchange of fire between the Greeks and the Turks, caused tremendous suffering to many people and diminished the possibility of a peace settlement between the two communities."

"Incidents involving an exchange of fire between Greeks and Turks happened many times before. Why was this one different?"

"For some reason this incident led to major fighting between Greek and Turkish irregulars and many, on both sides, lost their lives. As a result, the number of ugly atrocities committed by both communities increased substantially throughout the rest of the month of December."

"My God, this is the first time I hear about this escalation of community fighting in the young republic. Did the American press cover the event at all?"

"*The New York Times* did provide some factual coverage of the events. However, the paper's explanation of what caused the incident was minimal and too general."

"Did you ever find out what was the real cause?"

"In a nutshell, this is the cause as I understand it by reading Greek-American papers: President Makarios was seeking a way out of the impossible situation created by the Zurich and London Agreements. As you know, these agreements imposed an unworkable constitution to the republic's Greek majority by giving veto rights to the 18 percent Turkish minority."

"I remember reading about the London agreement which was signed by Britain, Greece and Turkey and eventually by the leaders of the two communities in Cyprus. I also recall reading last summer, while I was in Greece, that the constitution was found to be unworkable after the government tried to rule under it for about four years."

"That's exactly the point. Last fall President Makarios introduced a four-point plan for the solution of the problem by suggesting revisions in the constitution. The rejection of the Makarios plan by the Turks is believed to have caused the rising of tension and the eventual exchange of fire between members of the two communities."

"I think your explanation is probably right because it makes sense. But tell me, what other events brought sadness to your life recently? You referred to 'a couple of things' earlier in our conversation."

"My friend Luke, in fact his whole family, is moving to California in March.

In a personal way, this brought more sadness to my life than the recent community fighting in Cyprus."

"I think I know what this means...you are going to lose your weekend employment and the Saturday breakfast at the diner... but, on the other hand, what about your teaching assistantship? Doesn't that make you independent of such concerns?"

"Yes, the assistantship does provide for all my needs and . . . "He finished his thought in silence: *I even manage to send some money to my mother and sister in the village.*

"So, why all the fuss?"

"Because Luke and his diner have been more than just a refuge for my comfort and convenience, they have been my home away from home."

"Did he say where specifically in California and, even more importantly, did he say why?"

"It seems that a family friend informed Luke of a good business opportunity, a profitable family restaurant in San Diego. This restaurant appears to be busy not only for breakfast and lunch, as in the case of the Canal Diner, but also for dinner. In addition, Luke is excited about living in an area with a Mediterranean-type climate."

"Hey, Nick, did you notice the coincidence? I hope you are not superstitious but it is obvious to me that the city of San Diego conspired to steal two dear friends of yours in the last few months." Nick nodded positively and added only in his mind: *Of course I noticed the coincidence and if I am a bit superstitious, I have a good excuse...I lost two guardian angels to that town in a short period of time.*

The car service for the airport arrived. Stanley and Nicolas hugged and kissed and made their final promises to write to each other and even see each other again. As the car sped away from the pavement on Amsterdam Avenue, Nicolas whispered to himself, "There goes a good friend out of my life."

Six days before the start of the spring semester, Nicolas visited his department in Schermerhorn Hall. The administrative assistant handed him a letter from the chairman. It informed him that his thesis proposal was approved and that his thesis director, Professor Garnet, was hence forward his program advisor as well.

Dr. Garnet's secretary, made an appointment for him to see his advisor later in the afternoon. He was somewhat apprehensive about a one-to-one meeting with this world renowned mineralogist/geochemist who did pioneering work on metallic mineral deposits as well as on the mineralogy of clay minerals. Nicolas was interested in using acquired clay mineralogy techniques in his study of archaeology, specifically geo-archaeology, his main area of concentration.

Nicolas had met Professor Garnet briefly during a departmental seminar the previous fall. The professor, a portly man with a full head of white hair, appeared somewhat intimidating in his formal apparel of a dark blue suit, white shirt and black tie. However, Nicolas was encouraged to approach him since many of his students described him as "a very friendly professor." His advisees often referred to him as "poppy."

Prof. Garnet did show interest in Nicolas' idea of using clay mineralogy in the study of the compositional nature of archaeological tools and artifacts made of clay, such as pottery shards, and encouraged him to submit a more detailed thesis outline.

"I can see why you are interested in clay mineralogy and geo-archaeology, young man. I guess I better call you Nick, o.k.? Your birthplace, Cyprus, has a long and colorful history and it's rich in archaeological finds...your thesis proposal is quite impressive. I shall be happy to work with you."

"Thank you sir."

"You have been assigned space, including a desk plus cabinet and shelf space, in the clay research lab, room 229 downstairs. You can pick up the key to the lab at the department office. You will also be issued a pass to access Schermerhorn Hall in the evening or on weekends when the building is essentially closed."

"Thank you, sir, I am honored and indeed privileged to work under your direction."

"We shall put together a thesis committee this spring and hopefully you can begin your thesis lab work this summer. The first order of business is to have you write up a grant proposal. We need to get some support, some grant money for your research project."

Grant money, indeed. The professor's reputation for securing grant money for his students' research projects is legendary. He has a couple of dozen Ph.D. students, all fully funded from several federal and other agencies.

"What about my course program and my Teaching Assistantship, Dr. Garnet?"

"The course schedule you submitted is good but remember that you need plenty of chemistry for your research project. I would add an analytical chemistry course, perhaps next fall."

"I think I can add an evening course this semester."

"Probably not this semester because you also have to consider another six credit equivalents for your Teaching Assistantship. I am assigning you the laboratory teaching of a three hundred level course, Optical Mineralogy, and that of an introductory course, Historical Geology. The administrative assistant should provide you with the schedule details and the forms you need to sign."

"Oh, Dr. Garnet, you can't imagine how good this makes me feel. You actually have confidence in me that I can do the job... apparently you are not concerned with the 'language barrier problem' of Dr. Bower."

"Didn't Bower inform you about his change of mind on that 'barrier idea' of his? Well, here it is. During that seven-week substitution you did last fall for the laboratory in mineralogy, you must have impressed the students considerably. They wrote to the chairman, as a group of sixteen, declaring you as the top T.A. of the semester. They also petitioned that you be appointed their T.A. for the spring course in Optical Mineralogy."

Nicolas' body was moved as if earthquake waves were propagated through it. He chose to remain silent for a while in order not to betray his deep emotions through a trembling voice. After he partially revived, he shook hands and said,

"Sir, I am grateful for your confidence in me. I very much look forward to working with you and I shall try not to disappoint you."

He exited his advisor's office. In the corridor, he ran into Len Davis, his former teaching assistant.

"Len, you won't believe this, but Dr. Garnet accepted me in his research group and recommended my appointment as the T.A. in the Optical Mineralogy laboratory, the course you taught me three years ago."

"Actually, I'm not surprised at all! You're a good student, but you're also very lucky to be invited to join poppy's group. He takes good care of his students."

"According to the catalogue, he only teaches one course per year...his seminar course."

"He is so busy administering his grants, writing progress reports on the multitude of projects he directs, or reviewing new or additional proposals by his students, that he hardly has time for teaching formal courses any more."

Nicolas did feel lucky, indeed. Later on at home, as he lay all alone on his bed, he let his thoughts come out loud as if he wanted to hear himself speak.

"Thank You, God, for making me look good in the eyes of my teachers...for giving me hope for the future." Then he thought of his mother and continued his soliloquy. "Thank you too, mother, for your confidence in me and for praying for me...I want to see your face, mother, when you find out that I will actually get paid to teach at a great university...when you find out that I'm taking the first step in my life's goal of becoming a teacher."

The end of the spring semester had arrived and the final exams completed by mid-May. Nicolas felt quite relieved, at least in terms of the burdens of course work. He was looking forward to devoting all his time to his thesis research during the summer months. Prof. Garnet put him on a temporary Research Assistantship for the summer months since his Teaching Assistantship for the school year had ended.

The professor even suggested that Nicolas should continue on the R.A. for the following academic year. This would allow him to concentrate totally on his research instead of spending time preparing and teaching laboratories as a T.A. He turned down the suggestion, though, without hesitation, because he loved to teach. However, the reason he gave his advisor was quite different.

"Dr. Garnet, I have plenty of time to get on a full-time R.A. I very much prefer to wait until my own research proposal is funded...according to the National Science Foundation rules, we should hear whether my project is funded by the end of next semester...could we talk about it then?"

"I'm sure we can. You may have the right idea to wait for your own grant funds."

On the morning after his last exam was completed, his body resisted getting out of bed until almost noon. As he lay in bed, he spent most of the time reliving highlights of his experiences during the past semester:

No matter how he looked at it, the semester's work was tough and demanding. However, within a few weeks into the semester, the courses, the long hours in the laboratories, the library research, the teaching, all became routine.

Nicolas didn't mind the hard work, even when he had to stay overnight in the petrology lab on Fridays and even Saturdays to complete the weekly assignment of microscopic mineralogical analysis. He kept a sleeping bag in his laboratory/office just in case.

His social life in terms of dating was practically nonexistent. He did socialize with several fellow students, especially with Don and Maury who shared space with him in the clay mineralogy lab, but only in terms of an occasional lunch or coffee break. Also, he never missed the afternoon tea and cookies at the Graduate Student Lounge.

One afternoon, as he sat on a comfortable sofa sipping tea and leafing through a magazine, he looked up for a moment and then casually across the spacious lounge. He took a double take. The young woman, seated on a chair by one of the little lamp tables reading, looked very familiar. By the time he realized he was staring at Yiasmin, his old Turkish classmate at the Academy, she got up and left. There was no exchange of even glances.

After that day in early April, he looked for her every time he entered the lounge.

He recalled that, during his graduation reception when he first saw her in the States, about a year earlier, he was informed by her cousin Nora that Yiasmin was entering the School of Architecture during the upcoming academic year.

Nicolas was at a loss trying to rationalize his interest, his desire to see and possibly talk to the Turkish woman again. He even brought lecture notes with him and stayed in the lounge much longer than usual. Coincidentally, the Graduate Student Lounge was on the first floor of Avery Hall which housed the School of Architecture. He expected to run into her sooner or later. However, she did remain elusive all through the remaining part of the spring semester. His wandering thoughts finally got around to one incident that he very much wanted to forget. It was during spring break, the fifth day of March, when he accidentally discovered that he had been the victim of fraud which was perpetrated by somebody he thought of as a good friend.

Nicolas was in the apartment fixing lunch in the kitchen when he saw a piece of paper pushed under the entrance door. He casually picked it up, thinking it could be a message for him or his roommate. Upon close examination, his eyes bulged as if ready to fall out of their sockets. He took a second and third look just to make sure. It was a rent statement from the landlord, reminding Sanjay that the monthly rent for the apartment, the sum of $165, was due on March 1st.

"My God, this is unbelievable, this is incredibly deceitful and cruel," he exclaimed in anger. "This Indian guy actually took me for a fool for trusting him...he actually had me pay the full monthly rent of $165 for the last six months after convincing me that he was paying a similar amount per month as his share...as a fellow foreign student, he knew very well about my financial situation, my limited budget, my struggle to make ends meet...God, how can anybody be so devoid of conscience?"

By the time the confrontation of the two roommates took place later in the evening, Nicolas' anger subsided considerably but his words and tone of voice were far from being friendly when he spoke to Sanjay.

"What would you have to say for yourself if I were to tell you that I found out about your devious scheme to have me pay your monthly share of the rent in addition to mine for the last six months?" With that, he threw the rent statement in his face. It was as if lightning struck the young Indian, causing his foundation to collapse.

"Nick, I'm truly sorry about this...I thought I was going to do it for a month only, only for September because I had financial difficulties at the time...but then I continued to have problems and kept thinking I would tell you the next month and then the next..."

"I have a feeling your so-called financial problems have been part of your scheme, part of a fabrication to convince me that you were paying your share of the rent. I do remember clearly how you always made sure to emphasize personal problems, claiming difficulty in raising your share of the rent every month, always right after I had handed you my check."

"I promise you, I'll pay you back the money as soon..."

"Oh, no! You do not pay me back that way. I can't trust you to do that...I shall stay here in this apartment for another six months...you will have to pay the full rent every month for the next six months all by yourself...that's what you owe me and that's how you pay me back."

"I guess I can go along with that."

"You may add another element to our future cohabitation," concluded Nicolas. "Just do me a favor and stay completely out of my way, just simply stay out of my sight."

Those last words would produce an unpleasant echo in any person's ears, especially in those of one as gregarious as Nicolas. He placed his hands over his ears and forced himself to come back to the present. He got out of bed with an important mission in mind: to look for another roommate for the next academic year.

The Hellenic Student Association is a good place to start looking.

Chapter Eight

Nicolas found himself packing his apartment belongings during the final exam period in the middle of May. It was the second semester of his second year in graduate school. Why would he do such a thing in the midst of a period that demanded every second of his time and every bit of his brain capacity for concentration? He had no choice. The eviction notice demanded that he and his roommates vacate apartment 6B at 618 West 114 street in twenty-four hours because they failed to pay the one-dollar-per- month rent designated by the City.

The move to a new apartment at 434 West 120th street, on the corner of Amsterdam, was completed well within the time allocated. The new place was upscale and so was the rent. Nicolas' roommate, Alecos, thought it was about time to bring a little luxury to their lives. He also intended to impress his girlfriend.

Nicolas, once again, managed to earn good grades. His cumulative average was not as high as in his first year of graduate school but, nevertheless, it fell into the very good-to-excellent category. His mother referred to her son's accomplishment as "evidence for continued divine guidance in my Nicolaki's life."

On Memorial Day, Nicolas found himself all alone in the new

apartment. His roommate was visiting his girlfriend in Jersey City. After a late afternoon excursion to 42nd Street where he sat through a triple feature of war movies, he returned home bent on going to bed relatively early. He didn't even watch the eleven o'clock local news which he seldom missed.

As he lay flat on his new firm mattress, he began enumerating certain situations he faced during the past academic year. For some of those, he was proud of the way he handled himself, but for others he wished, in retrospect, that he had acted differently. And then there was the letter from a close friend, without a doubt the saddest and most moving letter he ever received.

It was very much a colorful year but a wild one too...too much socializing, obviously done at the expense of academic performance...I can't believe I even participated in what some people may describe as an orgy...I guess I was trying to make up for the paucity of socializing in my first year in graduate school.

With that thought completed, certain incidents of the last nine months began parading in front of his mind's eyes:

⁂

Nicolas' two-week search for a new place to live, perhaps a new apartment and a new roommate, remained fruitless. With only four days left before fall semester classes were scheduled to begin and he was still living in Sanjay's apartment. With the exception of a quick "hi" here and there, he did not speak to his Indian roommate for over six months, or since the discovery of what he liked to sarcastically refer to as "the great Hindu rent-fraud incident."

One day before classes Nick was having breakfast at Choc-Full-O-Nuts feeling gloomy because he had no new roommate prospects on the horizon. He had met and talked to three candidates the day before, but he didn't feel quite right about any of them, even though one of them was Greek. He even began considering the idea, no matter how revolting, of making a deal with Sanjay to extend his stay in the apartment for another semester.

He was about to leave the restaurant, to go talk to Sanjay, when Costas, a Hellenic Society member he had met through Stanley a couple of years earlier, walked in with another young Greek that Nick had never seen before. After the necessary hellos and introductions, Costas and Alecos occupied two counter stools adjacent to Nick and indulged themselves into the famous coffee and whole wheat donuts.

"Nico, you haven't seen me in a couple of years because I transferred to the NYU Washington Square campus, just about two years ago," explained Costas. "I can see you haven't changed a bit...same hairstyle, same clothing...with that navy blazer and the button-down shirt you've always looked like a WASP ivy leaguer rather than a foreign student."

"Well, not all foreign students dress as casual as you Costa...I happen to subscribe to the saying, 'When in Rome, live and dress like the Romans.'" He paused to laugh out loud. "You seem to abide by the saying too, Aleco, to a certain extent. But, since I just met you, how about telling us something about yourself, your background."

"I come from Zakinthos...after a semester at Columbia, I also transferred. I just completed my junior year in the College of Engineering at NYU, the uptown campus."

"It must be a trend. I must have met at least half a dozen students who also transferred to NYU at one point or another," observed Nicolas.

"Actually it's a little cheaper at NYU and life is more exciting on the village campus," explained Costas. "Of course there is another reason...my program there is not as demanding as on this campus."

"Aleco, you must be very good in math and the natural sciences to survive three years in engineering, no matter what type of engineering," interrupted Nick.

"It's electrical engineering and I'm no more than just an average student."

"But he is an A student in certain elective courses, especially in the humanities such as comparative literature and history," intervened Costas.

"They say that you perform better in those topics you love most," added Alecos. "I would rather read a good epic poem or, better yet, write a poem myself, than work with differential equations. It's true for so many of us...we have to sacrifice what we truly would have liked to study for the sake of a subject that is believed to create a more practical and fruitful career for us...a career that is perceived as providing better financial prospects for the future."

This guy is a good thinker, perhaps even a philosopher...he is right about career choices that we all have to make...in the beginning, I also had preferences for literature, for creative writing...but eventually science looked more promising for providing a good income-producing career.

Before long, Nicolas was impressed with Alecos' background, his balanced attitude about education and life in general, and especially his pleasant personality.

"By the way," Alecos added as he was getting ready to leave the restaurant, "I'm looking for a roommate for an apartment on 114th Street which I leased a few days back. I work part-time at the Paradise Restaurant but I still need to share the rent of $120 with someone..."

Nicolas responded with an immediate and loud, "Eureka!"

Alecos was very happy to help Nicolas move into his three-bedroom furnished apartment, a couple of blocks down Broadway, by early afternoon of that day. The 6th floor walk-up, like the building itself, appeared somewhat dingy. However, as far as the two students were concerned, the apartment's assets, particularly the fact that it was cheap, conveniently located and only temporary, outweighed its numerous liabilities.

A couple of weeks into the fall semester, the two roommates

rented the smaller of the three bedrooms to an American youth. His overall appearance, his lean and tall frame and his long blond hair, presented a sharp contrast to that of his two Mediterranean roommates. Terry Murphy, an Irish-American in his late twenties, was an aspiring actor who did a couple of semesters at Columbia when first out of high school. He explained,

"I still consider myself a Columbia student, a theater arts student, and I plan to take more courses one of these days. I wait tables at a downtown restaurant, but I need to continue living here on campus."

Terry's passive manner and totally laid-back disposition painted a portrait of a gentle and somewhat naïve young man. His roommates nicknamed him "cool Terry."

By the middle of the semester, routine and a bit of boredom settled in the life of the three roommates. Then things began to happen. It was as if one goes through a very long drought and then, suddenly, the rains come, first light and then much heavier, with flooding becoming the norm for days and days.

The first couple of incidents had to do with landlord services. At first, one of these incidents appeared to be just a small inconvenience but quickly changed to an irritating nuisance and eventually to a life-threatening situation.

The six-floor building was quite small by neighborhood standards. It had only two apartments per floor and its corridors were short and narrow. It boasted a concrete stairway, wide enough for two but badly foot worn by many years of sole impact. It extended above the sixth floor for access to the roof. A single 40-watt bulb in a near-flat ceiling socket, dimly lit each floor corridor.

When all the corridor lights went out at the same time, the tenants knew that it was not because of burnt-out bulbs. Jim Cronin, the part-time super for this and other buildings on 114th

Street, explained that the electric bill for the corridors was the responsibility of the landlord who probably had not paid it. After three or four days of dark corridors, everybody was carrying flashlights. Alecos and Terry and tenants who worked till very late at night and came home alone, began to be openly concerned and visibly annoyed.

Some tenants thought it was inevitable that something terrible, something criminal, would happen if and when crooks found out about the loss of lighting in the corridors. They were right. The tenant of 2A, a middle-aged man who worked as bartender at the nearby West End Bar, was robbed at knife-point by two men who were hiding in the dark lobby. Concern and annoyance quickly changed to fear and panic.

Alecos, who signed the lease for the apartment, tried to get in touch with the landlord, but had no luck. His next step was to acquire a 22-caliber handgun. The tiny gun, fully loaded with one solitary bullet, became his constant companion, day and night.

"What are you going to do if your single bullet misses?" asked Terry.

"I hope I don't have to fire the gun...I'm not sure I can actually shoot anybody. The idea is to simply frighten the intruder...make him run...I hope..."

Nicolas tried to solve the problem differently. He personally invited all the tenants to a meeting. They unanimously decided to assume responsibility for the payment of the corridor electric bill. Con Edison turned the power back on. The tenants also shared the cost of replacing the broken lock on the entrance door of the building.

The meeting of the tenants produced an additional bonus for both Nicolas and Alecos. They got to meet the tenant of 5A, a young undergraduate, the son of a well-to-do physician from Athens, Greece. Paul turned out to be the quintessential good-looking and self-confident Athenian, full of social graces and extremely gregarious. He became a lifetime friend.

"You guys should be ashamed of yourselves. You have been living right next door to me for weeks and never bothered to come over for a visit? I want to see both of you right after this meeting and I don't want any excuses." Paul spoke in a tone that became his trademark, one that mixed intimate familiarity with friendly sarcasm.

This is the best sounding Greek dialect I have ever heard...I guess this is the beautiful Athenian accent...what a friendly guy...ordinary clothing and yet it looks great on him...it's the way he carries himself, thought Nicolas.

For a few days things were back to normal, a little quiet before the impending storm. Then came the invasion of the silent radiators. The building's heating system went off at the time it was needed most. Once again the super explained the situation to the tenants—this time it was that the landlord had stopped having coal delivered for the building's furnace. Electric heaters brought some comfort. Water for the kitchen and the bathroom was heated on the stove. Extra clothing and additional blankets, including the piling of overcoats on the beds, made conditions slightly more bearable.

A little after Thanksgiving the NYC Housing Department determined that the tenants of 180 West 114th Street were being subjected to great hardship and, therefore, were not obligated to pay more than "one-dollar-rent-per-month until further notice."

The City's decision sweetened, somewhat, the tenants' soured mood. On the first day of each month, for the next several months, the three roommates alternated in sending one dollar to the landlord.

Nicolas continued his mental journey through the past academic year. The late fall, the winter and early spring months left their frigid and uncomfortable mark on the minds of all three roommates because of the absence of heat in the apartment.

I entered into a new love affair at Christmas time...my relationship with Maro was unusual and somewhat strange at times, but it brought lots of excitement into my otherwise dull life. It also taught me a lesson about honesty and responsibility.

Nicolas had the latter thought in his mind as he rode the "A" train to Brooklyn, on his way to his Aunt Eleni's home on Christmas day. He looked forward to seeing friends and relatives as well as to enjoying a traditional home-cooked meal.

The Mavros family Christmas feast was rich and varied. Two main entrees: roasted fresh ham plus *pasticcio,* a delicious Greek version of lasagna. The appetizers included Cypriot smoked sausage links fried with *halloumi* cheese, plus three varieties of olives and plenty of Greek country salad. Yiayia baked three loaves of Cypriot bread.

A spectacular assortment of desserts plus coffee or tea were presented at another family sit-down in late afternoon, this time with a few invited guests who brought additional sweet creations of their own. The lavishly displayed offerings included several types of cookies, phyllo pastries of *baklava* and *galoktopoureko,* a fabulous Greek version of baked custard, *kadaifi*—shredded wheat filled with nuts and honey, plus several all-American fruit pies.

Aunt Eleni welcomed the Pentaris family and explained the absence of the Savvides family as being caused by a last minute change of plans due to illness in the family.

They must have found out I was coming...they probably didn't want to face me since I refused to go along with the recommended match between their Tina and me.

Aunt Eleni did not appear to be overly concerned with the Savvides' absence or the unfulfilled match that she herself had proposed. She was still busy practicing her art as the quintessential matchmaker. Most of her conversation was directed towards her pride and joy, her older daughter Dora, but she also commented about Nicolas at the dessert table.

"Nicola, don't you agree that Dora is more fabulous than ever?"

She did not wait for an answer. "As you know, she's been working in Manhattan, with ABC television ever since she graduated from high school...since she became an Americanida. All kinds of people have been knocking on our door...I can see great things in her future...I make sure of that by screening..."

"I agree with you Aunt Eleni, Dora is an exceptional young woman. You know I see her once in a while in the city, we had lunch together just the other day. Aunt Eleni, your daughter is also a mature young lady...I know, and everybody else here knows, that you want the very best for her...but I think you should not only love her but also respect her...respect her opinion about her future once in a while..."

"You college types, you think you know everything better. Of course I respect my daughter and I do respect her opinion on many, many things...but there are certain things that a mother knows better, things that have to do with her children's future. Ask her, ask my daughter as she sits here next to you and Maro, her best friend...ask her if she agrees with me." Seemingly unaffected by a response of silence, she continued,

"And don't forget to ask Maro as well. She is a sophisticated young lady, a senior at Hunter College...ask her if she respects her mother and ask her if she agrees with the idea that her mother knows best about what's good for her future."

Nicolas continued to keep his silence because he thought of his aunt's questions as simply rhetorical. On the other hand, Dora lowered her head and wiped a couple of tears. Without answering her mother's question, without saying a word, she left the festive table and ran towards her upstairs room. Maro followed her friend immediately.

The mother showed no sign of being upset or even being surprised at her daughter's behavior. She calmly explained,

"Don't mind Dora, she gets emotional every time I discuss her future...it's obvious she is most concerned with the idea of having to leave her home and her family sometime in the near future...she does this all the time."

Eventually Nicolas joined Dora and Maro upstairs. This time the three young adults did not talk about old-fashioned parents or pushy mothers. Dora dominated the conversation with superlative descriptions of her secret beau's character and personality and their secret communication exchanges.

"Nick, you must swear to me, you must swear you never say a word about Tony to my mother...she will probably kill me... actually, she will probably kill herself...one of these days Tony will come up from Virginia to pick me up...I'm ready...I am ready to elope with him..."

"This is news to me, of course, but tell me Dora, tell me how you met Tony and especially why you think your mother is against him."

"He came up here by himself last spring, Easter time, for a week, and then again last summer, for over three weeks with his mother to visit the Laghos. Mary Laghos is his mother's sister. He has a good rapport with his Aunt Mary who never had any children of her own. He visited his aunt many times, but I only met him for the first time last spring. Later on in the summer several of us neighborhood friends invited Tony to beach parties and drive-in movies and birthday parties. That's how we got to know each other...that's how we fell in love with each other."

"But I'm still curious why your mother would be against him... he is one of our own...I would imagine he comes from good stock, his family is Cypriot American..."

"My mother referred to him once as 'a bum without any future.' She thinks he refuses to go to college. He is three years older than me and has been working as a waiter at a seafood restaurant ever since he graduated from high school. My mother doesn't know, of course, that he is saving for college and, eventually, law school. His parents are devoted to their only child but they are not well off... they do not own a business. His father and mother work for two different diners, both owned by another Cypriot."

"I can see how you are in big trouble, cousin Dora. I hope

things work out for you. But what about you, Maro? I know your parents are conservative and, in your case, your father is especially strict and over-protective. But a beauty like you cannot remain uninvolved for too long…any secret romances to share with us?"

"Honestly, I have nothing of the kind to report…I am not as popular as Dora."

"But I do have something to report," interjected Dora. "It's about time cousin Nick finds out…think about it Maro, he has to be told." Maro protested both with words and physical gestures, placing her hand over Dora's mouth. It was all in vain since Dora added,

"My friend Maro has a crush on you, cousin Nick, a rather severe crush—ever since she met you at St. Demetrius church almost two years ago, right after your college graduation."

Maro was very much embarrassed and ran out of the room. Dora followed her. She thought it would be best if she went after her friend whom she put on the spot. Nicolas remained in the room trying to digest what he had just heard.

This is good news at a time when I seem to have lost my touch with women. This is good for my confidence…my ego. She is a good-looking and proper young woman, perhaps her complexion is a bit too dark, but she is still a striking brunette with beautiful and expressive black eyes…

"Nick come down and join us. Maro and I are going down the block to visit a mutual friend, a member of the Greek Orthodox Youth Association. You are welcome to come with us," shouted Dora from the bottom of the stairs.

Nicolas right away knew that his cousin threw in the GOYA association in order to impress or perhaps even secure the approval of the parents who were no doubt listening to their daughters' conversation.

"Give me a couple of minutes, I'll be there in a couple of minutes." He entered the upstairs bathroom but his thoughts about Maro followed him:

Now I remember what bothered me the first time I saw her…her

mustache, she needed to get rid of all that dark hair under her nose and, thank God, she did...but what about her legs? I got a glimpse of her legs, way above the knees, when she sat on that low armchair earlier...lean and perfectly shaped legs, but unfortunately badly in needs of a shave there.

Nicolas joined the two women at their friend's home and managed to have some private time with Maro. He suggested that they should visit each other in the city, perhaps for a tour of their respective campuses.

"I would love to do that Nick. I would love to see you in the city, I can't wait."

"That's great. Lets do it the first week of classes in mid-January. Of course, personally, I'm available earlier, even tomorrow. Can you find an excuse to come to the city before the spring semester starts?"

"Perhaps I can convince my mother that I need to check grades or visit the school library...I will call you." And then she added, "Nick, we can only meet a couple of times...after that, you have to visit me at home, talk to my parents...once you do that, they will think you are serious and they will allow us to see each other more often. I can tell from your expression that you are puzzled, perhaps concerned...please do not be afraid...talking to my parents at home does not mean we are about to be engaged...they just want to feel they are in control...they want to know where we go and what we do..."

"I know, it's a matter of control...parents need to feel they have control...I imagine we can continue seeing each other for quite a while, or until your parents suggest that we introduce the word 'engagement' in our relationship...when that happens we can each go our own way very quickly, right?"

Within seconds, her exhilaration, her anticipation of future happy moments, all changed to a moment of total depression, a moment filled with miserable anxiety. The transformation was recorded in her eyes, on her face, in her movements. Nicolas had to act quickly.

"My dear Maro, you know I'm kidding, of course. If you are willing, I'm even more willing to carry our relationship to wherever it takes us...engagement could be part of our future...one never knows."

Nicolas and Maro became an item. They met several times in the city and took tours of each other's campus. They visited Riverside Park and sat on the same bench where he used to make out with Vivian. However, Maro was uncomfortable about indulging in passionate necking. Their kissing was quick, clean and simple. She was self-conscious about kissing in public.

Whenever he suggested the privacy of his apartment, she became even more visibly disturbed. Her excuse was the same every time:

"Nick, you know I would love to spend time with you, but not in your apartment. I told you how I had to make a promise to my parents, I had to swear on my baptism cross, that I would not enter your apartment and spend time alone with you there or anywhere else...unless I was engaged to you..."

Every time Nick thought of the idea of spending time with Maro alone, his raging hormones took control of his imagination. He envisioned himself making love after arousing the passions and desires of a "sleeping" maiden. Such scenes brought the notion of engagement closer and closer and made it more of an acceptable solution to his problem.

A semi-formal engagement, a ten minute blessing by Father Philotheos of St. Demetrius, took place after the liturgy on the last Sunday in January. Maro's parents and sister and Nicolas' Aunt Eleni and cousin Dora attended the ceremony. During the blessing Nicolas' mind was trying to justify the engagement.

I know my mother will love the idea of my getting engaged to Maro... she is a lovely maiden from excellent stock, from a well-to-do Greek

Cypriot family...after all, Aunt Eleni made the match...I seem to like the idea too...but what about Stella? An engagement leading to marriage will mean the end of all prospects of ever getting together with Stella...on the other hand, this is not marriage...the engagement can be broken up quite easily...it's not altogether binding.

Maro's first private visit to Nicolas' apartment took place two Fridays after the engagement. She couldn't believe how primitive and how unbearably cold the place was. He suggested to her to go under the bed covers and she eventually consented but remained fully clothed. When he joined her, also fully dressed, the bed temperature rose considerably and the covers had to be removed. He undressed down to his shorts and T-shirt but she only took off her sweater.

The young man was fully aroused but could only make first base. She would not remove her long girdle which tightly encased everything from her waist down close to her knees. She blamed the room temperature for refusing to remove her blouse.

Of course nothing could keep Nicolas' hands from exploring everything under the skirt as well as everything under the blouse and bra. He tried, but could not get too far under the tight girdle. And he was definitely turned off every time he felt the hair on the area of her legs not covered by the girdle.

During their second rendezvous in his apartment, a week later, he was pleasantly surprised, to say the least, by her unexpected change in behavior. After he was asked to leave the room for a few minutes, he was called back and was invited to share the bed with her. When he lifted up the covers, he was somewhat shocked to see her without her skirt and blouse and, most amazingly, without her "armor," the girdle. She was lying flat on her back, her legs tightly crossed but surprisingly clean shaven, still wearing her panties but no bra.

Nicolas was ecstatic and speechless and kept raising the covers for yet another glimpse at the "peep-o-rama." After he seemingly had his fill, he undressed quickly down to his briefs and placed his agitated body by her side. While he was devising a systematic plan of "attack" in his mind, his conscience, or what was left of it, was demanding proper consideration and respect for the maiden's virtue.

How lovely and innocent she looks...what a sad picture she makes, waiting like a helpless, unsuspecting lamb about to face a wolf in disguise...

His conscience gave it a good try—but the attention and recognition it sought were not forthcoming. Conscience lost to the formidable power of lust. He did not remove the panties even though she did not object to the idea in so many words. Somehow he sensed body vibrations that revealed her silent wish to wait a bit longer for the final curtain. The setback, assumed to be temporary, did not seem to bother him much. They both appeared to thoroughly enjoy the long introduction to each other's body and sexuality.

Nicolas was physically and mentally suffering while he waited for Friday evening, his next weekly date with Maro. The anticipation of another romantic episode with her, perhaps even more fulfilling than the previous, caused him to daydream and totally neglect his studies. His students detected a change in his focus and concentration in the classroom.

On Friday afternoon, he recruited his roommates to help him clean the whole apartment for his big date that evening. Even the late February weather was co-operating. The temperature climbed up to the high forties in comparison with the frigid twenties of the previous week. Alecos, who was a veritable gourmet, showed him how to trim and marinate two shell steaks and gave him detailed instructions how to grill them and serve them with a baked potato and salad.

Maro was expected at 6:00. The roommates cleared out of the apartment around 5:00. Five minutes later, the phone rang.

"Nick, *agapi mou*, my love, it appears very unlikely that I can see you this evening. My mother became quite ill during the last hour or so. It looks like the flu to me, even though her temperature is very close to normal. But she coughs and throws up and is now in bed suffering with nausea. Unfortunately my father won't be home till ten and my sister is at the county library with her friends."

"Did you tell you mother anything about spending the evening here in my apartment last week?"

"Nick, are you suggesting that she is faking it? Because she is concerned about my visiting you in your apartment? You know very well that I share everything with my mother, she is my best friend. She has always been concerned and has been advising me about out-of-wedlock sex and pregnancies ever since I was fifteen."

"So, did she ask you if you risked becoming pregnant?"

"She only wanted to know if I was still pure or if I did anything that I shouldn't do until I was married. I assured her that I didn't do anything that I would be ashamed of. Nick, I guarantee you, she would not do something like that, she would not fake illness so that I will be forced to stay home."

"I think she is trying to protect you in her own old-fashioned way. Even if she is truly sick, she may have caused her illness herself, subconsciously, as part of the motherly instinct to protect her offspring."

"But she knows very well that, after all, you are my fiancé. She told me many times that in Cyprus, once engaged, a couple lives together."

"Yes, true, but in Cyprus they do a formal church engagement, with both families signing a binding contract which also outlines the girl's dowry…remember how your mother insisted that we do a formal church engagement with signed documents?"

"Yes, I do. But, at the end, she accepted the idea of a blessing instead of a formal contract because your family could not be present."

"True, but don't you also remember telling me how your mother took you aside, that same day, and explained to you that this 'engagement blessing' is a license for us to date and get to know each other, but only under the assumption that we conduct ourselves properly?"

"Yes, I do remember that and also the fact that when I asked her to expand on the word 'properly' she bluntly said, 'without engaging in pre-marital sex.'"

The two young lovers ended the call by promising to see each other the following Friday, if not before. A minute later, his door bell rung. When he did open the door, he did not expect, not in a million years, to face two smiling women standing in front of him. Two small suitcases and a duffle bag were lying on the floor beside them.

Cousin Dora right away introduced her friend, a former high school classmate named Christalla, who seemed to be totally out of breath.

"It's not that easy climbing up six floors, especially when you carry a suitcase," said Nicolas while hugging both women.

"It's even more difficult for me because I do carry some excess weight and I also smoke," responded Christalla. "By the way, I did meet you once before at Dora's. You were a shy sophomore then."

He took another close look at her but did not respond to her comment. He did remember meeting her at Dora's naturalization party a few years back. He was quite surprised, however, that Dora brought her along, remembering how his cousin and others in her group made fun of Christalla's big breasts and big tush at the party.

"My God, Dora, I never imagined that you would be knocking on my door. I'm actually very pleased to see you but I'm also very curious. To what do I owe this pleasure?"

"Can we move inside first? I will tell you all about it as soon as we catch our breath."

As if I cannot guess, thought Nicolas. *She has decided to elope with Tony ...*

"O.K. Nick, here it is. Me and Tony cannot keep apart anymore. He should be picking me up from here tomorrow, early afternoon. I confided my plans to Christalla. She insisted on accompanying me to New York for support. I hope you don't mind our company for a day or so."

"No, not at all if you don't mind the place, the cool atmosphere and the luxurious accommodations. In fact, I appreciate the company. I had plans to be with my fiancée Maro tonight, but she cancelled the last minute. What concerns me, though, is your mother. What do you think she will do if she finds out I helped you elope by letting you stay here?"

"I can't imagine my mother finding out that I'm here with you and I can't imagine you telling her, even if she calls you. I did not leave her a note. I plan to call her after me and Tony arrive in Virginia and get married there in a civil ceremony so that we can live together legally. After that, we can easily arrange for the church wedding."

"Don't tell me, let me guess—you do plan, to invite your mother to the church wedding, right?," he asked.

"You can be sarcastic and you may not believe it will be possible for her to forgive me that easily. But I'm sure she will miss me and forgive me in time to even help arrange things for my wedding."

"I really hope I'm wrong, but I doubt it. I believe that I know and possibly understand your mother better than you do. My gut feeling is that she will probably never forgive you for ignoring her wishes and betraying her trust in you. If you really want your mother at your wedding, cancel your plans to elope with Tony. Turn around and go home before she even finds out you left."

"You know I can't change my plans because it's the only way to be with my Tony...maybe I shouldn't say this to you because I know how much you love and respect your mother but here it is: At this point, Tony is more important in my life than my mother."

"I can understand that. It's natural for you and every young woman in the world, or every young man for that matter, to feel like that after the choice of a partner in life has been made. When that happens, the mother's role in one's life becomes secondary."

"But that does not mean that I don't care about my mother. I do and I want her to forgive me and embrace my new life. But what can I do to convince her?"

"I can think of one thing that you can do that would eventually convince your mother to forgive you and embrace you in your new life. Give her a grandchild or two."

The discussion ended moments later when Christalla pointed out that she could use something to eat. Nicolas took them for a meal at the Caravan. The young Greeks working there took a good look at beautiful, proper Dora, but dwelt on voluptuous Christalla and her obvious assets.

A short tour of the campus followed, including a visit to his laboratory space in Schermerhorn Hall. Nicolas showed off all the fancy equipment that he used in his research, including the X-ray diffraction and fluorescence units, the infrared spectrophotometer and of course, his polarizing microscope, a late model Zeiss assigned personally to him.

Dora tried hard to appear interested, but was mostly absent-minded throughout the tour. Christalla, on the other hand, hung on Nicolas' every word and asked probing questions about his research. Nicolas was impressed with her analytic capabilities. He was even more impressed when he found out that she was attending Brooklyn College on a part-time basis.

Their last stop on the campus tour was Butler Library where they spent a few minutes in the smoking lounge for a cigarette break. There, Nicolas was awakened to the fact that Christalla projected a certain sexuality that apparently attracted a lot of men. While the three Greeks were sitting at the sofa facing the east-end wall of the lounge, a few Ivy Leaguers went out of their way in a detour around the sofa, obviously in order to more closely check out all of Chistalla's endowments.

Back at the apartment, they had very few options about sleeping arrangements. It made sense that the two women took Nicolas' double bed while he fixed up the cot, which normally served as a sofa, in the adjacent room. The two rooms had a partial-wall partition but no door. The electric heater was placed next to the women's bed. They also secured the lion's share of available blankets and bed covers.

Around 3:00 a.m., Nicolas woke up, feeling semi-frozen. He got out of bed, put on socks as well as a sweater on top of his pajama top and went into the kitchen. He turned on and lit all of the gas stove burners. He also turned on the oven, leaving its door open. As he began feeling a little more comfortable standing by the hot stove and the oven, Christalla walked in. She was barefoot but otherwise fully dressed in jeans and an oversize sweat shirt.

"It's only fair that you come and join Dora and me in your bed. She is asleep, her face smack against the wall. I'll lie next to her and you get the edge of the bed, close to the heater...even though the bed only seems to accommodate two, we can't afford to let you freeze."

It did not take much more to convince him. Christalla took off her jeans and gently placed herself next to Dora. He took off his sweater and lay on his side, his front and face turned away from the young woman. After a while, they drifted closer together and he made contact with her breasts and felt the heat of her body penetrate his spine. Overwhelmed by the sensation of her touch, his body began to experience intermittent shivers.

She must have sensed his discomfort and turned away from him. He had to change his position too, so he turned around, facing her back. But body sensations became even more enhanced when his torso drifted slowly towards her and made contact with her softly accommodating rump. He knew he had to act quickly. He left the two women and went back to the cot. He had to get some sleep.

In the morning, Nicolas got up at nine, relatively early for a Saturday. The women, as well as his roommates, appeared to be asleep. He warmed some water on the stove, in a large aluminum bucket, and had a washcloth body wash in the bathroom. He left the stove on to warm the kitchen. He then left a note informing his roommates and guests that he had gone out and would be back with donuts and Danish for everybody.

After a short visit to his lab to check out the progress of sedimenting clay mineral particles on glass slides for X-ray diffraction analysis, he returned to the apartment before eleven.

His two women guests and his two roommates were seated at the kitchen table sipping coffee. The atmosphere in the kitchen was rather warm, but everyone seated at the table was overly quiet and serious. Nicolas pretended not to have noticed the non-jovial mood of the gathering when he first spoke:

"Here are some goodies that go along well with your coffee… and here is the mail, two for Alecos and two for me…sorry Terry."

Nicolas took a spot at the table next to Christalla who was the first to offer him a cup of coffee. He was preoccupied with his letters, though, as he took a few sips. "This is great…I have a letter from my mother and one from my friend Rusty Weisman. I look forward to reading these a little bit later on…now, tell me, why is everybody so serious? What transpired during the last couple of hours?"

"Tony called, he is on his way from midtown. He should be here any minute now. Don't you think I should be down there, in front of the building with my two suitcases, so that he doesn't have to worry about parking or about climbing up all those stairs?"

"I'm certain that we—three strong guys around this table—

can take you and your suitcases down all those stairs in a minute or so. But what you just said does not answer my concern about everybody's apparently sad disposition at this table...what else happened?"

Aleco spoke up: "Just about an hour ago, your Aunt Eleni called. I answered the phone. She asked me if her daughter Dora was here in the apartment with you. I had seen Dora earlier on her way to the bathroom, so I told your aunt that she was here."

"Thanks a lot Aleco. I guess I'm now on her blacklist. I can imagine..."

Dora interrupted in order to explain her part in the drama. "I had to tell mother all about Tony and me. She was so upset, she could hardly talk." She stopped to wipe tears which came in spite of her valiant effort to appear calm and divorced from motherly pressure.

"Did she ask you anything about me and my role in this affair?"

"Yes, she did ask me whether you, cousin Nick, helped to arrange things for me and Tony. I emphatically said that you had absolutely nothing to do with my plan to elope...I even told her how I surprised you by coming here last evening on my own...I didn't mention Christalla's part at all."

"Thanks, that sounds good, Dora. I guess I have to assume that she was satisfied with your explanation and that she no longer suspects my participation in the planning of your elopement."

"I wish I could tell you that what you just said was true. Far from it. Her last words were: 'Nick has stabbed me in the back in spite of what me and my family have done for him...I don't want to see him in this house or anywhere else ever again.'"

Nicolas' face betrayed his deep concern. His spirit was practically destroyed.

"How can I face my mother after she hears such things from her cousin Eleni? I promised my mother that I should always obey and honor my Aunt Eleni. In this case, will my mother believe me or her cousin Eleni? Excuse me, I need to read my mother's letter." He entered his room, closing the door behind him.

Nick was still in his room when word came that Tony had arrived and was waiting in his car, parked in front of the building. The young lover avoided climbing up all those stairs—instead, he sent a message with Joan, the tenant of 4A, that his fiancée Dora should move fast and meet him down there as soon as possible.

The two women knocked and entered Nicolas' room. He was sitting on the bed, his eyes red and swollen from wiping tears. They were obviously much concerned but didn't have time for any questions or explanations, so they took turns to hug him and say goodbye. Alecos and Terry took the two suitcases and led the two women to the waiting car. Christalla left her duffle bag upstairs.

A few minutes after the girls said goodbye to him, Nick realized that he would have liked very much to meet Tony. He quickly wiped his teary face on a towel and literally jumped his way down the stairs. He was too late, the two young lovers had already taken off. His roommates and Christalla were still standing on the sidewalk. She approached Nick and whispered close to his face,

"Nick, is it alright if I stay a little bit longer with you before I take the subway back to Brooklyn?"

"Of course, if that's what you want."

All four found themselves once again seated at the kitchen table. Alecos placed a carton of crackers on the table and brought out a dish with *feta* and one with *kasseri*.

Terry took out the coke cans and the ice cubes. Before long, everybody was enjoying the light lunch as if nothing serious had taken place in that room minutes earlier.

"Nick," asked Alecos, obviously unable to wait any longer, "the girls told us that you were crying hard in your room when they came to say goodbye…am I to assume that you took your aunt's attitude towards you that seriously? Or is it something else?"

"You were holding a letter when we saw you sobbing… is everything alright with your mother, your family back in

Cyprus?..." this time it was Christalla whose concern was voiced.

Nick took an envelope out of his pocket. He emptied the contents, two different sized cards. The first, a 4 x 2 white card, contained five lines of printed blue words. Nicolas read the lines before he passed the card around.

> **Rusty Weisman passed away**
> **On January 19, 1967**
> **From lung cancer.**
> **He asked that you be notified.**
> **HE SENDS LOVE!**

"Any idea as to who wrote the card?," asked Alecos.

"Rusty addressed the envelope, I recognize his handwriting. Unfortunately nobody signed the card announcement. But I'm pretty sure it was his girlfriend Janet. She is the type who would add 'HE SENDS LOVE.' I don't see his lawyer adding that kind of a phrase. I'm sure Rusty left instructions concerning the contents of the card."

The second, a blue 6 x 4 horizontally-folding greeting card, showed an embossed white dove holding an olive branch in its beak, on the outside front cover. Inside the word PEACE was printed in five different languages, with the words forming a wreath. The Greek word for peace, *IRINI*, was hand written inside the wreath. Below the wreath there were two lines of hand-written words. Nicolas passed the card around after he read it out loud.

> *Dear Nick,*
>
> *I am truly sorry I have to leave behind good friends like yourself. But I am also glad to leave you peace and love.*
>
> *Rusty*

Nick could no longer manage his emotions and sought refuge in his room. Silence and sadness ruled over the rest of the group for a while. Christalla appeared much more shaken than the others. She later joined Nicolas and sat next to him on the bed.

"Nick, this is incredibly moving for me not only because it's the true story of the sad, untimely death of a good man, but also because it represents and illustrates a beautiful friendship between two people that, on the surface, appear to be so different, from two such obviously different worlds." He was impressed once again with her observation and comment. He drew closer to her and put his left arm around her.

"Nick, would you like me to stay here with you one more night?"

Her proposition took him totally by surprise but it also brought him some badly needed positive excitement.

"Are you sure you want to do this? I don't know whether you have a steady boyfriend or not but I'm engaged to Maro."

"In a way, I'm engaged too. I'm promised to an older man in Cyprus…he is expected to arrive here this coming summer. My parents arranged the whole thing. As for Maro, I leave it up to you, up to your conscience. Dora told me that you are not formally or contractually engaged…in a way, you have a pledge to go steady with her…you have to make the decision."

"I guess it's o.k. if we are strong enough to refrain from becoming too intimate. You think you can do it?"

"I'm sure I can if you can."

So, essentially, they agreed to endeavor to control their passions, their desires. They sealed their agreement with a quick kiss and then started thinking about dinner. Nick suggested that they should have the two steaks he marinated the day before when he expected Maro. She suggested that he should invite his two roommates if he could get a couple of more steaks. Both roommates had to decline because of work at their respective restaurants.

Nick and Christalla enjoyed the steaks and were working

on jelly donuts and coffee when the phone rang. As soon as he recognized Maro's voice, sensations of guilt and betrayal took control of his body and soul. But the minute she stated that her mother was still indisposed and that she couldn't see him that weekend at all, not even at church the next day, his happy libido juices were flowing through his veins once again.

Once in bed, cozily together, their endeavor to control their passionate desires failed miserably. They made love throughout the night, between naps, and in the morning, before breakfast. They thought they were in a desperate race with limited time. They knew they had less than a day to enjoy each other, probably the only time they would ever have for the rest of their lives. They conveniently allowed their fiancés to vanish from their consciences and their thoughts, for the duration of that lusty affair.

At the end of March, the weather became spring-like, with temperatures well above average for the season. Consequently, the problem of heating the apartment eased considerably. Nicolas saw Maro several times during that month but wouldn't invite her to his apartment. That was because his conscience wouldn't let him forget his infidelity, the terrible betrayal of her trust. But, as far as she was concerned, the reason for not being invited was always the lack of heat in the apartment.

Eventually, time heals and allows all kinds of events, good or bad, to be partially or totally forgotten. By Easter time, the second week of April, Nicolas once again had allowed scenes of passion, involving him and his fiancée in his apartment, to dwell in his mind. He set up the "trap" for Maro for the Saturday after Orthodox Easter. However, his plans were to change when a totally unexpected visitor arrived.

"Dear friend Laki, this is indeed a very pleasant surprise...I never expected to see you here and now...I thought you were studying health and nutrition in London."

"I didn't plan it either, it happened very fast. Before I left for England, I had applied for a Fulbright Scholarship to do graduate work in psychology in the States. It was approved last month, so I'm here to set things up. I've been temporarily staying with a cousin in Little Neck, Long Island—since Easter Holy Week. I'm already accepted at Long Island University beginning with Summer Session in early June."

"I still can't believe it...one of my best friends, from my Academy days in Larnaca, here with me...how long can you stay with me? I have to show you around campus and, of course, around the city, the exciting city of New York!"

"At this time, I can only stay this one weekend, perhaps till Tuesday morning. I hope I didn't spoil any of your plans."

"No, nothing serious. I changed plans the moment I received your call."

"How is your love life? Are you still getting involved with virgin-types?"

"No, not really. I guess you remember our correspondence concerning my first girlfriend, Vivian. On second thought, you are probably right. My new girlfriend, actually my fiancée, Maro, fits that bill as well."

"I didn't even know you're engaged. What kind of a woman is she?"

"To be honest with you, nobody in Cyprus knows yet that I'm engaged...not even my mother, unless my aunt wrote to her...but I can tell you, confidentially, I do not look at it as a serious or binding engagement. It's an informal arrangement strictly for the sake of her parents, so that we can date freely. She is a Cypriot American, born in Queens, but her parents are very conservative folks from a small village in Cyprus. You guessed it right, of course, I have not taken advantage of her yet."

"Where do you find all these Doris Day types? In London there's plenty of sexual freedom. I doubt if you can find a virgin there above the age of seventeen...it must be the puritan American culture...

but then, on the other hand, our friend Yiannis experiences lots of sexual freedom in San Francisco. Come to think of it, one of these days you and I should visit Yiannis and Andros in California."

"I very much like the idea of visiting Yiannis and Andros... can you imagine? The four Cypriot musketeers together again, this time in beautiful San Francisco."

"That sounds great, but right now lets get back to our topic of sexual freedom and virgins...maybe it's you, you must have a phobia..."

"O.K., Mr. psychologist, we all have phobias. You yourself admitted in one of your letters from your college days in Beirut that you had recognized more than twenty phobias in your psyche. Go ahead then, describe the one I have with regards to making love to virgins."

"Your problem, as well as that of most Cypriots of our generation or those before us, is that we were brought up in a conservative, religious society, one that thinks of sex as 'dirty or unholy' unless it's part of our marital duty to produce offspring."

"The Catholics, as in the case of my girlfriend Vivian, and some other religious cultures have similar ideas or restrictions."

"True but not as extreme as ours. We celebrate our women virgins as personifying purity or even a certain holiness which they lose the moment 'they are destroyed.' You have a 'virgins phobia,' you have what I call 'parthenophobia.'"

"Maybe I do...but enough about virgins and phobias. Let's take the subway down to Times Square and let me show you the unique sights of midtown Manhattan."

"That's a great idea. I haven't been able to visit most of the midtown area yet. I want to see Broadway's dazzling lights, the theater district..."

"You shall see that and much, much more...the brightly lit marquees of the 42nd Street row of theaters showing more than twenty films at any one time, the art deco buildings of Rockefeller Center...perhaps we'll see the spectacular show at Radio City

Music Hall, or visit the observation deck of the tallest building there."

※

The tour of midtown could not have been more awe inspiring and utterly satisfying. Furthermore, the two friends agreed that one of the more satisfying of the evening's pleasures was the great American snack they had at the corner of Broadway and 42nd Street—a couple of grilled, dark red hot dogs—plump and bursting with flavorful juices, accompanied by a cold glass of smooth, draft lager.

Instead of taking the IRT Broadway local to 116th Street at the 42nd Street entrance, they decided to walk to the 50th Street station for another close encounter with the lights and sounds of the broad boulevard. At the corner of 48th street, while waiting for the green light, a young, very petite woman, with the "lost generation" expression and the overall appearance of a sixties "flower child," approached the two friends.

"You mind if I tag along with you guys? I'm visiting the city, I'm all alone and I have no place to stay tonight…a couch, a room corner, any free space would be just groovy."

"Where are you from, and how old are you?" asked Nicolas.

"I'm Linda, and I'm old enough. I'm over 21, and I come from Ohio where I attended college for…"

Lakis interrupted, "I bet that this is not your first night in the city…I can tell from the way you approached us to…"

"The last few days, I had no problem finding a place to stay. Last night it was this nice older man, the night before three college buddies let me crash at their fraternity house…"

"We get the point Linda…this is Lakis and I'm Nick…you are welcome to crash at my apartment, but I have to let you know that I have no heat, even though you may not need it tonight, and no luxuries…you have a choice between a wash from a bucket of warm water or a cold shower…are you still interested?"

She was. When they arrived at the apartment, around eleven, they showed her to Terry's room since he was away visiting relatives in upstate New York for a few days. She said she was tired and wanted to go to bed right away. She closed herself in the tiny room.

Nick and Lakis had a lot to say to each other, about old times and new times, as they sat at the kitchen table sipping tea. At about ten minutes before midnight, they were joined by Alecos, back from his late restaurant shift.

"Do not be surprised if you see a young woman moving around our apartment tonight or, more probably, tomorrow. Her name is Linda and she is sleeping in Terry's room…she appears to be a free spirit and…"

Nick was interrupted by a loud call of his name. It was Linda's voice. He hardly had time to respond before Linda appeared at the kitchen entrance. One quick look at her, and all three young men were essentially petrified with astonishment. She was standing there stark naked.

"I feel lonely and neglected. Nick, I have a feeling you may want to join me in my room," she said with a very serious, matter-of-fact expression on her face.

He was at a loss of words for several long seconds. It was very uncharacteristic of the talkative and articulate young man.

"Nothing personal, but I'm unable to join you…I'm engaged."

She immediately extended the invitation to the others. "Anyone will do," she said in a non-discriminating tone and walked away towards her room.

After a short discussion among them, Alecos agreed to go first and "check the waters." He came back in about twenty minutes, apparently exhausted, with Linda following right behind him, still undressed and full of energy.

"Next," she said as if she was calling the next patient in a physician's waiting room. "Don't take too long now, there's plenty to do tonight," she added as she walked away.

Lakis went next. When he returned, she came along and repeated her demand for the next "lover."

"She is asking for the next victim to enter her lair," said Nicolas, still insisting that he was unable to oblige her. At the same time, he was vividly feeling a growing excitement in his body, the notion that he was about to experience what his roommate described as "the exciting lay."

After about five minutes of waiting, she returned to the kitchen with an angry look on her face. "I'm going over to that window, open it and shout 'rape, help me, rape,' unless somebody comes to me, in exactly ten seconds." She started to count backwards from ten but Nick was still playing hard to get. Alecos saved the day, he went for seconds.

Eventually all three men, including Nicolas, went at least twice each. Furthermore, Nicolas called a couple of fraternity houses for reinforcements.

It was after five in the morning when Linda took a break for toast and coffee and then declared she needed some sleep. The two roommates and their guest Lakis expressed a sigh of relief. Peace and quiet reigned in apartment 6B once again. During a period of five hours, Linda was able to suck out the virile energy of the three young men plus that of another eleven Ivy Leaguers recruited from two different fraternity houses.

It was well after lunchtime when the three young men began drifting into the kitchen. There was much concern, perhaps even fear, especially on the faces of the two roommates who felt they had to take responsibility for the behavior as well as the welfare of Linda, an invited guest sleeping in their apartment.

There was also considerable debate among the three as to how to handle her after she woke up and, more importantly, as to how to get rid of her. They decided to take a peek into her room, all three at the same time. After a quick glance inside the room, their three faces lit up with considerable joy. The young nymphomaniac was gone.

Nicolas' mental trip back to the memory lanes of the last couple of semesters ended rather abruptly as the curtain closed on the strange saga of Linda. He was back to the reality of having to spend a lonely Memorial Day holiday in his new apartment.

He thought of his roommate Alecos who loved to relive his "incredible adventure" with Linda and enjoyed telling her story to anyone who would listen.

For Nick, the Linda story represented another one of those shameful incidents which brought him feelings of betrayal and guilt and contributed to his inevitable alienation and separation from his fiancée.

What really contributed to the failure of my engagement? I admit I entered into it with one foot outside the gate, ready to exit...on the other hand, I may have stayed and gone all the way to the altar if I was strong enough not to allow those shameful incidents to take place...first came the one-night stand with Christalla and then the all-night orgy with Linda. But the straw that broke the camel's back was Catherine.

As soon as Catherine came to mind, that terrible incident, that fateful encounter between her and his fiancée came along and demanded attention. It all started with an unusual phone call on campus. Nicolas had access to a phone in the clay analysis lab, but hardly ever received outside calls.

"Bonjour Nicola, *c'est moi*..."

The voice, the accent, the French, all pointed to the tall and lean Dutch beauty named Catherine.

"Catherine, it's great hearing from you...*mon Dieu*. It's been over nine months since we spoke."

"*Oui, oui, c'est vrais*...I came back from Florida sometime ago. After I met you at Michelle's party last fall, I got back with my boyfriend and moved to Florida...I broke up again with him, this time for good...I moved back with Joanna. We share our old Brooklyn apartment again and we both work at the same hospital.

I'm coming to Manhattan this afternoon with a friend who is meeting her husband near the Columbia campus. I would like to visit with you if you care to see me. We can stay on campus if you like."

It was all arranged very quickly. She was to pick him up at the lab around four.

I can't believe she finally called me back after I left two messages with her roommate several months ago...it feels as if I met her only yesterday. It was at that dull party in Brooklyn, I was getting bored and looking for an excuse to exit when she walked in. Before long, she and I became inseparable...we talked mostly about Europe and the French cinema...we promised to see each other again...it never happened.

The idea of spending an afternoon, perhaps even an evening with Mademoiselle Catherine enthralled him. He felt his excitement growing by the minute. At first he didn't even think of his fiancée. But then he realized it was Friday and they had their usual weekly date. He waited till mid-afternoon, around three, and called her home.

"Good afternoon, Mrs. Pentaris, it's Nicolas."

"Good afternoon my son, everything fine with you? You know my Maro is not home until four..."

"Yes, Mrs. Pentaris, I know Maro's schedule. I just want to leave a message for her with you, if you don't mind...it's kind of an emergency...as you probably know, we have a date this evening. I'm to meet her in the city, at the Pantheon Restaurant, at seven-thirty. Unfortunately, I came down with something this morning and it's still with me...I have stomach cramps and a headache and, in general, do not feel well at all...I have no choice but to cancel our date..."

"I understand, my son. I will tell Maro...I will give her the message. Please take good care of yourself."

Nicolas was not surprised at all by the change in Mrs. Pentaris' tone of voice when she realized that her daughter's date was cancelled. She sounded more upbeat and relieved. *Her little girl's virtue was saved once again.*

"Goodbye, Mrs. Pentaris, and please tell Maro that I'm going to bed right away. She doesn't have to call me till tomorrow."

⁂

Catherine arrived on time.

She looks ravishingly French...simple but elegant dark blue skirt ending a few inches above the knees...beautifully coordinating yellow knee socks and yellow sweater and, thank God, flat loafers...high heels would have been a disaster.

"How was your extended Florida vacation?"

"At first it was like a dream of a honeymoon but soon enough we were back at each other's throats again...mainly because he wouldn't get a divorce as promised. He is back with his wife now...I hope he is happy. Right now I enjoy my life and freedom once again...how about you? Are you in a serious relationship at this time?"

He answered the question with, "I enjoy my life and freedom too."

Understandably, she interpreted his statement as a negative answer to her question. Nicolas gave her the usual tour of his Department's Schermerhorn facilities and his lab equipment. He was very proud and pleased, indeed, to see how well she was impressed. Like the first time they met, they seemed to enjoy each other's company immensely. Dinner and dessert and coffee at the school cafeteria was followed by more coffee and a couple of cigarettes at Choc-Full-O'-Nuts. Finally, around seven, a visit to his apartment.

She was definitely not impressed with the apartment and said so. She even made several sarcastic comments about "the beautiful antique furniture." But her last comment on the dwelling facilities was very encouraging:

"This kind of living is fine for students with a future...it's only temporary..."

She appeared happy to oblige when Nicolas invited her to sit next to him on the cot. She appeared even happier when he made a move for a quick kiss on the lips. She reciprocated with her own move for a more passionate kiss. After a couple more of such kisses, his hands went to work searching for hidden delights under her clothing. She offered no objection. In fact, she did something similar with her hands which seemed to dwell on caressing his spine.

She was also the first to begin removing clothing. She motioned to be allowed to stand up and then proceeded to remove her skirt which she folded slowly and placed on a chair. She looked absolutely stunning in her long and beautifully proportioned tanned legs. The yellow knee socks and white, lacey panties provided an incredibly fascinating contrast. She then proceeded to take off her sweater, but not her bra. When she joined him again back at the cot, his first move was to try and remove her bra. She appeared to object by crossing her arms around her chest.

I can understand her concern, she is entirely flat-chested...of course that doesn't bother me at all...I am not too much of a mammary glands person...her long, lean legs and her cute, petite ass are much more sexually attractive to me...the way her bikini panties cut into her round little cheeks is most enticing...

Before long, he had her lie flat on her belly while gently massaging her back side. His favorite spot was around the buns, occasionally slipping a finger or two under the soft panty edges and the waist band. When he finally managed to pull off her panties, the doorbell rang. They decided to ignore it but the ringing continued more aggressively.

"I have the feeling it's probably one of my roommates, probably Terry. It happened before. He forgets his key and comes home at all hours and rings the bell without any hesitation. I hate to move from this spot right now but I better go and let him in...he will never give up."

He put on his cotton briefs but could not completely hide

his point of arousal. However, his main concern was how to get back to the cot as soon as possible, hopefully before things cooled down too much. His point of arousal disappeared instantly and simultaneously with the opening of the door.

"Surprise, surprise...agapi mou..." she kept saying as she continued to kiss and hug her totally petrified fiancé. He remained motionless for a long moment or until she began pushing him towards his room saying,

"I'm sorry I made you come out of bed, Nicolaki, but I'm putting you right back and I'll take good care of you...you don't look sick, you look concerned or frightened. Don't worry, today you can have anything you want..."

It was Maro's turn to become totally petrified as she entered the room and faced the unexpected horror of finding another woman in the bed of her trustworthy fiancé. Catherine stood up, similarly surprised and utterly disgusted. The perfectly contrasting picture of two young beauties—one brunette and the other a dirty-blonde, one beautifully dressed in a light blue, spring-like dress adorned with little pink flowers and the other practically stark naked, one a picture of disappointment and the other one of disgust—could not have escaped the observing eyes of an artist.

The two women never showed anger or animosity towards each other. They knew they had a common enemy. While Catherine was getting dressed, they became acquainted with each other. They did not say it in so many words, but they both appeared to be aware of the fact that they were victims of the selfish, male ego; victims of the uncontrollable male lust.

As he sat in a corner of the room feeling miserable and cheap, Nicolas did not get any attention from either one of the two beauties, except an occasional look of disappointment or disgust.

When ready, Maro and Catherine, each in her own way looking calm and spectacular, walked out of the room without giving Nick the benefit of a last look of any kind. He watched them walk side by side through the corridor, very much like a fox eyeing grapes just out of reach, until the apartment door closed behind them. He never expected to see or speak to either one of them ever again.

Chapter Nine

At the beginning of his third academic year in graduate school, Nicolas made up his mind he would go for the highest degree instead of just completing the work needed for a masters. By the end of the fall semester, he would have completed all course requirements for the Ph.D. degree. Of course he would still have to pass the Oral Comprehensive Exam, popularly referred to by students as "the Orals," as well as complete and defend his Ph.D. thesis, a research dissertation that required at least several points of original contribution to his chosen area of concentration.

The fall semester of his third year was also to be his last as a teaching assistant. He was already scheduled to become a research assistant beginning with the spring semester. As an RA, he would work full-time on his dissertation research, but he had mixed feelings about the change. He enjoyed teaching immensely and had evidence, through classroom evaluations of his teaching effectiveness, that his students similarly enjoyed having him as their instructor.

The fall semester moved with the pace of a running gazelle primarily because Nicolas was able to concentrate on his final course requirements without too many social interruptions. He was definitely happy with his new living arrangements, sharing an apartment with his friend Alecos, but he missed life's dessert—the personal exhilaration of being involved in an ongoing and exciting romantic relationship.

Towards the end of the semester, about a week before Christmas, he telephoned his mother in Cyprus for the first time since he came to America. The village of Ora had finally installed a public telephone on Main Street, the first in the village.

"Kyriaki's son is calling from America," shouted Pavlos, the coffee shop owner. "Taki, go get the widow Kyriaki, tell her to come down the hill, her son is waiting to talk to her on the telephone."

Uncharacteristically, Mrs. Kyriaki was surprisingly soft spoken on the phone and couldn't hide her emotion and tears for actually being able to talk to her son for the first time in two and a half years.

"This telephone is truly God's miracle. I can talk to you and hear you clearly even though you are at the far edge of the earth."

"I'm happy to hear your voice too, mother. But please tell me if you are happy, if everything is alright with you, and if everything is fine with our Nina and all our family."

"Oh, we are all doing very well, my son. You keep sending Nina and me all that money, how could we ever complain...we got 36 pounds for the hundred dollars you send us last time...and almost every month before that...and even more for Christmas and Easter and St. Marina's day. I hope that you have enough left over for your needs, my son, and I pray to God that He gives you everything back double and triple."

"Don't worry mother, I have plenty left over for all my needs. In fact, next semester I expect to be able to send you much more since I will be part of a research team with a grant that pays very well and the income is not even taxable."

"From your mouth to God's ears, my son...in any case, I do have one good piece of news for your ears, my Nicolaki. I managed to put down money, near half of the asking price, towards the purchase of a decent house for our family in the village. Our old "palace" has deteriorated beyond repair and I'm now using it as a chicken coop. I'm sure you remember the nice Tomazos house just off the main street, near the school. The old man died three years ago, may God bless his soul, and his sister sold us the house for 900 pounds."

"Mother, how can you do that? I'm sending you a few dollars whenever I can for a better living for you and Nina, for buying necessities, not for buying a house at this time."

"My son, this new house is primarily for your sister's security. Before long, I have to go to my Maker. What will then become of our disadvantaged Nina? She needs the house because we may be able to attract somebody who may want to marry her…it's the only dowry we can offer…she needs somebody after I'm gone…you are actually doing a good thing for your sister…and don't worry about our everyday necessities…do you think I'm sitting around counting my blessings? I can still put in a good day's work out in the fields."

"O.K. mother, I can understand your concern about our Nina. I will slowly send you the rest of the money for the new house…I can definitely promise you that. And I will try to send a little bit more than I planned because I don't want you to work that hard out in the fields. Mother, you may think you are still strong and tough, but please remember that you are 63 years old."

"One last thing, my son. You know I am not educated, I never attended any school, and most probably I cannot fully understand what you are trying to do in America."

"Don't concern yourself, mother, about the benefits of formal higher education. You probably know and understand more about life than many educated people do."

"You explained to me, son, when you came back a couple of years ago that you had graduated from one of the best universities in America. You also explained to me that there's much more education you can get for free because you work for the university.

But do you really need that much education to make a good living here at home?"

"It depends on what your goals are, mother."

"After your college diploma, you have been back in America for more than two years. How much more education do you need, my son? I need to have you back, to enjoy your company for a while before the Lord calls me to appear before Him."

"Mother, I did try to explain to you in a recent letter…didn't Nina read it to you? I explained that I committed myself for the highest degree, the highest diploma in education, because it can make me eligible for a top job in education. This means at least another two years in America. If you take care of yourself, you still have many more years to live…I'll continue to take care of you and Nina, mother, and I'm sure I'll even help the rest of our family when I get a permanent job."

"I'm so happy, my Nicolaki, because you are determined never to forget your family. Do whatever you think is best for you, my son, but please hurry back home. I hope that the Lord will keep me until I see you back home…we have several young and proper maidens in our village…I can help you choose the right one out of these beautiful girls…she will give you the respect and love you deserve, and will also respect and honor your family."

"I have to finish this call now, mother. My very best wishes and all my love for our whole family for Christmas and the new year."

The beginning of the spring semester brought considerable changes to Nicolas' lifestyle. His course work had already been completed and, with not having to take any more courses, it meant that he no longer needed to do his daily routine of spending most of his time studying in the library or at home, often till two or three in the morning.

In addition, he was no longer obligated to teach two or three laboratory sections every week. These and other changes provided what seemed like a tremendous amount of leisure time but it was part of a deliberate plan—more time freed up in order to concentrate on his dissertation research.

This wonderful country never ceases to amaze me. This system of allowing any student from any social or ethnic or racial background to apply for a competitive grant in order to do research for a degree is so incredibly American. In a way, a student is given the opportunity to earn a high degree and is getting paid very well in the process...the federal government does not even tax income from an R.A. that supports Ph.D. research.

Nicolas did work hard, as expected, and by the first week in March he submitted the first progress report on his thesis research project to his advisor. After Dr. Garnet read the report, he called in his student for a review of the data.

"This is very good, Nick. Keep up the good work." The professor would have liked to praise the work much more, especially the discussion and conclusions section which reinforced his opinion concerning the student's exceptional analytical capabilities, but past experience forced him to be cautious about using superlatives in evaluating students' progress reports.

"Thank you, sir. Your confidence in my work means a great deal to me and I appreciate your continued support very much." He stopped for a moment to swallow his saliva and wipe his eyes. "Professor Garnet, there is something else, call it a favor if you like, there is something else I decided I must ask of you, after arguing with myself continuously for the last couple of months whether I should or not."

"Sorry son, but this sounds familiar. I heard this preamble quite a few times before," interrupted the professor in an obviously cynical tone. "Usually this means that the student receives a great job offer and cannot afford to work fulltime on the thesis...after all, one can always come back and complete the work later on a part-time basis if I approve the application for a leave of absence."

"No, nothing like that, Dr. Garnet. I did not get a job offer and I do not want a leave of absence. I do want to continue to work towards a Ph.D. but I want a different research project. Specifically, I want to join your group of students who work on uranium mineralization, with the financial support of the Atomic Energy Commission."

"We may be able to accommodate you, work something out for you because your timing is perfect. As you know, Tom Davies decided to abandon his uranium geochemistry Ph.D. project in order to enter medical school. But I'm curious as to what brought about your request for the change."

"The uranium geochemistry research provides for many more practical applications, for better employment opportunities in the future. In addition, I was told that the Atomic Energy Commission grant allows for a more generous budget that provides more funds for student investigator support."

"I must agree that the uranium industry does provide good-paying jobs, especially in the area of mineral exploration and processing. But the clay industry is not far behind, as you probably know. So, it comes down to the point that the A.E.C. grant has a generous budget and a higher level of support for its student investigators...I have to assume, then, that your move to change research topic is simply powered by the desire for more money for the next couple of years."

Nicolas guessed that his move would probably be interpreted that way. He did not want his professor thinking that he was greedy. For the first time, he began to tell his advisor about his mother and helpless sister, their financial situation and their dependence on him alone for financial support.

He also mentioned the telephone conversation he had with his mother last December and pointed out how his mother's words have haunted him since then. He further explained that this relentless haunting was not simply because he realized he had to help pay for their new village home, but primarily because his mother pointed out, and rightly so, that he was spending too much time on education, perhaps for the glory of it, instead of getting a job in order to support himself and his needy family.

"What about all the work you put in and the data you obtained on your clay mineralogy project?" added the professor. "I suppose you can always put everything down in the form of a more formal report which we may submit for publication."

"No sir, that's not what I was hoping I can do. Again, this is another special request, another favor if you will...sir, I would like to write the formal report but not for publication...I would like to submit the report first as the partial requirement for a graduate degree, the thesis requirement for a masters degree."

"I don't see why not, if that's what you want, but I'm a bit puzzled. Why take time out to write a thesis for a masters when you were accepted into the graduate program as a Ph.D. candidate?"

"Sir, for a foreign student like me, the M.S. degree will serve as a kind of security. The Ph.D. is three years in the future...if something happens and I'm called back home to Cyprus, unable to return to complete the doctoral thesis, the intermediate degree will represent something tangible for my three-year effort in grad school."

Nicolas worked extremely hard for two months, literally day and night, in order to complete and submit the master's thesis by the deadline, for a June degree. However, before submitting it to the department and the university, his advisor had to review and approve the thesis first. The student expected to see lots of comments and recommended changes on his 58-page thesis but he received none before the deadline.

Dr. Garnet is a very busy man...obviously he didn't get to review my thesis...no matter, an October degree is as good as a June degree...I can wait a couple of more months...he did not hide the fact that he doesn't believe that I should take time out for a master's when I can work for a Ph.D....maybe he'll never approve it.

Approximately a week after the thesis submission deadline,

Nicolas received a letter from the Dean of the Faculties of Political Science, Philosophy and Pure Science, informing him that he satisfied all requirements for a Master of Arts degree. The student had the choice of attending graduation ceremonies or receiving his degree privately in person or by mail.

The young Greek Cypriot was obviously happy to receive a graduate degree even though he was expecting to become a Master of Science instead of a Master of Arts. Nevertheless, he was satisfied with the official explanation that M.S. is conferred by the applied fields such as Engineering whereas the M.A. is the domain of Pure Science and Philosophy.

Nicolas' thesis was eventually placed in the library of the Department of Geological Sciences. He checked it out with Maury, his co-researcher on clay mineralogy.

"Maury, it's obvious to me that Prof. Garnet did not read my thesis...nor did anyone else for that matter...look at it... not a single comment, not even a single suggested correction or change...it's exactly the way I submitted it to my advisor..."

"This doesn't surprise me at all. This is a pure science department in a major research university...they only accept top Ph.D. candidates and support them well. They do not believe in wasting time and money on intermediate degrees. I guess they couldn't refuse the request of a well qualified foreign student for a "security degree." It's good public relations, in this case international relations, to just hand you one without making too much fuss."

By mid-June, Nicolas moved into one of the "uranium laboratories" and occupied the desk and lab space vacated by the departure of Tom Davies. He had to share the lab space with Dan Mason, Dr. Garnet's post-doc from South Africa. It took several days before Nicolas found an opportunity to say more than just a hello to the South African.

"It's a pleasure to share this lab with you, Dr. Mason. I read you paper on the Rand Conglomerate gold and uranium mineralization in the *American Mineralogist*. Very impressive work."

"Thank you. It's my pleasure too to be here. Please call me Dan."

"I must tell you, this is an incredible coincidence meeting someone like you from South Africa. My thesis project is concerned with the nature of uranium mineralization in urano-organic deposits."

"Yes, I do recall hearing about that from Prof. Garnet."

"I'm supposed to analyze samples from major deposits representing uranium-organic matter associations from the Colorado Plateau area and, hopefully, from around the world. I would very much like to include the urano-organic material known as 'thucholite' from South Africa."

"I can easily arrange for some thucholite to be shipped here by contacting my geology department in South Africa. My wife is still a graduate student there."

The thought of making his sample group truly international by including one or two samples from South Africa, made Nicolas very happy indeed. He invited Dan Mason for lunch and took him to his favorite pizzeria. Later on, in the afternoon, he introduced his new South African friend to tea and cookies at the Graduate Student Lounge.

While the two scientists were sipping tea and discussing their uranium research, Nicolas's eye caught a glimpse of a statuesque young woman in a long colorful dress approaching their sofa from the left corner of the room. When she finally stopped in front of the sofa, she stared directly into Dan's blues, with a pleasant-surprise look and a smile on her face. The young Greek followed his friend's example and stood up immediately but not before he managed to whisper a wondrous, "wow !"

Dan made the introduction, "This is Anika Van-Aken. She is also from South Africa. We met at the South African Consulate last

January. This is the first time we meet on campus." After allowing time for handshaking, he added, "Are you still trying to enter the graduate program in sociology here at Columbia, Miss Van-Aken?"

"No, I was actually admitted to the program, starting this coming September, but I still have to make up some undergraduate deficiencies by taking a couple of courses at General Studies."

The introductory comments were short and quick. Anika was on her way to a late afternoon course. Nicolas was completely taken by her exotic look. He spoke to Dan seconds after she left.

"When I met you, I could see right away that you are most probably a descendant of British settlers. But I can't quite make out Anika's South African heritage. She has a European name, a Dutch name, but her overall physical appearance, her lean figure, her symmetrical facial features, her black curly hair, her gray eyes and, above all, her light, milk chocolate complexion suggest a mixture...but what specifically?"

"She is actually a member of over two million people of mixed race in my country, the so-called 'Coloureds,' who are mainly living in the Cape area of South Africa. They are descendants of the first Dutch settlers and the native population of the Cape, the Khoikhoi, or the Malays who were brought to South Africa as slaves from East India in the 18th century."

"What an unbelievable combination of elegance and beauty. In many ways she reminds me of Audrey Hepburn, the quintessential fair lady."

Dan Mason had the last word on the topic. "I don't think I would compare her to the famous film star. Audrey Hepburn has an obvious pure white complexion."

For the next few weeks, part of June and the whole month of July, Nicolas went back to the lounge on a daily basis, always hoping to see Anika once again. He had no luck. Dan Mason was no help either because he had no idea where his compatriot lived and never asked for her telephone number.

In the meantime, Nicolas worked hard on his research topic, as expected of him, but he also allowed a little extra time for things he loved to do but did not have much time to enjoy fully during the previous semesters. This time he was able to spend more time at the great city museums, or watch more movies, or visit more often with his friends. He loved the competitive excitement of playing poker with his friends for nickels and dimes.

During one such poker night, usually held at his friend Paul's apartment near the downtown NYU campus on Saturday nights, Nicolas had a winning streak and was up several dollars. At a few minutes after midnight, a fourth NYU man, a pre-med from Persia known for his playboy lifestyle, joined the group. He was accompanied by two gorgeous and well endowed women, both clad in pink, semi-transparent, crinkle cotton blouses and culottes.

Putting on airs of amour-propre befitting a conquering lover that even Casanova would envy, the Persian hunk Darius introduced his escorts:

"This is Doreen, also known as Celine, from Istanbul, the most popular belly dancer in New York and the love of my life — and this is her baby sister, Rhonda, still a high school student, but already an accomplished exotic performer herself."

Darius joined the poker game for about an hour, lost some money and then retired to the bedroom, behind closed doors, with his exotic dancer. The young Rhonda was invited to join the game but was reluctant to play for money. Paul suggested switching to "strip poker." Rhonda gladly accepted the challenge.

The four male players were totally surprised with Rhonda's performance. They didn't expect a young girl, a high school junior, to be a veritable poker connoisseur. They kept shedding their clothes while she remained fully dressed. When all three were down to their briefs, she stopped the game and called out to her sister telling her that she was ready to go. The response out of the bedroom was loud and clear,

"We're not ready yet, sis…keep yourself busy a little longer."

Rhonda addressed her male companions with a semi-serious disposition,

"This is getting boring…you guys look pitiful in your underwear." She laughed out loud before she continued, "Let's change the game a little bit. I want to start all over again, this time with only one opponent. We go all the way, but I choose the player."

She pretended to look over the players, trying to make a wise selection, but everybody was sure that her choice would be Paul, the friendly host of the evening with his handsome, consummate Greek lover looks. Her choice of Nicolas then shocked most of them, including Nicolas. Darius and Doreen, who just came out of the bedroom the moment Rhonda's choice was being announced, expressed their disbelief.

Paul's happy-go-lucky expression and smile never left him. Apparently he was not shocked at all by the choice but offered an explanation:

"Most women, apparently even teenagers, tend to go for the nice guy with brains."

"The rest is not so bad either," added Rhonda rather quickly.

After a few deals, the results qualified perfectly as déjà vu. Nicolas was down to his briefs again and she was fully dressed. She was going "for the kill" when the cards began to change. Eventually, Nick got practically even with her—she was down to her bra and panties. The next deal was expected to be quite revealing no matter who turned out to be the winner. The men moved their chairs around their hero, openly rooting and praying for a Nick win.

God in heaven must have heard and granted the men's request because she did lose the next deal. Without any obvious hesitation, and in spite of her older sister's objections, she slowly and methodically removed her bra. Her young, exposed breasts formed perfect symmetrical cones which pointed straight into the men's eyes, all overflowing with passionate delight.

The cards were being dealt for the final game. Rhonda exhibited her usual poker face, but her sister's showed serious concern. The men, including the Persian lover, were loud and obvious as to their choice for a winner. Nicolas' mind was already well into the world of his fantasies, but his face appeared blank.

"Nick, you made a great comeback, you won fair and square, but don't expect me to remove my panties here, in front of all these hungry wolves…"

The older sister's face assumed its happy state once again but the men were projecting uncontrolled disappointment. However, with one exception, they made no specific complaints to the young belly dancer or to anyone else. The exception was Darius who bent over the poker table to directly face Rhonda as he spoke,

"Rhonda, dear, we all appreciate the fact that you are much younger than all of us. But somebody has to point out to you that you should not participate in adult games if you do not intend to abide by the rules."

"Age has nothing to do with my decision. I never said I will not abide by the rules. The winner can have his prize, but not in front of all of you guys who did not participate in the game…I will call Nick from the bedroom as soon as I am ready. The prize is for his eyes only."

Nick, the winner, spent over twenty minutes with Rhonda, the loser, behind locked doors. The people in the living room heard a few giggles but none of the other usual sounds and noises of an active bedroom. He emerged first, greeted his friends, but said nothing about his bedroom adventure. He didn't have to. The revealing expression of ecstasy, frozen on his face, and his glowing, wandering eyes personified perfectly the man who had just lived through one of his most exotic fantasies.

After the belly dancer affair, it took Nicolas days before he could settle back into the routine of his research without being preoccupied with sexual fantasies. Right at that time, he also discovered that Tom Davies, the student who began the urano-organic project before he quit for medical school, did not obtain field occurrence information on La Bajada, New Mexico, one of the key urano-organic deposits in the study.

Dr. Garnet advised Nicolas to personally visit La Bajada as soon as possible in order to do a geologic map of the ore deposit and obtain good representative samples. It was also agreed that Nick should do a quick field inspection of other occurrences in New Mexico (the Gallup hogback area and the Ambrosia Lake area near Grants) and in neighboring Utah (the Temple Mountain area deposits).

The professor's secretary did all the travel arrangements. Two days later, by mid-morning of Thursday, Nick was checking into the Holiday Inn on the outskirts of Albuquerque. After an early lunch he was on his way to check the location of the study area in a rented Travelall station wagon. He traveled about 45 miles northeast of the city, mostly parallel to the Rio Grande channel, to reach La Bajada. Before returning to the motel in late afternoon, he traveled another 20 miles northeast from La Bajada along the Santa Fe Creek in order to pay a quick visit to the colorful, historic town of Santa Fe.

Nick had scheduled four days for the La Bajada ore deposit, but he was ready to spend more time there if necessary. By the third day, he had established a daily schedule. First, at dawn he would have breakfast at the motel restaurant. Sweet-pickled Kadota figs were a must, plus either cereal or eggs and fries. Then he would pick up a sandwich for lunch and proceed to fill several containers with water and make it to the uranium ore deposit by eight thirty. By four thirty in the afternoon, he was back at the motel. Two to three hours at the motel swimming pool made the best part of a hot and exhausting day. He found that he always looked forward to dinner, usually at around seven. A couple of relaxing after-dinner cigarettes at the pool and then back to work in his motel room. He would study his field notes, write down his observations concerning the nature or origin of the deposit, and enter data on his base map till eleven. His sound sleep was interrupted only by the alarm at six.

On his second afternoon at the motel, Nicolas could not help but notice an incredibly attractive and voluptuous young woman, probably in her early twenties, reading a book at the pool side.

She stood out like a cardinal among several sparrows, a dozen or so other people making use of the swimming facility. A wide-rim straw hat covered most of her light brown hair except her neat pony tail. After a long, hot day in the desert, she was truly a welcome apparition, a sight to behold in her red, snug-fitting one-piece swimsuit.

The next time he saw the woman was on Saturday afternoon. She was in the same outfit as the day before, but this time she was not preoccupied with a book. She appeared totally consumed by the charms of a good-looking man, at most a couple of years older than she, in white shorts, pink polo shirt and sneakers.

At one point the man stood up while she remained seated and continued his mostly one-sided conversation, this time appearing more animated and perhaps even slightly agitated. Finally, he placed a quick kiss on her lips and left her there, face bent and hidden under the brim of her hat. She remained like that, seemingly depressed, for several minutes. Nick rationalized that it was his duty, as a good Samaritan, to cheer her up.

"I hope I'm not intruding, Miss...my name is Nick. I come from New York City...you have probably seen me around here the last couple of days. They say that a tall, cool drink does wonders for one's mood in a climate like this...I would like to invite you to join me for one, as my guest."

"Thank you very much...a cool drink sounds good," she responded with a smile, extending her arm for a handshake. "My name is Peggy, I come from Chicago. I just need ten minutes to change."

Ten minutes later: *She is definitely sexy in her casual, provocative sundress.*

Both seemed to enjoy the cool flavor of their Pina Coladas. Nicolas was talkative as usual, mostly lecturing on the regional food and culture. Peggy held back, listening politely but scarcely commenting, as if unable to make up her mind whether she should really be there or not. Her posture changed abruptly, however, after he explained who he was and what he was doing in the area. Her face was livened with a broad, lasting smile and her dark brown, almond eyes betrayed her pleasant surprise.

"This is an amazing coincidence. Part of my heritage is Greek—my father is a first generation Greek American. His parents emigrated from Northern Greece, the town of Thessaloniki." With that, she threw into the conversation several Greek phrases representing greetings and good wishes. Nicolas, too, was pleasantly surprised and amused.

"What about your mother's ethnic origin?"

"Her grandparents emigrated from Germany, the city of Hannover, in the early 1880's."

Peggy and Nicolas had more than one drink. Around six-thirty, they simply moved over from the bar into the dining room. They both paid very little attention to the food but savored each other's company with considerable fascination and delight. Neither mentioned anything at all about the young man who accompanied Peggy at the pool earlier that day.

After a couple of Marlboros by the poolside, they both went directly to their rooms around nine. It was unusually early for a Saturday night, but Nick had to work on the data he obtained earlier that day and needed to go to bed early in order to be ready for another field day the next day. "When working out in the field, geologists treat all days, including Saturdays and Sundays, as work days," he explained.

On Sunday afternoon, Nicolas was back at the pool an hour earlier than usual. He couldn't hide his disappointment that Peggy was nowhere to be seen. When she showed up a couple of hours later, she was wearing a light blue sundress and white leather sandals. She did not wear any hat. Instead of a pony tail, she had let her silky hair fall straight down below her shoulders.

Peggy was indeed a vision of beauty and sensuality, but Nick was quickly disappointed when he recognized her friend, her companion from the pool the day before, walking not too far behind her. This time he was wearing beige linen pants, a navy polo shirt and deck sneakers that matched his pants. His light brown hair covered the back of his neck as well as his forehead and he carried a small leather suitcase.

I can't compete with this guy...he looks like the perfect specimen of a male model. The couple stood motionless for a while, staring at the pool. They hardly exchanged any words. When they turned to face each other, they simultaneously extended their arms for a hug. He was the first to break the embrace. He landed a quick kiss on her lips, picked up his suitcase and turned towards the front entrance of the motel. Nick waited a couple of minutes before he approached Peggy. He was determined to get some information concerning her relationship with that man.

"I want very much to spend some time with you today, Peggy. Assuming you want to do the same, would you mind shedding some light on your relationship with that good-looking man that just left you? I feel a little bit uneasy about..."

"It was his decision to end our romantic relationship," she interrupted. "I can't tell you more about it now...maybe later, in a more private setting. I don't feel like a big sit-down dinner today, how about using room service?"

"That's fine with me. We can go to my room."

"No, let's use mine, if you don't mind...would you go for a pizza and beer?"

After consuming most of a large plain-cheese pie, they sat side by side on the twin bed closest to the window that provided a view of the motel courtyard and the swimming pool. They had at least a foot of separation space between them. Neither one said anything of significance until they put out their first after-dinner cigarette and opened their second can of beer.

"Dan and I met in college and have been happily dating, on a steady basis, for almost two years. During the last few months, however, I began to notice an obvious loss of interest, on his part, in our relationship. When he suggested flying down here 'for a taste of the Southwest desert sun,' I jumped at the opportunity of perhaps rejuvenating our romance."

"Just curious, why Albuquerque? Why not a more romantic Caribbean spot?"

"During the flight, I pressed the same question as to why he specifically chose Albuquerque. Eventually he admitted there was another reason for coming here besides the desert sun. He was determined to check out an old friend who moved here a couple of years after high school…"

"I can see it now. An old high school sweetheart."

"That's exactly what I thought, at first, and I started to panic. I calmed down immediately when he added that his friend's name is Richard. The visit made sense, especially after he revealed the fact that the two friends had kept in touch with letters and phone calls. One thing bothered me though…he had never mentioned the friendship to me before."

"Now, I give up, I can't imagine the reason for leaving you after visiting with Richard the last few days. By the way, did he introduce you to his friend?"

"I've been here since Friday, early afternoon. That's the only day he spent more than an hour with me…it was wonderful…he was very passionate…after so many passionless weeks in Chicago, we made love that afternoon. He said he would bring Richard over to meet me later in the evening, but he never did. In fact he didn't return to the motel until the next day. Today he simply came over to pay for the motel. I'm leaving alone for Chicago tomorrow afternoon."

"I think I finally get it...it's a homosexual relationship, right?"

"I suspected something like that on Saturday afternoon, a couple of hours before you approached me at the pool to invite me for a drink. I must have looked awful sitting there all alone. I hope you didn't invite me because you felt sorry for me after you saw my boyfriend leave me..."

"Far from it. You looked absolutely gorgeous to me. I was actually afraid you may reject my invitation...but, please, continue. What specifically made you think of him as a possible homosexual?"

"Dan seemed quite uneasy telling me that he couldn't spend Saturday evening with me, probably feeling bad for abandoning me the night before. He kept repeating that he had to spend time alone with Richard. When I pushed hard for an explanation, in tears, he claimed he couldn't explain the reason just yet."

"Did he or did he not admit, in so many words, his decision to abandon you for a homosexual relationship?"

"That's what he revealed to me this afternoon. His face was blank, expressionless...his voice betrayed no apparent evidence of any guilt or regrets as he told me that he had made up his mind to share his life with Richard...he then added that he had been 'in love with Richard, in love for a long time.'" Repeating Dan's last, cruel phrase was too much for her to bear—she covered her face with her hands and began to sob out loud.

Nicolas moved closer and put his arms around her. She placed her head on his shoulder and continued to cry. He began pushing his fingers through her silky hair. Slowly but surely she moved until she was seated on his lap, with her upper torso leaning against his chest and her face resting on his, cheek to cheek. After a while, his neck, wet from her tears, and her weight forced him to signal for relief with his arms. They both stood up.

"I think I better go," he said softly, moving towards the door. "You probably need to be by yourself…you probably…"

"The worst thing that can happen to me now is to be by myself…please stay. I won't cry anymore…I want you to make love to me…I want to make sure that someone wants me…I assume that you want me, that you want to make love to me as much as I want to…"

"Making love was the first thing that entered my mind the moment I saw you."

"Great! Let's make love," she whispered close to his ear and then proceeded to undress. He did the same. For a few moments they stood still in their birthday suits, their eyes studying each other's body as if exposed to the panorama of a naked torso for the first time. She made the first move. She pushed him towards the bed. He placed himself lengthwise on the bed, on his back, facing the large mirror on the south wall. She bent over him, placing her weight on her knees and capturing his hips between them. She was in control.

"I enjoy lovemaking most when I initiate the moves," she informed her lover.

He did not mind the situation at all. The room was dimly lit, but his wide-open eyes were focusing in the direction of the mirror. With his head slightly raised, he was determined to visually capture her titillating stance, the whole intense sexual scene as it unfolded in front of his eyes. Like most, he wanted to have as many of his senses as possible participating in the act of lovemaking.

It was not meant to be. She kept his head down as her lips met his and locked into an endless, turbulent kiss. His sense of vision lost out, but his sense of touch took over as his hands began their own expedition, purposely looking to discover every erogenous part of her soft body.

Peggy was uninhibited, totally giving and passionate, but Nick had a funny feeling about her total mental participation in the current affair. She appeared to be far away, perhaps involved in a scene where she was making love to her beloved Danny instead of her current lover. Nevertheless, Nick thought it was the most unique and incredible night of lovemaking he had ever experienced.

The next morning both lovers woke up late. For the first time, the meticulous and highly disciplined Cypriot student, failed to wake up on time and do his work, as per schedule. He spent the whole day with Peggy and even drove her to the airport.

As they said goodbye, they did not exchange promises to meet again. They never pretended there was anything between them except perhaps an accidental occurrence, an instance of great mutual passion. They both knew, without having to say it, that fate had brought them together for a short moment in life, a moment that would probably never be repeated again.

During the month of September, the first month of the fourth academic year in graduate school, the first true all-research academic year, Nicolas became convinced that he could finish his research earlier than he had thought. He established a new, more ambitious working schedule.

His working day, any day of the week, began around nine in the morning, after breakfast, and ended well after midnight. Two thirds of the time were spent on the analysis and testing of samples in the laboratory. The remaining third was spent on reading journal and other relevant articles as well as on evaluating analytic and field data and writing down ideas and conclusions.

There was always time in the schedule for lunch and dinner as well as an afternoon break for tea and cookies at the Graduate Student Lounge. Time for socializing was also allocated. Ever since his roommate moved out, he got married in early September and moved to Jersey City, the need to go out once in a while became a necessity.

Friday evening was designated "pizza and movie night." He enjoyed it immensely whether he was doing it alone or with a friend or two. Saturday evening was "Greek socializing time," the most exciting time of the week. It was usually dinner at a Greek restaurant followed by a card game or, occasionally, a party with his many friends living around the downtown NYU campus.

When the weather was pleasant, lunch took place on one of the many well-kept campus lawns. Besides a sandwich and a drink, the typical lunch break included some reading and sun bathing or simply watching students study or flirt or play.

At times students, usually undergraduates, had rallies on the campus grounds around lunch time. Nick made sure he sat close enough to listen to the speeches and, if interesting, extended his lunch period till the end of the rally. Most of these rallies protested the Vietnam War or something or other relating to university policy. The most interesting of these student groups was the SDS (Students for a Democratic Society). In its early stages, the organization typically demanded that the university do more for the surrounding community.

At one of the SDS noon-time rallies in early October, the main topic of protest was South Africa, specifically its adopted policy of apartheid which imposed strict racial segregation and discrimination practices against its native Black Africans and its mixed race peoples, referred to officially as "Coloured." The students demanded that the university administration and the United States government stop dealing or trading with the apartheid regime of South Africa. The protest rally reminded Nicolas of Anika, the beautiful mixed race South African he had met the previous June at the Graduate Student Lounge. Instinctively, he looked around the Sun-Dial area for her. He had the same lack of luck finding her at the rally as he had spotting her at the student lounge during the last few months. He was about to leave the rally and return to his lab, thinking that the protest speeches were becoming too repetitive, when the speaker announced,

"A citizen of South Africa, Miss Anika Van-Aken, who represents her apartheid government's official racial category known as the Coloured, will join us here in about five minutes. She is a graduate student here at Columbia and, as a foreign student, she is not going to criticize this university or the U.S. government. She will be here to answer your questions concerning life under apartheid."

Nicolas changed his mind about leaving the rally early. He was determined to see and hear the woman that occupied his mind on and off for several months after only a ten-minute encounter with her last June. He could sense the fact that his interest in gorgeous Anika was somewhat different, perhaps not as sexually oriented as usual when he met an attractive woman for the first time. But he couldn't quite explain his feelings, especially since he didn't really get to know this woman's character or personality to any reasonable extent.

The third question asked of Anika was by Nicolas. "Miss Van-Aken, would you please explain the difference between the terms 'Coloured' and 'Brown,' often used to describe various people in your country?"

"Thank you...Mr. Maos, right? We, the Coloureds of South Africa, are a mixed race people who primarily descend from the earliest European settlers and the indigenous Black peoples. The term 'browns' refers primarily to the Asians who descend from Indian workers brought to South Africa in the mid-19th century to work on the sugar estates."

A little bit later, Nicolas got another opportunity to ask an additional question. "You stated earlier that, as a teen-ager, you faced poverty and, in addition, discrimination from your own government in terms of education and other opportunities for improving your life. How then, did you, as an officially discriminated person of mixed race, manage to get a college education which proved good enough to qualify you for graduate admission to this institution?"

"We Coloureds, like the Browns, have a cultural heritage of our own, of which we are proud. We have our own community institutions, including our own schools of middle and higher education. The college I attended is believed to be as good as most of the government-supported institutions."

When the question and answer session was over, Nicolas had to wait for over half an hour to get close to Anika. Several students surrounded her, asking additional one-to-one questions on life in South Africa. She agreed without any apparent hesitation to meet Nicolas in the Avery Lounge for tea at four.

He arrived about ten minutes early in order to "reserve" a two-seater sofa. Anika arrived on time. They were both very much interested in learning more about each other's background and plans in life, but she could only stay for half an hour. As he escorted her on her way to a class in Hamilton Hall, several students approached the South African beauty on College Walk to comment on her rally participation and sometimes to ask additional questions.

"I think I became a campus celebrity," she said with a smile, assuming the posture a model during a photo shooting. "I didn't realize how many students attend these lunchtime protest rallies."

"No doubt, you are the new campus queen...please, your majesty, do try very hard to allow yourself to have tea with this commoner tomorrow afternoon. I'll definitely be there early... waiting to serve you."

"As I promised you earlier, my subject, I'll try to do my very best, but it will be tough for your queen to get out of the seminar before four thirty. Even royalty are required by the Sociology Department to write an analytical synopsis on the guest speaker's presentation. I'm sure you understand that I have to attend in order to do a good job of formulating a synopsis..."

"Yes, Anika, I do understand. Just in case I don't see you tomorrow, I do hope you will accept an invitation to spend Friday evening with me, the day after tomorrow. We can have a casual dinner on campus, perhaps pizza and beer, and then watch a superb film together, the great love story of *A Man and a Woman*, with Anouk Aimee, at the nearby Thalia. "

"I would love to do that...very much...but I don't know if I can manage it. I'll explain tomorrow. If I don't see you at tea, I will definitely call you in the evening." She extended her arm for a handshake, adding, "Thanks for your company at tea and for escorting me to my class."

He reciprocated with another handshake and a hand kiss, expressing his own appreciation for her royal company. As she walked away from him, gracefully climbing up the steps towards the hall entrance, he remained motionless watching her long legs and petite, round bum moving harmoniously under a tight, below-the knee skirt.

⁂

Anika did not make it to afternoon tea on Thursday and even failed to call later in the evening as promised. During work the next morning, Nicolas had Anika on his mind. He normally felt depressed whenever he thought he was being rejected by a woman but, in this case, he was also deeply concerned about his infatuation with her, the fact that he was paying too much attention to a woman he had just met and with whom he spent only a small part of one afternoon.

It must be her exotic look...I'm attracted to a woman who is beautiful but also quite different.

He had just about settled in his work routine by mid-afternoon when somebody knocked on his lab door. When he saw Anika standing in front of him, sporting a smile across her face, his first reaction was to pretend that he was neither surprised to see her there nor affected, in any way, by her presence. His second reaction, however—to smile back and joyfully hug a gorgeous woman who was there to specifically visit him—was the response that took total control of the situation.

"I'm so relieved to see you smile, Nick. I apologize I didn't keep my promise to call you yesterday…"

"That's alright, your majesty, a queen should have the prerogative to forget her promise…"

"Actually, I did not forget…I can explain the situation some other time. Right now, I want to talk about tonight, your invitation for dinner and the cinema…I'm terribly sorry to disappoint you once again…I cannot make it tonight but I…"

"Do not be sorry, my dear, because as it turns out now, I couldn't make it either," he interrupted, assuming a tone that reflected total disappointment. "I realized this morning I have to work till late tonight and be back very early in the morning tomorrow. Special experiments require my undivided and continuous attention for the next couple of days."

She detected the sudden change in his mood right away. She could see his overall disposition changing from jovial to sad, but she decided to pretend otherwise.

"You can't imagine how relieved I am…I was afraid you would be disappointed or even become angry with me for turning down your invitation. A moment ago, I was about to suggest to you that perhaps we could spend some time together this afternoon, perhaps the next three or four hours…but we can always do that some other time since you have experiments to take care of during the…"

"Actually, it's not a bad idea," he interrupted again, this time sounding much more upbeat. "I'll need to break for dinner anyway, and I also need to have a couple of hours of rest before I come back, preparing samples for analysis all night."

They agreed on early dinner at the Caravan. She definitely wanted to experience the food and atmosphere of the Greek diner-like restaurant that Nick had just described. They walked across campus and down Broadway side by side. About half a block from the restaurant, he finally found enough courage to hold her hand. She reciprocated by bringing her entire left arm closer to his right.

His Greek friends suggested a fish-fry special. Fish was not one of her favorite dishes, so she opted for a special cheeseburger—a thick homemade patty grilled with blue cheese and served on a hard roll. They also shared a Greek country salad.

Tony, the Greek waiter, brought the check to the table and bent over to ask Nick, in Greek, "This woman must be something special...I never saw you go out with a colored woman before...she is light-skinned and very good-looking...she must be a mixture... is she anything like a Linda type?"

Nicolas was visibly angry but tried to control himself and hide his anger with a fake smile as he responded in Greek, "I guess you heard about 'nympho Linda.' Nothing like that here. This is a special lady, a graduate student from South Africa. Yes, she is a mixture, but I'm proud to be with her and I'm crazy about her... you can tell the others about my feelings...I'm sure they're curious, like you."

"Did that Greek man talk about me? I could tell by the tone of his voice and by the way he kept looking at me as he talked to you that he was probably asking you if I sleep with you, right?"

"Yes, you are absolutely right, you've got this man's number... he was asking me if we sleep together and, when I nodded positively, he then asked me if you are as good in bed as they say you are, explaining to me that he was referring to the reputation of black or mixed race women. Of course I indicated that you are as good as they say you are."

"My God, I can't believe you said all that about me...I see now that you are laughing, so you must be joking about the whole conversation...I guess a bad question deserves a bad answer."

On their way back to his lab, he held her hand for most of the way. At the entrance to the campus on 116th street, he came a little closer to whisper in her ear, "I'm not joking at all about making love to you, I'm now taking you to my room...we enter Amsterdam Avenue at the end of the College Walk and then go four short blocks uptown...my building is at the corner of 120th Street..."

"You know, that's a great idea. I would love to see your apartment," she responded seriously. Nick was totally surprised and at the same time encouraged to ask,

" I can't disappoint my Greek friends who think I'm sleeping with you, I have a reputation to uphold...and, according to them, you have a similar reputation too."

She turned to face him but said nothing at all. Her wily smile, the smile of a veritable temptress, said it all. He was very pleased indeed but, at the same time, felt a bit uneasy as thoughts did flash through his mind that perhaps she was teasing, but she entered the apartment with him without the slightest hesitation.

"Is your roommate here?" she said pointing to the closed bedroom door.

"No, Alecos is not here any more. It's incredible that you do remember my mentioning Alecos when I first met you, last June. He got married a couple of months later, in September, and moved to Jersey City with his bride. I now live alone. How about a drink or perhaps some Greek coffee? "

"The Greek coffee sounds good but we don't really have time for that."

Her words encouraged him. *I guess she wants to make out rather than spend time on something else.* He had no sofa in the living room, it had been Aleco's and he had taken it with him. He thought that any of the three small chairs would be inconvenient and uncomfortable for any kind of love-making. He suggested sitting on the bed, in the small bedroom and she readily accepted the invitation. The small bedroom was poorly lit and looked uninviting, especially since the bed appeared neglected and unmade. *Just once...just once I fail to make the bed and look what I get as a reward...a beautiful visitor.*

Without asking for approval, she proceeded to tidy things up. After she finished, she looked at her watch, assumed an air of disappointment and announced,

"I hate to use the phrase, 'I'm sorry,' once again but it's time for me to get going. It would take me at least half an hour before I get home, all the way down to Greenwich Village. I can't afford to be late."

He was badly shaken up, his pride taking a terrible beating, but he managed to keep an air of unconcerned calmness. "Whatever you say, of course, it's fine with me. After all, you did say you only had four hours...I'll walk you to the 116th Street subway entrance."

The walk to the subway appeared cozy, they were holding hands, but both remained essentially quiet. *I finally got myself involved with a real teaser,* he kept thinking. He broke the silence when they were about to exit the College Walk.

"I still do not quite understand why you cannot go out in the evening, any evening it seems...why the early curfew, for lack of a better word, especially since you are of age, a graduate student... why?"

"I already promised I will explain fully one day, one day soon I hope, but only if we continue to be fond of each other. I use 'if' since it's rather obvious to me that you are quite upset and disappointed with me. All I can tell you now is that I live with my father and younger sister and I have to be home before he comes home from work...I have to prepare dinner for them."

Her answer did not provide all the information he wanted but it did calm him down considerably and helped elevate his ego, especially since her earlier "strange" behavior could be attributed to her sense of family responsibility. It left him thinking she may not be a tease after all.

Between October and Christmas time, Nicolas and Anika saw each other a couple of dozen times. Whenever her course schedule and home responsibilities allowed, they met for lunch, usually for a cream cheese sandwich and coffee at Choc-Full-O'-Nuts, or for mid-afternoon tea in the Graduate Student Lounge.

On Fridays she was not available for an evening date, but was always willing to spend three or four hours with him in the afternoon hanging around the campus, mostly the tea lounge and the library and occasionally even his laboratory, but only if Dr. Mason was not expected to be there.

They never made plans to share time together on Sundays until they accidentally met one afternoon in early December at the Museum of Natural History. After that, a museum visit on a Sunday afternoon became one of the activities they most enjoyed sharing together.

The right moment for him to invite her to his apartment during those Friday and Sunday afternoons never seemed to materialize, even though he didn't lose hope and made sure he was always prepared by making his bed and tidying up his bedroom early in the morning.

Nicolas often hinted about a casual Saturday evening together, but she was not available until, to his great surprise, she introduced her new social schedule at tea the day before Thanksgiving.

"We can get together on Saturday, if you like. I'm available between four thirty in the afternoon and nine in the evening this Saturday and, hopefully, every Saturday from now on."

"This is good news. What brought about this major change?"

"I convinced my family, actually my father, that I need to do library work at that time. I also promised to clean up the apartment and cook for the whole weekend by four in the afternoon, before I leave for the library."

"That's terrific! We can spend more than four hours together... there are so many enjoyable things we can do together..."

"Actually, to make things look real, I must spend at least an hour or so in the library, take out a couple of books, write down some notes, just in case my father checks up on me...he is known to do just that..."

"How about your teenage sister? Can't she help with cleaning and cooking so that we can even meet for lunch once in a while?"

"My sister Marien, who is 14, is always willing to help but she is limited since she is paralyzed from the waist down...she moves around in a wheelchair most of the day."

"I'm terribly sorry to hear that. Does she attend school at all?"

"We've been trying to register her in a school for handicapped children ever since we arrived in this country almost a year ago. It looks like she can begin next January, but we must make arrangements for her transportation back and forth to school. She cannot ride the bus or the subway."

"Since you do not drive, I imagine your dad will have to drive her back and forth every day."

"Actually we contracted for special van transportation for the handicapped. Since my father works all day, it fell on me to accompany Marien on the bus until she becomes more independent, perhaps after a couple of weeks of experience."

"What does your father do?"

"He drives a delivery truck for a home appliance firm. He leaves the apartment at six in the morning and does not return until after eight at night on most work days. On Saturdays he comes home much earlier."

"I'm glad you finally told me something about your family, even though some of it makes for a very sad story. I told you quite a bit about my family, you always knew about my mother and handicapped sister. Tell me a little more about your sister and your father and especially about yourself. How did it come about that all three of you came to the States?"

The conversation went on for another ten minutes, with most of the talking done by Anika. When they parted, his mind was full of new and interesting information about her family, but he learned only a couple of new facts about Anika herself. As soon as he was back in his room, many of these new pieces of information kept buzzing in his head. He tried to connect them in the form of an organized tale:

Once upon a time, a South African man whose family heritage was designated as belonging to the official racial category of the Coloureds, fell in love with a South African woman whose racial category was officially designated as white. In the eyes of his government, he could not legally marry her, but he did so secretly. She died giving birth to their first child, a beautiful girl of light-chocolate complexion. Mr. Van-Aken named his little girl Anika.

When Anika was eleven her father was married again, this time to a woman of his own racial category who was already heavy with child. In a little over two months a little girl of dark chocolate complexion came into the world. She was named Marien. Seven years later mother and little daughter were in a bus accident that killed Mrs. Van-Aken and injured Marien, causing her to become paralyzed from the waist down.

Anika excelled in high school and managed to win a community scholarship to a college specifically created for the Coloureds. She graduated with a concentration in sociology at the age of 22 and went to work for the government's agency on social welfare. During a three-year tenure at the agency she was promoted twice.

However, soon after her second promotion, her father managed to obtain an immigrant visa for the United States and brought her and her sister to New York City about one year ago.

The tale affected Nicolas' sensitivity immensely, making him sympathize deeply with the Van-Aken family and their history of discrimination and bad luck. But after a few minutes of rehashing and analyzing the facts, a new concern, a new question popped up in his mind and took over his thoughts: *Why did Anika abandon a good job, where she apparently excelled, in order to follow her father and half sister to America? There must be more to her personal story that she is willing to share...perhaps she left things out inadvertently, or perhaps by design...probably the latter...I'll have to find out.*

☙

Spending Saturday late afternoons and evenings with Anika did not allow Nick much time to visit with his other friends. He couldn't meet them for the usual dinner at a Greek restaurant and only occasionally could he join them for a couple of hours of poker late at night. Before long, his Greek friends began to complain among themselves about "the incredible stranglehold this South African Coloured woman has on Nick."

On Christmas eve, Nicolas was alone in his apartment. He felt happy and content because he had telephoned his mother earlier that day and everything appeared to be just fine. Also, the anticipation of Christmas dinner at Anika's the next day added more happiness to his agenda, even though it also brought certain feelings of uneasiness. After all, he was scheduled to be introduced to her seemingly strict father.

As he sat on his comfortable armchair listening to Christmas carols, his mind went back and forth on his three-month relationship with Anika. He had no doubt that their relationship was different from any other he ever had. But was it simply platonic friendship or true love, finally? Then again, it might be a lonely man's infatuation with an exotic beauty disguised as love. He couldn't tell for sure. He didn't even think it was necessary, or even appropriate, for him to mention the relationship to his mother when he telephoned her earlier that day.

He was quite certain, however, that whenever he was with her, he felt deliriously happy and, whenever he was apart from her, he was euphoric with the anticipation of seeing her again. He was undoubtedly proud of the way she looked and the way she carried herself. He was thoroughly impressed with her articulation and began to appreciate her unique sense of humor.

For Nicolas, sex and sexuality were an important part of any real romantic relationship. He was very much attracted to her sexually and could hardly ignore her eye-popping hourglass figure. However, unlike his previous relationships, sex was not his main preoccupation every time they came together. He had opportunities to bring her to his apartment, but he never felt the pressure to rush it.

Christmas day with the Van-Aken family was a delightful experience for Nicolas. Anika and the wheel-chair-bound Marien greeted him at the door when he arrived around two in the afternoon with warm hugs and kisses. He handed each a present, a handkerchief embroidered with the famous Cyprus lace. He received a Merino wool sweater. More hugs and kisses before they showed him to the living room couch and offered him a glass of white wine from South Africa.

"This is good wine, Anika...a little sweet but fruity and pleasant."

"I'm so glad you like it...please enjoy your wine for a while. Marien and I still have a little more to do for dinner..." They started towards the kitchen, but Anika turned around to add, "dinner will be ready soon...my father should come out to say hello in a few minutes."

At first glance, as he approached, Mr. Van-Aken could not be more intimidating to his guest. He was a big, tough-looking man with a wrinkled, weather-beaten face and a full head of graying, curly hair. His intense, penetrating stare produced a deep frown down his forehead. His complexion, like his younger daughter, was dark but, unlike her, his facial features gave only a hint of his black heritage.

"Happy Christmas, young man—welcome to our home," he said, with a smile and a surprisingly soft voice as he extended his arm for a handshake. "I hope you enjoy our family Christmas celebration...we want you to feel at home."

Nicolas couldn't believe his senses as he witnessed the man's incredible transformation from a perceived intimidating brute to that of a man with the mildness of manner and overall disposition of a true gentleman. In addition, the man was dressed more like a fashion-wise executive rather than a redneck truck driver, sporting a herringbone gray jacket, neatly-pressed khaki pants and a white button-down shirt and red tie.

"Merry Christmas to you too, sir. I appreciate your warm welcome very much. Thank you for the invitation to celebrate the holiday with your family...please accept this Cyprus sherry, it's considered a good Mediterranean dessert wine. They say the queen of England drinks it all the time."

Both men laughed heartily and exchanged pleasantries for quite a while. Nicolas felt very comfortable with his surroundings, indeed as if at home. In a polite way Mr. Van-Aken was asking lots of questions, some of which centered around Nick's studies and future career. *I hope he doesn't think I'm in a serious relationship with his daughter. Perhaps he thinks I'm here to ask for her hand in marriage...I wonder what Anika told him about me.*

"At one point in my life, I did some work in geology...I worked in one of the gold mines in my old country," Mr. Van-Aken commented.

"In a way, my studies and some of the work you did in South Africa are related. I work on the origin of metallic ore deposits, including uranium ore from South Africa, and you helped mine gold ore there."

"I see your point, Nicolas, but I'm curious about one thing . . . did you ever go down into a deep mine?"

"Yes, I did visit several underground mines in the Colorado Plateau and other areas, and went down some deep shafts in the gold mines of the Porcupine District of Northern Ontario. But nothing as deep as some of the deepest gold mines in your mother country."

As soon as his host excused himself, Nicolas took the opportunity to visit the girls in the kitchen. Anika looked simply stunning in her red velvet Christmas dress which reached close to her ankles, exposing her flesh-colored tights and red loafers. Under the kitchen fluorescent light, her jet-black, shoulder-length hair reflected millions of silvery rays. It was kept in place with a coordinated and very becoming red ribbon. Her off-white apron, tight with a bow in the back, further emphasized her petite waist, completing the painting of a lovely maiden by the stove.

Her handicapped sister's smiling face and bright, dark brown eyes reflected happiness with no apparent sign of bitterness for her misfortune. In the kitchen she was more of a participant rather than an observer.

First he complemented the two sisters on their good looks and their very becoming outfits and then added,

"That roasting goose smells real good, young ladies. You both must be good cooks…by the way, I brought you a couple of unique Cypriot products for your festive dinner, if you care to include them. Halloumi cheese, which you can grill or fry and some smoked sausage."

"It sounds great, we'll be happy to include them, but you have to show us how to prepare them…better yet, you too can help prepare them…where did you find them?"

"I bought them in Astoria, the Greektown of Queens. I'm sure you remember my telling you that I go there with my friends for a Greek dinner once in a while. One of these days I will take all of you there for a taste of Greek food. Now that the goose is out of the oven, maybe I can use your broiler to prepare the Cypriot food."

As far as Nicolas was concerned, the dinner couldn't be more delicious and the company couldn't be more pleasant. He praised the work of the two cooks incessantly. In their turn, the three South Africans had nothing but praise for the Cypriot delicacies. Mr. Van-Aken used superlatives to describe the "unique culinary experience of tasting grilled halloumi cheese."

Nicolas never felt so much at home away from home. It appeared that all three of his hosts were competing for the privilege to please him. Anika served baklava for dessert and even prepared Greek demitasse coffee.

"Where did you learn to prepare Greek coffee?"

"My father bought the coffee at the Greek general store on 42nd Street, near 8th Avenue. He even bought the required brewing pot and the serving-cup set. He taught me all about making the demitasse this morning…"

Mr. Van-Aken took over to explain further. "We were close friends with a Greek family in Cape Town. A couple of times we were invited to their home for the traditional Easter dinner, a spit-roasted, whole baby lamb in their back yard. It was quite a sight and quite a party. My friend Yiannis, the head of the family, showed me how to prepare the coffee."

The Christmas dinner party lasted for close to three hours. Everybody helped with the cleaning of the table and the washing of the dishes before moving into the adjacent living room. Everyone looked forward to a taste of the Cypriot cream sherry. They were not disappointed. Two hours of merry conversation and laughter went by very quickly. Nick felt he should be on his way in order to allow the family some privacy on a special day.

Anika then suggested that perhaps Nick should stay for the night, describing her living room couch as a "comfortable convertible." To Nicolas' amazement, her father seconded the idea. The young man politely declined, but thanked his hosts for the opportunity to celebrate a most joyous Christmas.

Anika escorted him to the door. After a warm embrace and a quick kiss on the lips, she handed him a tiny gift box, explaining that it was a personal gift from her.

On the subway train on the way uptown he closed his eyes and let all kinds of thoughts about the Van-Akens occupy his mind for various periods of time:

Interesting family, these Van-Akens...not too different, really, from my family. At the right time, I could easily become a member of this family. Anika looked so lovely tonight...what a picture of an ideal wife—practical and accommodating and yet gorgeous and loving! But probably not ideal enough for me...I'm not ready of course, but I will also have to convince my mother...yes, my mother can be a major problem if I were to decide to make a commitment here...for her, the ideal wife should be any one of several proper maidens from the village of Ora...

He took a break from his thoughts to open Anika's present. It was a beautiful silver tie clip with a light-blue Columbia crown attached in the center. Accompanying it was a little card with a personal note wishing him success in his studies. It was signed,

With Lots of LOVE and Admiration.

Yours Always,

Anika

Nicolas became quite emotional. He found the whole idea of a personal gift, especially the personal note, very gratifying and moving. The combination of an exceptionally pleasant evening and a revealing note pushed his thoughts towards a new direction:

I must love this girl...I'm quite convinced now...how else can I explain this incredible feeling of joy as I think of her now?...or at any time?...the feeling of elation is present whenever I think of her...

But soon enough, his thoughts changed direction:

But I still need answers...is there a special reason for her coming to America? Leaving a good job, a career, to come here? I have a feeling that graduate school is only incidental...where do they get the funds for that gorgeous apartment in a relatively upscale area of the village? Who pays for her tuition? What is the source of funds? It can't be the wages of a truck driver...I must ask her, first thing, next time I see her.

Nicolas saw Anika a week later, on New Year's Eve. They attended his friend Agop's party and had a marvelous time. During the celebration, their kisses were more frequent, lasted longer and were certainly much more passionate than they had previously been.

They continued to see each other, as per their regular weekly routine, until the middle of April. Throughout that period, sexual intimacy eluded them, as if by design. At the same time, Nick never had the opportunity to ask any of the questions he always wanted to ask about her personal life. He decided to forgo all socializing for the rest of April to prepare for his "orals."

On the first Friday of May, the Good Friday of Greek Easter, Nicolas was scheduled to take his Oral Comprehensive Examination. All graduate students considered this exam to be the most dreaded and most critical event of their quest for the highest educational degree. They all knew that they only had one chance to pass this exam. A failure usually meant that the student's association with his graduate program would be ended.

Nick consulted with several students who had survived what they all referred to as "the oral inquisition." Just about every one of these students described the proceedings as "a two-to-three-hour torture during which a dozen or more professors try to show off by asking esoteric questions on any topic or sub-discipline in the broad area of geological sciences, whether the student is expected to be familiar with the topic or not."

Even though a student was not required to specifically study for such a general- background exam, it was recommended that one should at least review notes on all graduate courses taken. Nicolas did just that and, in addition, included his notes on all upper-level undergraduate courses.

Throughout his life, Nicolas had confidence in himself and his abilities when it came to academic performance. Even though he was quite concerned and exceedingly nervous, he still expected to come out a winner at the end of the oral exam.

The orals were scheduled to begin at one thirty that Friday afternoon, so he made plans to meet with Anika after the exam, at four-thirty, at the student lounge. She agreed to make an exception and stay with him longer that evening for "a celebration befitting the occasion."

In addition to his mineralogy/crystallography advisor, Prof. Garnet, eleven other professors representing geological sub-disciplines and the departments of chemistry and mining engineering participated in the orals.

After all participants were allocated enough time for "questions" and "more questions," and after they all, in turn, declared "no more questions," two hours and twenty minutes had passed. Nicolas was asked to step out of the room until called back. In easy, straightforward cases, the professors usually took about fifteen minutes for a "pass" vote. The advisor would then call the student back into the room to announce the happy results of the vote.

For Nicolas, the fifteen minutes of anxious waiting in the hallway felt like ages. But nobody came out to invite him back into the exam room. Another five minutes and then another ten, and Nicolas felt he was about to collapse. Several of his student associates started gathering in the hallway. They all had encouraging words for him but it didn't make any difference. His mind could only see pity in their eyes and the word "doomsday" was written across their foreheads.

Finally, after thirty minutes of absolute torture, his advisor came out to invite him back into the exam room. For a moment, they both stood side by side in front of the room, facing eleven pairs of eyes staring at them. The student must have gone into some kind of mental shock because he stood there expecting the worst without showing any emotion.

Prof. Garnet said something to his colleagues and then turned around to face his student. "Congratulations, Nicolas," he said calmly, extending his arm for a warm handshake. One by one, the rest of the exam committee passed by to congratulate the student. No word about the delay in their deliberations that almost killed the candidate.

Nick followed a few steps behind his advisor who appeared to be on his way back to his office. They did not exchange any more glances or words until Dr. Garnet asked his student to take a seat in front of his desk.

"Please give it to me straight, Dr. Garnet. Did the discussion include a recommendation to fail me?"

"No, not at all. Davison of geochronology asked a question about your background and lots of discussion followed about the

Troodos massif in Cyprus, its composition and age. Time went so fast, nobody realized how anxious you would be out there in the hallway waiting for the results. We all assumed you would know that you did an outstanding job. I can see now you were seriously concerned. I apologize...it was up to me, the chairman of the committee, to stop the discussion short and push for the formal vote within the expected time frame."

Nicolas left his advisor's office feeling much better about himself. But significant damage had already been done, with both his confidence and his pride having been devastated for a big part of an hour. On his way to his rendezvous with Anika, he felt ill and unable to control his stomach which felt as if tied up in knots. He no longer looked forward to meeting her. Both his body and mind were apparently rejecting food or any other kind of celebration.

Anika was waiting in front of Avery and ran over to Nicolas as soon as he exited Schermerhorn. He managed to display a sign of victory and a smile as she came closer. Their body contact was somewhat violent. She jumped on him, almost knocking him down on the brick pathway. Her words followed as soon as he regained his balance.

"Congratulations, Nicolas Maos! I'm very happy for you... I'm very proud of you! Shall we begin the celebration? Everything's on me today...I insist and my family insists too..."

"Thank you very much, you're a sweetheart...I appreciate your kind words and your generosity, my dear, but I'm afraid I'm going to disappoint you...I feel quite sick right now, mostly strong abdominal pain and nausea and general ill-feeling, perhaps an anticlimax response syndrome due to the exam stress...I need to lie down...can we postpone the celebration, perhaps until tomorrow? I know I'll feel better tomorrow."

She suspected a rough ride of some sort during the exam but did not say so.

"I can understand the stress of going through such a critical exam, such a career-defining exam…but I want to come with you… you are an essential part of my life now…please allow me to take care of you…"

He agreed. He just couldn't turn down such a considerate, loving offer.

As soon as they entered his apartment, he excused himself and dashed for the bathroom. He thought he was about to throw up, but it was a false alarm. He came out to tell Anika that he was going to lie down on his bed for a while, perhaps even take a nap, since he slept for only an hour or two the night before.

He was putting on his pajama bottom when Anika knocked and entered fast, way before he had a chance to respond. She began to help him get into his pajamas in spite of all kinds of animated protests on his part. He got under the covers fast. She bent down and kissed him first on the forehead and then on the lips. Before she retreated, she tucked him in tight, much like an infant.

"I'll be out there watching t.v. I'll be very quiet. But I'll be coming in to check on you every once in a while…please call me if you need anything, anything at all."

It took him a while, perhaps an hour or more before he fell asleep. It was a deep sleep because he could no longer sense her presence when she came in to check on him. Around midnight she decided to also retire herself but where? Nicolas did not have a sofa and she did not want to disturb him by joining him in bed. She looked around for extra blankets and sheets and pillows and created a rather cozy sleeping corner on the living room carpet.

He woke up first, around seven in the morning. He was surprised he felt as good as any Saturday morning. He was also very much surprised to see that Anika was asleep in his living room. He was tempted to go lie next to her, perhaps surprise her for gaining back his wellbeing, but he opted to get ready first. After a shave and a hot shower he even felt better than before. In fact, he felt unusually hot, perhaps because he was aware of the presence of a vulnerable beauty on the premises.

He sat down next to her. He was wearing a pair of blue briefs and matching t-shirt. He knelt and lifted up the edge of the blanket with the intention of getting under but what he saw caused him to freeze in mid-process. It was the vision of a spectacular body sculptured out of milk chocolate. White cotton and lace provided an exciting contrast in places. He stretched his activated body by her side.

The prolonged cooler ventilation forced her eyelids to open. She was indeed pleasantly surprised to see his happy face. She moved quickly and stood up beside him. Towering above him, her statuesque frame produced an even more intoxicating vision.

"Please excuse me, Nick, I have to use the bathroom," she said softly as she walked away. She took her clothes and handbag with her. Sadly, Nick got the message. He went back to the bedroom to dress up.

When she came out, fully dressed, he was already frying eggs and halloumi cheese for breakfast. He greeted her with a quick kiss on the mouth and labored to appear happy and jovial. She sensed his mood, but said nothing. She busied herself preparing tea and toast and setting up the table.

I can't believe she rejected me like that...a cold, total rejection.

They began breakfast with polite conversation. Towards the end, when they were just sipping tea with lemon, she totally transformed the mood at the table by saying,

"Nick, I can no longer see you like that...I can see you are upset...I do owe you an explanation for my earlier behavior when I sort of brushed you off. It so happens I couldn't help it... I'm in the middle of my period, always very heavy bleeding...it would have been very uncomfortable for me, and perhaps so for you, to let you make love to me. I want us to have an ideal situation when we first make love."

He was instantly transported to the highest elevations of self confidence. They said very little after that. Instead, they sealed their understanding of the circumstances with several kisses. Finally, they agreed to go for a walk on campus.

Holding hands, the two lovers traversed many of the campus promenades as if programmed to walk in slow motion. The brilliance of a sunny mid-spring day combined with the classic beauty of the campus Acropolis to enhance their appreciation of each other's company. For him, the total feeling of romantic exhilaration was not only endless but unique. He could sense the desire of the flesh as usual but he could also recognize something new—a powerful sense of belonging and protecting. He decided to reveal his feelings.

"S'agapo," he whispered in her ear softly.

She recognized the Greek phrase for "I love you" because she looked it up a couple of days earlier, just in case.

"S'agapo para poli," she responded in a similar manner, adding more personal feeling into the phrase by incorporating the qualifying words for "very much."

"I'm impressed. You are not only very beautiful but also amazingly clever."

"Efcharisto, agapi mou, you are amazing yourself."

Her last Greek phrase, "thank you, my love," was even more impressive because it was so well pronounced. It represented the only additional romantic words in her Greek vocabulary. At one point, while seated on the grass under the shade of a tall plane tree, the conversation became more serious and forward-looking, especially for Nicolas who began to talk about his plans for the future and the value he placed on his family. As a result of the day's romantic interlude his feelings for her were enhanced considerably, and a part of him was pushing him to take a more formal stance.

"Since we have proclaimed love for each other, I want to be the first to cap our romance with a personal commitment to you, a commitment to remain true to you always…at the same time, I want…"

She quickly interrupted with, "Please count me in with my

own personal commitment to be yours and yours only...forever," and then initiated a series of kisses.

As soon as he managed to come up for air, he added, "Anika, I want you to know that my commitment to our love is forever true...my only problem right now is that I cannot make any definite commitment about our future together in terms of formal marriage...I hope you understood my explaining to you earlier about my other lifelong commitment, that to my mother and my family...I hope you choose to be patient with me..."

"I choose to be patient with you, dear Nick, because I love you. At the same time, I want to suggest something that may provide a solution to your commitment dilemma. You told me recently that you were seriously considering getting a full time job after the orals were behind you..."

"Yes, and I still do. My dissertation research is halfway completed but I still have to do a lot of writing and revising along the way towards the degree. Maybe in less than two years if I'm lucky. But I can work on my dissertation part-time, provided I manage to get a good-paying job. It would be great for my family...it would mean help for my family much earlier..."

"Yes, I agree it would be great for your family, but the problem of getting a full-time job, legally, still remains with you..."

"But I did mention to you one available option or easy solution to my problem of replacing my student visa with the highly sought-after green card...all I have to do is enter into a "financial marriage" with a permanent resident or a citizen, apply and get the green card within six months or so, and then dissolve the fake marriage..."

"This is where I wanted to suggest my personal solution to your problem...a solution that will not cost you an arm and a leg. Since my father won the lottery for an immigrant visa I have permanent residency. I'm willing to enter into a fake marriage with you so that you can apply for your permanent residency through me...and the best part is that it will cost you nothing..."

"I can't believe you said that...your suggestion it's too outrageous...too demeaning for a beautiful person like you...why sacrifice your dignity with a fake marriage?"

"Perhaps I subscribe to the idea that true love is not afraid of sacrifice. I also believe I can help you achieve your goals because I love you...I have no doubt that true love, along with respect and devotion, will eventually win you over and convince you to stay for the whole ride."

"I still think your suggestion is incredible and perhaps a bit disturbing, but I feel I'm beginning to be convinced...it may turn out to be a convenient way of getting us to make an early commitment for a permanent relationship."

"I'm ready to swing as soon as you are."

"Let's be a bit more serious, for a moment. If we do go through with the idea of getting into this fake marriage, we have to announce it to your family, and to no one else, as the real, true thing. I will explain later why it is not a good idea to make a similar announcement to my family and friends...I want to keep the fake marriage a secret from them until we decide whether we want to declare it real and permanent."

Anika's face showed deep disappointment with his latter statements, but Nick never noticed. He was involved in his analysis of the situation and continued with, "We also have to come clean about our past since our fake marriage arrangement has a good chance of becoming permanent. Is there anything in our past that would affect our future relationship as a married couple? If there is something, let's share it now and then forget it...we cannot afford to have regrets later on..."

"Do we really need to do this now and perhaps spoil the memory of this beautiful and romantic day?"

"I'll go first," he declared, as if he did not hear her comment and without noticing the increasing expression of concern in her face, her total uneasiness with this new trend in their conversation.

He began by pointing out that he really didn't think he had

anything out of the ordinary in his past life, anything that would affect his present relationship, any secrets that he needed to reveal. Nevertheless, he went on to talk briefly about his former girlfriends and romantic affairs, chronologically, until he mentioned Maro, his Greek American ex-fiancée.

"I guess I do have something I need to confess, after all... about three years ago, I entered into an engagement, with Maro, half-seriously and half-heartedly, even though it represented a commitment sanctioned officially by the church. Why? Perhaps for financial security and most definitely for selfish reasons. I cheated during our engagement, seriously hurting a beautiful and innocent young woman. I feel ashamed of myself...I also know I'll never again take such a commitment half-heartedly."

"Thank you for being frank with me...I don't think you should feel ashamed for contributing to the breaking of your engagement...we all do foolish things when we are young. As far as revealing something about my past, I do have something I want to share with you but not today...I hope you will understand my position...I hope you'll give me the benefit of the doubt."

"There's no problem here, I do understand...I can wait until you're ready, but we'll also wait till then to announce our intended marriage to your family."

She was not happy at all with the latter statement. To her it sounded too cold, too much like the business transaction that it probably was. She was also very much disappointed for not being able to share the good news of her engagement with her family, especially her sister.

"Nick, I think I better go home now..."

"But it's only four in the afternoon...today is Saturday..."

"I've been with you for twenty-four hours straight. I'll tell my family that it took that long for you to feel better. I told them all about your exam results and your stomach discomfort last night, while you were asleep. Of course we shall see each other again tomorrow afternoon at the Metropolitan. Since it's very important to you, I promise that during our walk in Central Park I'll tell you all about my past, or about anything else you want to know about me or my family."

⁓

The Sunday afternoon walk in the park was exceptionally pleasant. The early May sun was bright, fruit trees were in full blossom, the grass was thick and emerald-green and the flowers were varied and colorful, with the color yellow of the daffodils and the dandelions dominating the landscape. As usual for a warm Sunday afternoon, the park was quite crowded. Anika and Nick could not find an empty bench so they chose an isolated rock outcrop on top of a hill.

"I can see that you are not your usual self, you look sad, you definitely look unhappy...please, Anika, if you don't feel like it, you don't have to say anything about your past...you don't have to relive any sad or traumatic events. I know your family had lots of bad luck...I can do without..."

"Please do not make any promises that you may regret later on...I made a promise to you yesterday about telling you...actually, I feel as if I'm about to make a confession to you, to become your penitent...but I plan to keep my promise anyway, so here..."

"That's fine, if you insist, but first let me get us some ice cream," he interrupted. As he walked down the hill, he added, without turning around, "two toasted almond bars coming up."

After the ice cream treat he settled down by lying flat on his back, his head resting on her lap, as if expecting to hear a long and interesting fairy tale. She sat with her back straight and her head slightly bent over his.

"I decided to start with the most shocking aspect of my confession first. You may not want me to continue after you hear this...I accompanied my father and sister to New York close to two years ago, shortly after I gave up my child for adoption, at birth."

There was no doubt that he was shocked, even worse than she thought he would be. He stood up, towering above her as she remained seated. His whole body appeared to be shaking. They both purposely avoided each other's eyes. He managed to blurt out, "How did it happen? Who did it to you?"

"I did it to myself...I was fresh out of college, I was young and foolish and confident about myself, my prowess...I felt invulnerable...I was used to men of all ages complimenting me on my beauty and salivating over me. When my boss made a pass at me, I thought it was normal because he appreciated the best of youth and beauty."

"It was normal, alright," he interrupted. "I can see him appreciate youth and beauty, but only for his own selfish needs."

"I admit I was naïve and foolish...perhaps even worse than that because it didn't matter to me then that he was fifteen years older than me, or even that he was married with two small children...it didn't even make any difference to me that he was white. You can probably guess the rest, can you?"

"I can guess, but I still want you to finish the story in your own words," he replied in a demanding tone of voice.

"I'm not very happy at all with the way you said that, Nick, but I guess I owe you the full story...I became his mistress. When I found out I was pregnant and decided to keep his baby, he went berserk. His aim was to avoid a scandal that would jeopardize his job and destroy his family...finally, he convinced me to give up the baby for adoption at birth and then leave the country...he made it very easy for me to leave, especially for my father who was unemployed at the time. He gave our family plenty of financial security."

Perhaps Nicolas should have noticed Anika's trembling voice, her teary, red eyes, her sad face...or perhaps he should have expressed sympathy with her misfortune, the loss of her child...or perhaps he should have given her his total support by hugging her and kissing her...after all, he did proclaim true and lasting love for her just the day before. Instead, he only whispered,

"He gave your family plenty of money…this explains the apartment, the fact that you can afford your tuition, your lifestyle…"

Anika finally stood up and faced Nick, staring straight into his eyes. Her pleated white skirt and light blue blouse were somewhat untidy and wrinkled, but that did nothing to diminish her perfect posture. As she stood for a moment—motionless on top of the sun-drenched hill—the enticing lines of her statuesque figure were clearly outlined by the penetrating rays. Her eyes were no longer filled with tears and her radiating face showed nothing but pride.

"Goodbye, Nick," she said softly and ran down the grassy hill, holding her red sweater and black loafers in her hands.

Nicolas stayed alone on top of the hill for quite a while, his head buzzing with negative thoughts. *Her story is way too much for me to digest right away…It's a disturbing revelation…I need time… yesterday I managed to convince myself that I could share my life with Anika and that, with time, I could also convince my mother, my family and my friends to accept her…*

His thoughts continued to dwell on his mother. *It would have been very difficult for my mother to fully accept the idea that her precious son would marry someone who is not Greek, who is not Greek Orthodox, let alone a mixed-race woman…my mother is so tuned into tradition, she places so much value onto cultural heritage… now the situation had become even more difficult, if not impossible… she would have to make peace with the idea that her daughter-in-law had an illegitimate child and then gave it away.* He started walking slowly down the hill. His pace appeared artificially animated as if he had no destination in mind. His expression revealed deep concern. He had absolutely no idea as to his next move. He exited the park, walked down 5th Avenue to 42nd Street, and then crosstown to the IRT station. He did not descend into the subway station. The bright marquees of the 42nd Street movie theaters kept him glued on the surface. A good film had always been the best remedy for whatever ailed him mentally.

Close to two hours later, he exited the theater after watching *The Graduate*. The romantic comedy/drama brought him back to his senses. On the way home in the subway all he could think of was Anika and how to get her back. He got off at the 59th Street station and crossed over to the downtown side on his way to her apartment.

My mother has to accept Anika for what she is. She is, after all, a beautiful woman both outwardly and inwardly, and her race and culture do not alter that fact. I cannot afford to lose her...I pray to God that she agrees to come back to me...I pray to God that she ignores the pitiful, selfish way I responded to her story concerning the biggest personal tragedy in her life.

Chapter Ten

At first the road back to romance with Anika appeared to be quite rough for Nicolas. He was absolutely devastated when nobody would answer the door on that fateful Sunday evening after the Central Park incident. She obviously refused to see him or even talk to him. The phone was constantly busy, probably off the hook, or if not busy, no one would answer it.

Anika did not show up on campus for her morning class on Monday. Since she wouldn't answer her phone, he decided to call on her at her Greenwich Village apartment later that day. He was there three hours before the end of the workday. He just wasn't ready yet to face her father. He thought it was a very good omen when her sister opened the door and invited him in.

Marien was friendly, flashing her usual charming smile, but she couldn't produce her sister.

"I'm sorry Nick, Anika is not home, she told me she has a date…but you can visit with me," she said in a rather loud voice, winking at him several times.

It was plain obvious that Anika did not want to see him. To somebody who was as proud and self-confident as Nicolas, possibly even over-confident, it was quite devastating for the ego.

He didn't have a long visit with Marien. On his way out, he asked the young girl in his own deliberatley loud voice, "Marien, please do me a big favor, since you seem to understand me better than your sister does. Please tell your sister that I love her very much. Also, please tell her that I'm anxiously waiting for her to get in touch with me...life is not much fun without her."

After he closed the door behind him he hung around the hallway for a few minutes, hoping that Anika would run out after him. No such luck.

Nicolas decided to change his tactics. He would refrain from running after her on a daily basis. He would not call on her until Saturday afternoon, or perhaps even Saturday evening.

We had some good times together on Saturdays...actually we had some terrific times together every time we were together...she is so much fun to be with...maybe she'll remember the good times and respond positively to my calls then.

On Saturday, five days after his last attempt to contact her, Nicolas left his lab early and returned to his apartment. He was there by three in the afternoon, debating whether he should call her at that time or wait a little longer when a knock on the door postponed his decision. As soon as he opened the door, Anika rushed to hug him and kiss him.

"I couldn't ignore you any longer...I love you...*s'agapo poli*...I miss you so."

"I love you too, *s'agapo para poli*...I was about to call you...I never could have given up on you...you are such a beautiful person," he responded with equal warmth and excitement.

They spent the whole afternoon together walking through the campus and the neighborhood, hanging on each other's words as if they had just met for the first time. They took the subway to midtown for a Greek dinner. During dessert, she announced that she could stay over at his place for the night. His adrenaline surged to a new high. He bought her a magnificent pink rose from the vendor near the campus subway exit.

At the apartment, they took turns to freshen up a bit. He was the first to come back to the dimly lit living room, barefoot but otherwise dressed in a white T-shirt and khaki pants. He was carrying the bed comforter and two pillows. He placed the comforter in front of the TV and lay flat on his belly, using one of the pillows to cushion his chest. He turned on the Late Show.

A few minutes later, she joined him and assumed a similar position close to him. She was also barefoot but dressed only in a matching set of light pink panties and bra which appeared to fluoresce under the glow of the television light. For a few moments, they both appeared to watch the show but it was much harder for him to pretend. It wasn't clear who made the first move, but it was inevitable that their bodies would eventually become intimately united. It took much of the night and a strong desire to sleep before the two young lovers became completely disentangled from each other.

She got up first and woke him up only after she prepared breakfast. He was pleasantly surprised to see the kitchen table neatly set with table cloth and matching napkins, and with the solitary pink rose serving as centerpiece.

"This is beautiful, sweetheart…where did you get the tablecloth and napkins?"

"I brought them over in my bag last time I visited. I hid them here in the table drawer, which apparently you never use, thinking I would surprise you some day when I stayed over for dinner or breakfast."

The two plates of fried eggs with golden-brown halloumi and sliced tomatoes, plus the accompanying glasses of orange juice and the two mugs of tea, were immensely inviting. Nick was impressed beyond belief.

Anika left soon after breakfast. The rest of the day was gloomy and lonely without her. Immersing himself into old movies on t.v., each one a different love story, made him even more nostalgic for the time they spent together the night before. She felt the same way, lonely and miserable without him, even in the presence of her family.

Before long it became routine for Anika to spend Saturday and most of Sunday at Nick's apartment. One Sunday morning in early July, halfway through breakfast, Anika finally noticed the intended surprise when her eye caught a bright reflection from the ever-present rose centerpiece. She stood up to investigate. It was a ring, semi-hidden in the flower's petals. She picked it up and found herself holding a brilliant cut diamond in a white gold setting. She stood speechless for a while.

"I'm sorry it's so tiny...it's only a 32-point stone...but it's devoid of any color tint or bubbly inclusions or dark impurities...even under 10X magnification...it has exceptional clarity and brilliance," he explained with the obvious expertise of a mineralogist.

Apparently, the tiny size of the gemstone and its gemological appraisal were of no significance to the young woman in love. When the proposal symbolism finally sank in, she let out a deep sigh of exhilaration, followed by a slow, clear declaration from deep within, "Yes, darling Nick...I do accept."

Embraces and vows of never-ending love intermingled uncontrollably for several minutes. Her thoughts were clear and uniform: *This is the moment I've been waiting for, this is the beginning of true happiness.* The direction of his thoughts were unclear and variable: *I guess I do love this wonderful and fascinating woman...but perhaps I should remind her that, as per our agreement, this proposal represents a fake marriage of convenience...at the end, this fake marriage may end up being the real thing, but right now we should not lose track of what this proposal represents...unfortunately I don't dare remind her now...maybe later.*

Twelve days later Anika and Nicolas got married in a civil ceremony. The bride looked stunning in an off-white, below-the-knee chiffon dress, and the groom was dressed in a double-breasted navy suit, white shirt and matching tie. It was an exceptionally hot and humid Friday afternoon when Mr. and Mrs. Maos exited City Hall. The weather was the last thing on the minds of the newlyweds, but it seemed to take its toll on the two witnesses, the father and sister of the bride, who were never told that the wedding was essentially a fake.

The wedding celebration was held at the bride's apartment and was strictly a family affair between the married couple and its two witnesses. Nicolas and Anika had already agreed to keep the fake, temporary marriage a secret from anybody else, including his mother, until if and when they decided to classify it differently.

The celebration began at lunch time and lasted well into the night. The food and drink was a melee of Greek and South African delicacies and wines plus ginger ale for the young teenager who, nevertheless, appeared to have as much fun as the others. Mr. Van-Aken never seemed happier and was the soul of the party. He talked almost incessantly, proposed a large number of toasts to the married couple at regular intervals, and sang or hummed several traditional wedding songs from his native country.

Around ten Marien kissed everybody goodnight with tears of joy in her eyes. By then, the father of the bride had slowed down considerably and appeared to lapse into short naps. Nicolas suggested that it was time for him and Anika to also say goodnight.

"I'll get ready first, love. Our room has been ready since yesterday evening. Please join me there in a few minutes," she said, moving towards the master bedroom.

Nick had moved his belongings into the Van-Aken apartment the day before, but he hadn't slept there yet. On his wedding night, he was to begin sharing the master bedroom with his wife.

"I have a surprise for you, sweetheart...I'm not going to join you there..."

She turned around with a puzzled face. He continued, "I

booked a room for us at the Waldorf...it's our special night... our first night as Mr. and Mrs. Maos...just pick up some essentials for one night."

"It sounds great, love...did you plan anything for tomorrow?"

"After brunch at the hotel, we'll come home to dress more casually for an afternoon walk around the city since they expect better weather tomorrow...perhaps we can visit Bloomingdale's, Central Park and then have 'high tea' at the Plaza."

"I can't wait to share all those things with you...what about the evening?"

"Well, don't you think that by then we should begin spending some time here at home also?...Just kidding...I plan to take you to a new Greek restaurant in Astoria. And I also have tickets for the 9:30 showing of *The Odd Couple* at Radio City."

Everything went as planned for the newlyweds. For one day and two nights they were completely lost in each other. Nothing else existed in their world...they were literally in seventh heaven. On Sunday morning they began to share their new world—they had breakfast at home with the family. It was a memorable event not only because they all breathed a thick atmosphere of family love, but also because Mr. Van-Aken made an unexpected and gratifying announcement:

"I have a small gift for you, my daughter Anika and son Nicolas. I couldn't give it to you earlier, I only managed to finalize it yesterday," he said, handing an envelope to his son-in-law with pride in his eyes.

"My God, two airline tickets to San Francisco! Leaving next Friday morning and returning Tuesday evening...here Anika, take a look...how did you know it's been on top of our favorites list as a place to visit?"

His answer was delayed because Anika was all over him. At the same time, Marien brought her wheelchair close enough to embrace him, placing her head on his lap. Finally he replied,

"You talked about San Francisco a couple of times and mentioned the fact that two of your closest friends live there... you've also mentioned that you visited your friends a couple of years ago and were very much impressed with many aspects of the city... if I remember it right, you referred to it as 'the only city in America with a European-like look and atmosphere.'"

"You remember my comments perfectly...a veritable European flair, but not so much in the central business district or some of the tourist areas, but the surrounding residential outskirts like Pacific Heights...beautiful townhouses on tree-lined streets, cafes with outdoor, sidewalk facilities and of course, the gourmet restaurants and boutiques. I remember Vallejo Street...my friend Yiannis had an apartment there, a short walk to the shops and cafes of fabulous Union Street."

The newlyweds were delighted with the gift and started planning for it immediately, referring to it as their "unexpected honeymoon."

Nicolas got in touch with his high school buddies in San Francisco. He was surprised to hear that Yiannis was divorced and living alone. Andros was still happily married to Christina, his first love, and had two daughters—a five and a three year old. Both friends immediately invited Nicolas and his "girlfriend" to stay at their place.

Nick was not yet ready to tell his best friends that he was married. Anika had already assumed the role of the loved and loving wife for several days, so it was only reluctantly that she agreed to go back to playing the role of the girlfriend.

"These are your best friends ever...why keep it a secret from them? You should be proud to introduce your wife to your best friends...sorry, your fake wife. What are you really afraid of? Them or your mother?"

Nick was startled by her expressed doubts concerning his sincerity as well as by her tone of sarcasm. Nevertheless, he understood her concern and her frustration. He took her in his arms while he explained once again, "Sweetheart, you know I'm proud of you and I do plan to abide by our agreement...and I'm not afraid of my mother...I just want to tell her personally when we are ready...I owe her that much."

"I'm terribly sorry, love, we do have an agreement and I shouldn't have doubted you...please..."

"I still want to explain my position once again concerning my friends," he interrupted, "with them, the situation is a little bit different. They are in constant communication with their family and friends back home in Cyprus. If they know about our marriage, even if they try to keep it a secret, there's always the possibility of a slip-up..."

"I understand, you don't have to explain any further."

"If my mother finds out from a third party that her son got married without telling her first, she will never forgive him, no matter how precious he may be in her eyes...it's bad enough she will probably never understand why her devoted son got married without asking her opinion in the first place."

"Please, I feel bad already...let's change the subject..."

"One more thing. After I get a good job and earn some money, perhaps a year or so from now, we may be able to make a decision about the status of our marriage. At such a time, I'll make plans for a trip to Cyprus to personally inform my mother."

⁂

Yiannis and Andros came to the airport on Friday, around noon, to pick up "Nicolas and his girlfriend." They had nothing but compliments for the exotic beauty of Anika. Then they asked several questions in Greek: "Where did you find her? What is her ethnic heritage? How did you manage to impress her? What are your intentions?"

For the benefit of Anika, Nicolas replied in English: "I didn't find her, she found me, and she insisted that I should notice her...

she is the beautiful outcome of a mixture of South African Dutch and native Khoikhoi blood." He paused for a moment. "As far as who impressed whom, I believe I impressed her first," he added, breaking out into laughter. The two friends as well as Anika appeared to have enjoyed the joke.

In the car, on the way to the city, plenty of jokes were exchanged and joyous, loud laughter was quite frequent. In the midst of all the merriment, Nicolas noticed something out of the ordinary. There was an obvious coolness between Yiannis and Andros and, uncharacteristically, they would not play jokes on each other. Nicolas decided not to bring up his observation or ask for an explanation at that time.

The couple was taken to Yiannis' townhouse on Vallejo. The property consisted of two floors, each separated as a different six-room luxury apartment with a private entrance. The upper, recently renovated apartment was Yiannis' residence and the lower was used as a guest house. Upon entering, Nicolas recognized the décor of the lower apartment where he stayed for a few days during his first visit there a couple of years earlier.

Andros, whose residence was outside San Francisco in Marin county, said goodbye after he told the couple that he would pick them up the next morning for a scheduled visit with his family. The fact that Andros would not stay to celebrate a rare reunion of the three friends was extremely unusual and reinforced Nicolas' suspicions of a probable rift between Andros and Yiannis.

After a couple of hours' rest, Yiannis gave the couple a tour of his downtown office and warehouse facilities for his import business. He imported mainly women's fashions, both clothing and leather accessories, as well as fashion jewelry, mostly from Italy and Greece. He was primarily a wholesale distributor to boutiques and department stores. He appeared to have well over twenty employees working for him, including several spectacular-looking young women. His two guests were both extremely impressed.

"For lunch I'll take you to a romantic place with excellent

seafood and great gin fizzes in Sausalito. I'll show you some of my property there too," Yiannis told his guests and then directed them to his car, a midnight-blue Mercedes 300 SE. This time he invited a girlfriend along. Suzy was the personification of youth and model-type beauty. Perhaps a little too much youth. Throughout the trip, Yiannis was driving using the left hand only. His right was occupied, holding his girlfriend's left in a tight grip.

"I guess you still enjoy your late teen habits, right Yiannis?" Nick asked in Greek.

"Why not?" Yiannis responded in Greek and then added in English, "Those were the best, easy years of my life...and you were an important part of those years too."

"I'm sure you meant to include Andros and Lakis too," commented Nick, hoping to bring something to the surface concerning his friend's current standing with their mutual friend Andros. "Sure, why not? At that time things were different," he responded and left it at that, much to Nick's disappointment.

The food, the drinks and especially the view from the terrace of the restaurant, high up on the coastal hill overlooking the bay were unique and impressive. Nick and Anika were even more impressed with the tour of Yiannis' property in picturesque Sausalito.

Later in the evening, as Nick and Anika lay in bed thinking of the day's events, they almost simultaneously had a similar thought pass through their minds.

This has definitely been a taste of the good life.

The day with Andros was low key but quite pleasant. It was a family day, four adults and two little girls having a great time playing games, eating barbecued meats and drinking plenty of soda or beer in the small backyard of a modest ranch-style house. Andros and his wife Christina appeared to personify the ideal young couple with small kids, all-loving and all-happy. Anika was very much impressed.

"Love, this is the kind of family life I can dream about, the kind of family life you and I can have...do you think we have a chance?" she whispered in Nick's ear.

"Sweetheart, I've been having the same thoughts throughout the day," he whispered back in her ear.

"When do you expect to get your Ph.D., Nico?" asked Andros, interrupting their whispers.

"I hope in about three semesters, a year and a half from now, if things go smoothly."

"Well, you can probably start planning for a wedding now...it's quite obvious to me that you two are in love. In fact, you act a little bit as if you are a married couple already...a good family is the most satisfying thing in life," commented Christina.

"You are right, we have been thinking about marriage...it shouldn't be long now before we make it legal, before we start a family," said Nick looking straight into Anika's eyes, asking her to continue to be patient for a little longer.

The topics of conversation became more personal as evening approached. Nicolas took advantage of the situation to ask,

"Andro, I hope I'm wrong, but I noticed yesterday that things do not appear to be the same as they used to be between you and Yiannis...for me, and for all who know us, you two have always represented the best in friendship...you have always been the quintessential devoted friends...is it possible that your friendship has cooled down, or even possible that there is a rift between you?"

"All I can say is that Yiannis seems to have forgotten many of the things that formed the bond in our friendship...the great devotion between us that you just mentioned, the oath we made to support each other unselfishly forever as well as the respect for each other—all have apparently diminished or perhaps even disappeared..."

"We helped him come to the States, he stayed here with us for several months...we even provided for all his needs, his pocket money...until he got a job in the city. Now of course he is a big shot, he doesn't need us...but we don't need him either...I guess he thinks we're after his money," interjected Christina.

"Honey, please, this situation has very little to do with money... it's mostly about diminishing loyalty and respect between lifelong friends," explained Andros.

"Andro, how about the incident or incidents that started the loss of loyalty and respect between you two great friends?"

"About a year ago, I lost my job as an insurance salesman and had some difficulty getting another one. Yiannis found out about it and immediately offered me a job in his company. He said he needed a security officer for his three-story building right away. I accepted the position, thinking that it was only temporary..."

"I'm sure it wasn't a good-paying job, especially for a family man with two kids," interrupted Nicolas.

"No, actually he was so generous, it was embarrassing. My take-home salary was close to twice what I made in my previous job."

"He kept you in that position too long, is that it?" asked Nicolas.

"I was kept as 'gate-keeper' for close to six months which, in itself, is not very long. However, it was somewhat demeaning because of the way the other employees looked at me. They were told that I was the boss' best friend and yet I had a position that represented the bottom of the barrel...they thought I was a loser...I could see it in their eyes...and the situation got even worse when Yiannis added to my duties...I was to see to it that all bathrooms never ran out of toilet paper and paper towels..."

"It's very difficult for me to comprehend this situation," interjected Christina once again. "How come your best friend, your brother, as you have often referred to him, couldn't see what he was actually doing to you?"

"That's exactly what I would like to know," added Nicolas. "I'm shocked to hear that our Yiannis behaved this way."

"Wait until you hear the rest of it...during that six-month period Yiannis conducted interviews for three positions for which I knew I qualified to one extent or another..."

"Did you approach our friend about your interest in these positions?"

"I approached him about one of them which sought a Greek-speaking person to act as liaison between Greek exporters and the San Francisco office. He told me that he needed somebody who would take the job seriously, somebody reliable—he told me in no uncertain terms that I did not have the right personality for the position because of my laissez-faire attitude...he further explained that I tend to make a joke out of everything."

My God, strictly speaking, Yiannis is right in the way he described Andros' personality...that's the way we all used to describe him during our Academy years...some of us even referred to him by the nickname of 'Mr. Laissez-faire' at times...nevertheless, it was still wrong of Yiannis to treat his best friend in such a insensitive way...it appears that friendship and business do not mix very well.

After dinner, Andros drove Nick and Anika back to the city.

The next day, during breakfast, Yiannis continued to show his exceptional generosity to his friends. He offered his Mercedes for the couple's planned three-day trip down south along the California coast via Route One. Their final destination would be San Diego. There Nicolas looked forward to a visit with his old friend Luke, his one-time guardian angel.

The couple's visit with Luke and his family in San Diego was most gratifying. Nick bet five dollars with Anika that he knew exactly what his friend would say as soon as he saw Nick enter his restaurant, a much fancier version of the old Canal Diner. He won the bet. The moment Luke recognized his friend, he called out loud, "Hey, Nick, are you hungry? Of course you are...what do you want to eat?"

Nick and Anika had a wonderful time during their short visit with Luke and his family. During their goodbyes, Nick was quite surprised at Luke's last words, in Greek,

"You ought to marry that girl, Nick. She appears to have the best of everything."

Back in San Francisco, Nick and Anika spent their last day with Yiannis. He appeared most interested in Anika's background and, at one point, he told his friend, "Nick, you are a very lucky man to have the attention of such an extraordinary woman…if you want my advice, you should do something about it very, very quickly."

Nick agreed with him and came extremely close to revealing his marriage secret. Anika appeared intoxicated with the compliment. At the end, Nick did not bring up the problem with Andros. He wanted to believe that he never found the right opportunity to do so but, in reality, he did not want to disturb the calm and pleasant waters at this time. During the flight back to New York, one sad thought refused to leave his mind:

I grew up thinking that the tower of friendship is solid and permanent…however, time appears to weather everything, including the seemingly most weather-resistant friendships.

⁓

Nicolas' trip to Cyprus one and a half years later was a total surprise for his family. First, he surprised his sister Marina, who had moved from Larnaca to a Nicosia suburb, not too far from the Nicosia airport where he landed. After a two days' visit with his sister's family, he traveled by bus to the village of Ora, accompanied by his nephew Andros, now an athletic high school sophomore.

Mrs. Kyriaki answered the knock on the front gate. When she saw her son and grandson standing tall in front of her, under the midday sun, she practically had a heart attack because of the sudden, intense joy that rushed through her veins and heart.

"Thank you, Lord, for yet another miracle," she shouted on top of her voice while running forward to embrace them.

Soon after, she started pointing out the beauty and practicality of her new home by giving the boys a quick tour. She then led the two young men towards the small pine table and chairs placed in the thick shade of the lemon tree in the middle of the courtyard.

"Relax here for a while, my boys. I'll bring you some fresh bread and cheese and grapes from our vine for lunch…Nina, bring the boys plenty of cool water."

Nicolas was impressed with the layout of the new house he had helped purchase. Its four rooms were spacious, with freshly plastered walls and white marble floors, a veritable luxury for the Maos family.

He was most impressed, however, with the large courtyard of the new house. Its neat, oval-shaped floor was covered with interlocking slabs of limestone. This was unlike their old house, the "cave," whose yard was only partly covered with rough cobble stones, leaving exposed a large area of the original semi-hardened clay.

The gigantic lemon tree, in the center of the yard, was loaded with its indispensable fruit whose green and yellow color tints represented various stages of maturity. The tree provided plenty of semi-circular shade, an essential requirement for a climate that boasted sunshine for over eight months of the year.

On the southern side of the yard, a well-established grape vine was trained to climb a wooden lattice built in front of the room that served as combination kitchen and dining area. The vine's leaves and large bunches of ripened, dark brown fruit hanging from the lattice roof, provided additional protection from the sun's rays.

Numerous annuals as well as perennial flowering plants in red clay pots and white-painted cans of all sizes and shapes were placed all around the edge of the courtyard floor and on top of the front stone wall that paralleled the village main street. Their leaves and flowers added plenty of green plus a multitude of other colors to the surroundings.

"You must be proud you bought this house for your sister

Nina, my Nicolaki," said Mrs. Kyriaki as she pulled a chair to sit close to her son. Her daughter Nina had already joined her brother and nephew a few minutes earlier.

"If you must point out that I bought this house, mother, why exclude yourself as one of the beneficiaries? How come you still insist that I bought it for Nina only?"

"Are you going to tell him, mother, or shall I do?" interjected Nina.

"Son, you probably recall that the second I saw you standing at that gate a few minutes ago, I thanked the Lord for a miracle..."

"I'm not surprised at all. I've heard you refer to the Lord's miracles many times."

"Well, that's true, my son, the Lord never ceases to perform miracles. But listen to this story and tell me if you don't agree with me that a miracle was performed. Just yesterday evening, we finalized an agreement—we signed church documents for your sister Nina's engagement and then..."

"My congratulations, dear Nina," interrupted Nicolas, standing up to embrace his sister. Andros, in turn, also congratulated his aunt with hugs and kisses and then excused himself for a visit to the village square where young people congregated. Mrs. Kyriaki continued her miracle story as if nobody interrupted her,

"And then, right there in church, I faced the icon of the Virgin Mary holding the infant, my Lord Jesus Christ, and prayed that you come back home to celebrate with us this important event, as soon as possible. Less than twenty hours later, you were standing in front of me. Wouldn't you call this a miracle?"

"It is indeed a miracle, mother, no doubt about it. But please tell me more about the agreement...and about my brand new brother-in-law, of course."

"Before the wedding takes place, we have to transfer the deed of this house to him...this home became part of your sister's dowry."

"Now I can see why you referred to this house as having been bought for Nina. I will also assume that you probably agreed to sign one or more of our three remaining pieces of land holdings over to him...I don't much care about the other two, but please don't tell me that you plan to give him my favorite, our nearby Laxia, with its decent olive grove and fruit trees and especially its cool water spring."

"I'm sorry son, I never mentioned or offered him the property but he insisted on Laxia...it appears he was well informed about all our properties before he came to see us, according to the matchmaker. Since I made it very clear to everybody that one of my biggest aims in life has been to secure the future of our Nina, I couldn't very well refuse him..."

She stopped for a moment to ask Nina to go do a few chores in the kitchen. "I plan to slaughter and prepare a young chicken for dinner, son. I remember how partial both you and Andros are to macaroni and chicken with lemon sauce."

"Thanks, mother...the idea makes me feel even more at home."

"Now that Nina can't hear me, I want you to know that we are lucky we even got one man seriously interested in your handicapped sister. You'll meet him tomorrow. Please welcome him—if we chase him away, I don't think we'll ever attract any others."

"You're probably right, mother. In any case, I know that whatever you do, you do it for your loved ones, without any selfish notion behind your actions. Because of that, I'll always respect and support you."

"Thank you my son...may the Lord always keep you and protect you."

"Speaking for myself, I lay no claim to this house nor to any of the land property. My interest in Laxia was in terms of keeping some original property of the family in place...something for the future...something that would historically and symbolically represent the Maos family."

The conversation between mother and son continued for quite a while, covering all kinds of topics. During a short break, Mrs. Kyriaki left her son in order to consult with her daughter in the kitchen about dinner. When she returned, Nicolas became literally animated with excitement to see her bring back a tray full of fresh figs.

"I recognize these figs by their delicate taste…Aunt Marina's, right?" He didn't wait for an answer. Instead, he had a serious question to ask of his mother.

"Mother, I want you to he honest with me about something, now that we're still alone. Please do not try to evade an answer, as you sometimes do, in order to spare me from perceived harm or sadness…"

"I think you're mistaken, my son, about my evading answers to any of your questions…but go ahead, ask me."

"I noticed that you walk with a slight limp or imbalance, as if you do not have full control of your left leg or perhaps even your whole left side. Also, your left eye appears smaller or half closed…and your energy is not even close to what it used to be only four years ago when I last saw you. You would have never even considered having Nina do kitchen chores for you, let alone ask her. What is the story, mother?"

"I'm sure you remember Dr. Karaolos, our district doctor who visited our village every Friday for many years…he treated you many a time…"

"Of course I do, mother. Did he examine you for the symptoms I mentioned?"

"I wish he did…he passed away last fall. Our new district doctor, a young man close to your age, visits Ora twice a week. He insists that I had a small stroke four months ago…he says it helps that I'm skinny and active, but I'm still a candidate for a major stroke unless I change my diet. Imagine cooking without lard! I tend to agree with midwife Salomi that I probably had a bad virus or the flu instead of a stroke."

"Mother, please listen to the young doctor…we're in the space age now…we've already been to the moon…the age of the midwife is over…"

Nicolas had planned to stay in Cyprus for about a month. He knew he couldn't risk losing more valuable time or the momentum he established in the writing of his dissertation. The original idea was that thirty days in the quiet, non stressful environment of the village would be sufficient for him to find the right opportunity to talk to his mother and sister about his marriage to Anika.

Unfortunately, contrary to what he had expected, the village environment made it very difficult for him to make a quick revelation, particularly because of the relentless efforts of his mother to set him up for marriage with one of the village maidens. On the one hand, he regretted the indecision and, on the other hand, he loved the personal attention he was getting from many sources.

Marriage by arrangement was part of his cultural heritage and, in many ways, he felt quite flattered to have been offered the privilege of choosing from among so many beautiful young women with a known village pedigree. At the time, and for many years in the past, village parents would be highly honored and proud to arrange to have their daughter marry a man with an excellent education and, therefore, with outstanding prospects of giving her a good and privileged life.

Nicolas was absolutely determined to please his mother, at any cost, especially since her stroke made him more aware of her mortality. Therefore, he promised her he was seriously considering the young village women she proposed as possible prospects for marriage. He also promised his mother that he would extend his stay for a couple of weeks in order to attend his sister's wedding which was pushed forward for his sake.

Certain things about his sister's forthcoming wedding bothered Nicolas immensely. It was bad enough that the groom was getting the house and the property of Laxia, but in addition, Nick thought that his future brother-in-law appeared to have zero prospects for giving his sister life security or support of any kind.

Physically, the groom-to-be was not an attractive man and appeared to have difficulty breathing, probably because of his chain-smoking habit. As a 63 year-old widower, 26 years older than his bride-to-be, he was the one most probably seeking support and companionship from a younger woman in his later years.

Out of fear of probably offending his sister's sensitivities, Nicolas did not reveal any of his concerns to her about her future husband. He had a feeling his handicapped sister valued the idea of marriage more than the groom himself. He did confide to his mother, however, but she either could not or would not see the drawbacks of the match.

"Son, I had to face a similar situation in life when I was matched with your father. Yes we had our difficulties, and surely I had to take care of him most of our lives together. But I have no regrets because marriage is a holy institution and we all enter into it unselfishly."

Nicolas did not respond to his mother even though he was certain she was being naïve for making a statement that nobody would enter into marriage for selfish reasons.

On the other hand, he thought, *life in a small village is simple and somewhat sheltered and maybe people do see the institution of marriage very much like my mother does. After all, I've never known or heard of any married couple in this village that even wanted to get divorced, let alone go through it.*

⁂

Both Nicolas and the groom, plus the groom's 30-year old daughter from his first marriage, preferred a simple wedding which would consist of a church ceremony after Sunday's liturgy plus a reception—dinner at home for close friends and relatives.

The bride and her mother insisted on a traditional village wedding which involved a four-day celebration of food, drink and music at a coffee shop plaza, with everybody in the village invited. Under pressure, the two women compromised for a two-day celebration, but with a guest list that included all village residents.

On Saturday morning, the bride and her mother, with glass rose water dispensers in hand, went door to door to every household in the village for a personal invitation to the next-day wedding. The invitation was sealed with a few drops of the aromatic rose water on the invited guests' open hands.

On Sunday afternoon, after the hour-plus church ceremony and the congratulatory greetings, everybody gathered for dinner. The large coffee shop plaza, a former wheat field left uncultivated for such occasions, was set up with long, picnic-type tables for at least two hundred adults. Additionally, separate tables were set up for children of all ages. The menu consisted of two entrées: hand-made macaroni-type noodles served with plenty of grated halloumi cheese mixed with mint flakes, and lamb with whole, peeled potatoes—all baked in an olive oil and tomato paste sauce with tiny, whole onions and garlic cloves. Several members of the Maos family served the dinner portions to the rest of the village residents.

The Monday wedding celebration menu consisted of baked chicken with rice pilaf and a salad. According to tradition, all chickens were contributed by the village residents. They were picked up by a pair of men who hanged the chickens by their tied legs on a long wooden bar placed across their shoulders. Fiddle music accompanied the chicken collection through the streets of the village.

The evening's celebration ended with the dance of the bride and groom. As the couple moved slowly around the dance floor, a small wooden platform in the center of the field, the wedding guests threw paper money of all denominations over their heads.

At the family breakfast the next morning, Mrs. Kyriaki proudly declared that her son paid not only for the new house but also for Nina's wedding. When Nicolas questioned the latter part of the statement, she explained that she paid for everything through savings from money sent to her by her son. Everybody cheered.

The groom's daughter also made an announcement concerning the Laxia property. She declared she was taking over the olive grove, as it "was promised to me by my father, the new owner." This time nobody cheered. In fact, for the first time since the arrangement of her daughter's wedding, Mrs. Kyriaki lost her facial expression of pride and satisfaction and was exhibiting worrisome disapproval, perhaps even anger.

⁌

Four days later, after most of the wedding guests left, peace and quiet reigned once again in the Maos household, actually the new Ponticos household. John Ponticos had agreed during the wedding negotiations that Mrs. Kyriaki could live in his and Nina's home for the rest of her life.

Nicolas was planning to stay for another three days in the village before returning to the States and was sharing his mother's room after placing an extra cot there. For Nick, the Ponticos household didn't quite feel like home. The old Maos household, the primitive dug-out cave, where he spent his early formative years, would always occupy a special spot in his heart and soul.

Another day passed and Nick was far from finding a way to tell his mother about his marriage. On his last day an unexpected encounter took place. He crossed paths with Despina who was playing on the street with some of her friends. She was pointed out to him as Stella's 10 year-old daughter.

"Good morning, Mr. Maos,. Yes, I'm Despina, Stella's daughter."

Nicolas was amazed and very pleased, indeed, that little Despina spoke to him. He definitely wouldn't have recognized her on his own. He quickly found out that single mom Stella was working in Kyrenia as a hotel receptionist. The little girl was spending a few summer days in the village with her maternal grandparents.

Later that day, during a private afternoon coffee break with his mother, Nicolas posed a couple of hypothetical questions: "Mother, earlier today I met Despina, Stella's little girl. I got to thinking and I want your opinion as to how would you feel if I were to marry my first love, Stella?"

"Stella is a good woman and comes from a good family in our village. But she was married twice, and one of her men left her with his love child. Do you want to live with a woman as the third man in her life and raise someone else's child?"

Nicolas did not answer in so many words but nodded his agreement with her. He then posed another hypothetical:

"How would you feel if I were to fall in love and marry a foreign woman, an American woman, an outstanding woman in all respects except for the fact that her heritage is other than Greek?"

"That would probably kill me, my son. Can you imagine me not being able to communicate with my new daughter, my grandchildren...not being able to celebrate our great Orthodox holidays with them?...I don't think you can do that to me."

That's it then," thought Nicolas, quite disturbed, but managing to hide his frustration. *I'm not going to take the risk...I'm not going to tell her and probably kill her in the process. I can wait a little longer... perhaps after I give her a grandchild.*

Later in the evening, after Mrs. Kyriaki went to bed, Nicolas sat at the small table by the lemon tree, enjoying the cool breeze and having a last smoke before retiring. Nina joined him, bringing Greek coffee for both of them.

"My husband is still at the coffee shop, it's his gin rummy night. I was looking for a private moment with you, brother...I have something important to show you."

She handed him a sealed envelope. "FOR MY SON NICOLAS" was written on the upper-front edge.

"Our mother asked me to keep the envelope for you, not to give it to you until after she dies. She became concerned after the doctor told her she had a small stroke and that she may have another one, perhaps a much more severe one, if she is not careful with her diet...she kept lamenting that she may not see you again. I decided this may be as good a time as any to give it to you. Take it with you to America. It's up to you whether you want to open it now or abide by her original wish..."

"You know what's in the note, of course, since you are always the one who writes or reads her communications."

"No, not this time, brother. I don't even know who wrote this for her. She refused to reveal the person who took her dictation...I can't even imagine who it may be..."

He moved closer to the porch lamp and opened the envelope. He took out a neatly folded ruled paper containing a six-line, handwritten paragraph. After he read it, he crumpled the paper into a tight knot in his fist and began walking up and down the porch, throwing out a medley of words and phrases in synchronization with every two or three steps he took.

Nina couldn't make out what he was saying in English, but she could clearly see his face under the glow of the bulb. She could tell from his strained facial expression and his body movements that he was extremely disappointed and somewhat irritated, but not really angry. She approached, blocked his pace, and asked face to face:

"I can see you are quite upset, brother. Can you share the message with your sister?"

He handed her the paper knot. She slowly unscrambled it and turned it towards the light bulb. As soon as she read it, she literally went into shock, unwilling or unable to say anything. She dropped the paper. It landed straight up on the porch floor. Simultaneously, as if by telepathy, they sat down and, again simultaneously, they began staring at the words, reading them silently:

My dearest son, Nicola:

I hope I do not shock you terribly with my words and if I do, I pray to the Lord that you forgive me. You are the greatest gift that God has given me but I had to commit adultery in order to get you. Your real father is Tassos Kamilaris. I did lifetime penance for this sin and I hope God has forgiven me. I pray that you too, in time, find it in yourself to forgive your mother.

Eventually, Nicolas regained his composure. He carefully folded his mother's letter and put it in his pocket. He made up his mind to tell his mother everything about his marriage. *My beloved mother revealed to me that I'm a bastard. Why shouldn't I reveal that I'm also a sneak...I sneaked behind her back and married a woman that she probably won't approve of.*

"I have something to share with you and our mother," he said calmly to his sister who still appeared to be in shock. "Let's join our mother," he added, walking slowly towards her bedroom. Mrs. Kyriaki woke up easily but looked quite puzzled.

"I'm always ready to hear what my son has to tell me," she said as she pulled herself up to sit on the bed.

"I'm not sure you will like what I have to tell you, mother, but here it is. A few months ago, I married the girl that I love...her name is Anika. It was a simple civil ceremony. I hope you forgive me for not telling you earlier, for not asking your permission..."

Mrs. Kyriaki began trembling with excitement and uncontrollable tears. She got off the bed and moved to embrace her son. She managed to respond, whispering close to his ear,

"There's nothing to forgive you for, my son...there's plenty to congratulate you for...you're happy because you married the woman you love...tell me more about your Anika...our Anika."

Nicolas, who expected and dreaded the prospect of his mother's disapproval, received, instead, her quick and loving endorsement. He became ecstatic with instant happiness and joy. Of course he expected and got the complete support of his sister who cherished the idea of her brother being married. He decided this was the best time to push the envelope further.

"Mother and sister, I want you both to know that my Anika, our Anika, is a mixed-race woman, originally from South Africa..."

"They say that these mixed-race women are often striking beauties," commented his mother. "But what about your children? Could they be totally black?" she added with concern in her voice.

"Anika is indeed an incredibly beautiful woman, mother, both in body and in spirit. I know you will love her the moment you meet her...and I wouldn't be concerned about the color of the children. She has an appealing dark complexion...our children should be lucky to have her complexion."

He excused himself for a moment to look for something in his suitcase. He brought out two six-by-nine inch photographs of his wedding—one for his mother and the other for his sister. Nina came out with several superlatives to describe her sister-in-law. Widow Kyriaki kept kissing her "beautiful new daughter."

"I have one other thing to tell you both about my wife, something she revealed to me before we got married. She admitted she had made a terrible mistake in her life—a few years back she had a child with another man...he was not her husband..."

"If she is a good Christian and if she prays to God...well, God tends to forgive all sinners who repent and pray to Him...do you have her child living with you back home, my son?"

"She gave the child up for adoption at birth, mother. As far as forgiveness is concerned, I'm sure God recognizes sincerity...I'm sure He forgave her already...and her family and I do not hold it against her...we all love her very much..."

"We all love her too, we all love your wife, son...personally, I cannot wait to meet our Anika...I cannot wait to embrace my new daughter."

On the flight back to New York, Nicolas had plenty of time to think about the recent events in his life. He was still trying to digest the idea that everything went so well with the main mission of his trip to Cyprus...it was so gratifying and so liberating to see his mother accept his marriage and practically declare her willingness to adopt, to embrace his Anika.

He couldn't wait to tell his lovely wife that they were liberated as a married couple...he couldn't wait to see her consequent bright, smiling face...they could literally go around telling one and all about their love vows, about their marriage.

His mother's letter and her confession about committing adultery, on the other hand, could only produce sad notes in his memory. He decided he would never tell his mother that he saw the letter. He also had Nina swear that she would never tell either. In his mind, he began painting a new icon of his mother's character and personality:

During my early formative years, I thought of my mother as pure and perfect. The incident of almond stealing early on and now her confessed infidelity have made me realize that she is neither pure nor perfect, but simply human...yet, there is no doubt in my mind that she represents maternal love that is perfectly unselfish and pure...Mrs. Sunday, for me you will always be the quintessential loving mother...and I will always be privileged and proud to be called Sunday's son.

Epilogue

During the next five years, Nicolas and Anika had the best of everything that life had to offer.

He received his Ph.D. in Mineralogy in 1969 and landed the job he always dreamed about–a tenure track teaching position as an Assistant Professor at a state university. She received her M.A. in Sociology and began a career with the city's Social Welfare Department.

Their love and respect for each other never stopped growing. Towards the end of this period, they were blessed with their first child who was baptized in the Greek Orthodox church as Kyra, short for her paternal grandmother's name of Kyriaki.

The couple's life in paradise came to an end with a series of catastrophes that took place during the sixth year of their life together. Ironically, during that same year Nicolas was promoted to Associate Professor with tenure.

Nicolas' mother, Mrs. Kyriaki, died of a stroke during Easter Holy Week, just days before she looked forward to seeing her eleven-month old granddaughter, Kyra, for the first time. With the passing of his mother, his handicapped sister Nina began living all alone in the village since her elderly husband had died of a massive heart attack a few months earlier.

Undoubtedly, the worst tragedy that could ever befall Nicolas surfaced during early June of that sixth year when Anika was diagnosed with ovarian cancer. She passed away five months later, eleven days before Christmas. Her husband and her family were devastated.

Nicolas barely managed to complete the academic year that was in progress. At the end he took a leave of absence and, together with his infant daughter Kyra, joined his sister Nina in the village of Ora in mid-June of 1974. He wanted his daughter to experience life in the village, to live her formative years where her father did.

Life in the remote, mountainous village was pleasant and peaceful as usual.

However, the times were not the best for the island as a whole. Continuous communal conflicts between the Greek-Cypriot majority and the Turkish-Cypriot minority, plus intervening outside forces, made life on the otherwise beautiful island of the goddess of love, Aphrodite, miserable.

One of these outside forces, Turkey, caused a disaster of immense historical proportions when, on July 20th of 1974, it invaded and occupied the northern section of Cyprus, close to 40 percent of the island nation. The brutal Turkish invasion created 200,000 Greek-Cypriot refugees and, in addition to the thousands of casualties, over 1,500 Greek-Cypriots and others were officially listed as missing.

Stella and her daughter Despina had to run for their lives. They became refugees by fleeing from the beautiful resort town of Kyrenia, on the northern section of Cyprus, a couple of days before it was occupied by Turkish mechanized army units. Eventually, mother and daughter joined Stella's parents in the peaceful and safe village of Ora.

Less than a year later, Nicolas and Stella were married in St. Marina, their beloved village church where they had flirted many a time during their elementary school years. Three weeks after the wedding, Nicolas had to return to his teaching job in the States. Eleven months later, his wife Stella and their two children, Despina and Kyra, joined him in New York City.